WAR IN SPACE

During my freelance period, before meeting up again with the English Empire in Space, I was briefly weapons officer on a Peewermums Inter-Galaxy Class Destroyer. The Peewermums were difficult to work for. Each unit of Peewermums grew from a Peewermums plantpot, in which some score of Peewermums lived together, making noises like grouse on the Glorious Twelfth. I never knew, to be truthful, if a score of Peewermums made an individual Peewermums personage or if a score of Peewermums were a family of 20 different Peewermums. It worried me once but I find I have now ceased to care! They had faces like worried Pekinese, stuck on the end of stalks, but which could detach themselves and roll around the room during periods of hiatus. During their flowering season they sighed continually. Worst of all, they were fervent pacifists – hence me as weapons officer! – and their first impulse in any conflict was to surrender. As they were at war with the Bunnypeople this meant certain death – but tell them that! I understand, anyway, that they have since become extinct – no wonder! Evolution hates a coward . . .

Also by Steve Walker in Coronet Books

21st Century Blues

About the author

Steve Walker, playwright, poet, artist, novelist, teller-of-tales and historian of the future, was born in Gateshead in 1956. He travelled extensively throughout the 1970s. Returning to Britain in the 1980s, he held 64 one-man shows of his paintings and embarked on a stupendously successful radio drama career – he has written over 30 plays for radio and is the only playwright to have won two consecutive Giles Cooper Awards for Year's Best Radioplay. He has also written scripts for major television animation series.

22nd Century Blues

Steve Walker

✳

The Book of the Century, Being the Life and Incredible Times of Muggeridge Chaffinch, who left England during the Final Days of the Anita Government to Travel Far into the Stars, First as Prefect of HMS *Billingsgate*, Later as Archbishop of Bunnyland, Written in the Year 2199 on the Planet Cats-by-Nowhere, Witnessed and with a Prologue and Footnotes by J. W. Mathis, False Man.

CORONET BOOKS
Hodder and Stoughton

First published in 1996 by Hodder and Stoughton
A division of Hodder Headline PLC

A Coronet paperback

British Library Cataloguing in Publication Data
Walker, Steve, 1956–
22nd Century blues
1.English fiction – 20th century
I.Title II.Twenty-second century blues
823.9'14 [F]

ISBN 0 340 66663 3

Typeset by Hewer Text Composition Services, Edinburgh
Printed and bound in Great Britain by
Cox and Wyman Ltd, Reading

Hodder and Stoughton
A Division of Hodder Headline PLC
338 Euston Road
London NW1 3BH

CONTENTS

✳

Contents

Appendices 357

FOREWORD

by His Excellency Hippity Rumbaba III, Shogun of Bunnyland.

It gives me great pleasy-do to write these few words in recommending a book which teacheth us muchsomemost about the Bunnyland of the recently deceased century, and also raresome informationy-doos about that peculiarish planet which was the birthdayplace of the various religions now swaying in Bunnylandia. Speaking as a rabbit, as I must, I find all humany doings too-too-too amusant, oui-oui! But in these writings of J.W. Mathis and M.C. Chaffinch (both of whoms I knew as a young buck) I chomp beyond this to findeth hoppings of spiritual inspirations to soften and enlarge my warrior soul. Had I read this book before coming to powersomeness I would have slaughtered the previous administration with more compassion. It hath strengthenethed also the political philosophy of mine – in seeing the vastness of this our Universe evoked hereinly I conclude that every choice is a limitation of life's boundless possibilities, and that therefore no choices should be allowed. Plusly, it hath whiskered my heart that these two oddbod creatures, not even rabbits, knew suchmost friendshipy-

*doos in t'other. A Shogun is lonesomedone by his heavy office –
he knoweth no friends, except his books. This is one of mine.
May it be yourn in joydooerlysomeness. U-huh! Be you Bunny,
unite behind Rumbaba – be you owt else, sayeth I in toothy
fraternality, and no sex intended, beware the Bunny.*

**B'bubbadub Palace
Christmas Day, 2201**

Prologue

or

The Book of Mathis
which he also, with deepest humility,
calls 20th Century Blues
– a true book by a false man

'The changes that are sure to come, I do not fear to see.'
David Lloyd George, Earthling Statesman

My First Day

I, J. W. Mathis, false man, was advancing through the smoke of No Man's Land. It was November 11th, 1918. Those 2 fine men, my manufacturers, I had left behind in the trench. They watched me with the other observers as I trudged forward with my fellow Tommies. At the suggestion of Mr Randy Botswoodie, my Canadian father, I wore the uniform of a Canadian regiment over my brass body. But my tin hat was part of me. It did not come off. I advanced, aware of nothing, a mere machine. If I performed my part well that day, my 2 fathers would be commissioned to make more like me, millions more – then only false men need die in wars. A noble ambition, wot!

I was slow in the mud and was being left behind. Tommies, grim and fearful, turned while overtaking me, saying: 'Cor, what the bloody hell is that?' It was I, J. W. Mathis, false man. But, as yet, I had no consciousness. I was unborn. I was, as I say, mere machine.

'Haven't yerh ever heard, Jack!' cried one, 'that where there's muck there's brass!' Laughter in the jaws of Hell! How brave they were! How proud I am of them, even now!

Many died ahead of me, felled by Hun machine gun fire, dropping without cries. As I approached the German wire I was hit myself, in both thighs, in my clockwork chest. But I had been made to be dogged. I stood at the wire and fired my rifle, then advanced. Others joined me. We cut the wire. But the Hun fusillade was too great. Those around me were felled. Their

3

blood bespattered me. It drenched me. It filled my expression-less eyes. I was on the lip of the German position, throwing Mills bombs into it, vanquishing the hated Hun, when I stopped being a thoughtless machine and became myself, J. W. Mathis. I was blooded, grief-stricken for the loss of my comrades, exulted by my victory – all these things at once – as I looked around with new eyes. In my head was no brain. In my chest no heart. How could I live, think, as a man did? I still, these hundreds years on, do not know the answer to this. Except to say that the mind does not reside in a body, but in some other place, and that though 2 men made my clumsy clang-clang-clang frame, something else awarded me the gift of a mind.

The Hun were all dead. So were my comrades. I did not know what to do. A barrage was shooting over my head. I thought it beautiful. I walked back towards our lines, discarding my uniform, so sodden with English blood, and walked naked, free for the first time as a brass man, bathed in butchery, bespattered with mire. The barrage stopped and within moments, as my steps pulled themselves from the mud with rude noises, a thrush began singing a song of peace. Foolish bird, I thought, how can there be peace when even one German remains in this world! I looked for it, readying my rifle, but saw instead, shining back at me from a bloodied pool, my own reflection. A certain vanity which has ever been a part of me caused me to linger by the pool, and look into others as I threaded my way back. Where there's muck there's brass, I chuckled. A wounded man, Private George Wilkinson of the D. L. I., screamed at my approach.

'Fear not, comrade,' said I, "Tis only J. W. Mathis, false man.'

Although I had spoken words in my prototype days in the Ipswich workshop, these were my first as myself. I also did something else I had never done before: I whistled. I threw Private Wilkinson over my shoulder and struck up an original tune. But all music left me as with difficulty I climbed down an unavoidable hole. This was where our trench had been. Not 30 minutes before, I and my comrades had gone over the top from here. My 2 fathers, my makers, those brilliant young men, along with 5 colonels, a General and 14 representatives of the coalition government, had been sheltered here. But in the barrage it had taken a direct hit, and they were all gone. I have always wondered if my muddled consciousness descended upon my metal body in the same moment that they lost theirs. I have speculated that when they, filled with so much promise, lost their lives, that something left them, some dream of a man, some idea of life, that a passion hurried across No Man's Land and entered my brass.

When I put Private Wilkinson down, I saw that he was dead. For a while I studied his poor silly face. I whistled at it. I spoke to it. It seems to me that I was having my profoundest-ever thoughts just then, and that since I have become something of a flippant and emotional creature, whose thoughts about himself have prevented profundity from arising in his clang-clang-clang.

I had been constructed to obey orders, and not, in the absence of orders, to act upon my own initiative. But, as proof to myself of my new consciousness, I returned across the mud to the Hun lines. I had, above all else, been made to kill Germans. And that is what I did. For 3 days I wandered, shooting them, invading their trenches, battering them to death with metal fists as they slept in their holes, impaling them upon their own picklehaubes. Good honest work, wot. But I found them always strangely relaxed, jolly even, before my attack terrified them. At last, when I was attacking a multitude upon the Nancy road, some cried in their hideous tongue (I understand all languages save Welsh) that the war had been over for 3 days. 'Armistice! Armistice!' they cried. 'Kein krieg! Ist Friede! Wir sind in Frieden!'

My disappointment, I confess, led me to kill a dozen more,

throwing them as high in the air as I could, which was 300 feet for the lighter ones. I may have killed more, but I was suddenly gripped by the fear that this new consciousness of mine would give out, that like a clockwork toy I would run down. Still, centuries later, I have this same fear. Sometimes it has me useless, sobbing with the terrors it inspires. For a week sometimes I am free of it, but never longer, and for years on end I have chuntered with the frights. On that day in 1918 I hurried away from my enemy, terrified of death, but as I walked towards the British lines my vanity bolstered me with the idea that my own arrival on the scene had caused the Hun to surrender. The Kaiser had heard of my first fight and said to his Hun Generals: 'Vat is zee point in going on, mein Herrs – zis Mathis is too strong for us!'

I reported to a certain Major Devcoter, who was of an unscientific mind, and kept frapping on my chest.

'Bally marvel you are, soldier!' he kept saying.

I was put to work pulling artillery about. Some weeks later, as no one knew what to do with me, I was demobbed and sent back to the Ipswich workshop. The train home was rattled by winds. Always penny-pinching, I travelled 3rd class, and listened to soliders telling tall stories of their exploits in the late war. How I applauded their bravery! I shook their hands and pressed their cold cheeks to mine. Much laughter we had. But when I told them the story of Private Wilkinson, who had so very nearly survived the war, they remembered their own lost comrades and a sombreness filled our compartment. Someone started up a sad song. We joined in, but slowly fell silent, so that the starter finished it alone. Full of swearing it was, but beautiful in context. At Ipswich station those still aboard waved me goodbye, and skimmed their tin hats at me, which I caught in a flashy manner on my magneticized fingertips. When I arrived in the workshop at Nacton I was wearing ten tin hats, one atop the other. Foolish creature! But the atmosphere was gay in those special days of England, wot.

Mr Ogden, the foreman, was drunken when he found me sitting on the bench where I was made. I was reading the poems of Kipling, the only poet I could ever tolerate, in a tattered pocket edition.

'So you're back, yerh tin bugger!' he said.

'I am back, Mr Ogden.'

Ordinary man that he was, and quite drunken, he recognized immediately the change in me.

'Well, war's over, int'it, y'bugger. I don't know wot to do with yerh, lad. I really don't.'

Then he fell upon the bench, filling his fists with metal shavings, gripping them tight. Blood seeped through his fingers. He wept.

'I loved them queer lads, tha knows, Mathis. I loved them like they were my own.'

The loss of my fathers struck me heavily and I fell back in a faint. In a dream I saw myself clanking down an endless metal road. My dream-self was jolly, kicking nuggets into the muddy seas beside the road, but my dreaming-self was in agony. Each clank was a terrible pain. I remained in this condition, dreaming this dream, for 2 years and 5 months.

Marvellous Boys

The marvellous boys who made me were Mr Randy Botswoodie an.¹ Mr Simeon Crumply. Individually, each was brilliant. Together they found an intimacy of mind which I have no doubt was the most exciting scientific instrument of all human time. Had they lived I am sure humanity's story during the 300 years that have passed since they were whizz-banged would have been different beyond all recognition: better, wiser, easier. Thus, the moment that light dawned inside me was one of the most unfortunate of all moments. As it is, they are entirely forgotten. Their contribution to science is preserved in a few equations. Otherwise, the vain false man who writes this down is all there is of their brief life's work.

Mr Botswoodie was born in Saskatoon, Canada in 1892, into a wealthy farming family. He was a hugely fat and prodigious child, fascinated with the natural world, a 2-foot long polymath, who spent much time constructing mechanical toys. He told me, when I was still a senseless jangle of bolts and chunks, about his foot-high clockwork soldiers who would do battle in the wide wheatfields, seeking each other out with all their whirring energy, and upon finding each other, falling over, but continuing their leg movements upon their backs until they were found or their mechanism stopped. Sometimes I think of these little ancestors of mine, and worry that one was never found at the end of a day's play, that he lies on his rusty back in some Canadian gulch, looking up at the stars where lives J. W. Mathis.

Mr Botswoodie's genius was soon bothering itself with the improving of farm machinery, and on a bench in a wide barn he constructed all manner of gadgets. Happy early days which make me glad for him. Then the train steamed him away across the plains. He never returned. First he attended school in Montreal, then university in Boston for a year, then, at age 16, 1908 this was, he shipped to Cambridge, England to continue his studies. On his first night there he was sitting in bed eating from a bag of buns, looking out the window at a sweet English spring night, when he heard a peculiar whirring which aroused his curiosity. Walking about the building he found Simeon

Crumply in his rooms, busy with experiments in perpetual motion. From their first howdeoyoudos in that nightshirted peaceful night they hardly stopped talking for 10 years until the whizz-bang silenced their fast and brilliant dialogue. Nor were they ever out of each other's company. They slept in the same bed. They ate always at the same table, forever talking excitedly about one idea or another, laughing, arguing, fired by each other's flashes of genius, the trains of their thought colliding a hundred times a day with insights new to man. In some invisible metal room inside me, I fancy, I really do, that they continue their excited talk even now, at this moment.

Simeon Crumply was born in 1893. His father was a greengrocer in London, who, in a pencil-written letter to me in 1929 from a retirement home especially for greengrocers, confessed that his first clue that his son was exceptional was when he found him leaning out of his pram counting Brussels sprouts in the shop window. He was a silent, solitary boy, whose pleasure was to wander foggy London counting people, horses, paving stones. This pastime was very nearly a nervous affliction, and somehow was passed on to me. Sometimes I find that I am counting things and can't stop – for months at a time I will simply count things. No one denied Mr Crumply's brilliance. But he was lost in alcoves of highfalutin mathematical thinking, much of which amused him no end, causing a private giggle which made folk think him mad. It was only on the insistence of W. E. L. Purvis, the great mathematician, that the low-born genius was given a scholarship at Cambridge. There he sat writing equations all day, sending some to Professor Purvis, who spent the rest of his life pondering over them, plucking at his beard. When I met the Professor, at Brooklands in 1925, all he could do was chunter and weep. He showed me an equation on a triangular scrap of paper and asked for my comments. I was all cars in those days and didn't bother my cogs with it. My last sight of him was while zooming around the track. He was pulling the buttons off his waistcoat and throwing them at the cars. I have often thought that I missed an opportunity that day to find something out about myself. When Professor Purvis died of an apoplexy the following year his papers were bequeathed to me. 50 boxes' worth. I memorized them all, but the scrap he'd had with him that day at Brooklands was nowhere among them.

Professor Purvis was delighted by his protégé's new friendship. Mr Botswoodie's playful genius and Mr Crumply's faraway genius joined to make a single practical genius that set about explaining the universe in mathematics. They wrote almost nothing down. Just an occasional tantalizing note to Purvis. Nor was life spent in lab or frowning over a desk. They spent their days sitting in Cambridge cakeshops, where Mr Botswoodie became ginormously rotund. Each carried a small blackboard slate, upon which mathematical conversations were chalked, rubbings-out done with the leather patches on their jacket elbows.

At the outbreak of war in 1914 both young men attempted to join the army, but Mr Botswoodie was too fat and Mr Crumply too unbalanced. They returned to the cakeshops and their sums. But the deaths of thousands of fine Englishmen, including every last one of their contemporaries who had poked fun at them in Cambridge streets, caused them to write a letter to the Prime Minister, David Lloyd George, promising that they could construct metal soldiers, false men, who could then fight in the stead of flesh-and-blood all-too-mortal boys. The P. M. was a very great man, full of foresights and instincts bordering on the magical. Knowing that anyone else would laugh at such a project, he financed it from his own private funds. Thus Lloyd George became my third father.

Now he lies beside the Dwyfor in Llanystumdwy, an empty world around him, and I, the prototype of that amazing project in a long-forgotten war, somehow endure at the other end of everything, on the planet Cats-by-Nowhere, full of love for those who made me, and undying hatred for Germans.

I Find a Home

On September 21st 1921 I awoke from my breakdown in a tumbledown shed. Jammed in around me were a hundred legs and arms of unfinished metal men whose construction had been halted by the Armistice. My mind was worried that Germans might be abroad, so I kicked my way out of the shed, making a din like an axeman sabotaging a brass band. A heavy shower of rain was outside. It washed the cobwebs from my dull skin until I stood golden, shiny at the edge of a newly-ploughed field. More English fields rolled away towards the sea. Oh, joy! When the rain stopped, a rainbow looped from one copse to another and rooks were flying in both directions, copse to copse. Geometry filled my mind, but also, as I stared into the beads of rain on the back of my hand, where the reflections of rooks flew, I was more impressed by the complexity and majesty of existence than I have ever been since, though I have seen, I suppose, more remarkable things.

The horn of a Talbot-Darracq peeped me out of my idyll.

'I say, burwnt-up in the war, were you?'

(There were lots of disfigured servicemen in those days, and people explained my extraordinary appearance to themselves in this way – they assumed that I was a war-damaged skinless person, hurt flesh covered in a new brass skin.)

'I was in the war, yes, sir.' I attempted to doff my tin hat,

11

then remembered I couldn't.

'Damned shame. Still, no weason to stand about in the bally woad like an idiot, wot!'

'I most sincerely apologize.'

'Quite all wight, old chap. Lovely day. Can I give you a lift?'

I looked around at the workshop. It was deserted. The big doors were gone and the floor was cleared. Nettles grew in cracks in the forecourt.

'Thank you, yes. Kind of you to offer.'

I climbed into the automobile and its driver, Captain Stoves, drove off as fast as he could. It was very exciting. Later, of course, I was a famous driver myself. But this was my first spin, and I loved it – the automobile, like all automobiles, I felt, was my brother. Unable to smile, I can laugh with the best, and flung open my jaws and laughed for joy. Captain Stoves enjoyed showing off his Talbot-Darracq. He was a very jolly fellow and we parted firm friends. He dropped me miles-out-of-his-way in Ipswich where I set about looking for Mr Ogden, the works foreman, my only other friend.

I went on a pub crawl, expecting to find Mr Ogden in one of these establishments. I clanked in, amazing the drinkers, asking for my quarry. I was at last told by a strapping ex-soldier that he usually supped at The Butcher's Arms. He was not there. So I sat in a corner and waited. The landlord, taking pity on what he also took to be my war-woundedness, made me a gift of a pint and a pork pie. But, being a false man, I could not eat it. This caused him to sigh in further pity, assuming my digestive parts were war-damaged.

'Trouble inside have yerh, soldier?'

'I'm all cogs,' I admitted. 'It's a wonder I work at all.'

He showed me pictures of his sons, both killed on the Somme. I sang a rude song, one I'd learnt on the train coming from London in '18. I told him he should be proud of his sons and his backbone was immediately much stiffer.

'Bugger in Hell's flames!' It was Mr Ogden dropping a farthing in the swearbox. 'Mathis! That you, lad? Whey, it must be – wot bugger else! Thought you'd bloody conked out for good and ever. Whey!'

He drank my beer, bit at my pork pie, while we reminisced about my construction. The landlord overheard our chatter with an increasingly befuddled expression between his wagging ears.

'Thing is, lad,' said Mr Ogden, 'wot the ruddy bloody sodding hell does werh dee wi'yerh now, eh? I mean . . . you could live with me, but the wife wouldn't take to the likes of you. We've five kiddies and only two rooms.'

'I wouldn't dream of being the slightest trouble, Mr Ogden. I shall find a quiet place to reside until I am needed again.'

'Needed? Wot for?'

'To kill Germans, of course!'

And I thumped the table, sending our pork pie three feet into the air, to be caught by a stranger at the bar. This person took a bite out of it, an act objected to by Mr Ogden. The resulting fight was very exciting. But Mr Ogden lost.

I carried him home over my shoulder. His wife blamed me for this latest trouble in their lives. I sat in their small living room, feeling quite enormous, with 5 frightened children screaming with terror at me, their mother's sharp features scowling at me from above her folded arms. I was allowed to spend the night. But Mrs Ogden wanted rid of me, and it was her idea to send me off to Lloyd George. He had financed my making, she argued. Therefore I was his property, his responsibility. This scheme the man and wife discussed all night, arguing above the screams of their children, who were terrified to sleep with a monster in the house. The monster, my good self, read the latest *Police Gazette* by firelight and worried about his future.

Next morning Mr Ogden took me into his yard and started

hammering planks around me. I was crated up, very distressed.

'Sorry, lad, but I dunno wot to do wif yerh. Marjorie is usually right about wot to do wif people. It's either this, or I don't know wot. Mr Lloyd George will have a use for a metal man, I'm bloody sure he will. You'll be awlright, kidda!'

My expressionless face was watched during its fencing in by a cat, sitting on the wall. I shall never forget its smugness. I have hated cats ever since.

Finally Mr Ogden picked up the last plank. He shook my nose in a friendly goodbye, then hammered over my face, completely encasing me. I whistled to pass the time. Later that day men lifted me onto a waggon and I began my journey to the Prime Minister's residence, Chequers, in the heart of England.

The crate was placed in the Prime Minister's study. It stood there for three days, with me looking out through a crack at the doings of the house when they came my way. Miss Stevenson, L. G.'s secretary and later his wife, kept coming in with letters, opening some, leaving others on the desk. No sign of the great man. He was in the London Parliament. At last, on the morning of the 3rd day, the house was in a flurry. How nervous I was! I found that pork pie which Mr Ogden had fought over. It was in the secret drawer that is in my chest. Though I need no sustenance, I commenced nibbling it, terrified, waiting to see my only-surviving father for the first time.

He swept in, still in his coat, his mane of white hair flying, a speed of oratory coming from his little body. Such a spirit he was! Hurrying after him came Sir Austen Chamberlain and Lords Beaverbrook and Curzon. Around their feet were a number of dogs. These settled down on and around sofas, while the gentlemen lit cigars and poured brandy. Lloyd George neither drank nor smoked – he spoke! They were discussing the Irish question, then in high crisis – great vehemence, determined inspired speech from L. G. with the others chipping in footnotes. I was very moved by the things these good men said and dropped the pork pie. A dog came sniffing. These events alerted the gentlemen to the huge crate in the middle of the room which, due to their absorption in matters of state, they had not previously noticed.

'Someone has sent you a pressie, L. G.,' said Sir Austen, the most honourable man I ever had the pleasure to know.

'There now, I wonder wot it is!' said Lloyd George.

'5 bob says it's an Egyptian mummy!'

'10 says it's a wax statue of L. G. in a toga!'

Lloyd George rubbed his hands together in boyish excitement.

'Cummon, Max, Austen, boyos, give me a hand here!'

So it was that these distinguished statesmen used letter-openers, scissors and fingernails to pull away the creaking planks. Lord Curzon, above such doings, stood watching like a humourless walrus, kissing his cigar. He was the first to see what was inside the crate. He hurried forward beyond his own smoke, coughing, gagging, amazed.

'Dimmee!' he said. 'Dimmee! By Jove! Dimmee!'

Lloyd George's face was red from his exertions. I felt an idiot just standing there, with all my strength, while these gents toiled needlessly. I lifted my arms, butted with my knees, and the crate fell into splinters all around me. Lloyd George let out a stream of muttered Welsh. I stepped into the middle of the carpet, apologized for the mess, handed Lord Curzon the remains of the pork pie, then bowed deeply to the Prime Minister.

'J. W. Mathis, false man, your humble servant, sir.'

I handed him my keys as a sign that I was indeed his to command and control. With a wag of his finger he asked me to walk around the room. I did so, past pricked-eared dogs and astonished statesmen. Lloyd George grinned widely, slapped the cheeks of a bust of Gladstone 3 times, fizzed with delight.

The unflappable Miss Stevenson entered. She stared at me, then apologized for doing so and asked me if I needed anything.

'Nothing, thank you, miss.'

I looked around for my pork pie, but Lord Curzon, in his distress at meeting me, had absent-mindedly eaten it. Lloyd George stepped right up to me and frapped on my chest, as so many people have done. I looked down from my 6 feet 4 to his 5 feet nowt, very embarrassed. I showed him my hands, how well the fingers moved.

'Very good. Excellent, see. But can you sing hymns?'

I made one up, there and then, a beautiful one – very Welsh, I thought. He put his hands in his white hair, chortling with amazement and joy. I had found a home.

The Fall of Lloyd George

I became Lloyd George's permanent houseguest – in Chequers, Churt and Downing Street during 1921–2, thereafter for over 20 years my 'parental home' was at Churt, L. G.'s country home in Surrey.* Though I have lived in many places, some for donkey's years, when I think of home it is Churt that I picture in my brainmatterless mind's eye.

---

* L. G.'s Welsh domicile at Criccieth, where his wife lived, I never visited. I suppose I was part of the ménage of Churt, Frances being his mistress, me the child of their secret life. His daughter, Megan, often at Churt, snubbed me her life long. She never explained why. Jealousy, I expect, for although he was proud of her, dare I say that he loved me more.

Thursday October 19th, 1922. I was walking in the fields beyond Churt, deep in thought, and was surprised by the dropping of night. But there was no point in going back into the house, because I was suffering from an embarrassing attack of 'spoons'. Just as human flesh catches colds in winter, my brass catches spoons. This was my most serious attack so far. In its sickness, my body had become an attraction for spoons. Wherever I was, they found me. But indoors was terrible. They flew from their drawers or settings and stuck themselves to me, spooning and clonking under my clothes with no pretence at table manners. When I felt better they would drop off and be put away, but when I felt worse they would return, quite capable of breaking down doors to get at me. At that moment every spoon in Churt was attached to my person, and in the sinking day I saw silver flashes coming towards me across the fields – the spoons from nearby estates were intent on joining the infection, to fly cold up my trouser legs, or whack me on the face, still half-filled with a spoonful of some yeoman's supper. (Once, on the planet Bilickers 4, I had a particularly bad attack, but only one spoon found me. On leaving the planet, my shuttle-craft approached a silvery asteroid belt, which turned out to be nothing but spoons, half the spoons in creation, stuck in orbit due to my recovery.) So there I was, trotting across fields away from flying spoons, when I heard the horn of Captain Stoves' Talbot-Darracq on the darkening road.

'It's bad news, I'm afwraid, wot, J. W.,' said Captain Stoves. 'L. G. is out. Bonar Law is in, damn the man. Dimmee, but the countwy's going to the dwogs. I say, you're covered in spoons.'

Just then, the spoon complement of a considerable dinner service totally covered my expressionless features. Lloyd George had fallen. The Tories had killed the ogre. He never held political office again, though he was a better man than everyone.

I clunked into the life of David Lloyd George just when his star was about to fall. I firmly believe, and said so in my 1952 biography of him, that he was the greatest man ever to bestride British politics. But when I arrived upon the scene the qualities which had made him great were working against him. The coalition members of his government were grumbling, many plotting his downfall. He was fighting like a tiger, or in outer-space terms a rampant Bunnyperson, to stay in office, to remain in Downing Street at all costs. But crises came at him from every direction, some, it must be admitted, entirely of his own making. And in the background, always, was the sly figure of Bonar Law, waiting to pick up the crown.

I, J. W. Mathis, have seen the re-establishment of the British Empire across the galaxy. I have witnessed the blotting out of vast civilizations, and talked philosophy with creatures more subtle than any human ever was. I have clunked through wars more terrible than all Earth's wars rolled into one. But what heats my pipes more than anything are the events and issues of 1921–22 in British politics, planet Earth. It could hardly be further away, but I only have to think of that time for a moment and it is all powerfully alive within me. My winders click.

My own involvement was minimal at first. I spent most of my time reading adventure novels, mainly set in WW1, full of evil Germans slaughtered by the hero. John Buchan's stories were among my favourites. I saw L. G. only at weekends, and although he and Miss Stevenson chattered continually about politics, I politely stayed quiet on the subject and when I was addressed it was usually upon some other topic. But there was a government crisis which cut me to the heart. L. G. had been selling titles to anyone who could afford one and putting the money, huge sums, into his private political fund. It was not quite corruption, as I explain in Chapter XXVIII of my *Lloyd George As I Knew Him*. Stuck in a coalition government, made up mainly of Tories, his own party split, with only his personal prestige to back him up and meagre party funds behind him, Lloyd George was on his own, an independent force. He needed the money from selling titles to continue his political fight with might. But in 1921 it was a scandal, and painful for me, because the financing of my manufacturing had come from this iffy fund. When, one day at table, Lloyd George asked me what I thought about this particular crisis, I told him what I thought. He didn't like it. He bent his spoon in two in fury. (That very spoon was the one that found me that time on Bilickers 4.) My opposition set the great orator off on a tirade that continued for 3 hours around the table. Lord Birkenhead, Sir Arthur Griffith-Boscawen and my good friend Winston Churchill, then members of the coalition government, came in during the tirade and each smoked two cigars down to stubs before it finished. I had often watched L. G. listening to these very men's opposition with a thoughtful considerate face. But for me, always, were reserved the full furies of his dynamism. This first occasion caused a breakdown in me lasting 3 weeks, followed by a minor attack of spoons, and a whirring in my chest that I imagined presaged my conkout. I awoke just in time for the Addison Crisis.

L. G. was in trouble in Cabinet, always in danger of being outvoted and therefore forced to resign. So he made the useless Dr Addison minister without portfolio to give himself an extra vote, paying the man £2,700 a year for the job (the equivalent of £700 billion in 2199 money). Meanwhile, he was appointing men in their early 90s to important junior posts under his cabinet enemies to keep them overworked in their departments rather than causing trouble without. (My friend and employer, Archbishop Mugg, the author of the better part of this book, is currently 117, still young of body and mind, but in the 20th century people were getting ready for their grave in their 60s.) These nonagenarians died with tedious frequency and were succeeded in office by ever older duffers, or by barking-mad aristocrats – Viscount Trimbles kept a tortoise under his bowler hat and only spoke in quotes from the poet Tennyson. I thought this a dreadful business, and without being asked, said so.

'Owh, I see,' said L. G., walking around me in a flap, 'so I'm wrong again, I am, issit? Mr High and Mighty Tin Head thinks Dr Addison should resign, does he?'

'I do. It's the only way out for the Government, sir. Your only chance of surviving Tuesday's vote!' (Had L. G. lost that vote he would have been out of office a year earlier.)

'Well, perhaps you'd like to be Prime Minister yourself, is it! Mr Man-of-the-Future!'

He commenced snatching at my hairpiece. (I had cut off the brim of my tin hat and donned a Henry Irving wig the week before.) I was compelled to stand at my full height. L. G. was compelled to jump up, like a terrier after a tree-clumb cat. He failed, left the room, and returned a moment later swinging a golf club (this was 100 years before golf was declared illegal by much lesser politicians than L. G.) He chased me around the grounds of Churt, swinging at me fierce blows, missing every time. At last I gave up and knelt before him to accept his wrath. He was confused for a moment, puffing like a toy train, then he brought the club down hard upon my head. There was a clang as loud as the drop of the French knights at Poitiers. My tin lids closed. Was I conked? No. They opened again, to see a worried L. G. holding a broken golf club in his hands.

'You all right, boyo?'

'For a moment, sir,' I said, more sombre than usual. 'I saw the whole of my future life, hundreds of years, the distant stars, strange creatures.'

'Did you see me anywhere?'

'No, L. G.'

He chuckled. Still playing with the broken club he sat in a bower. Roses were on all sides. The air was dangerously enlivened by bees.

'I'm going to fall, know you, Mathis. Owh, yes. If not Tuesday then soon. I don't know if there's anything I can do to save myself.'

I presumed. 'Why not, sir, declare war on Germany! The country will arise to support you and all opposition will melt away! Please, let us return to our God-given task – to wipe Germany from the face of the Earth!'

He thought I was joking. His doomed face chuckled again. 'If only I can hold on long enough, see, to get the Irish Treaty signed.'

Then he sneezed. I felt a premonition. So did he. We looked into the air . . . sure enough, there it was: a spoon. I was having a mild attack.

L. G. worked day and night on the Irish Treaty. He was the greatest negotiator of all time, and needed to be. When De Valera left No. 10, Michael Collins, the Sinn Fein leader, would arrive. When he left, the Orangeman Carson arrived. For weeks this went on, all the while the country teetering on the verge of Civil War, and me sending warlike memos to L. G. advising him to crush the Irish with force of arms. Finally, on the night of December 5–6 1921, while I was washing a corgi in the P. M.'s bathroom in No. 10, the Treaty document was signed. Miss Stevenson hurried in, very excited.

'Come quick, J. W.! You must see! He's done it! They're signing now!'

The signatories were in the hall as I clunked down the stairs. Lloyd George gripped the unfolded document, its ink barely dry. Michael Collins had, L. G. told me later, signed as if he was signing his own death warrant. He watched me walking down the stairs, his coat in his hands. I helped him put it on.

'Thank you,' he said.

A year later he was assassinated.

'Here you are, Mathis, there now, see, ha, ha!' said Lloyd George.

He handed me the document. I folded it up and put it away in my secret chest drawer. It is there yet. And far away Ireland is indeed as extremely peaceful as can be. There isn't a soul there! Odd, wot.

There was a conference in Geneva that Christmas. I drove L. G. down. My first continental drive. Splendid. The icy roads. The Jura and the Alps. I felt like a character in one of Buchan's stories. Too exciting for words. I was then fanatically anti-Free Trade, being under the influence of Lord Beaverbrook's Empire Protection scheme. L. G. and I argued about this matter all the way, fiercely from both sides. No, I was no longer reticent. I was proud of my developing mind, and my opinions, once fixed, were powerfully felt and expressed. Much more so than now, when I care for nothing much at all, for or against, excepting Germans.

The conference concerned the peace of Europe, threatened by the power struggle in the Balkans, the so-called Graeco-Turkish war. The Turks had broken the Versailles Treaty, written by L. G., and were expelling the Greeks from territory granted them under the treaty's terms. They were also shooting at British and French troops put there to maintain the treaty. Bally awful mess! The French were pulling out – the cowards! L. G. intended to make the Turks (and French) submit. He would go to war if necessary. My suggestion about Germany had been the seed for this new policy. L. G. intended to pull Britain and Empire together by going to war against Turkey. He hoped to re-create the unity of his WW1 glory days with a new war spirit. I encouraged him in this with all my new-found oratory. My hatred of Johnny Turk was briefly equal to my Hunophobia.

But the policy failed. The conference broke up in shambles and, apart from myself, no one took L. G.'s side in the matter. His courage was admirable, but his every act from then on was seen by many as a dynamic force out of control. He was seen as a danger to peace, an autocratic figure whose day was done. Plus, the King hated him and was plotting against him at every step. 1922 was a year of argument, crisis and exhaustion. L. G. was pursuing his policy against the Turk, but the British people did not rally to him as he had expected. They were tired of wars. He was alone. On October 19th, while I was suffering agonies with spoons in the Surrey fields, there was a meeting of the Tory big boys in the Carlton Club. Only the be-monocled Sir Austen Chamberlain, who always fought bravely, and always lost, spoke up for Lloyd George. They pulled out of the coalition, putting Bonar Law into Number 10. Shame on them! The disloyal swine!

Lord Curzon, the plotter whose greatest hope had been to succeed L. G., stamped about in a fury for weeks, strangling his servants, making speeches to his dogs, until he dropped dead across his billiard table. Bonar Law himself was rewarded with death within the year. Baldwin succeeded and stuck fast. I chuckle now at how I detested Baldwin. I wasted years in attempts to prove my theory that he was a German spy during WW1.

So it was that my paterfamilias, David Lloyd George, lost the thing he cared about most. In the general election which followed, his Liberal Party barely survived, winning a paltry 4 seats. He was wiped out. They were sorry days at Churt. I had spoons for months on end. I only spoke the most essential pleasantries.

Then one day Captain and Mrs Stoves, their daughter Jennie and I came out of that delightful operetta *Bright Pudding*, they in good spirits, I a sorry cloud of tune-humming brass in the Strand.

'Look here,' said Captain Stoves. 'No need to be at a loose end, wot. You're such a spiffi-o dwiver, J. W., and no better gwease-monkey. Why don't you have a go at a few wallies?'

'Wallies?'

'Car wallies, nitwit!'

My spirit soared. L. G. was thwarted in his vocation. But I, standing in the rain-washed Strand, ridiculous in top hat and tails, had found mine. Brumm-brummmm!

The Rally Driver's New Face

It must have been early in 1923, wot! I was dining alone in the Criterion Restaurant, a popular spot occupying the top floor of a building in Piccadilly. I did not, of course, eat. But I had installed in my throat a rubber bag into which food could drop, thus giving the semblance of eating. I should add that though I rarely bothered myself to chew, only the specialities of the best chefs in England were forked into my throat bag! Often I forgot to empty the thing and I'd find myself sitting at table beside swanky folk forcing *coq au vin* into a space without room for it. But that day in the Criterion my bag contained but a few prawns and a carrot swallowed whole. The Duke of Westpelton tapped my shoulder with a spoon – which, with my medical history, caused a start whose effect was to make that carrot to shoot out of the bag and rest between my jaws like a cigar. The 25-stone eccentric million-aire Duke was entertaining the Dolly Sisters, a famous theatrical act from New York, then appearing with much success in London. He invited me to join them.

One of the sisters, I forget which, while studying my brass face, politely suggested that I should visit a renowned make-up artist of her acquaintance.

'He's worked with Lon Chaney in Hollywood, hon. Gawd, he

can make a pig look like a chicken or a chicken a pig.'

'Is there much demand for such a service?' I enquired.

My unintended witticism made my companions chortle. Much laughter came also from all around the restaurant, as everyone was ear-wagging the glamorous sisters and their odd escorts.

'Honest injun, hon – he could do wonders with that face of yourn. Make it look more kinda human, if you take my meaning, huh. I'm sure yerh doctors did all they could for yerh, but this guy's a genius. He'll make yerh into Valentino's brother.'

After luncheon we adjourned to the murky backstage of the Drury Lane Theatre, where Adrian Hewitt, the genius in question, was found sodomizing a rather old chorus boy. We waited outside his room for him to finish, during which time I said, my voice raised over the groans of Mr Hewitt and his friend: 'I cannot find it in me to despise homosexuals. Both my fathers were of that persuasion.'

This was thought to be another of my witticisms. I was somehow gaining a reputation for humour. In their hilarity the Dolly sisters kept slapping my knees, and continued to do so after their gales had subsided – I think because they liked the clanky tunes they could make there.

At last we were admitted into the company of the great artist. Somewhat beetroot-faced from his exertions, he examined my face and hands. His lips quivered. Tears fell from his bloodshot eyes. His fingertips caressed my brass like a jazz virtuoso might a wonderful trombone. His compassion was a surprise and moved me deeply. I grasped his hands tightly.

'Thank you,' I said.

Adrian Hewitt was very important to me. He was a close friend, one of the few who have shared the secret of my nature and with whom I have discussed my mystery. And, of course, above all else: he made me a face. Red rubber, painted over in greasepaint with the sensitivity of a Gainsborough. The face was the only part of my identity which my fathers and God's gift did not give me. I was changed. No longer a golem, but a man – a false man, but for appearances' sake, very nearly a man.

Let me describe that old face of mine. It was handsome, very. The nose, which had to fit over my jutty-out brass one, was long and noble. Its nostrils flared like a horse's at all times. The mouth in its relaxed state had a debonair smile, but I had a way of setting my teeth which caused the smile to turn knowing and grim. I could make any woman on earth weep with that smile, and sometimes tried it out on complete strangers. Perhaps she, my smile victim, would be trying on a hat in a hatshop and see me through the window, giving out that smile. Day ruined, poor dear! My eyebrows were of sable, very beautiful. My moustache of hog bristle, tough as needles. My chin was severe, I admit. But by stuffing a handkerchief under the rubber – my own idea, that – I gave the chin's outline something of the English softness. Adrian's final masterstroke was to add a manly scar to my left cheek, and a fizzingly rakish beauty spot to the right side of my nose. My Henry Irving wig was put aside for a new one: raven's wing black, short back and sides, curls on top, with a large kiss-curl crossing the deeply etched lines of my masculine brow.

The face had a personality of its own. How blank I felt when I took him off at night and stared at my tin-can reality in the mirror. He, the face, had become J. W. Mathis. I was the bronze statue of my own mask, wot! I lived inside the face's personality in one way or another for 40 years. He was not me and I was not him. We lived together, the face and I. We shared the delicious vice of vanity. We loved and married a woman together. We left our home world together. Even now, when he is as dead as everyone else from the 20th Century, I dream of him, the face, the same dream always. He sits beside a forest pool and begins to undress. For most of the dream he is undressing. When he is finally naked, I see that he is flesh from head to toe, no burnish of brass at all, not a boltsworth. Invariably, just as he dives into the water, I awake screaming like a kettle.

Adrian was killed by a tram in Trafalgar Square in 1929. I had by then lost so many of my rally-driving friends in smash-ups that I took one more little tragedy in my stride. My face, remember, had glass eyes, cold and tearless, and anyhow a certain coldness was a feature of my new personality. But the man had loved me and now I feel ashamed that I didn't even attend his funeral. By then, of course, I didn't need poor Adrian – I was my own make-up artist, making new rubber faces from Adrian's mould whenever needed – plus I fancied myself a better painter than he: his work added a sentiment to the face, failing that mine added a kind of whimsical severity which was altogether more in keeping with my martial nature.

Life was a whirl in the Twenties. Spinning tyres. A cascade of wild corners. French and Italian countryside slipping past. Brooklands, always Brooklands. But also Le Mans. Boyish faces cheering. Cups held high. Wonderful days. I was on the road most of the time, and had my own cottage and workshop near my 'birthplace', Ipswich. But when not busy or racing often I was back at Churt.

Since Lloyd George's fall from power and the dawning of my new face we had grown apart. L. G. was embattled in one-man political campaigns, full of busy, never stopped talking. My political stance had moved to the right, influenced by a horror of the great unwashed, from which I remain uncured. I joined the Conservative Party in 1924. Being a rally ace made me yet more haughty, a regular old-fashioned club Tory. When L. G. said to me one day that God loved the common people, that's why he made so many of them, I replied that he made even more fleas. How the old Welsh wizard was outraged at that remark! We barely spoke for a year. Whenever I arrived at Churt, L.G. would mutter through his toast: 'So it's Mr Mathis the tinpot Tory car-crash expert, isssit? Win any more races, have you? Or disqualified for tinpottery, was it?'

Our opinions were so different that it was impossible to

27

speak without causing argument. So L.G. read the newspapers to me, usually in a voice so sarcastic that often as not we both broke down laughing before long. More than once he screwed up the paper and kicked it around the room, conquered by his all-powerful sense of fun. One thing, wot: he never did read to me from the sports pages! He exhibited no interest whatsoever in my frivolous motoring career. But after his death – he died in 1945 when I was a prisoner of the Germans in Colditz Castle – Frances sent me a dog-eared scrapbook he'd kept of my exploits, each newspaper cutting annotated in his own hand. It can be imagined how deeply moved I was when turning its pages.

In his never-ending search for new political ideas, social concepts, ways of organizing the chaotic world, L.G. was usually brilliant, but he had a few hideously shameful croppers. Worst among them by far was his advocacy of Germany! He was forever meeting Huns in London or visiting them behind their lines. He counted Germans among his most intimate friends! He insisted that a strong Germany was essential to the peace and prosperity of Europe. Hah! Germany must be destroyed, said I! If no one else would do it, then I would do it myself, German after German I would kill till the Fatherland was fatherless. L.G. laughed. He took my outbursts for an old soldier's idle threats. He was, as in everything else connected with Germany, utterly in the wrong.

In 1925, I was at Churt resting after my famous crash in that year's Le Mans 24-hour race, in which Captain Stoves was killed. L.G. and Frances were attending the whelping of Labrador pups in one of the outbuildings. I was alone in the house when the doorbell ding-donged, so I put down my magazine and went to answer. I had never answered the door at Churt before. That I did on that occasion cost a man his life.

The caller was a German diplomatist, Heinrich von Stumph

by name, come to see L.G. on some matter concerning the future of the German economy. His heel klick was his last action in this world. I tore up his proffered card and took his bull neck in my gloved hands. The gloves squeaked. The astonished Hun squeaked his own squeak. Little had he expected retribution that fine day!

'Die, German swine!' I cried. 'Die! DIE!'

His neck broke in my hands, making a sound like a horse biting a bitter apple. I tossed him onto the gravel with a sneer, then kicked his last intake of breath out of him, rolling him onto newly cut lawn, and was about to commence stamping on his face when I heard voices in the house. I swiftly scooped up my German and bundled him into the boot of my Bentley.

L.G. was in the doorway.

'Six!' he cried. Meaning six puppydogs.

'Congratulations, old pip!' said I.

'Come and see!'

I hurried after him, stopping briefly to pick up the pieces of Heinrich von Stumph's calling card. I had murdered my first German and although I have since murdered many more, that was by far the most exhilarating.✳ He stayed eyes-wide in the Bentley for a fortnight, before I drove back to Ipswich. I took him out in a rowing boat, made a virulent speech to his long-dead face, and threw his weighted body overboard near Orford Ness. Here I am in another age, half the universe away – how it thrills me to think that his bones are still there, in a sea that teems with fish, in a world deserted by man.

✳ I do not, of course, include as 'murders' Germans killed in wartime, or in preparation for wartime. My secret career as a serial killer of Germans between 1925 and 1965 was purely a private matter, but inspired by my duty to my country and my anxiety about its future, especially after the lamentable loss of our Empire.

The Man I Hated Most of All

I took Pontlieue Corner faster than I should and felt that strange sense of balancedness that comes over you when you're right on the edge of turning over but know you won't. I had the feeling on a spacecraft once, which was about to explode, but then did not. It is a feeling with immortality in it – something momentous of eternal significance is about to happen, but history, your history and everyone else's, goes another way instead. Did my 3-litre Bentley, my good friend, my metal-brother, my jolly green girl, feel this in her carbs? I'd been caught whispering questions to her more than once, while taking her to bits looking for signs of a mind.

'Who's to know,' I said to Monty Otty, my partner in this, the '26 Le Mans, 'that motorcars don't think thoughts in their engines, wot, just like men do in their heads.'

'Egad, J.W., I'm too squiffy for such talk s'morning, wot!'

'Wot!'

'Wot!'

'Ehwot!'

'Ehwot with knobs!'

'Wot!'

'Who wotted that wot, wot?'

This was our little 'wot game'. It was utterly pointless, and totally delightful. We did it at breakfast, in corridors, on the phone, and when one of us jumped out at the pits for the changeover. We'd just won the British Grand Prix, not to mention the Essex 6-Hour Race, where we'd wotted endlessly, but we never tired of wotting, ehwot, wot and wot. We drivers

30

were a dotty breed, overburdened with superstitions – Monty and I had wotted ourselves into truly believing that the more we went 'wot', the better chance we'd have of at last winning Le Mans.

And so the race! The car was performing beautifully, no disasters, everything felt right. Reaching the end of my second 200-mile stint, I passed a Bugatti and took 2nd place, a good second. Wiggling down in the seat, I let the old girl have it for all she was worth. The revs went up splendidly. The Aries in the lead was way ahead up the long straight. With my acute hearing I could make out, over the noise of my own girl, that something was dicky with the Aries. Its exhaust didn't have that crisp sound. My Bentley did. Brumm-brummm! But from the Aries, a sound equivalent to one wrong instrument in an orchestra – a futtering which meant dicky. I was sure. Dicky. Perhaps this year the race would be ours! I daren't hope, then gave in to the hope! We'd win it in the night drive! Yes, siree! This was for poor old Captain Stoves! Wot! WOT!

The sun was red, sinking to its death as I pulled into the pits for the changeover.

'Wot!'

'Ehwot! There's something dicky with the Aries, Monty, wot! It's in the exhaust.'

'Good-o, wot! Wot!'

'Wot!'

'Ehwot!'

'Ehwot with knobs!'

'Wot?'

Whooosh, he was gone. We'd forgotten to say 'who wotted that wot?' Damn!

I sat in a corner, resting, letting the shadows darken over me, listening to the drone of the exhausts of passing cars, until all had passed. I was terrifically excited. This year would be ours, I was damnably sure of it – I was fully expecting Monty's next pass to be as race leader. When the time came for the cars to pass us again an excited hummer arose from the pit crews. But I did not arise with the others. Something had wafted through the empty helmet that is my head – a very definite impression of a soul, I thought, on its way to Heaven. I prayed from the hard core of my soggy faith, and during that prayer the excited hummer died down. Jinks Wilkerson, timekeeping, looked at his watch, stupefied. Officials gathered at the side of the road, then wandered into it. There were 22 cars in the race! Where had they gone? Never have I heard such a silence, not even when I've been alone on a world with no lifeforms. I could stand it no longer. I jumped up and ran down the road towards White Horse Corner.

I ran at normal speed till I was out of view, then went up a gear to inhuman speed. Running in darkness, at 65 m.p.h. I felt that I was running away from the world, from life itself – or a coward, was I, failing my prototype's test and fleeing from Jerry guns across No Man's Land? It was all around me again, my one true day of battle. But I could hear frogs, a myriad, beep-beeping in the humid air, like a trillion little cars in a jam – they brought me back to present reality. Just in time, for skidding from a start out of a forest cut roared a Merkel-Schnatz, its lamps so bespattered that they had less beam than a glowworm's. It was attempting my life – my instincts could not mistake it! But I span out of its way on one heel. Saved, but then I tripped into a ditch. For a minute I was befuddled in the dark, senses lost to the reek of wild garlic. At last I poked my head out, looking for more cars. None came. But my ears picked up a dread sound – creaking metal, hissing. And around the bend through the trees there was fire. I ran towards it, fists clenched to my heart, and sank to my knees in the middle of the terrible scene.

'Wot!' I said to Monty as I lifted him.

'Who wotted that wot,' he said, weakly.

The Bentley had managed to throw him clear before it skidded into the Aries and thence the ditch. But Monty's soul was still in him, or connected to him, or however it works. So, as none of the other drivers were killed that night, the soul that had flitted through my head must have been that of the Bentley. Yes, I was sure of it – my conviction that every machine, indeed object – every pin, pencil and toy train – has a living soul of its very own, was born in that moment. But the Bentley wasn't the only deaded car. The other Bentley in our team was there, on its back. Two Irats, two Licornes, two Salmsons, a Schneider, the Aries, a Peugeot all lay wrecked all around, blocking the road. As I carried Monty to safety, a Bugatti, its brake pedal on the floor to avoid the wall of calamity, skidded into the back of us.

I was in a state of unconsciousness from June till 3 days past Christmas, during which time I dreamt of nothing except driving in my dear old Bentley, always in good weather, through Cannes and towards the Italian Riviera, but also in Suffolk, between Yarmouth and Chaffinch Hall, singing *Tipperary* and other airs of the Great War. I awoke in my room at Churt, tinsel on my bedhead.

L.G. filled me in on the bad news. Monty Otty's injuries were severe. He would never walk again. Only 4 cars were finishers. The Merkel-Schnatz had won the race, driven by Baron Werner Schmernercreutz. In a flash I understood it all! I was sure that this vile Hun had engineered the pile-up at White Horse Corner, in order to eliminate all opposition and emerge as the only possible winner of the race. Not only that, but I saw the death of Captain Stoves in a new light. He was, poor dear, found up an apple tree in the same orchard beside White Horse Corner into which the Bugatti had bumped Monty and myself. His Talbot-Darracq was bent around the tree beneath him, its seats littered with a scrumping of bruised green apples. Not hard cheese, no: murder!

Monty's mother told me that he did not wish to see me – no, not ever again. He would always be my friend, she said, but wished that I should remember him as he had been. I honoured the wish and we never communicated again. A broken man, he turned to his mother's cakes, alcohol and the occult for solace. Rarely leaving his home in Penge, he was still alive when I left Planet Earth in 1965.

But I was not depressed that Christmas of 1926. I was elated by the thought that sometime very soon I would kill Baron Schmernercreutz. I considered journeying there-and-then to Munich, to shoot the swine while he insulted Jesus by yodelling his Hun carols at his fireside. But I decided to wait until next year's Le Mans and take apt revenge.

I declined to join the Bentley team, thinking it best that with murder as my real business I should go it alone. The good old Duke of Westpelton helped out by presenting to me a big 12-cylinder Sunbeam. A sheer animal of a car, it had a murderous intent of its own – to assassinate its driver! Yet in its day, it was the most wonderful car in the world, going at 140 m.p.h. down the straight. It gave a thrill of speed like no other car of its day, and which I never felt again until I happened to fall out of a shuttlecraft while entering the atmosphere of Bilickers 43b.

I took young Pikey Turpington, recently released from prison, as my co-driver. I have no room here to dwell upon Pikey's problems, mental, sexual, ethical. He was a damned good driver and I was glad I could give him a chance where others had spurned him.

I occupied the big garage in the Hotel Moderne yard at Le Mans. There was much work to do, getting the car ready for the most gruelling race on Earth, and Pikey was useless under the bonnet. So there I was, all alone, busy installing 2 experimental carburettors, when I heard a sinister cough in the archway that led to the street. A man stepped from cool shadow into bright light. He wore a black leather coat down to

34

the ground, a black leather cap, jackboots, a silver scarf, and carried a swagger-stick with a gold double-headed eagle on its top. His moustache was all under his nose, in the style later made infamous by Adolf Hitler. He was about to speak when I struck him in the forehead with the largest spanner to hand. Then, summoning all my tinman's strength, I grabbed him by the collar and threw him out of the yard, over the hotel, and into the copse beyond. So much for the evil Baron!

But three days later at the commencement of the race, he was among the drivers at the start, grinning in a shiny black leather one-piece suit. Just before the gun went, signalling us to dash for our cars, he said to me: 'How is your friend, Mr George Spigleys, please? I borrowed to him an outfit of mein clothes 2 days before yesterday and have not seen him after then. Is it possible that he is unwell?'

I checked the faces of the Bentley team. George wasn't among them. A new fuzzy-chinned lad had his car. The gun went. We dashed to our cars. Of course! – the Hun knew my game! He had sent George to see me disguised as himself, convincing George 'twas a jolly jape, but Schmernercreutz knowing full well, wot, that I would clonk poor George an eternal clonk. Damn my metal hide! – I had mistook that most English of Kentishmen for a blasted Hun! I had killed George Spigleys. My good friend, he had put my name forward to join his Masonic lodge, making us sacred brothers in that noble organization. I was godfather to his son Clarence, and I had killed the man! No guilt, of course, could be felt on my part, and indeed was not. The guilt was the Hun's! A foul Hun trick killed George! That Bavarian Devil, Schmernercreutz, killed him, not I! Not I!

In my first turn, of 214 miles, I couldn't find the Merkel-Schnatz. But Pikey, on his first turn, soon found it. He came back to the pits with a right headlamp missing, rear mudguards scraping rubber off the tyres and, worst of all, the axle bent.

'The Merkel-Schnatz, I suppose?'

'Aye, how'd you know?'

'Lucky guess, ehwot.'

'It was stopped at t'side of road and suddenly pulled out. Mind you, he had t'worst of't.'

Just then the Merkel-Schnatz sped past our pit-stop into its own. The Baron hopped out and his co-driver took straight off. The car was pristine, undented.

'Mebbes it t'weren't the Merkel-Schnatz after all.'

'It was, Pikey, I promise you, wot.'

There was little chance of us winning now, even finishing. The Sunbeam was a shuddering wreck. The axle might go at any moment. Without the right headlamp night-driving would be suicide. But I took off with a smile, one soon rattled into a grimace by the front shock absorbers which were badly in need of adjusting. Plus, the battery box was loose on the running board and my knee was all that kept the dashboard from falling off.

Despite all that, and driving half blind all night, Pikey and I kept the Sunbeam going, just. Next morning, only 8 cars were left in the race. A Bentley was in the lead, the Merkel-Schnatz second. We were fifth. I came around Pontlieue corner alone, nothing ahead or behind. Then, going down the straight I spied Stuffy Hopwood in the lead Bentley. I gave the big Sunbeam everything it could take. 140 down the straight, the Bentley a blur in the road ahead. Madness. The car would never survive. But it was now or never. I took the next corner well, but from nowhere a spatter of fist-sized stones pranged on the bonnet and bounced over the wire-windscreen, tearing my face, shattering my right eye. At the same time I was swerving to avoid the Bentley, which was on its side in the middle of the road. My wheels bumped over Stuffy Hopwood, I mounted the sandbanks and cleared the ditch, landing with a terrific crash among the trees. But the car wasn't dead. It kept on going, swerving through the trees toward the Merkle-Schnatz parked on a farm-track. I rammed it. Turned it over. Both cars fizzed and steamed. I staggered out of the Sunbeam and found my opponent. This wasn't Baron Schmernercreutz, but a double of same – one of many he employed for his elaborate cheatings and double dealings! And the car was a double of his own car, the very hellcart which had duffed up Pikey earlier and driven 2 other likely rivals off the road. Amongst all else, your German has no sense of sporting honour! The Baron's double was badly shaken up, but could still stand. He was fumbling in his coat for a weapon of some kind when a brass fist – I wonder whose! – ended his shenanigans forever. I threw him into the tree where Captain Stoves had landed 2 Le Mans ago.

The Merkel-Schnatz won the race for the 2nd year running. I arrived at the grandstand in time to see the Baron's face wet with champagne. I would have killed him there and then, damn the consequences. But Pikey was taking our loss badly. He had turned up in women's clothes and was accosting the Duke of Westpelton with claims that he had impregnated him during the Battle of Mons. A small French child, obtained who knows where, was an accoutrement of this hectic improvised charade. I somehow became involved in saving Pikey from himself, to his dismay tearing up the £5,000 cheque the worried Duke had written him. In all the fuss I suddenly felt a bony leather hand in mine.

'Hard cheese, mein old fellow, please,' said the Baron. 'Better luck next year, ehwotto?'

I turned my unshattered eye upon his dapper figure, looked it up and down with utter contempt. 'You absolute swine!' I said.

Despite many proud achievements, I never did win Le Mans. Baron Schmernercreutz, as every schoolboy once knew, won the great race a total of 11 times.✳ I throttled, shot, poisoned, exploded him a score of times, but it was always a double that

---

✳ I should say CHEATED his way to victories which should have been mine! Vile HUN!

died for him. He was, at long last, executed by order of the Nuremberg War Crimes Commission for his Nazi career. But that wasn't him either!

Latterly, of course, he has made himself notorious in ways then impossible, destroying places, peoples then unknown. If Rupert Brooke might be judged the ultimate Englishman, Schmernercreutz can be called the flaw in the German character personified.

A Cats-by-Nowhere Marginal Note

My good friend and employer, Archbishop Muggeridge Cod Chaffinch, Lord of all he surveys on Cats-by-Nowhere, woof-woof, God bless his little bald nut, has been reading thus far and is mightily irritated with J. W. Mathis, false man and sole member of his flock. He remonstrates I have been busying my pigboggn mornings writing a pigboggn autobiography, rather than pleasy-do mending his pigboggn mechanical cats – they being his only solace after a ruined life, he says. My instruction from the aforementioned Eminence in writing this prologue to his *22nd Century Blues* was to be as brief as possible about my earlier history and move straight on to my acquaintance with space travel, wot, thereby adding an element to Mugg's in-progress writings to maketh a book describing the entire history of the English experience beyond our home planet. But I have taken the argument to him, have I not, that it will be a bonus to his chronicles of the 22nd Century to have the contrasting element of my own humble beginnings in that very different atmosphere of 20th Century England added to it. He has reluctantly agreed to the sense behind my reasoning. But first he commands me to make at least 3 conked-out wire-whiskered pussies miaow again. No easy job, even for an old grease-monkey like myself, with an attack of spoons coming on.

My Old-Fashioned Life Between the Wars

1931, wot, found me in the United States for the first time. I was racing at the Indianapolis track. No Huns in evidence, the contest was mainly between an energetic Stutz driven by Hoss Bravelli, and my handy little Riley. Bravelli was on his home turf. He knew the individual character of the four corners of the track better than anyone. But 'twas I, J. W. Mathis, false man, true ace, who won. Three cheers for that chap, I say, wot!

While I basked in glory after the race, a reporter asked me a question which changed my life. He asked me when I was going to retire. I realized something, believe it or not, for the first time – how could I possibly continue with my charade of being a bona fide flesh-and-blood human man when I did not age? Egad, but most of the top drivers from my early days were by now either dead or watching their roses grow. I looked at my mechanic, Hares, an excellent man, been with me since I started racing. I recollected the day he first walked into my Ipswich workshop – he'd been in a fight with two socialists on a bus and his clothes were all ahoo, but he was a picture of working-class health, solid, rough, his flat face ruddy as a pork chop, and a shock of dark hair sticking up off his head like a black ice-cream cone. Now that cone was half grey. He looked tired, old, his body sagged. He wouldn't stop coughing.

'How old are you, Hares?'

'Dunno, sir.' A cough.

'Older than me, though.'

'Not by much, shouldn't fink.' A worse cough.

'Ever think of retiring, Hares?'

'Me, sir? Never, sir! I've years of work left in me. I'll see you win Le Mans yet, sir, bugger if I don't!' A tremendous cough.

'Of course you will, Hares.'

I shook his hand. He was very moved.✳

This was a dreadful fix. Especially, when I was in truth only 13 years old. But my mask, worn right through the Jazz Age, had given me the appearance of being a mature man, a vigorous 45-ish. First notion was to explain to people that due to a hormone imbalance I would remain 45-ish forever. Nope, I could imagine their faces during the telling! Better idea was: what if I deftly age my facemask – a line here or there, just enough to keep in step with the new decade? But to so do would mean adding corruption on a regular basis until I looked like the portrait of Dorian Gray. No, no, no! Plus, I should also have to ape the movements and behaviour of an ageing man, and eventually a grandpop, and then a Methuselah! For a chap like myself with an iron constitution, capable of enjoying life to the full, this was a bally damned silly situation to get himself into, wot!

Obviously, I needed an occupation less in the public eye, a more obscure but still interesting life where I could remain my normal 45-ish self through the Thirties, no questions asked. If,

---

✳ Gladstone Hares was among the five killed the next year, '32, when Crawford's supercharged Amilcar 100 c.c. skidded into the crowd at Phoenix Park. Old age never wearied him.

40

indeed, in the long term, I was fortunate enough to live a span far in excess of the norm, I would eventually recreate for myself a new life, with a new mask, always awaiting the time when my country would need me again. The prospect was not an unpleasant one. It gave me a feeling of freedom, adventure.

So by the time I returned from the United States I had sadly accepted that my dashing rallying days were over. I made preparations for my retirement from motor racing. One final race, the Paris-Madrid. I allowed Baron Schmernercreutz to run me off the road in the High Pyrenees – he probably would've anyway. I virtually came to bits. So, true to my plan, when I retired after the race, no one was surprised.

A week later I accepted a commission in the British Army. I was a Captain of the East Anglian Foot and settled down to a dull routine at Colchester barracks. But I enjoyed riding, shooting, cycling, canoeing, training my men. Not a bad life. Years passed in this way. Years of reading, contemplating my mystery, which led in 1933 to me being received into the Catholic Church – a new home – though the theological implications of tossing the holy wafer into my throat bag was a problem I dared not discuss with Father Mickananan. I was so grateful to God for his unique gift of life to me that I felt I simply had to worship, sing his praises and all that rot.

My leaves I usually spent at Churt. L.G., unlike me all too human, was ancient now, troubled by his prostate gland, in constant bad tempers, a one-man political movement, no friends, nowhere to go, all his greatness behind him, but still full of the old energy and fire. A tragic figure, spurned by the nation that needed him, warped by the futility of political brilliance without hope of power. At table he'd be ranting wonderfully on some current topic – we shared a happy detestation of Baldwin – then suddenly he'd flare up with an argument of long ago, denouncing yesterday's men like Asquith and Bonar Law, Haig and Kitchener.

One day at high tea he veered off his usual hobbyhorses for a lengthy, angry lecture on the humiliations suffered by Napoleon on Saint Helena. I broke in, very jolly: 'You know, L.G., back in '22, you should have seized power the way Napoleon did on 18th Brumaire.'

He stood, slowly walked across the room to where his dreadful corgis snoozed away eternity, picked up his favourite, cradled it and . . . yes, sobbed. When Francis came in, he dropped the pooch and buried his sobs in her bosom.

'What on earth did you say to him, J.W.?'

'Something about Napoleon. I forget what, wot! Nothing vile, I assure you. I was comparing him with Napoleon, 'tis all!'

Shortly thereafter I was promoted Major with a posting to India. I came home wearing my proud new pips. L.G. hurrumphed at them.

'One day you might be stupid enough to be a general, issentit!'

I knew his contempt for army officers, how it was born dealing with donkeys like Haig in the Great War, but I was deeply hurt. He saw that I was, but didn't know how to remedy the situation. Sorry would have helped. He just got on with packing away papers. It seemed he was off on a trip.

'This new Chancellor of Germany is a very great man, J.W.'

'Tosh!' He was going to Germany! My cogs ticked over like drumming fingers.

'Oh, yes, I know what you think of Germans, boyo. But this fellow will solve all the economic problems of his country, just you wait. Germany is the great eternal power of the European continent. Her prosperity, issentit, is vital to our national interests. She'll be our largest trading partner by 1940, see!'

'To blinking blue blazes with Germany. We don't need trading partners. We've got the Empire!'

He stood under my nose, twinkling, with his kindly-explaining-to-an-idiot expression: 'The Empire, see, it's an old fashioned thing. It'll not be there forever. But Germany will. I'm off to visit with Herr Hitler in Berlin tomorrow. Why don't you come, J.W.? You'll see the boche aren't so bad as you think.'

Believe it or not, I was tempted to go. If I accompanied him to Berlin I'd have ample opportunity for murdering Germans, perhaps even nipping this Hitler creature in the bud with moves from the jujitsu manual I'd recently mastered. If only I had gone! How different that distant century would have been for those marooned in it!

Late in the afternoon we were standing beside the pig pens in our wellingtons. Grunts filled our ears – a sound like comical gunfire.

'Well, boyo, are you coming to Berlin or not?'

I almost said yes. Instead, hardly knowing why I was saying it, I asked Lloyd George to return to me my keys. I had given them to him the day I broke out of my box as a sign of filial obedience and affection. I had 3 other sets, as I needed to be wound on a regular basis like any toy soldier – L.G.'s set was presented purely for symbolical purposes, and for new symbolical purposes I had asked for them back.

L.G. could express outrage like no other man. I'd watched him from the gallery in Parliament ruin Baldwin's day by a single sigh of oratorical outrage. But I'd never seen him, perhaps he'd never been, as outraged as this.

'KEYS IS IT! THEREHAVEYOU, KEYS, OH, KEYS, SEE!'

He stamped into the house, swiping at corgis with his stick, and returned to the same spot by the pig pens, from which this false man had not moved. He cast the keys down hard into the mud. Their silver sank so instantly that they seemed to disappear.

'THERE'S YOUR BLOODY KEYS, BOYO! I'D TELL YOU TO STICK THEM UP YOUR ARSE, SEE, IF YOU HAD A HOLE THERE TO STICK THEM IN!'

Then he growled like a small polar bear, waved his stick under my nose, and stormed off across the fields, scattering sheep with puffs of his anger. A day later he was discussing the future of the world with Adolf Hitler. He was photographed giving *Heil Hitler* salutes. Gad, the shame of it! It did not then mean what it later came to mean, but he did it, all the same. Twas the final moment of his downfall. His reputation never recovered.

I had left Churt before L.G. returned from his sheep-puffing walk, his highly offensive remark playing in my head like a stuck 78. I didn't return to my home till after WW2. I never saw Lloyd George again.

The posting to India was entirely unsuccessful. My original hope was that the change of scene would do me good, that I would break out of the inertia of thinking the same thoughts over and over which I'd been in for some while and develop as a person, as indeed I have here on Cats-by-Nowhere. But I missed England most awfully and despised the Indians no end. I found them petty and ungrateful. Their demand for independence I took as an insult to the King, then nearing the end of his quarter-century of service. Without the English to rule over them they'd be nothing but beggars, at each others' throats, their fate decided by the whim of Maharajas. Besides, I was damned sure their leader M. K. Gandhi was in the pay of the Germans. Unhappy, fidgety, I barked at my subordinates, cursed the climate, and told anyone who cared to listen that the Empire should be swept clean of its snakes, its temples, its various aborigines and made to look like Surrey!

In Bombay in '35 I lost patience with an unruly crowd demonstrating at the dockside as the new Viceroy, my old friend the Duke of Westpelton, arrived. He was now some 40 stones in weight and I was sure the chanting by the increasingly ugly assemblage was making rude reference to his weight in their silly language. I ordered my men to shoot into the crowd, expecting the usual few casualties. 142 Indians were killed – an astonishing number! Shows how well I'd trained my men, wot! I was sent to a hill station in Kashmir, out of the way, until the fuss settled.

The station was an old fort from the Afghan Wars. A damned pretty setting, rather mythological-looking, and everything neat and whitewashed and proper. I shall never forget that first night. I walked out onto the veranda of the officers' club, my throat bag full of curry, to be greeted by Colonel Chaffinch, ancestor of my present friend and employer.

'I say, Major Mathis isn't it? Wally dwiver, weren't you? Can't be the same chappie, arh-ha-harrr. I say, heard all about your twouble. Still, bet the wogs deserved it, ehwot? Oh, sowwy, wude of me – this is my daughter Maud.'

She was a slip of a thing, swish, twizzling her pearls in the twilight. She turned, no smile at all. Eyebrows plucked, painted on again surrealistically high.

'Howdyoudoooo.'

So haughty, so beautiful! My cogs raced! My subsidiary motor somehow kicked in, giving me an electric shock and creating a field of static around me which made the wings of the Colonel's moustache beat like a seagull's wings. Meanwhile, my wires had crossed themselves and, despite myself, I was dancing, right there on the veranda in front of the Colonel and a dozen Hooray Henrys leaning out of the club windows with whisky and sodas.

'Oh, I say, how charming!' said Maud. 'How awfully funny, how superdupery, har, har, hoooooooooooooooooooooooo! Life will never be dull with your new Major around, daddy!'

I couldn't stop. Some wag brought a wonky gramophone out, put it on a wicker table and wound it furiously. Something very like Bing Crosby came out of it. I twirled and took Maud, my Maud, dear Maud, in my arms. The static made her hair rise on end, denuding her long neck, revealing her nibbleable ears, making her look exotic, desirable beyond all women.

'I love you!' I whispered to her, steam filling my cavities. 'I have never said this to a woman ever, not ever – I love you! Oh, darling!'

She giggled furiously, making a sound at the back of her throat like a Zolistian mudcrawler's mating call – not that I had acquaintance with such creatures back then: suffice to say her hiccoughing thrilled me. Perhaps I would have gone on forever, dancing that timeless moment away with that most wonderful example of femininity, had not the Colonel shot five times into the air, killing three small monkeys on the roof, then once into Bing Crosby, ceasing all musical entertainment in the station till the end of the Raj. At the same moment Maud's string of pearls broke. They bounced and slipped away between the boards. All eyes were on these little scattered worlds, then they were gone and eyes saw the burgundy-cheeked Colonel Chaffinch and his smoking gun.

'Oh, daddy,' said the woman I loved. 'We were having such a wheezy time. You always have to spoil things!'

'NEVER IN MY LIFE HAVE I SEEN SUCH OUTWAGEOUS BEHAVIOUR! GET TO YOUR QUARTERS AT WONCE, GIRL. AND YOU, MAJOR TWINKLETOES – IF I SEE YOU DANCE ANOTHER TANGO OR EVER AGAIN MAKE A FOOTSTEP THAT LOOKS TO ME IN ANY WAY ARTISTIC I SHALL SHWOOT YOU WITH MY ELEPHANT GUN TILL THERE'S NOTHING LEFT FOR THE FLWIES TO POO ON!'

Having so promised, he picked up those dead monkeys and shoved them one by one under the jacket of my uniform. Then he dragged Maud away, but before she was completely gone she cried from the moth-haunted night: 'I don't care what daddy says, I think you are a sweetie.'

My desire for Maud Chaffinch, to possess her body and soul, was a mania of a kind I have never felt at any other time in my life. It was complicated by the fact that Messrs Botswoodie and Crumply had constructed me for one purpose only – to fight Germans in the Great War. No thought had been given, in the urgency of their commission, to make me a complete man. What I'm saying is: I did not have a penis.

No penis! False man, indeed. In my previous 17 years I had given womenkind no real thought, except lately an enthusiastic admiration for the singing talent of Gracie Fields. I did, admittedly, play the part of the ladies' man, but that was just my public face. In truth, I never went near the creatures, had barely spoken to one other than as briefly as possible to assistants in shops and red-heeled housemaids. Wasn't interested in women, didn't think them an important part of life – not like cars and cricket! But now my being was crying out for sexual satisfaction with Maud, dear skittish Maud – and I had no penis! Just a small bolt protruding from my pubic plate which gave me a peculiar sensation when polished with cloth and brasso.

I could see no alternative but to try to make myself a usable sexual organ with which to consummate my sudden libidinousness. So I set about it, full of expectations and anxieties. Most of all I was concerned that the continuation of my consciousness was somehow dependent upon penile success. So, terrified of failure, gripped by surges of sudden passion, I was an emotional hotplate bubbling with roasting aphrodisiacs.

This, the first penis I made, was a rather brutal, obscene object. As I worked on it in an old dhobiwallah's hut I was embarrassed to look at it. Made of a shaft of solid copper, covered over by a hundred elastic bands, then a sheath of thick rubber which I painted bright red – the length being some 18 inches, but poking only 11 inches from my body after it was

47

attached. It was, necessarily, permanently erect and therefore potentially dashed conspicuous. But when clamped to the inside of my left leg it hardly showed, except for causing me a slight limp. When needed, rather than simply unclamping it, causing it to wag most uncomfortably on its hinge, I installed a small winch at its base by which I could wind it up to the required angle. I removed 2 ballbearings from my chest cavity for use as testicles – their previous function was unknown to me, but the change caused no breakdown elsewhere.

The only other drawback, apart from convincing Maud to go to bed with me – but she had already, dear girl, called me a 'sweetie', had she not – was that I could not undress in front of her because stripped I was all metal (years later I developed an all-over bodystocking). Therefore, unless I abandoned all pretence of humanity and appeared to her as my monstrous self, I could only make love through my undone flies, which seemed to me at the time, and even more so now, a disgustingly depraved procedure.

We had slipped away, Maud and I, to a charming little pagoda in the grounds of a deserted palace. A dozen tiny lizards skipped off as we entered.

'I've never brought anyone here before,' she said. 'I come here to think. I once saw a tiger sleeping beside the orchids over there, licking his paws.'

I wasted no time. 'Oh, darling, tell me it's true – do you love me?'

'I . . . well, gosh, I'm not sure. I think so, yes. Yes, I do.'

I kissed her with my cold lips. She kissed back, grasping my epaulettes with all her might. She giggled and sighed, then frapped on my chest, which made a sound like a horse counting under a thick blanket.

'Your muscles! They're so hard. Like iron!'

Suddenly, she was passionate, her every kissing hotter than

the last flurry. Amazed and excited by this delightful little animal pawing my previously unpawed torso, I meanwhile had my hand fumbling deep in my pocket trying to turn the tiny handle of my winch. My new penis began to arise in my trews.

'I say, what ARE you doing?'

'Excuse me, dearest, but I am having trouble with my winch.'

'Winch?'

'A winch is required to get the . . . you know, thing, into an erect position.'

'Is it? I never knew!' (Poor dear, this was her first time, also.)

I shall never forget her cry, a mixture of delight, amusement and, yes, horror, when my new accessory twanged into the light. She seized it with both hands.

'Oh! Major, Major, Major!!!' she said.

Maud and I lay on a pagoda floor criss-crossed by the sticky trails of snails, and abandoned all morals in a writhe of frantic outrageous sin. She was delighted, fully thrilled and satisfied by the congress. I was not. As I thrust carefully into her a wave of sorrow crashed over me and I felt accursed in my un-humanity. I knew that no crescendo of ecstasy was possible for me, that I was condemned never to feel the satisfaction I craved, and though here I was heaving away on dearest Maud, I was still aching to be heaving away on dearest Maud. I was nothing but a piece of farm machinery drilling in a field.

So it was a dismayed J. W. Mathis who winched his false phallus down. Maud had shaken droplets from a big green leaf and was patting her face with the water. How beautiful she was.

'Didn't bruise you, did I, darling?'

'A few bruises, darling, are to be expected.'

'Awfully sorry, darling.'

'Quite all right, darling.'

'Was it . . . for you, darling . . .?'

'Exquisite, darling.'

'Oh, darling!'

'My divine darling Major!'

'Mmmmmmm!'

'Mmmmmmmmmmmmm!'

On the pagoda step we held hands and stared into each other's eyes. How I ached to press her naked body on my bare metal!

'Look here,' said Maud, sounding very army, 'I have to go to Kathmandu for a few days tomorrow. I know – terrible bore!' A shy pause. 'Could we meet here and do this again next Friday, and could I have a go winching your thing next time?'

Indeed, Maud left the next day, but her destination was not Kathmandu, but England. Her father, the Colonel, saw the change in her, the devirginized glow, when she skippped back home and greedily scoffed down her tiffin. She was sent away from me by force, bound hand and foot, locked in a cabin all the way to Southampton, bossed over by two cruel Indian nannies who delivered her, heartbroken no doubt, to Chaffinch Hall.

The following Friday, quite unaware of the new situation, I was waiting at the pagoda, fiddling with my winch with one finger-&-thumb and a box containing a wedding ring with the other. Yes, I was going to propose marriage! When Maud didn't arrive I went to her billet to enquire of the servants if the young lady had been detained in Kathmandu. The Colonel burst out onto the veranda with his service revolver at his own head.

'YOU CAD! YOU WOTTEN CAD, YOU! YOU ABSOLWUTE STINKER!'

Marriage into one of the great families of England without parental consent was in those days almost impossible. I knew in this very instant that my romance with Maud was over. In a way I was relieved, as its intensity had been too great to bear.

'Please, sir, don't shoot yourself because of anything I may

50

have done. Your country needs good officers like yourself!'

He was a broken man. Anger, yes – I had deflowered his little girl. But this I did not understand. The gun trembled in his trembling hand, his eyes darted from it to me, from me to it, and then I saw what had broken him – I understood the depths of the man's passion for his daughter. He had wanted her for himself, to possess her utterly, and her affection for me had made that forever impossible.

On my own return to Blighty I was quickly embroiled in the gathering storm of war, and did not attempt to see my first love again. I often skimmed the society pages searching for the name Maud Chaffinch, but never found it.✷

That afternoon in the pagoda with Maud, however, had made something of a monster of me. But a monster who better understood the passions of men. I especially thought of L.G. How often was I out dining with him when some flapper with boop-boop-ee-doo lips swanned in, cutting his intellectual flow dead, summoning up that other L.G., his monster, called by his detractors 'the goat', with an eye and consciousness all its own. What a curse this sexual desire was! And now I had it too!

The fear was this, and it was considerable: that my new

✷ It was over 200 years before I discovered the fate of pretty Maud Chaffinch, when my friend and employer Archbishop Chaffinch lent me a copy of his grandfather's autobiography *21st Century Blues*. This goes into some detail about life at Chaffinch Hall and tells of family members called 'the Others' who were locked in cells on the top floor of the Hall for their whole lives long. Either mad, unruly or the secret children of incestuous liaisons, there were at times over 100 of them. I am sure that this is what happened to Maud, that, when returned home, she was imprisoned on the orders of her jealous father and never again walked in an English meadow. These 'Others' developed their own philosophy of life. They spent their long solitary confinement dwelling upon one moment in their lives, gaining a certain enlightenment by forever focusing their thoughts. If Maud practised this I have no doubt what her moment would have been. That gorgeous day in the palace ruins with Major J.W. Mathis, while tigers slept nearby.

sexual consciousness, with all its tingling power, was a person in its own right, that it would simply take me over. It would depose me from my tinpot kingdom and reign in my stead! Warped as I was by its presence within me, I thought that the only way of conquering the libidinous spirit was to let it have its fill. But how to achieve this in an obscure hill station on the borders of Thibet?

The ginger, befreckled Captain MacReikie was a very keen hunter and was often off doing that very thing, leaving his wife Helen alone in their billet. This was a little removed from the others, on the other side of our quad. She didn't mix much with the other wives, preferring to go out painting by herself or staying home to practise dour tunes on the cello. I had no idea as to her personality, but she was handsome, broad and fleshy with big blue eyes and lots of tied-up white-blonde hair. I agonized for weeks, then at last I found the courage. I winched my penis upright and walked through the night to her window. A cool breeze was slipping down from the Himalayas. The humming music paused.

'I say, I listen to your cello every night, you know. It's all that makes life here bearable.'

She came to the window. My winched-up penis was pushing hard on my flies. Suddenly it broke out.

'Oh, do excuse me,' I said. I put my hat over it.

Her expression didn't alter. 'Maud Chaffinch was my friend, Major. She told me everything about your love for each other. It was beautiful! Beautiful!'

'But she couldn't tell you, could she, how desolate I am without her.'

'She stopped off here on her way to tiffin the day before she was sent away. She told me that when she was a gal at Poona she used to spy on the officers' bathhouse through a crack in the wall, but that she never saw, in all her 16 years of spying, a 'thing' half as impressive as yours.'

She looked down at my hat, sighed, then averted her face to say: 'Captain MacReikie, perhaps you know, was wounded at the Cape. He's not a proper man.'

'I didn't know.'

'We don't broadcast it.'

'No.'

'Do you mind me asking, Major, but are you very lonely?'

'I am, yes. Very.'

'So am I. Do come in.'

Absent-mindedly, I hung my hat on a peg behind the door. Mrs MacReikie's whole body heaved. 'Oh! Major, Major, Major!'

Moments later we were in each other's arms. But this wasn't like the last time. This time I was earnest to dispel the demon from my body. I let it rip. I allowed it to take me over. No restraint was asked for and soon none was possible. My brass body became a wild machine and I was lost inside it, powerless. There was no pleasure in it. I felt like a suicide whose afterlife is a continuous car crash, rolling over and over, exploding again and again, metal crunching, tearing. A destructive natural force had been let loose from some filthy sweating pit of Hell.

When it was over I fell into one of my dream-filled conkouts. This could well have lasted years, but in fact was only a few minutes long. I awoke to see that Mrs MacReikie had given her life to extinguish my demon. Her flesh was smeared all over my naked brass. Her gore was dripping from the furniture all around the once tidy little billet. Everything was bright crimson. One of her feet lay embedded in her broken cello. I had lost my facemask and wig among the steamy offal in the hot room. In a smeared mirror I could see my true identity – a murderous automaton – exposed in all its unbearable horror.

I fled, threw myself in a mountain stream and let the cold

water clean me. Soon my metal was shining in the morning sun. But nothing could forgive what I had done. The guilt, I felt, was a thing I could not and should not recover from. I should be disassembled.

Returning unseen to my quarters, I donned a spare face and wig, dressed in my best uniform and marched to HQ to give myself up. Murdering Germans was fair do's, but not innocent and obliging Scotswomen. I was indeed the worst sort of bounder.

Colonel Chaffinch was at his desk looking helplessly into the phone.

'Ah, Mathis, it's you – I suppose you've heard about Mrs MacReikie. Some sort of ritual killing, it seems. Egad! Look here, they're connecting me with her father, a Herr Muller in Düsseldorf. I'm no good at this sort of thing. You speak to him, wotho?'

My guilt disappeared in an instant, replaced by a wry shame that I had made love with a German. Yes, Helen MacReikie by marriage, but née Helga Muller, daughter of the Fatherland! Dimmee, but MacReikie had taken himself a German squaw! I wasn't going to own up to killing a Hun and ruin my army career. No fear.

But several officers, pixilated on the veranda of the officers' club, had seen me enter the late Mrs MacReikie's billet. They announced this to the Colonel and I found myself accused of being the High Priest of some diabolical order. Next thing was a court martial. I was on trial for my life in a sweltering court in Delhi. Dreadful business!

But Major Camberwell, defending, produced my facemask and wig – plucked from the gore – as evidence that not J. W. Mathis but someone disguised as he had committed the grisly act. Touché! I was acquitted. This was, however, my second scrape in India, so it was thought best I return home.

After my return, I read in the London *Times* that the entire officers' mess, including Colonel Chaffinch, had been found guilty of killing Mrs MacReikie during a Satanic rite.✳ After several appeals they were hanged in Delhi in 1937.

On the boat home, heading towards a Europe teetering towards total war, I tossed my first penis into the sea. There would, of course, be others.

A Foggy Night in London Town Halfway Through the Wilderness Years

January 1937 I was walking in my new Colonel's uniform through a real pea souper on my way to the Albatross Club. Dim headlights of cabs moved like ghosts beside the Thames Embankment. Approaching Parliament I was aware of two voices in the fog ahead of me – stone me if they weren't speaking bally German! I could almost smell the sauerkraut! They were lewdly discussing the Abdication Crisis, so recently resolved, but their Germanic natter was interrupted by bumping into a towering Englishman – myself!

'Enshuldigungs, mein Herr,' said one, and attempted to pass me.

I took off his titfer and skimmed it into the river.

✳ Captain MacReikie, away hunting, was, apart from myself, the only officer at the station not among the accused. But he was spared the news of his wife's death, being so trampled by a buffalo on this same expedition that he lost his memory for good. Simple minded, he spent the rest of his days attending to the gardens of an Indian potentate and died from snakebite in 1959.

'Excuse me, but are you two gentlemen perchance ... Germans?'

'Ja, ja – why did you do this to mein hut, please? Did you see what he did to mein hut, Helmut?'

I took his friend's titfer and skimmed that into Father Thames also. Then, before they could lodge a protest, I summoned all my inhuman strength and threw them as high into the foggy night as they would go. I listened carefully to discern exactly where they fell, hearing the lap of the river for some while before a faint distant sound told me I had thrown them right over Whitehall and into Saint James's Park.

This encounter set me on my way whistling popular tunes of the day. I was gung-ho breezy as I entered the Albatross Club and hung my albatross around my neck.✶ After a big dinner I was even jollier when I slipped into the Gents to empty my throat bag into a bog. I heard someone straining in the next cubicle.

'Winston, that you?'

'Mathis? J. W. Mathis! Harrr-harr! I've been looking for you everywhere, old boy!'

'Well, here I am, large as life and twice as handsome!'

I had known Winston Churchill all my life, but we had never been intimate friends, largely because he suspected I held Lloyd George to be the greater man. I did. But Winston's spirited opposition to appeasement, his advocacy of putting the country on a war footing and his enthusiasm for the Empire had made him a hero for me.

Winston's bird had a wingspan of 8 feet. He needed help extracting himself from the cubicle. We then adjourned to the

---

✶ Rule One for Members of the Royal Albatross Club is the most strictly upheld: members must wear a stuffed albatross around their necks whenever on the premises of that said institution. The club was founded by Admiral Jellicoe in 1924 and now has 72 affiliated Albatross Clubs across our galaxy.

library and sat in big leather chairs under a stained glass window of the Relief of Mafeking. We smoked cigars, Winston tipping his ash onto the already grubby albatross hanging around his neck.

'The boche will take over all Europe if we let them, J. W.,' he said in a drawl more drawlish since last I heard him speak. 'Our island race is on the precipice of a great calamity. Though I try my best, I am but a voice crying in the wilderness. If something isn't done to rearm, we shall not be ready when the time of testing comes.'

'They must be stopped! Blasted Hun!'

Winston smiled. 'Didn't think you'd be an appeaser, J. W.'

He chuckled for a while, then fell asleep. I snoozed also, soon waking to help Winston put out the fire on his albatross – his cigar having fallen from his mouth into its feathers.

When the conflagration was well doused he gripped my arm and said: 'Some friends and I are trying to prepare the country for the inevitable war – on the quiet, you understand, without government knowledge. Do you think you might help us, J. W.?'

'Anything, Winston. Just say what you want me to do!'

'Do you think you could make more "men" like yourself?'

I was astonished. 'Like myself? England is full of men like myself – patriots!'

'You are a robot, Mathis.'

'Am not!'

'Are too!'

'Not!'

'You forget, I knew you before you put on that matinée idol's mask of yours.'

'Mask? Wot mask, wot! Stop this scurrilous talk, Winston! You know very well that I'm a man, same as you.'

'Come, come . . .'

Fog was creeping through cracks in the Relief of Mafeking. I shall never forget watching it curl while Winston told me an old Jewish folk tale, about a certain Rabbi Loeb, how long ago in the Polish ghetto he fashioned a man out of clay to defeat the enemies of the Jewish people. Winston described in his dramatic voice how the Rabbi put life into this golem by whispering secret words into its mouth, then how it ran amok in the night, smiting the enemy till none were left. The golem then returned to the Rabbi and became mere clay once more, but was kept in a room for the day it might be needed again. I was England's golem, said Winston, but in the terrible conflict ahead we needed more, many more. He spoke to me of my destiny: again and again he used that frightening word.

When he was finished I stood up, haughty, insulted, confused. Winston stood before me, legs wide, determined. The beaks of our albatrosses fenced. He gripped my hand. I could have squeezed it dry, but I shook it.

'Good man!' he said. 'I knew you wouldn't let me down.'

'I can't promise anything, Winston. There may indeed be as much magic as science in making a man like me. But I'll give it a go, wot!'

My Robot Platoon

At last, after my long years of hard work perfecting the manufacture of robotic soldiery, my outfit was being trusted with an important mission. Success in this would mean (A) mass production of my kind, the fulfilment of my fathers' dream of 30 years ago, and (B) a major contribution to the winning of this terrible war on a planet now obscure and far away.

We were cooped up in a De Havilland bomber, flying from Gib towards the Alps, heartily singing *Sommernachtslieden*, a Tyrolean folksong we had mastered especially for the mission. 2 hours of this same song and it was beginning to get on my nerves, so I went up front for a looksee and looksaw the mountains dead ahead. It was July but their tops dazzled with snow.

My interview with Field Marshal Underdoggerly kept running through my mind.

'Mechanical men!' he'd kept saying while reading the file. 'Wot will you boffins think up next, ehwot?'

'Not merely mechanical, sir. They have souls, sir. Souls, like you and I.'

'Souls? That's a conchie word! Don't want to hear it! Guts, that's the word I want to hear. Do they have guts? Guts for a mission that they probably won't come back from but which may very well turn the tide of this war!'

'I think my men are up to it, sir.'

But I wasn't sure. He'd hit a raw nerve when he said 'conchie'. Something not in the file. My first batch out of the blood tank had proved quite effete, like a set of bally chaplains. After a week of preliminary training, in which they behaved like chorus girls, they sent a spokesperson to see me who made a long speech about how WAR was wrong, that they wished to devote themselves to LOVE and when would they be issued with penises. It hurt to do it, but there was a war on: I dismantled the lot, then melted down their parts and had the RAF boys drop the material into the Atlantic. Even then their ghosts whoooooooed effetely in the barracks all night, so that we had to abandon the Ipswich workshop to them and move to Ashford. Damned tricky business, making robots!

'Mountains coming up ahead, men. Won't be long now.'

'Good-O, sir. Can't wait!'

'That's the spirit.'

I looked up and down the line at my score of men. Funny, they were my own kind, but I could never trust them. Any flesh and blood soldier, yes, but not these. Or was I being unfair? In '41 I took a batch of 6 on a raid on the Norwegian coast to help blow up some German shore batteries. The moment we were ashore, they overpowered me, tore off their uniforms and ran to join the enemy. I have never, before or since, been so mortified. If they hadn't been destroyed when the batteries went up, the Germans would've had themselves 6 of the best crack troops to pin Iron Crosses on. That also was not in the file. Destroyed in the line of duty, said my official report. But such an experience meant that I could never quite be sure of my metal men, and this was why I had secretly installed in every Jack of this new batch a bomb big enough to blow up a house, which I could set off with a remote control I kept in my secret drawer.

It was also the reason I had brought Mr Ogden along. He had worked on my own manufacture in 1916–18 and had worked beside me making all these men here. His had been the suggestion that instead of using Army issue bloodbank blood to bathe the newly constructed metal men, we use blood freshly brought from the battlefields of Europe – this had been crucial in our success in making thoroughly martial men! Ogden was, furthermore, an excellent judge of men, and knew the chaps inside out. If any thought of betrayal or cowardice crossed their minds I felt he would be able to discern it before I could. He was now 87 years old, and quite frail, but the risk of bringing him along was balanced by the affection that the men held for him – they would stick together just to protect him, I was sure.

The red light flashed. Egad, this was it, wot! I opened the door. The wind filled the aeroplane, blew the girlie magazines out of the hands of the men. They looked at me, all 20, with the handsome eager faces I had given them. It will break my heart,

I thought, if they let me down. Then again the clipped voice of Field Marshal Underdoggerly played in my mind like an unforgettable tune:

'It's a mad idea, Colonel, but it may just work. We happen to know that the German Führer is attending a folk-singing festival at Innsbruck in his native Austria on the night of July 12th. What we intend to do is drop you and your men in the Stubai mountains, here, disguised as a troop of folk singers. You are to infiltrate the festival and kidnap old Adolf, gottit?'

And my own voice saying: 'Seems pretty straightforward, sir!'

Now here we were doing that very thing, jumping out over enemy held territory in our lederhosen. Funny to think of that whole planet at that moment, us in the air, and everywhere else humans engaged in war, dying, escaping, opening telegrams, bobbing in life rafts in the sea, and Adolf Hitler on his way to a folk-singing festival in Innsbruck. Early on I had elected that we should jump without parachutes – meaning much quicker to earth, therefore less chance of being spotted, more accurate drop, and no yards of silk to hide afterwards – but the training was hard on the men, and I don't think I've recovered from it yet myself! We simply jumped into the wide blue yonder with nothing but a small cushion to break our fall – the cushion being eaten upon landing. I had the added burden of carrying Mr Ogden.

'Whey, lad – I must be bliddie daft doing this – and them's very likely me last words 'n all!'

He'd watched us jumping off the tower often enough in training, but he'd never actually practised being a passenger. In the end, he enjoyed the descent – the long slow ride, a moveless feeling, quite the most peaceful minute I'd spent perhaps ever. Ogden said 'Y'bugger!' 103 times and no need to have worried about him for twas he, with a big grinning doggy face, who helped me to my creaking feet on Mother

61

Earth, or near enough to same . . . We'd landed, as planned, on the Stubai glacier, a good hike from Innsbruck. It was permanent ice where we stood at 3,000 metres, but way down below were meadows full of violets, green valleys bright with summer.

'Remember to eat your cushions, men! Everyone accounted for?'

'Clem's head's come off, sir.'

'Mr Ogden, see what you can do. If he's too badly pranged we'll just have to leave him.'

While we bit into our cushions, scoffing them feathers and all, Mr Ogden did what he could for poor Clem. He came back to me with a doctorly shake of the head. Last I saw of Clem he had his head in his hands, yellow and grey cogs lying in the snow all around him, his fingers picking at his mask as if he were a schoolboy and it a scab. We had to leave him. As we trotted along the valley floor, singing our song in our perfect Tyrolean accents, waving to peasants busy in fields, I surreptitiously opened my drawer and pressed Clem's number on the control. The crack of the explosion echoed from mountainside to mountainside, getting smaller and smaller all the time. The men were curious about it, but had no idea what it signified.

It took us an hour on the trot – taking turns to carry Mr Ogden – to reach Innsbruck, where we goggled at baroque cathedrals and snarled behind our masks at the swastika flags which hung every few yards and at the German troops who ambled about in twos and threes. I noticed that people were especially admiring of our knees. Of all the work I'd done in the field of robotics, I found myself most proud of the little rubber knees I'd made us, to fit between sock and lederhosen.

We marched down Maria Theresien Strasse singing our song, then whistled it through the old town and had just turned into the plaza where the festival was being held when a leather coat with a small bald head sticking out of it blocked our way.

'Enshuldigungs, please, but I have been listening to your whistling. It is most charming, an almost inhuman quality about it which reminds me of Schumann when he was irretrievably insane. I am Herr Spaß, one of the judges in tonight's contest. Which village are you coming from, please?'

Due to the German deference to the old, Her Spaß addressed this sinister speech to Mr Ogden who was the only one of us without perfect German and who just nodded saying 'Aye, y'bugger,' to every point.

I did the answering: 'Ve are from ze village of Puffenshrinkle.'

'Puffenshrinkle? I have not heard of zis village. Where is it, please?'

'It is between Obergurgl, Imst and Piffenblatzen, please, in the Glockendinkental.'

His shoes tapped under his long leather coat. 'Zis is where I am from, please! I was born in Piffenblatzen! I have spent all mein life walking in the beautiful valleys zere – unt never, NEVER have I heard of a village called Puffenshrinkle!'

Swastika-shaped wrinkles broke out upon his face and he yelled for assistance like a dachshund in a well.

A Gestapo officer – of the blond, educated and cruel type – who was having a smoke nearby while gazing lazily at examples of the baroque, came over toot de sweet!

To be stumped so early in a mission was damned unlucky. My men looked from one to t'other, scratching their knees, wondering how I was possibly going to get us out of this fix. I had no choice but to resort to hypnotism. I had learned this from one of those War Office handbooks and tried it out a few times on young women in an effort to get them to remove their clothes. It had never worked. But Herr Spaß proved an excellent subject.

'Have you ein problem, Herr Spaß?' asked the Gestapo chap.

'Nein, nein, I was just wishing for to introduce you to the

Puffenshrinkle singers. Puffenshrinkle is near to my own home village of Piffenblatzen.'

'Ah, so. You will be singing before ze Führer tonight. A great honour.'

'Ja, ja, ja, ja, ja, ja, ja, ja, ja, ja, ja, ja, ja, ja, ja, ja, ja, ja, ja, mein herr.' We all said it.

The Gestapo officer walked up and down our lines, looking suspicious. Was some detail wrong? What had given us away? Crikes – feathers! Half the men had little feathers at the corners of their mouths – from eating those damned cushions!

He stared close into Diggers's face, almost with the expression of a lover.

'Unt vot is your name, pretty boy?'

'Diggers . . . erm, Hans, Herr Oberst.'

When Diggers spoke a puff of dry feathers hicced out of his throatsack and hit the Nazi in the face. He slapped Diggers with his gloves – then, his curiosity raised because no redness had been made upon the skin, he commenced to pinch the poor creature's facemask with his naked fingers.

'Bitte, bitte,' said I. 'The feathers are from the raw unplucked chickens I make them eat. Excellent for the voice, don't you know, ehwot?'

He was appeased. He patted Diggers's cheek. 'Ah, so! Raw unplucked chickens.'

'A tip given me by the great Furtwangler himself.'

'Nein!'

He was suddenly all laughter. We laughed with him, spraying the air with feathers, which made him laugh more. As we went on our way he slapped his gloves on his thigh and said: 'If your singing is as beautiful as your knees you will be receiving cups from the Führer's hand this night!'

We mingled with the dozen other troupes of singers in a huge tent in gardens behind the imposing theatre where the competition would be held that evening. Much eating of sausages, drinking of beer, excited talk about the Führer being in town. Men in feathered hats kept coming by carrying tubas. Herr Spaß brought over other judges and officials to meet us, some several times. He also introduced us to tubas, busts of Goethe, aspidistra plants and a carriage horse he'd met outside and taken a fancy to. My hypnotism, it seemed, had done something weird to his mind and I half feared he might start braying like a donkey, which is what all those girls did rather than remove their clothes.

We were on stage 8th out of the 12. So I had plenty of time to mope about, peeping at Hitler from the wings. He was seated not in a box but in the stalls, surrounded by bull-necked generals and their fat sensual wives. Strange to see in the flesh the creature whose evil face I had so often sworn at in the papers. He looked so small, so ordinary, so jovial and reasonable. How could this one man have thrown the whole planet into an utter darkness of mayhem, murder and tears? There he was accepting chocs from boxes offered him by fat wife after fat wife. A dapper, courteous little fellow, but also the Devil incarnate!

The 3rd troupe were about to go on when Mr Ogden pulled at my sleeve and said in his big flat North Country voice: 'Hey, lad, we've a flap on – half of oor lads have mickied!'

Damn! Binky, Stinky, Winky, Todger, Bodger, Dodger, Diggers, the 2 Corporal Robinsons (I'd made 2 the same by mistake), Bingo and Fido all AWOL! I should never have fitted them with penises. Only did so out of kindness! What a fool! Odds on they had charmed the frauleins serving at the sausage counter and were even now smooching them with unbuttoned lederhosen. The irresponsible blinking shower!

'You stay here, Mr Ogden – and don't you dare say a word, gottit!'

He called after me: 'IT'S ALL YOUR FAULT, YER DAFT BUGGER! YOU SHOULD NEVER HAVE FITTED THEM

BASTARDS WIV WANGERS! I BLIDDIE TOLD YER SO, DIDN'T I?'

I found Binky and Stinky and Winky in a little park on the other side of the Inn, snogging away with, as I'd thought, sausage frauleins, lederhosen unbuttoned. The Corporal Robinson twins were discovered taking turns on top of a very grand lady in a huge Daimler parked outside the theatre. While one thrust the other sniffed her feet. Very odd. Diggers I tracked down in a private bar off Boznerplatz, sitting on the knee of that Gestapo officer we'd met earlier. They were feeding walnuts into each other's cheesy grins.

'Awfully sorry to break up the party, Oberst, wot, but Diggers, erm, Hans is on stage in 10 minutes.'

'TONIGHT, MEIN LEIBLING, WHEN YOU ARE VICTORIOUS, WE SHALL SCREAM TOGETHER, NAKED UNDER THE BLOODSTAINED MOON!'

Funny, but that perverted parting shot from that Nazi swine came up in my dreams many times during the years ahead.

In the theatre the 7th act were taking their bows when I arrived back with a full set of my absconders.

'Other singers much cop, wot?' I asked Mr Ogden. 'Not a patch on us, I'll bet!'

'Naw! The last two lots were the bestest but some bugger at the back of t'stalls started braying like a donkey and it put them off no end!'

We sang our *Sommernachtslieden* with a strange unearthliness, its tone informed by a sorrow born of the Blitz, the whole suffused with an English lyricism, driven home by a mellifluous nostalgia as we remembered practising this song in our billet back in dear old England. Halfway through, we dropped the words and commenced a humming which began low, then rose, higher and higher, like the arrows of the English archers at Agincourt, then cut it suddenly as Mr Ogden's bass baritone took up the chorus and we whispered it behind him, raising our volume towards the crescendo, feathers in the air all around us, like thistledown on a night such as we sang about . . . where the young peasant lad loses his cow on the mountain and can never return until he finds it again. The Führer was in tears, the sinews of his neck twitching in emotion. I felt smugly confident that we had won.

As the coup de grace, Diggers stepped forward and, with me accompanying on guitar and Mr Ogden on tuba, sang in a soprano so high it worried dogs on the mountainsides ringing the town, a coda to the song . . . how the boy finds his cow, brings it home, marries his sweetheart and they eat the cow whole on their wedding night. Powerful stuff, ehwot!

I knew my Germans! When we were done the whole theatre was in an uproar of emotional furore. Hitler was banging his head into the ample bosoms of his generals' wives. Everyone was on their feet slapping out an overenthusiastic applause. But suddenly I was deflated . . . It is quite true what old stagers say, that just one unresponsive member of an audience can spoil a performance for a performer. Amidst all the acclaim all I could feel was a single ray of disapproval. My eyes scanned the cheering rows: THERE HE WAS! In the whole theatre only one figure was seated – grim, arms folded, a stony stare directed right at me. It was Baron Werner Schmernercreutz! The nemesis of my rallying days! When our eyes met I knew the game was up.

But the Führer in his enthusiasm, and in a typical despotic disregard for proper form, snatched the winners' cup from its table and climbed the stage to present it to us himself. The audience was out of its seats, pushing forward. I saw that Schmernercreutz's seat was also empty – I could only hope he'd been caught up in the crowd. That might give us all the time we needed. The curtain came down and we accompanied the Führer into a spacious reception room at the rear of the theatre – it was all pillars and fancy pink plasterwork, like a vile tasteless cake in a shop window in Brighton. The picture of this room in Field Marshal Underdoggerly's brief had been in black and white and therefore had given no impression of its true nature!

'Your singing!' exclaimed Hitler. 'It was like our ancestors singing from their graves, telling us that zee day of our greatness has arrived. Oy, vot a performance!'

'Nay, we weren't rubbish, wuz wer,' said Mr Ogden in English from behind his tuba.

Celebratory cake was handed around – to my surprise, cake exactly the look and texture of the room's ikky rococo plaster-work. My Puffenshrinkle singers ate cake. Hitler, his emotions having stirred his appetite, had a slice in each hand. High-pitched social chuckles from generals' wives. Chatter rising from a buzz to a buzz-roar as more and more people pushed into the crowded room. Meanwhile, I had opened a small door behind a pillar and was guiding the second Corporal Robinson in his reversing of the four-door 1934 Merkel-Schnatz provided by our local agents for our getaway.

I had just stepped back through the throng, the chloroform-soaked handkerchief ready to press against the Führer's cakehole, when Baron Schmernercreutz ran puffing into the room, his leather coat flapping over the uniform of a Gestapo general. The shock of seeing him made me hesitate. He represented my past, my private life, when nothing had been so intense or important as this particular moment – seeing him flooded me with memories. I remembered him saying to me once, when I was crashed in a ditch, my co-driver comatose: 'Don't look so sorry, mein friend – it is only a race.' Well, this wasn't only a race. It mattered! – But my hesitation seemed to have cost us everything.

The Baron took out his Luger and shot twice into the air. Silence. A dropped plate. The Führer coughed up a cherry.

'ZESE PEOPLE ARE NOT SINGERS FROM PUFFENSH-

RINKLE! ZERE IS NO SUCH PLACE, MEIN FÜHRER, AS PUFFENSHRINKLE!' His bony finger pointed me out. 'HIM, HIM THERE, HE IS NOT EIN FOLKSINGER!'*

Mr Ogden stepped forward through the stunned silence, like a piece hurrying across a chessboard, more sprightly than his 87 years should have allowed. He deftly took the Luger from the Baron. I thought he was going to shoot him with it. Instead he thrust his hand under his hair and pulled off his facemask! Uh? Mr Ogden was the only one of us without a facemask! Underneath was another facemask. What the . . .?

'Enshuldigungs, Baron, lad, but I think it is for me to expose these British agents,' said Mr Ogden in perfect German. 'Ja, mein Führer, British agents – but more than that: I bring you a valuable weapon for ze Fazzerland. They are fully operational sentient . . . ROBOTS!'

'Ogden, wot's come over you, old chap! You can't be a traitor, not you.'

'Whey, I am not Ogden, you daft bugger. He has been at t'bottom of the blood tank for 2 years. I am a man like you, secretly manufactured by those poor boys who didn't return from the Norwegian raid. Now I'm where I belong like, where me loyalties really lie, wif this luvly fella here and Mr Hitler there.'

I was about to make my move, but two of my own men grabbed me from behind. Not Todger and Bodger! Yes. And four, six, ten more gathered behind Mr Ogden, who was stripping Binky down to his bare metal to prove his assertion of robotitude. Yes, I saw it all now – the blood that, as hulks, these men had been bathed in to induce consciousness must have been German blood. I'd been Ogden's dupe all along! Damned tinheaded fool that I was!

---

* I was, in fact, an excellent folksinger, as I had just proved, out-folksinging the Nazis at their own game. But I knew what the swine meant.

Things couldn't be going more wrong! But I wasn't beaten yet. Binky had gone all shy when the generals' wives cooed at his penis – I'd given him a whopper – and had hidden himself behind a curtain, much to the amusement of the room. Though my arms were held by robots I'd made a tidge stronger than myself, I contrived to cough, bending my head forward, at the same time opening my secret drawer and with my prominent nose tapping out Binky's number on my control pod.

ZABOOOOOM! The room was destroyed, everyone flattened. I stood up first, in a room full of motes of pink plaster, like daphnia being sprinkled into an empty fishtank. I picked up the dazed Nazi leader from among the chunks of rococo extravagance, and with my only surviving loyal men – Diggers, Stinky, Jervase, and Nosher – we bundled into the Merkel-Schnatz. I bumped Corporal Robinson over and took the wheel. Driving skills learned in all those damned pre-war rallies were of vital use now, as we sped at 70, 80, 95, through the streets of Innsbruck with the boche on our tail.

'I say, where's the other Corporal Robinson?' asked Corporal Robinson.

'Sorry, old chap, not coming.'

– And I pressed a few more numbers on my control pad. That ought to slow those Nazi swine down a bit!

Blummy! We'd kidnapped Hitler – there he was, coated in pink dust, blinking from inside his daze, humming our *Sommernachtslieden* like a mad child on its way to boarding school, and gripping tightly onto our winners' cup, dented and with a big bit of plaster in it.

'Hold on, Adolf – we'll have you safely in your bed in Wormwood Scrubs before the night's out, ehwot!'

The Ghosts of Old Comrades
Can Appear When Least Expected

During my freelance period, before meeting up again with the
E.E.S.* I was briefly weapons officer on a Peewermums Inter-
Galaxy Class Destroyer. The Peewermums were difficult to
work for. Each unit of Peewermums grew from a Peewermums
plantpot, in which some score of Peewermums lived together,
making noises like grouse on the Glorious Twelfth. I never
knew, to be truthful, if a score of Peewermums made an
individual Peewermums personage or if a score of Peewermums were a family of 20 different Peewermums. It worried
me once but I find I have now ceased to care! They had faces
like worried Pekinese, stuck on the end of stalks, but which
could detach themselves and roll around the room during
periods of hiatus. During their flowering season they sighed
continually. Worst of all, they were fervent pacifists – hence
me as weapons officer! – and their first impulse in any conflict
was to surrender. As they were at war with the Bunnypeople
this meant certain death – but tell them that! I understand,
anyway, that they have since become extinct – no wonder!
Evolution hates a coward.

'There's a Bunny furball 61 gnars to starboard, sir. It's
attacking a Peewermums garden centre on Snarn 4.'

The plantpot with the captain in it edged over. He suggested
we run away or surrender – he couldn't decide which.

'We can't do that, sir!' I said. (I had never been more

* English Empire in Space.

vehement with him!) 'We can't just let the Bunnies destroy your beautiful garden centre! Have some pride, for God's sake!'

The mention of God was a major mistake. It set them off into religious mode. They clucked their flower-power hymns and rang little bells for an hour, while their sprinkler system watered them and drenched me.

Meanwhile, as ever with my natural grit, I was flying straight for the Bunny furball. Perhaps the most irritating thing about Bunnypeople is the way in which they enjoy being Bunnies. Their spaceships, true to this trait, are covered in fur, often with large bunny ears. Their weapons are also furry. But their fiercer warriors are usually shaved, to offset the somewhat cuddly appearance of what are, after all, despite being the galaxy's supreme military civilization, only rabbits – 7 feet tall without counting the ears rabbits, but still rabbits down to their big cotton tails!

The garden centre was destroyed along with half of Snarn 4 by the time I was close enough to put my gunports up. My final approach was from behind the sun. The Bunnies didn't see me. I swerved side on and gave them a full broadside. Their fur was burning! I pulled about.

Time to surrender now, the captain suggested.

I refused. 'I'll give you that Bunny's pelt for you to wrap your pot in, sir. Just watch me!'

He gave me a direct order: SURRENDER! I ignored it. I gave a second broadside, close to – my cannonballs ripped deep into the Bunny ship. With my captain apologizing profusely to the toothy Bunny Captain on the viewing screen, I flew through the gap between the ears and dropped our entire stock of S/343 bugbombs onto them. But the Bunnies za-zoomed at the last instant, the ears flicking back some of our own shot towards us. In the agonizing delay between the realization of doom and doom itself, the Peewermums had one of their sudden flowerings – vermilion, lemon yellow, turquoise blooms filled the bridge. Never before had I felt so many emotions in one moment. It was like seeing the flowers at your own funeral. Then we exploded. The Bunny furball exploded. I didn't feel much, just my facemask melting.

I was among the debris – metal, plantpots, chairs, blooms, fur, smithereens of this and that – but unharmed and alive. Not needing air I could float in space forever – but it was a terrifying prospect: alone with my thoughts till the end of time! Dead bunnies kept floating into my face. When I punched them away some squeaked. Peewermums petals were so brilliantly coloured. If you looked at a star through one the beauty was almost too exquisite to bear. Poor things!

After a while lost in my memories – car rallies, WW2, my marriage – I made efforts to reach Snarn 4. I ran with my legs as fast as I could – on Earth I'd be going 65 m.p.h. – while doing a vigorous dog-paddle with my arms. I got nowhere at all. I just kept on floating. I later tried to reach Snarn 18. It looked so close – I could see the little blue islands where I'd taken my leave the month before. The rows and rows of flowerboxes would still be beside the lapping waves. Paradise so near and so unreachable.

There was nothing left to do but pray. For a hassock I knelt on a length of Bunnyship furry debris and conjured up pictures of Father Mickananan. During my induction into the Catholic Church he had given me a talk on 'How to pray'. Did he ever think I might employ his advice in circumstances such as these?

How long did I pray for? Days. I slipped in and out of it, of course. Religious fervour is brief for a healthy mind. I spent more time daydreaming about my wife and I walking through the woods hand in hand. Or of Lloyd George at table buttering his toast. All the while my cold brass body floated helplessly, full of the blurred reflections of stars. Then I heard a voice.

'Hiya, Colonel, old bean! Remember us! Har-har! Ehwot!'

I turned in the nothingness and saw floating towards me strange grim spectral forms . . . transparent metal men! They passed through debris, sloppy grins on their naked brass faces. Then they were bobbing around me, humming a tune. Dimmee – if it wasn't the *Sommernachtslieden!* It was Diggers, Stinky, Jervase, Nosher and Corporal Robinson! My men! My dear boys! Ha! Ha!

Last I'd seen of them was that day in Austria 147 years before. We'd sped up a dirt road on the Patscherkofel mountain above Innsbruck, bosche on our tail. I turned the Merkel-Schnatz through trees onto a flat Alpine meadow. We jumped out, holding Hitler aloft like he was a triumphant rugger captain. I let off a flare and moments later we heard the engine of our lift home.

But by the time it landed, the trees behind us were full of Hun troops, searchlights cutting from their parked vans, and every man with a torch. They daren't shoot for fear of hitting their Führer, whose dazed face in the torchlight I shall never forget. But they were advancing through the trees closer and closer, a murmuring crowd of them, from all sides. They were like some terrible infestation of beetles – torches the eyes and helmets the carapaces – come to klep food in the night. When we made our dash for the plane they were all over us. Jervase got left behind – so, damn me, I did what I had to do. I pressed out his number on my pod. He exploded. But the hole he made in the mass of torchlight and helmets was filled in a moment, and the surge caused by the explosion helped more Germans to make the leap through our door and scramble aboard. The plane's nose had been pointed exactly towards our only free run off the mountain. But the crush of Nazis had shifted it just enough so that take off would mean crashing a wing into trees. The pilot swore with fury as he tried to taxi the plane into a decent take-off position. The propellers decapitated dozens of Nazis, reddening the torchlight. But their metal helmets going ching! ching! ching! into the blades like a bus conductor's bell would break them very soon and leave us stranded! Plus, they had managed a tight hold on our tail, preventing take off. I could think of only one thing to do – I grabbed Corporal Robinson from his iron fistfight with invading Huns and threw him out of the door towards the tail. He skimmed over helmets, bashing the wearers unconscious with his palms as he went. I pressed his number and the explosion ripped holes in our fuselage but made the Huns let go. The plane began to move faster, fast, bumping over bodies. Meanwhile, our battle inside the plane had reached crisis point. More than 20 of the Huns who had climbed aboard remained with us. Half of these had holds on Hitler and were pulling him all ways. I had a grip only on his upper lip, but my superior strength kept him my prisoner as Diggers, Stinky and Nosher – all that was left of my life's work in robotics! – brained the enemy with their fists. But when the plane took off, veering suddenly upwards, we were all thrown down. When I stood up again, an unconscious Hitler under one arm, I saw that Stinky and Nosher were gone. They'd slipped out the door along with 6 bosche during take off. I couldn't allow such unique fighting machines to fall into German hands. So I pressed up their numbers. We were already way above the mountains, so no explosions were heard. But Diggers, glancing at me while bravely fighting a dozen krauters single-handed, guessed what I'd been doing. His expression was blank and uncomprehending. Suddenly it hardened – he was a child who understood his father for the first time. Then they overpowered him. I heard strings snap in his arms as he heaved them off. But they quickly returned, denting him awfully with their rifle buts. They had overpowered the pilot also. Now only I fought on, bravely as ever, with Hitler under one arm, but the battle lost. A Hun officer had control of the plane. I kept throwing Nazis out of the window, but there always seemed to be one more. I never quite reached the Hun pilot, who made such a bad landing at Innsbruck airport that our battered plane broke in two. The survivors of our hellish flight were scattered over the runway like cornflakes spilt from a packet.

I sat up, my head ringing like orchestra tuning forks playing *Greensleeves*. Diggers was standing over me. He had never looked more handsome.

'What's my number on that thing of yours?'

I looked at the Nazis nearby, bundling their bashed-up leader into the back of an ambulance. He was still holding tightly onto our cup!

'Quick, Colonel. Okay, so our mission's gone skewiffo. But we can still kill old Adolf. That's something, isn't it?'

'442,' I said, and handed him the pod.

He ran after the ambulance, grabbed its back door, pressed himself to it and thumbed 442 on the pod. The explosion destroyed Diggers and blew off the doors of the ambulance, only to reveal its insides as it sped away, where Hitler was ranting a speech with a flannel on his head. Everything I had tried to accomplish had totally failed and all my precious men, some of whom I now realized I had loved dearly, were dead, blown to bits for nothing. I lay back, looked at the black night, and broke down – my cogs stopped, my winders clicked no more. When I came to again I was in a prison camp, and remained in one or another for the rest of the war.

The spectral Diggers, Stinky, Jervase, Nosher and Corporal Robinson flew me at incredible speed, faster than any ship I was ever on, out of Bunny Space across the Neutral Zone, and into so-called Pink Space, that belonging to our beloved Empire. I sobbed with joy at such a homecoming. God bless Queen Anita! At last, after so long lost in space, I had found my people again.

We slowed down and floated above a fleet of villages.∗

'Which village do you want, Colonel?'

'Ooo, I'm not sure, wot . . . I . . . '

'None you recognize? There's a nice Cotswold one over there.'

'Or a Yorkshire dales village?'

'THERE! I know that place! Billingsgate-on-Sea! The original's in Essex, you know! Clarissa and I went for a Sunday jaunt there once! Oh, Billingsgate-on-Sea, how happy we were there!'

Something frightened the souls of my friends. No goodbyes. They just shoved me downwards and flitted away. I fell fast and hard, bombing into a field just behind a row of shops. The field was newly ploughed and the earth soft. I went 6 feet under and remained stuck in English loam for 27 years. Which makes my 2½ years in Colditz seem like a doddle.

∗ Spaceships of the English Empire Fleet are made in the form of English villages. A central village section, with surrounding fields, all covered by a dome of English atmosphere – sticklers for authenticity, the British Villycom Company ensures that the weather is invariably bad. Quarters are in delightful cottages, and the HQ is generally in a public school outside the village. Crew go about their duties as on any other ship, but the space travel aspect is merely an overlay to a normal English village way of life. Thus, as ever, the English bring genuine civilization to the brutal beyond. These villages, I should add, are not replicas – like the identical versions of their home planet built by the Deanabatnas on Chomp 4, 5, 6, 7 and 8 – they are clones, created from samples of the original village in the manner that the Scots covered Mars with Scottish beauty spots. So these villages aren't homes from home – in a very true sense they *are* home.

My Morning Out
with the Shite Creatures

This account of my early life I have written at a wonky terminal in the icon-filled study of my friend and employer, Archbishop Mugg, while he busies himself further down the bench at the big terminal with the more important task of writing his own memoirs. Now and then he looks up.

'CATS?'

'I have attended to the cats, sir.'

'Boglyfala, Mathis! You couldn't possiblydoda all the cats! There's 763!'

'All the cats, sir, are attended to and are resting in the spotted knapweed around the statue of their god.'✱

'Prhumph!'

Then after perhaps 22 minutes with his eyes flicking up and down at my busy typing, he will come and stand behind me, looking vexed. Finally, it comes out: 'Pleasy-do, Mathis – that prologue of yourn seemeth destined to be longer than the book t'which it is designed to be attach-ed!'

'Is not the Old Testament a mighty read, your grace? But nothing nowhere near as much a thing, wot, as the Testament which followeth it!'

'Verily-be, Mathis, verily-be,' says he, crossing himself, thwarted. But the thwart wears off and after some minutes back in his place he will suddenly exclaim a loud: 'PRHUMPH!'

✱ My remark here is catty. Nothing ever upsets the Archbishop more than the idea his beloved mechanical cats worship a pagan deity.

But this morning the flow of my recollections about my 30-month incarceration in Colditz Castle has been interrupted by an outbreak of Shite creatures. These disgusting parodies of humanity first came into being during the days of the first space stations. The shite ejected from the plumbing systems of said establishments, having spent some time floating in energy pools created by the constant to-fro of computer SE-Mail, was in addition bathed in life-promoting cosmic rays – all this, and the presence of non-Earthling bacterial matter in human shitematter, plus, one must admit, the hand of God, turned ordinary human shite into human-shaped shite people, and six-footers at that! Although, in a sense, human beings laid them just as geese lay eggs, humanity feels no sentimental attachment to the shites. They have never been accorded recognition as life-forms, despite the obvious evidence, and are exterminated whenever encountered.

As one who creates no waste matter I have always been utterly disgusted by this aspect of human life – eurghhhhh! – and cannot imagine why it has been allowed to continue so long. I shudder to remember a Henley Regatta in the late 1920s when, while watching a particularly thrilling sculling race in the company of the distinguished author Arnold Bennet, the said gent plopped his pants, making a most hideous noise in the process. Though his works had theretofore afforded me much pleasure, I was never able to open one again without hearing that noise. I understand that in some of the larger villages they now have the shite beamed out of their bowels into the nearest black hole and that their toilets have all been converted into broom-cupboards. But this action was taken not out of a revulsion at the very idea of shiteing, but as a preventative measure against giving birth to more shite creatures.

They are morose and self-critical individuals, these shite creatures, whose greatest delight is to watch humans doing that very thing which created them. They travel always in bands and display a camaraderie I have witnessed in few lifeforms. Their shared sense of scatological humour dominates their every waking moment and seems to me to be their greatest hold on life – perhaps without the company of other shites to laugh with they could not endure. They earned my grudging respect years ago when I discovered that they will die for one another. While exterminating them I have seen this again and again.

Some weeks ago a band of 50 shites crashlanded on Cats-by-Nowhere in a purloined shuttle craft. I remarked to the Archbishop that the shite problem must be pretty bad in the Inner Spirals if shite creatures have spilled over to this obscure place.

The Archbishop was of the opinion that we should leave them alone and that they would soon go away. As he himself had been constipated since 2172, and I and the cats produce no shite of our own, they could afford no amusement from watching anyone on this planet defecate. They would get bored here very quickly and go away, he said.

But, dare I say 'As usual', he was wrong. For months they have been a pestilential nuisance – forever jumping out at us in the corridors of this abandoned city, blowing raspberries and pelting us with shite . . . or smearing themselves over the windows while we dine . . . or throwing themselves on the cats, which has been a major distress for the Archbishop. And of course the smell, wot!

'The flame thrower, sir?' I requested while washing several distressed cats.

'No. Mathis, I will not countenance such un-Christian cruelty!'

The Archbishop, I guessed right away, would be slowly seized with a fervour to convert these sad creatures – I knew for certain when I saw him stapling plastic sheeting to the chapel pews. For this last week of mornings he has ventured forth alone in full regalia to the sheds where the shites sleep. From our kitchenette window I have heard him singing *To be a Pilgrim* to them in his thin voice. Then his cries of 'Oh, shite!' as they threw themselves on him. There have followed 7 stinking returns home, casting off his robes onto the knapweed, watched by me (peepsomely) with a smile on my facemask but in my metaphorical heart a deep admiration for the evangelical courage of my oldest friend. But the miffed little voice from the dressing room affords much amusement to the cats and me: 'The regalia of an Anglican Archbishop, pleasy-do, replicator. Plenty of gold – and don't pigboggn forget the bunny motifs like you did yesterday!'

Finally, this morning, he had had enough, and burst into my meditation room with a ginormous crosier – it must have been 25 feet long.

'MATHIS! Have you been fiddlydoos with yon replicator! It keeps giving me bigger and bigger crosiers!'

'Probably one of the cats having a joke, sir. May I suggest, as a solution to all imminent problematicals: the flame thrower.'

His small bald head sank. 'Oh, very well Mathis, have it your way.' And off he went wielding his burden.

I went out to meet them in my bare metal. 7 shites were dressed in shitey Archbishop's outfits, picked from the claws of the knapweed. They put up quite a fight, but were no match for J. W. Mathis and burned alive. Like the most fervent martyrs of the strangest possible sect, they met the maker of their makers blowing raspberries. Some, as I have noted before and had expected today, threw themselves in the flamejet to save others from harm. What I had not expected this morning was an innovation in their behaviour: they attacked! I was clunked clanging blows with crosiers of various lengths and pelted with heaps of shite before I finished the job. It was a proper little battle! Great fun, I must admit! I whistled home from the smoking sheds as happy as if I'd slaughtered a trench of Germans.

But old Mugg has been depressed by this, yet another failure to convert the unconvertible. When I tried to cheer him up with natter about memories of our adventures in the 2060s, he waved me away.

'Tell it to your pigboggn prologue, Mathis!'

'Certainly, sir. But before I do, I thought you might like to know: one of the shites, he crossed himself before the end.'

'No? Not! Oh, Lordy! Hallelujah!' He wept. 'Oh, Mathis – I am so joyful, so, so joyful! Thanky-bees to God!'✴

Colditz

I was not happy as a P.O.W. and do not look back on that time with affection. The betrayal by half my robot platoon and the destruction of all of them had been a terrible blow to my pride, confidence, indeed my very life force – I was willing for the first and only time in my life to let it go. I felt that I had failed in my destiny. To be a prisoner, to be out of the fight, not to be doing my bit, was too terrible for me.

In my first camp I astonished the Escape Committee with this simple but brilliant scheme of of escape: I would throw

---

✴ Now that there is no chance of Archbishop Chaffinch reading my prologue, I am adding this footnote to confess that I was lying to him about the converted shite. It was a white lie which brought my dear friend much comfort and I do not believe I did wrong with it.

chaps out of the camp, over the wire. The S.B.O.* said he'd never heard such nonsense – nobody was strong enough to throw a 12-stone man 20 feet over an electrified wire fence! He wouldn't listen to another word and vetoed the plan. I took it to the Poles. They were a fine body of men and were willing to give it a go. Well, I threw 81 of them out of the camp just after the teatime sunset on Christmas Eve 1942, aiming at tree cover in the nearby forest. But my enthusiastic Pole-tossing was too great, and having jumped over the 20 foot wire with my superhuman legs, I found I had dashed the poor fellows against treetrunks. Not one was conscious. What could I do? I couldn't just leave them! So I kept on throwing them, 500 yards at a time. In this way, me and my pile of unconscious Poles made a painfully slow progress towards the Swiss border.

Of course, citizens of the 1000 Year Reich, seeing limp bodies flying across their landscape, were quick to inform the authorities, and we had some pretty close scrapes, with Jerry shooting at the aloft Poles as if they were skeet. The thing that finally defeated us was the snow. After I'd tossed my Poles from one snowy hillock to another I simply couldn't find them again – not without a team of St Bernards! The closer to Switzerland we got the more snow there was, and falling picture postcard fashion all the while. From my original 81 I was down to 27 Poles – less tossing time but ages spent hunting for them in the deeper and deeper drifts.

On Arlberg Mountain, with Switzerland within sight, I had my heap of unconscious Poles ready to throw, when a Nazi ski patrol whizzed right along the ridge above us, clocking us with their binoculars. Dashed hard double Gloucester! I managed one more throw and was collecting Poles from the snow to make what would have been the final toss into Switzerland,

* Senior British Officer

83

when the troop trucks pulled up on the road below me. Soon the mountainside swarmed with Hun, and I and my fellow escapees were captured.✶

Two camps, 14 more failed Pole-tossing escapes later I was sent to Colditz Castle, a bleak fortress in the east of Germany from which escapes were nigh-on impossible. During interrogation when I arrived the Gestapo made the brilliant discovery that I had tin legs. These were unscrewed and taken from me.

'You vill find escaping with your friends the Poles difficult vissout legs to be walking on, eh, Englander!'

Then they had their fun torturing me, never twigging that the rest of me was tin also and their efforts quite without painful result. But intent on keeping up my secret, that of being a proper flesh &-blood man, I howled along to their game. Afterwards, I was handed over to the prison camp authorities to begin 2½ years of unbearable tedium.

I rarely left the little library, high up in the castle. Without legs, I couldn't walk anywhere. I just sat in an old burst chair, 24 hours a day, reading and re-reading novels. I read *Middlemarch* 11 times and couldn't have hated it more. My constant companion was Squadron Leader Jennings Farquar. A native, like me, of Ipswich, he insisted that he was an alien from a planet called Neebaffatwoloa, this being a brave attempt to get himself invalided home on grounds of insanity. His fantasy contained the ingenious idea that although in Colditz he was simultaneously on his own planet, and while our guards earwigged he regaled us with

---

✶ After the war I received a letter from a certain Ignance Drozd from Zakopane in Poland, thanking me for helping him escape from Nazi Germany in late '42. Apparently, the projectile of my very last, desperate throw had been Mr Drozd who, unknown to me, had landed safely in Switzerland. He enclosed a photograph of himself, wife and 5 children taken outside his cake shop – which reminded me of my fathers, both great cake men.

descriptions of the parpamela trees and the pools where many bosomed maidens cooed lasciviously while dog-paddling. The Germans were never convinced by his act – too many eccentric Englishmen had passed through their hands! But by the time we were liberated Jennings had convinced himself – his mind was marooned forever on his other world. He was, in short, barking.✳ I last saw Jennings in 1952 in the Savoy Grill. He was ordering in gibberish, meant I think to be his native alien tongue, the order being translated by a twitchy man who was obviously his psychiatrist. Damn that war! It ruined so many lives!

Late in '44 I was waiting for the moment of the afternoon when, on a good day, the sun shone directly through the little slit of a window opposite my chair to flood the room with brilliant yellowness. My favourite moment of the day. While waiting I was aware of a strange sound on the stairs like a cricket bat batting stones. I took it for one of the boys' warning signals that a ferret was getting near one of their tunnels. It was, amazingly, Baron Werner Schmernercreutz on his new wooden legs. He entered just before the sun flooded the room. When it did, to his credit, he stood transfixed inside the moment of beauty.

Having failed to save his Führer from being kidnapped, the Baron was demoted and sent to the Russian front – along with his coven of doubles. He fought at Stalingrad until he ran out of doubles, then was wounded himself. A mortar blew off his legs and one arm. He also lost much of lower intestine, his right eye and ear. He was horribly disfigured. His upper lip was quite

---

✳ In 2120, when I had just passed my butler's exams, I was sent for my first duty to a Clobbic gentleman's somewhat gaudy mansion on a planet then called Slerdgggggggggggg, but whose previous name I discovered had been not Neebaffatwoloa but Baffneeatwoloa. Damned near thing to a spooky coincidence, wot! Plenty of parpamela trees, too, but the pools contained only a sort-of underwater parrot of the kind that emasculated Admiral Sir Rodney Bleans.

gone, leaving teeth bared in perpetual grimace and just one inch of waxed moustache, still cultivated with all the vanity of better days.

Clouds crossed the sun and the brightness left the room. Yellow to grey. Two old enemies faced each other.

Sinister and cheerful: 'J.W., mein old racing friend. How are you today?'

'Gad, Werner, wot a bally mess – wot HAVE they done to you?'

Defensive and Hitlerlish: 'I am bursting mit health! I am every bit the man I vas when I was beating you in Le Mans in zee '20s, ehwot, J.W.!'

God help me, I was sorry for him. 'But your legs?'

'And yours, I see.'

'Mine? Oh, they took them away yonks back. Don't miss 'em a bit, wot!'

'Do you remember White Horse Corner? '27, was it?'

I smiled. He laughed. Nazi swine.

'Chess, J.W.?'

'Difficult to cheat at chess, don't yer know!'

It wasn't. He managed. His favourite trick was with a magnet under the table. But I never confessed to noticing because watching him cheat was more interesting than merely playing chess. I should, of course, have strangled him at the first opportunity. If so, I would have saved myself, and the Empire, much future suffering. But at that time in my life, not on my usual moral plane, I took pleasure in Werner's company, and he – a shattered man who had briefly had his fill of cruelty – in mine. We had much in common. Not as much, of course, as we do today.

By spring '45 it was obvious that Germany was finished. The Baron disappeared, skipped it before the dangers of the final collapse. But not on his old wooden legs. He had found my confiscated legs propped up in a storeroom and had put them on. He was instantly a changed man – not for the better, however! No longer was he fully a flesh-&-blood person – he had become something like the sort of creature I am. My legs had worked a magic on him! He later, in hiding with Hitler and other Nazis in Paraguay, made for himself a steel arm. It worked admirably – he arm-wrestled Paraguayan Indians with it and crushed their hands. Gradually, as his body succumbed to the corruption of age, he replaced every part with metal. 50 years later, he was a 100% metal man like myself, fleshless, immortal, standing beside the little white crosses that marked the graves of his fellow fanatics. He was the last Nazi, and clonking on my legs! He is out there now, that falser man than I – somewhere in the starry sky my bogeyman flies, commanding his fleets of German warships in the uneasy truce with the Empire. On some nights I am awoken by the sound of my own chest ticking. So I sleepily jam the key in the winder to shut it up. But I still hear ticking – HIS ticking, though he be light years away: our dreams have connected, and I hear his mechanism, God help me.

– Is it not interesting to note that . . . had he not been in the Theatre that night . . . had I escaped the last half-mile into Switzerland and not ended up in Colditz . . . had that mortar either killed him outright or never been fired . . . any of these things and Baron Schmernercreutz would have been dead these 250 years and a hideous past dead with him.

Instead, the Empire is doomed to fall, and all because of my legs! Should I not, therefore, devote myself to the Baron's destruction? I will do this, I swear on the sacred soil of Albion! It is, after all, what I was made for. But first I wish to spend some time with my friend and employer, Archbishop Chaffinch, who is very old and who needs me. Of course, in any battle with my Nazi foe I will lose. Indeedy-be, wot! I was constructed in 1916–18. Werner was made with the knowledge of later 20th Century technology, and he has added and improved himself constantly ever since. I am, except for some innovations on my hinges (and my penis) just as I was originally made. Thus I am very much Werner's inferior, more even than in the '20s when he beat me in so many rallies.

So there I was when the Yanks liberated Colditz Castle – waiting for the G.I.s to find my legs. A black G.I. brought me the Baron's wooden pins: 'These yours, bub? Only ones we could find.'

I screwed on the short skinny legs, gave myself a good winding up, and went for a tripsome walk down to the town. I felt like a toy escaped from the cupboard – light and free, my own man again. But with each awkward step I sank deeper in despair. Within days the war would be over. What then? I had heard some weeks before of the death of Lloyd George, so I had no home to return to. Germany was destroyed, so my original purpose was no longer of any point. I stomped miserably through streets full of Jeeps and U.S. personnel, hearing a few sneezes but thinking nothing of them. Limping across fields to a forest whose rookeries I had for so long stared at from my library window, I heard a clinking in the air behind me, as of a lunatic eating vigorously off an empty plate. Turning around I saw the castle, grey and forbidding, and in the sky all around were spoons, thousands and thousands of spoons. I could not run at all on the Baron's legs.∗ I fell over backwards and the spoons fell upon me.

'Where in tarnation did yerh find all those godamned spoons, bub?'

'I am ill,' I told the American sarge who was standing over me. 'Please help me. I am seriously ill.'

∗ Upon my return to England I replaced these wooden Nazi warhero-issue legs with a rusty pair from the hoard of spare parts saved from my makers' workshop. The knees have been restrung a thousand times, toes added, rust expelled – otherwise these legs, made for a never-made false man, daily-burnished, have carried me about for all 1945's future so far, or rather 254 years of steps small and large.

Clarissa Devney

The immediate post war years, drear anyway, were my worst ever. I thought I had come to an end of myself. I wanted to live LIFE so much, but was unable to help myself partake of it, because I could find no interest or pleasure in anything at all. I was the victim of constant breakdowns, some lasting only hours, one a whole year. But I didn't return from my slow dreams of fighting Germans refreshed. I awoke with the frights, sad and lonely. My incomprehension at how a busy useful chap like myself could have descended into this pit of despondency led to such a confusion that I could barely decide which foot to put forward.

I employed a stout ex-RN man, Walter Dibley, to fetch me when I broke down. I carried a card sticking from the band of my trilby – not in my wallet, as that had twice been stolen when an opportunist thief saw me frozen in a stupor.

URGENT! EMERGENCY
PLEASE TELEPHONE MR WALTER DIBLEY
PONDERS END 72893.

Mr Dibley, often as not, was dragged out of a bar by his aged mother in order to accommodate my crisis. This 'robot break-down recovery' business was their only income, I believe, apart from occasional winnings from horse racing. When eventually Mr Dibley arrived at wherever I'd conked out – I'd be staring at the wall in an art gallery, or on my back in Hyde Park – he'd bundle me inside a taxi and, to the accompaniment of his drunken pub singing, I'd be driven home to my flat at Ponsonby Mansions, spoons pursuing us through traffic in their usual dogged way. Often as not I woke up with Mr Dibley snoring on the sofa next to me. But the effort of getting me up the 8 flights of stairs was hard going. He was worth every bit of the £12–18/6 a week I paid for his services. Some weeks, indeed, I was fine and he didn't have to do a thing, lucky man!

Just the other day, hacking spurge to make pathways for the Archbishop to waddle along to look at the breathtaking views beyond the abandoned city, memories of Ponsonby Mansions came back to me. I leaned on my rake and walked around the rooms in my mind. I picked up nick-nacks, smiling with painless nostalgia, turned the pages of 1940s picture maga- zines, saluted my Géricault* of a Napoleonic hussar on rampant steed hanging over the fireplace. Dear, dear Ponson- by Mansions! I do wish I could have been happy there. 'Twas the perfect place to be happy. But I was as miserable as a Gimbiak from the Planet Nonnonanonadab.

On May 2nd, 1950 I had lived 5 useless years, going to the pictures in the afternoons, long drives in the Morgan to nowhere and back, living comfortably thanks to the trust fund Lloyd George had arranged for me, but with no aim in life, when I wandered into the Geological Museum in Kensing- ton. I'd been in that part of town, having my best wig tidied, and dropped into the museum for no reason at all, having scant interest in geology. I was standing on a narrow 3rd floor gallery looking into a case of labradorites, feldspars and jades, when I broke down. – Kaplunk! Lights out! Gone! Not a whirr stirring within! – Behind me, over a rail, was the rest of the museum, a 50-foot drop onto rows of glass cases. I would have fallen if not for Clarissa Devney.

I had and have a tendency to fall over backwards – I was

* Bought for 800 guineas in 1929.

teetering! Clarissa, walking along the narrow gallery peering into each case in turn, suddenly found me teetering in her way. She had quite a struggle laying me down on the floor, picked all the spoons off me, then went downstairs to fetch my trilby, which had fallen over the rail during the teetering, and found Mr Dibley's number on the card. Mother Dibley answered Clarissa's phone call with profuse apologies but Walter was locked in his room with the DDTs – he could be heard yelling about mice – and, terrible inconvenience, but was it possible the young lady might herself take the broken-down gentleman home to Number 87 Ponsonby Mansions. If the key wasn't in one of his pockets, she would find it in the secret drawer in the gentleman's chest. Don't worry, no doctor necessary – he'll snap out of it right as rain, he will, always does.

Fortunately, the key was in my coat pocket. Clarissa took me home, got the taxi driver and a passing oaf to carry me upstairs, arranged me on my sofa, made a pot of tea and sat watching my sad mannequin's expression until, just as she was about to give up on me and leave my life forever – when she had embraced me (unofficially, during the teetering) but had not yet properly met me at all – my eyes twissled and my cogs burrrRRRrred. She was peering at the photos on the wall, of my rallying days, my famous friends. When she turned around I was wakefully adoring her.

'I'd left you a note. I was just about to pop orf. The war, was it?'

'Hm?'

'That gave you your trouble.'

'Trouble? Yes. The war.'

'Oh, um! When you fell over you squashed the box with your new wig in. I took it out, gave it a comb and put it on your pillow. Hope that was all right.'

'Thank you.'

'Some tea?'

'Hm?'

'I made you some tea. Better have a cup of tea, what say?'

'Please.'

She poured. 'Mr Dibley would have come but he's unwell today. His mother did sound worried.'

'Oh?'

'A nice lady, she sounded?'

'Hm?'

'Mr Dibley's mother.'

'Quite.'

'So I brought you myself.'

'How utterly hideous for you. Hope I haven't spoiled your day.'

'No, no. No. Not a bit. Really. Ha-ha. No-no.'

We drank tea. Clarissa suddenly removed her spectacles. She blushed. 'I only put them on to look at your pictures.'

'Pictures, yes.'

'A gum-golly-gosh of an exciting life you've had – cars and everything, and the war. Upsets you, I expect, me mentioning the war. Sorry. I'm a goose.'

'No. Not at all. And I rather like geese.'

'Really? Yes, I suppose they are funny, aren't they. Those feet.'

We sat in a silence of exchanging smiles. My throatsack had come unhooked and the sickly sweet tea I supped was splashing down over my workings. But still I smiled and supped more.

'Oh, well, mustn't dawdle!' she said.

She put her cuppa down! She was out of the chair! She was about to leave! But, yes, a moment's dawdle: she looked at her hair – her long fine fair English hair done up in a bun – in the mirror for just a blink's worth as she passed it on her way to the door. A moment of sublime femininity. I was hers then, hers forever.

'I say, don't go yet.'

'But I . . .'

I was across the room in a stride, close beside her. 'Please, you must give me a chance to thank you.'

'No need, really.'

'Let's go to Martino's ehwot?'

'Martino's!' It had just opened, the brightest thing in London since the Blitz.

'To celebrate.'

'Celebrate?'

'Oh, you know – LIFE!'

'Ha! Ha!'

Suddenly she remembered something, fished in her handbag and brought out a dozen spoons.

'Your spoons.'

'Thank you ever so much. You really are a most dreadfully kind young woman!'

'Gosh! Do steady on. I was only doing my bit.'

As we walked through the Temple I noticed for the first time that she was in uniform.

'Girl Guides,' she beamed. 'I have a troop.'

'An excellent organization, I believe.'

'Splendid, yes.'

And as we crossed the rather squalid little railed park in front of Martino's she stopped, took a breath, raised on tiptoes, swung her arms and said: 'Spiffing sort of a spring we're having this year, is it not?'

I was so moved I couldn't speak. I thought I was on the verge of a new kind of breakdown – I would crumple to the ground and hug her knees. She detected my bizarre distress.

'Oo-er, not going under again, are we, Mr . . . Ha! I don't know your name!'

'Lt-Colonel J. W. Mathis, MC, DSO and bar. But please, do call me Jerome!'

Pigeons were in the air all around us. We were laughing at them when she firmly shook my hand saying: 'Clarissa Devney, that's me! Dib-dib! Ha-a! Gosh, what a goose!'

We were engaged in June and married in August. No more misery, no more breakdowns. I dismissed Mr Dibley, gave up Ponsonby Mansions, bought a charming house in Oxfordshire where no spoons tapped on the windows at night, and settled down with my darling Clarissa, whom I loved with all the power of the rare soul God had gifted me. Oh, Clarissa, my darling! Clarissa! On the edge of the galaxy I whisper your name. I pet mechanical cats, wishing they were you. I stride through the spurge, the knapweed, and think only of you in those first happy days – so young, so beautiful, my own darling. I miss you so.

I Married an English Rose, She Married a Robot from Ipswich

My flippant chapter heading doesn't help me. Although it has been over and done with for 247 years I find my marriage far, far too painful to write about. But I will treat it as a shriving and have a go.

My new life in Goring-on-Thames with Clarissa was the first and only time in my Earthbound or Spacefree life that I lived what might be called an 'ordinary existence'. I was a chappie with a job in the city (a factotum in the Foreign Office), a nice big gardened house in the country, a pretty wife with whom I was delightfully besotted. We went for picnics and jaunts on weekends to the seaside, long country walks, candlelit dinners.

Clarissa was very horsey, so I took up riding and we hacked together. We rode with the hunt a few times. I helped wash the dishes. I mowed the lawn. I tinkered in my workshop in the evenings. I canoodled with my darling in front of the new-fangled television set.

My *Lloyd George as I Knew Him* was written during this period,✶ and as I contemplated the creature I had been in those pre-war years, full of pepper and grim hooray, I was delighted with what I had become. Never had I been less like the soldier I was made to be. Never had I aped real man more. But I had never been happier, and unlike happinesses I have had since it did not dissolve into mere contentment when it regarded itself.

During the engagement I had made myself a new penis – a married man's penis, modest compared to the stonking great wangers I'd made in the past. But on the wedding night a sudden madness made me change it for a bigger one. Clarissa laughed in fright when she saw it and hid under the sheets. I'm sure it was the first she'd ever seen. Our lovemaking did not give me that ultimate ecstasy I had always looked for in my sexy doings with womenkind. But it gave me something else – a sweetness, a tenderness whose existence I had been ignorant of, and which made a new man of me. During our first year of marriage we made love every night. Sometimes we woke each other up in the wee hours and did it some more.

✶ The book was written in a way unique to myself. I removed my buttocks and installed a typewriter inside myself. To this I attached a long roll of paper. I then 'thought' the book. It typed itself while I did the gardening or had a lie-in. True, thoughts nothing to do with the book crept into the typescript, some rather lewd. But I crossed most of these out during my revision. Only one serious one slipped through into the final book: on page 372, the sudden remark about warm thighs in jodhpurs, followed by a brief fantasy in a hayloft. It occurs to me now that, although the book was a reasonable success, no one ever mentioned to me, in their kind letters or to my face, anything about the nude scene on page 372, which suggests that although many people bought the book, not one of them read as far as page 372.

Bliss, indeed. My only complaint concerned her family – a vile crew, in whose presence my darling girl became something unlovable, became one of them, no longer any part of 'US'. Her father had been an eminent historian, writing a famous 63-volume tome on the history of China, a place he never visited. He at least was safely dead. Her mother, Charlotte, was a rotund muscular hag with none of her daughter's prettiness. Her only conversation was the weather – its wayward moods, its effect on crops and cricket. (Much fun for such types here on Cats-by-Nowhere where the weather forecast has been the same since creation!) The only words not connected with weather or tea-making which passed her lips were the words of her late husband – she read out his *China* in the evenings. My first visit to their house, in Pangbourne – just down the river from where Clarry and I settled – consisted of tea, weather and the triumphs of the Sung dynasty. It was a frightening experience, especially because when she read the old trout donned spectacles exactly like my fiancée's. After dozens of these dull-dull-dull Chinese evenings I hatched revenge: I sped-read Clarissa's set of the monsterwork, mem-orizing it, plus footnotes✳, which took a week, and on the next Chinese evening, just when Mrs Devney was about to read I closed my eyes, sat back with my hands behind my head and

---

✳ It occurs to me that my penchant for footnotes, and here as you see is another, derives from this experience. I once visited the Great Library on Carstairs Station when it was anchored off Paladron 2 and pottered about in the books, only looking at footnotes, wondering why I was doing so, but unwilling to stop myself because I was deriving so much pleasure from it. Or does this footnote fetishism perhaps illustrate a truth about me: that I am a footnote to history myself and therefore feel fraternity with other footnotes. My biography of Lloyd George is 250 pages of text and 400 of footnotes. Whatever, Prof. Devney's monumental *CHINA* still splashes about in my memory – sometimes I will find a sentence of it in my head which is like finding a broken piece of crockery while gardening: it is a memory of lost domesticity, shattered happiness.

began to rattle. I did 50 pages, fast as a talking Bren gun, to general astonishment.

Her Uncle Herbert was a drone. The only work he'd ever troubled himself with in his 60-odd years was to help his brother with research for his *China*. He offered to play the same role for me with my *Lloyd George*, and read through the typescript, but sleepily.* He'd been briefly in bombers in the war but his nerves gave out and he was sent home to Pangbourne, where he returned to his vocation of playing golf. Herbert usually played alone. He wasn't merely unclubbable – he was a sneering solitary misanthropist, and skulked about like a man with a nasty secret, which was his complete detestation of everyone he could possibly meet. His unspoken loathing of Mrs Devney showed itself in many subtle ways, but never in words or deeds. He was my favourite of the bunch.

Clarissa's elder brother Monty I really didn't like. He was a bald babyish ass of 35 with a room full of teddy bears. His pudgy blond face, peeping out from behind the *Beano*, was uncomfortably similar to Clarissa's. He called her 'Monty' and she called him 'Clarissa', which to this day strikes me as the damned unhealthiest item in any relationship I've ever known, Bunny-people included. Monty loved his sister beyond the borders of brotherly love – he therefore treated me as a rival. His innocent pudgy face, I was sure, hid a depth of hatred for this prologue-maker, J. W. Mathis. Perhaps it wouldn't have mattered, but Monty was a detective inspector in the Oxfordshire police – and, despite his unpolicemanlike demeanour, was on the rise, due solely – as his mother and sister said every time he plodded into view – to a genius at the craft of detection. I knew from the first that this jealous boyish sleuth was investigating me, and wondered how long it would be before he found a trail of slaughtered peacetime Germans leading to my door.

* No mention from him about page 372 either!

One night, almost exactly a year into our marriage, Clarissa had her hairbrush in her hand on the landing, as she always did when troubled. 'You don't like Monty, do you?'

'Monty?'

'Monty.'

'Well, bit of an ass, isn't he?'

'He's a dear. The police think the world of him. They say he's a genius at the craft of detection.'

She flounced into the bathroom. No shouting, no door slamming, but she shut the little bolt. She'd never done that before and I was mortified. For an instant I imagined I saw the Geological Museum all around me. Had my whole marriage been a good dream dreamt during a breakdown? And was that dream about to turn nasty?

'Clarryyyyyyy! Jerry loves youuuuuuuuuuuu!'

No answer.

'Goosey-goosey-do-dar-ookums-lovey-doves.'

This opened the bolt. She came out. But her face was strained. In a moment of irritation I snatched the hairbrush from her.

'Brute!' She snatched it back.

I was all a-shudder. 'Darling goose, what has happened to us?'

Suddenly she broke down, sobbing in my arms, dropping the hairbrush. 'Oh, darling, darling, darling, Clarry loves you, I'm so sorry, my big dumpling, so sorry. It's just something that Monty said, it's been worrying me, that's all.'

'Oh, I don't mind Monty. You tell him from me he's an egg but nobody likes policemen, however soppy they happen to look.'

'It's not that. It's the widdling.'

'Widdling?'

'Monty says that when chaps go into the loo to, you know, widdle, you can hear the noise their water makes in the loo. And

98

Monty says that he's listened at the loo door when you've gone in and that there's no widdle noise . . . and I've listened too, to Monty, Uncle Herbert, even Rev. Neeves, and to you in the loo – and Monty's right, everyone has a widdling noise except you.'

I laughed so loud that our beagle, out in the garden, began to howl. Clarissa was furious. She beat my metal chest with quick little fists till I could hear jingle-bells echoing in my empty head.

'You tell Monty that if he really wants to know the truth about me – I never widdle at all: I'm a robot!'

She laughed. 'Oh, Jerry, you are silly!'

I picked strands of her fine hair away from her face. I kissed her. The beagle came into the house, up the stairs and commenced howling again. We laughed. Happiness was restored.∗

But I saw clearly that Monty Devney would destroy that happiness, sooner or later, somehow. There was no moment when I actually decided that he would be the first person I would murder who wasn't a German. I just found myself daydreaming of ways to commit a perfect murder, and Monty was the victim.

First thing was to eliminate myself as a suspect, so I became his best pal. Up to the pub on a Sunday, me and Monty! Me, backslapping, full of natter – Monty quiet, with that little smile of his. I'd quickly tire of discussing that week's excitements from the *Eagle* but if I could get him to talk about his police

---

∗ Our only other 'tiff' concerned German music. She had a collection of 78s of German music – Beethoven, Mozart, that rot. I took them out to the bins and snapped them to bits. Clarissa was upset and called me names: 'rotter', 'Philistine', 'ninny', 'brute'. But when I explained that such music had created the emotional basis in the German character which led to the outrages of the Great Wars, she said she understood how I must feel, after my time in Colditz and all. I bought her a shining new set of Elgar, which was much better altogether and the soundtrack to our marital bliss.

work the time passed less slowly, and it really brought the little cretin out. I even tried my hand at solving his cases for him, though behind every burgled tobacconist's I detected a plot by Dr Adenauer and the new Germany. I even tried introducing him to girls, but he asked me please to stop – politely, yes, but I knew his private visions of me and Clarissa doing rumpy-pumpy-o were behind his complex distaste for the fair sex. My, what a leer he had if he thought no one was looking! He looked as if he was masturbating without using his hands. But the leer would change in a blink to the scowl of a church elder. Odd chap. But jolly good do's on me, though – I got him into the Albatross Club, helped him stuff his albatross, introduced him to members. I was a total brick where Monty was concerned. I took him to the Festival of Britain 3 times! His innocent moon face dared not show anything but open friendliness to me, or Clarissa would have scolded him something rotten. Meanwhile, I could tell, his hatred deepened. My pièce de résistance was for his birthday in '52 – I bought him a nifty little red MG! He was as happy as Larry with it – only I suspected the rage within and the foul and fouler words he called his brother-in-law while peeping down the lanes on his virgin drive.

'Oh, Jerry, you're so kind to Monty. And I thought you didn't like him. Aren't I a goose? The weather looks like it might turn nasty again.'

'Oh?'

'And the ground is very damp for this time of year. One thing you can never trust is the weather. Isn't that true, darling?'

'Sorry, darling?'

'The weather. I don't expect there'll be any cricket this weekend. And the poor farmers! Very bad for the crops, weather like this – almost any weather, in fact. Terrible thing, weather. I only like sunny summer days – like that day we went to Billingsgate-on-Sea last summer. Do you remember how happy we were?'

Suddenly, from my depths, I said: 'I like the fog. I like the way it wraps you up and leaves you utterly alone with your most secret thoughts. Fog is a particularly English pleasure. I expect Milton, after he went blind, used to grasp it in his hands and smell it. I do adore fog so.'

'Golly-gosh, Jerry, you say the oddest things sometimes! Fog's horrid, everyone knows.'

I handed her hairbrush to her and she smiled as she brushed her long fine hair.

It was, in fact, a cosy pea souper the day I killed Monty, February '53, end of a long hard winter. People were porridge-pale as their faces floated from the fog. Monty had followed me up to London. They say the best detectives have a superhuman instinct – they identify a wrong'un as easily as Saint Peter at his gate. Monty by all accounts, ass that he was, had this instinct. He knew I got up to some wickedness, didn't yet know what for sure, but was determined, I was certain, to expose me as a villain to Clarissa and ruin our idyll.

As I walked from the Foreign Office through the fog towards the German Embassy I could hear a policeman's feet behind me – those same policeman's feet I had seen so often, soft and plump in their teddy-bear slippers during Chinese nights at Pangbourne.

I stood outside the German Embassy, waiting for a victim. I was in confident mood, battle-minded, more my old rallying self of yore. A pot-bellied attaché I had met at functions came down the steps, a Herr Uwe Korff. He was surprised to see me, put out his hand to be shaken. Instead of howdoyoudoing, I took him under the armpits, bent down low, and threw him up with all my might. He was gone. Launched into the fog.

At almost the moment of his disappearance 2 plates of porridge floated out of the fog and hovered by the steps. One face was Monty's, t'other a young woman's.

For months I had practised throwing things, waiting for this moment. I found an old box of worn cricket balls behind the pavilion at Goring. I threw them in the general direction of Aberdeen. Next day I bought copies of Scottish newspapers at Victoria. It was there: HAIL OF CRICKET BALLS STUNS ABERDONIANS. Windows broken, no one hurt. But one ball had fallen short and killed a cow near Arbroath. I also experimented with, shame on me, cats – whenever I passed one I checked that we were alone, then threw it as far as I possibly could. The real problem, of course, with all murders is not the act but hiding the body. With this freakish talent of mine I had found the perfect method: I would dispose of Monty's body by throwing it into the middle of the Atlantic Ocean. If, in the unlikely event it were ever found, they'd never work out how it got there.

This was to be my moment – alone with him in the fog. But here he was with an unpleasant-looking girl. Damn the man! And crikes, what if they'd seen the launch of Herr Korff, even through a befogged haze of foggy fog!

'Monty, old bean, what the Devil . . .!'

'We came to see you at your office, but you'd just left and we've been tripping through the fog to catch up!'

They'd been to Hamley's. A new teddy bear poked from a bag.

'Sorry, got the better of me, I'm afraid.'

'This is Sandra.'

She nodded. Dimmee, I recognized her from the pub! A tart I'd introduced him to. But now she was dressed and made up to look the spit of Clarissa, except for a tasteless fur collar and a face that could never be anything but common and repulsive.

I kept looking around through the fog to see if anyone was coming. 'Sandra, yes?'

'We want to get married. But, well, we thought we'd better talk to you about it first, Jerry. First there's Clarissa. She'll not like Sandra.'

'People don't,' said Sandra.

'Then there's the religion thing. Sandra's a Catholic and I remember the fuss when Clarry married you. I thought, well, with you being like a father to me, a man of the world and everything, I thought you might advise us, help us break the ice, d'yer see.'

I was flabbergasted. 'Yes, yes, Monty, I see.'

Gad, if I hadn't misjudged Monty all along! He didn't have it in for me. He couldn't care less if I killed Germans as a hobby. The lad loved me. He was eternally grateful to me for introducing him to this dreadful bint! But there was something terribly irritating about his hopeful smile and his girlfriend was in the early stages of perfecting an identical one. So, in a mad wild moment, angry at myself for getting the situation wrong, I tore off my facemask, spat out my falsies and gnashed iron jaws at the lovers.

She opened wide in a silent scream. Monty's round-faced expression hardly changed. It was the same small beatific smile of innocence that I see in my mind's eye, which I do sometimes, because in struggling to remember his sister's face my memory brings up his similar fiz instead – guilt, I suppose.

I threw Monty first, then her. I'm sure they died before they hit the water. No final swims or anything. I stuck my face back on anyoldhow and went around to the Albatross Club. I sat with a Babycham looking down into my albatross's eyes.

'I say, you look done in, Colonel. Been overdoing it, wot?'

'Yes, thank you, Field Marshal. These damned long winters are a swine.'

'Should be grateful we're not campaigning, say I! Ha! Ha! Ha!'

Monty's disappearance was terribly upsetting for Clarissa. Story was he'd met an unsuitable girl and had run off with her to places unknown – Australia was mentioned. The family expected a phone call, a card. Nothing came. One evening Clarry came back from Guides. She'd been crying.

'Not Monty again?'

'If only he'd call, something, anything. But I understood today – he never will. Never! NEVER!'

She was quite hysterical. I slapped her. She fell into my arms and clung like a frightened baby monkey. I did not yet know it, but we would never be happy again.

Candlelit dinners were no comfort for Clarissa. Her sudden tearful departures from table ruined the occasion and were dashed embarrassing to boot. My pretty young wife now avoided all subjects except the weather and was beastly to the beagle. She took to going out alone for walks by the Thames. She'll soon get over it, I told myself. And she did, but not in the way I'd thought. She met Nigel. He was fishing by the river. He had a beagle, too. He was beastly to it also. He had an endless supply of anecdotes about the weather.

I only met him once. Clarissa introduced him to me in a butcher's shop at Reading.

'This is Nigel. Nigel . . . um!'

'Bostock. Nigel Bostock, ducklings. Is this your big husband the General? Oooooooo!'

'Howdyoudo. It's Colonel, actually.'

'Oooooo! It's going to rain,' said Nigel.

'Is it really?'

'I do think so, yes. Heeeee-heee-heee-heeee.'

'I met Nigel down by the river. He fishes.'

'But supplements his diet with meat, I see.'

Long nasal laugh from Nigel, in the middle of which a young blond policeman plodded past the window and Clarissa gripped the packet of sausages she was holding just a little too tightly. I noticed her pang of emotion and I noticed that Nigel noticed.

When I offered my two-fingered superior chap's handshake to him on parting, he leaned over, reeking of cough medicine, and whispered: 'She's much improved, I think, poor dear duck duckling. You must be pleased. Wasn't he a bugger, slinging his hook like that?'

I didn't know to whom he was referring or what about. Oh, Clarissa and her damned missing brother, wot!

'Bye, Clarissa,' she said.

'Bye, Nigel,' he said.

'Wot the blue blazes did you call him Clarissa for?' (I was outraged when she'd played this game with Monty, but with this lanky weasel!)

'Um, just an, um, private joke, Jerry. Nigel's funny, isn't he? Did you see his feet?'

It could only have been a few weeks later when Clarissa led me under the apple tree in the garden – there had been a frost, the roses looked bruised. She removed her spectacles told me she was going to have a baby. My world ended.

'A baby? No-no. No, dear. No. There must be a mistake. No-no.'

'Isn't it wonderful? Our happiness will be complete!'

I looked at the beagle and hated it. In its dumb stare was the knowledge that Nigel had been here, in my happy home, resting his rods in the porch – while I had been trustingly busy at the F.O., serving my country by planning against future German aggression. Oh, God!

'But you can't be pregnant, you silly goose. Can't possibly be!'

'Am! Cross-my-heart! Splendid, isn't it! Mother knew before the doctor did. She could tell.'

I was too hurt to bite my padded leather tongue. My sarcasm pounded the very earth: 'Well, now, this IS excellent news. Was Nigel pleased?'

'Nigel?'

'Nigel.'

'Nigel who?'

'The Nigel who fishes. The Nigel I met in the butcher's shop that day. The Nigel you have private jokes with.'

'I haven't seen that Nigel in yonks. I think he's given up fishing. Bad for his chest.'

It was her Girl Guides night. She was in her uniform, insulting it with her lies. How different had been that first beautiful day! My pain was so acute that I almost did that mad wild thing once more – I was about to tear off my face and show her the metal man I really was, a metal man who could not father children. But Nigel, gormless, lanky, weedy, effeminate Nigel, he could.

'You'll be off to your Guides, then.'

'Better had. It's how-to-light-a-campfire tonight.'

'How jolly for you.'

'Will you be here when I get back?'

'I hardly think so.'

She looked helpless, relieved, exhausted as she straightened her cap to leave. It was a gesture I'd seen senior officers make, and now her. She walked away through the cut where the bins lived, but suddenly turned.

'I can't explain it, Jerry, it's just that there's something cold, almost inhuman about you. It didn't seem to matter at first. You were a man and I thought men were supposed to be like that, not silly and soft like Monty.'

Ice from me: 'I suppose Nigel is like Monty, is he?'

'Yes, if you must know, he jolly well is. We're the same sort. He has a Scout troop, you know.'

'And a new member on the way, perhaps.'

'Goodbye, Jerry.'

'Goodbye, Clarissa.'

The beagle crawled under a rosebush and bit a ball which squeaked.

This was all so long ago, way back in the 20th Century. I never heard when Clarissa died or how, but of course she must have done. Did she marry Nigel after our divorce? I don't know. Was she ever happy again the way we were that first year? Did she mourn losing me the way she mourned Monty?

It also haunts me to think that there must have been a day when Clarissa lay dying, our marriage but a chapter in a long life, and I in those same moments was out in the stars, saluting the flag of Empire where there was always another sun to set course towards, Bunnies to fight, incredible discoveries, another lifetime to live.

I never met anyone who left Earth who regretted it. A liberation of the spirit takes place when you're out among the stars. You are at one with a stolid neutral God, a nature God who feels nothing but comforts all. Out here the kind of passionate love I felt for Clarissa all those years ago just doesn't happen to anyone. There is a freedom too in this lovelessness – God's subtle gift for man on his next great step. So am I a heretical old wreck for believing that an oak in Tutt's Clump in old England, if it yet lives, carved with the motto *JEROME LUVS CLARISSA* is more a vital remnant of mankind than all the cathedrals we abandoned there?

My Motion Picture Career

When I reported to Archbishop Chaffinch of Bunnyland to take up employment as his butler, he was sitting on his mission steps picking bunnyhairs from his chasuble. This was 50 years ago, 2149. We knew each other from years before on H.M.S. *Billingsgate*, so I expected a good reception. I was therefore deflated when he barked that he didn't want me. I was a Catholic and he detested them worse than anything.

'But I haven't taken communion for 183 years, your grace!'

He said nothing more and stormed angrily into the mission. I followed him inside. It was empty of converts. Just his curate, a large bluey-green Solperine, sitting on a table eating crisps.

'Pigboggn cheek. Asky-bees for a manservant and looketh what they hath sent me, Dominic!'

The Solperine, Dominic, looked at me with hauteur typical of its kind.

I turned my back on it and addressed the Archbishop: 'May I ask if the converts are out for their morning hop, your . . .?'

'NO, YOU MAY NOT BOGGN ASK! URK! P'BOGGN COTTONTAILS! THE GOOD LORD MADE ALL CREATION, BUT THE BOGGN DEVIL MADE THE RABBIT!'

The Solperine filled me in: 'Peterpeter'ik, the'ik candidate'ik for'ik Bunnyboss'ik hath'ik converted'ik to'ik Fat Elvisism'ik.✳ If'ik he'ik wins'ik the'ik election'ik, and'ik it'ik looketh'ik like'ik he'ik will'ik, then'ik he'll'ik outlaw'ik Christianity'ik. Our'ik converts'ik hopped'ik it'ik after'ik they'ik

---

✳ I knew Elvis as a spirited singer of Rock & Roll on Earth in the 1950s. But during my absence from Earth a personality cult developed around him, which when exported to the Heavens became a potent religious force. Alien creatures given a choice between Jesus and Elvis invariably, as every bishop knows, choose Elvis. The cult swept the Villages in the 2140s, leaving the pretty churches empty, and spoiling the vision of English Christian life which the Villages were established to preserve. Whereas in Space the Christian religion became united in a High Church Anglicanism (there being too few Catholics to matter) the Elvisism religion split, into two halves: Thin Elvisism was a nature cult, devoted to exploiting all the possibilities of experience and worshipping potentiality above all. Fat Elvisism has always been more popular with the Bunnypeople, with its feasting, intoxicants, excess in general, and its strange death wish. I abhor the whole business like any sensible right-thinking person! The annual Thin Elvis Gathering on Bilickers 4, with millions in their black wigs – especially over bunny ears – and their spangled outfits, walking around the giant Elvis statue chanting song lyrics is the most ludicrous sight I have yet seen. Damn all Elvisites! Damn them! Damn!

heard'ik his'ik speech'ik on'ik the'ik radio'ik. The'ik Lord'ik hath'ik sent'ik our'ik Archbishop'ik a'ik terrible'ik pigboggn trial'ik.'

'But surely, your grace, whatever the new Bunnyboss does, the Shogunate✳ will still protect thee. For thee art the only one who can cast out their evil spirits.'

'Verily, Mathis. But Dominic's bro is a clerk in the palace, is he not, and he sayeth that the Shogun hath been fitted for a black wig.'

'No!'

'We knoweth not if 'tis a Thin Elvisite or Fat. Either way, 'tis the end of all my work here. Triple sorries on you evermost, Mathis, for thee hast come here just in time to see my martyrdom.'

The Solperine was humming a tune I recognized as *Blue Suede Shoes*. It stopped abruptly, faking a coughing fit, when it saw my number 4 suspicious expression – the one where I bring my tin lids down over my glass eyes, rolling them to and fro in the slit.

'Is there perhaps no morally upright Bunny, your grace, able to command the respect of his fellow rabbits? A Christian candidate for Bunnyboss with the courage to speak the truth! God would guide him, wot!'

'No, Mathis. In the 16 years I hast been Bunnybish I have never come across one. The Bunnies are a violent sex-obsessed

---

✳ Bunnyland politics are too complex to comprehend, but it is nominally a Republic, electing a president, or Bunnyboss, every 2 years, and members of their parliament, the Warren, every 14 days, meaning a constant state of elective hiatus. To an outsider this seems wholly pointless, as the real power is in the hands of the Shogun, the rabbit who currently holds sway among the various military factions. If the president opposes the Shogun in any way whatsoever he is immediately assassinated and there is nothing anyone can do. Thus, if the president happened to be a Christian sympathizer and the Shogun was going through a phase of Fat Elvisism, the President would be forced with a choice of (A) martyrdom or (B) the spangled suit.

rabble. In their past they had great artists, thinkers – now they have no thinky-doos under their ears but self-gratification. I have failed.'

'Ik!' said the Solperine, and crossed itself, then ordered me to fetch it more crisps.

Not wishing to appear bolshie in my first minutes of a new employ, though as the Archbishop's man my duties did not extend to gophering for his curate, I complied, and when it said pickled onion flavour made its scales crawl I was so good as to take the packet away and bring 2 bumper bags of rabbit flavour.

Seeing the thing eating rabbit crisps in the middle of Bunnyland struck me as a wheeze. I couldn't help laughing. The Archbishop laughed too.

'Indeedy-be, Mathis. Chee! Let us laugh at the vanity of a man who thought he could bring rabbits to God.'

That night I was lying in the dark in my room listening to the radio – endless comedy shows full of jokes about hares – when the butler bell over the door dingalinged. The Archbishop wanted me. I put on my butler's suit and hurried across the quad into the refectory. All the lights were on. Dominic was sitting on a studded box with another Solperine who I took to be his wife.

'Mathis! We are saved! God hast sent us a champion in our hour of need!'

'HALLELUJAH!' from the Solperines.

'And who, pray, is this champion, your grace?' I looked up and down the tables for a compliant rabbit.

'You, Mathis, you.'

I had thought so. But the full horror didn't then twig.

'Your suggestion this afternoon of us finding for ourselves a candidate for Bunnyboss. You, Mathis, are it!'

I walked down the aisle, slowly, with butlerish aloofness, climbed a table to straighten an icon of St Floppity, the only sanctified Bunny, before returning to say, with a hauteur worthy of a Solperine: 'But as you see, your grace, I am not a rabbit.'

'HA! CHEE! HE!' went my employer, and nodded his crosier at Dominic.

The Solperines jumped off the box they were sitting on and opened it up. 'Twas full of the white pelts of Bunnies.

'As you see, Mathis, we don't just eateth rabbit crisps. Rabbit is the only meat to be had in Bunnyland, and forsooth there is nothing in the Bible against eating rabbits. But we saveth the fur, do we not, indeedy-be we do!'

He winked at me, it was a triumphant lascivious wink such as I never expected to see upon the face of a holy man.

'You don't mean, sir, not, not, not – a bunny suit! Me! In a bunny suit!'

'You were an actor, weren't you, Mathis – in the old films? Well, here's the role of a lifetime for thee. Mopsy Bunny, Presidential candidate of the Jesus Party.'

Dominic's wife held up a pelt for me to try for size. It was the most humiliating moment of my life. But I had long before caught the acting bug and the scheme had a wonderful conceit about it, did it not? I took the bunnysuit, feeling its texture with a butlerish finger and thumb.

An announcement: 'Very well, your grace, thou hast thyself a rabbit!'

Cheers and applause. After so many years, I was an actor again.

✵

Twas shortly after the end of my marriage. 1952. In those days I wandered the streets of old London a great deal, full of miserable thoughts. Rather than return to my office at the F.O. to stare out of the window till darkness revealed my own sad reflection in the pane, I took to frequenting the flea-pits of the capital. I liked anything with Doris Day in it. Or a good war

111

flick where lots of Germans were blown up. I also enjoyed science fiction – though without for a moment thinking that outer space really was populated with strange alien beings.✱ One rainy afternoon I saw a flick called *Destination Blue Moon* starring Franchot Tone, Melanie DeBruk and Chuck Connors as the robot. Mr Chiswick made a very unconvincing robot and the thought hit me: I could do better than that. Within the week I was in Hollywood, introducing myself to agents and producers as perfect casting for any robot parts that happened to be going.

This was a wonderful change of life for me. I felt more vital, more myself than at any time since my rallying days. But I was not overly successful in my interviews.

'Okay, so walk like a robot.'

I walked around the room in my normal way.

'Jeez! What kinda friggin geek are you, kid. Robots walk like this, see . . . Legs apart, arms out, head forward, see . . . clunk, clunk, clunk. Like Chuck Connors in *Destination Blue Moon*.'

'But robots don't walk like that. Unless they are extremely badly made, wot.'

'Ert, get outta here, Professor!'

I was sitting on the beach at Malibu with some other out-of-work actors. They were in beach wear, but I was in a 3-piece suit to hide my metal – they thought me very cool. We were sucking on cokes and reading through a play one of us had written. My character, Gus, was a crooked lawyer with a mother complex – which I found hard to relate to as I never had a mother. Gus had a line once every third page, until near the end when he suddenly takes over the play with pages and pages of clever chatter. We were just getting to this, with me all

---

✱ It is not, in fact, as generously populated with diverse creatures as Science Fiction prophesied. Space, to the surprise of explorers from every direction, is mainly the abode of rabbits.

geared up as Gus, when a chappie I'd met in line at an audition came hurtling across the sand.

'Say, Cody* – you wanna play robots, don't yerh, huh? They's casting this minute down at Paramount. Biggest robot picture ever.'

I handed Gus over to my friend and hurried away, tearing off my clothes as I went. I left a trail of gloves, pants, waistcoat and finally face all the way to the studio. They wanted a robot, did they – well, they were jolly well going to get one!

The director, King Pnarvelt, was looking at a host of acromegalic specimens when I came in, clunk, clunk, clunk, walking as I had been taught robots walked, and threw my rivals out of sight and contention with some handy robotic violence, slow and all-powerful.

'Howdoyoudo, Maestro Pnarvelt. Cody Belafonté.'

'Robot, huh?'

'Robot.'

'Swell suit you got there.'

He frapped my chest, by chance, just at the place that springs open my secret drawer. Its sudden appearance amazed the director's crocodile eyes. I fished inside and found a cigar – one Winston gave me in the Albatross Club before the war.* I offered it to Pnarvelt. He sniffed it, threw away the one he was smoking, and lit up mine. More than satisfied with the cigar, he walked away into the darkness, where several potential robots were waking up and checking their bones.

---

* I had taken the stage name Cody Belafonté on the advice of an agent.
* My friendship with Winston did not continue after the war. He was then out of office living on friends' yachts in the Med and I in my period of breakdowns. When the socialists were kicked out and he was restored to his proper place as P.M. in '52 I was among those who congratulated him at an Albatrossers-only do at the Guildhall. I was shocked upon shaking his hand to see that he did not recognize me – he was quite senile. The leader of the old Earth's greatest nation was a befuddled old man who talked about India and bottoms in the same breath.

From darkness: 'Whatya say yerh name was, big fella?'

'Cody Belafonté, maestro.'

'You got the part. And keep up the maestro. I likes it.'

I was in ecstasies, punching my fists together between salutes. Suddenly he was back again, in the light. He pointed with his cigar.

'One thing – lose the pecker, huh. What kinda movie do you think I'm doin here?'

'Oh!' I cupped my hands over my brass genitals.* 'I am so terribly sorry, maestro.'

My Bonk the Robot in *Robot Planet* proved a considerable popular success. Stills from my scene with Ingrid Tremaine, where she's swimming in a pool and I am holding the towel for her, were on the cover of all the weeklies. I was appearing as Gus in *Remains of Guilt* in a dinner theatre in Hollywood when King Pnarvelt and a clutch of studio cronies came backstage.

'Your Bonk's a hit with the kids, Cody. We wanna make another picture.'

---

* It was one of my stonking wangers, I'm afraid. In my early days in Hollywood I got the best use from my caseful of brass penises, making acquaintance with several attractive actresses and bedding them all, wotho! I knew the once thoroughly famous Marilyn Monroe, then on the cusp of fame. She met me in the canteen at Paramount on a day when I was in some distress. I had extricated the typewriter behind my buttocks, forgotten since the days of writing my *Lloyd George as I Knew Him*, and discovered on its roll of paper a long letter to Clarissa generated from my miserable trains of thoughts.

'What's wrong, honey?' she said.

'I discovered this letter in my buttocks,' I said.

She read it and was moved to tears within a few lines. She said she understood, that she too felt pain like this. We became firm friends and often went out together – for drives in my convertible, where I'd show off my driving skills. We usually ended up eating ice-cream, looking out at the ocean. Though she often sat on my lap and wiggled there, I regret we never actually made love. She sometimes wrote to me when I was in prison – cheerful notes on the back of pretty pictures of herself, long drunken sad letters on yellow paper. When she died I had a considerable crisis of faith – how could God make such beauty and gentleness and yet equip it with such pain? Her voice was like oil on my cogs.

'With Ingrid Tremaine?' (We hadn't got on.)

'Naw. Better. Bigger bazookas. Plenty dames ferh yerh. Waddayasay?'

I was aloof: 'In *Robot Planet* my name was not above the titles, or indeed, under them, wot – but at the fag end of the closing credits, by which time 'my' audience have brushed the rogue popcorn from their folds and are out on the sidewalk whistling the score.'

I whistled the score myself while they consulted. Finally Pnarvelt: 'How's about **Cody Belafonté . . . IN . . . "*Bonk's Earth Adventure*"**? Huh? Huh? Whaddayersay, maestro?'

I grinned. 'Well, yes, sounds splendid, yes, tophole, wot, harhar!'

They held the paper anxiously before me. I was fingering with a spoon on my dressing table and thinking how far I'd come in my peculiar life. Then I moved jerkily, robot fashion, which amused the cronies no end, and I signed a 3-picture deal. Over the titles! Dimmee, I was a star!

My 2 Best Acting Roles

That old happier self of mine – dear, dear Cody Belafonté – had made a comeback – inside a Bunnysuit, indeed, but back with all the old panache – pressing paws on an election campaign. My make-up skills, developed over many years of making masks for myself, had turned an unhappy rabbit pelt into a very convincing Bunny. I was undoubted as a Bunny, as perhaps I never was as a man!

115

Yes, this was my best ever role! I relished every moment! Though I had, through 6 years of butler school and 3 demanding appointments, been earnest to devote myself to a butlering career, I now wanted my role as Mopsy Bunny to go on forever. In short, I was desirous of winning the election.

This caused some friction between Mopsy and the Archbishop, presently my friend and employer but then just my employer. He was forever nudging me with evangelical notes to impress my Bunny audiences on the stump. Tedious as these were, I was compelled to use them – I was still under orders as his butler – but I contrived to mumble them or cough through them while waggling my ears in an entertaining manner, so did not bore like a droning Sunday sermon. This compromise elicited from the good Archbishop my greatest ever compliment as an actor. He said, as I descended a platform: 'P'boggn Bunnies – you're all the same!'

He had forgotten that I was J. W. Mathis! To him, I was just another pestilential perfidiously untrustworthy hoppity scamp! HA! HA!

Bunnies, though they developed spaceflight and numerous nik-naks which humanity never thought of, had at this time no flicks and no television.* This, I understand, is because they have trouble telling each other apart, making any narrative unfollowable. So the Bunnyboss election was more like those fought in Lloyd George's day than the TV-influenced elections I remember from my last Earthbound years. I was therefore, due to experience gained at Lloyd George's feet, well equipt to electioneer.

We zoomed here and there on the furry bullet trains, to Bunnyville after Bunnyville – and always Peterpeter was either arriving next day or just gone. Elvis wigs bespattered the white

---

* They now have the Elvis Channel, showing his dreary old flicks 24 hours a day.

forests of ears I addressed. Months were spent in this effort, and me, utterly ignorant of Bunny political issues, spoke in my big brass voice, sounding more and more Welsh, about the politics I knew best – those of 1920s Britain. Free trade! The Addison crisis! The ratification of the Irish treaty! Labour reform! My early crowds were merely bamboozled. But after reading the speeches in the press the later gatherings, larger and many with the wire haloes which Bunnies prefer as a symbol of Christianity to the cross, were vociferously worked up about the longago issues of the 1921–22 coalition Government. They even cheered my attacks on Baldwin and Bonar Law. But, of course, it wasn't what was said, it was the oratory! And I put 99.999% of David Lloyd George into Mopsy Bunny – whom I'd given a white mane of hair like L.G.'s, so effective when tossed during a pause.✶ Soon, even the Archbishop was tearing up his notes and cheering points the Welsh wizard made in the British Parliament 160 years before Mugg was born. Thousands of eager pink eyes, noses twitching in excitement! That strange padded rumble of Bunny applause – like excited suffragettes wearing muffs. Dimmee, but I was a sensation!

Peterpeter was biting his claws in desperation! He tried filling his speeches with wisdom about Empire Free Trade and the Lancashire Wool Industry, but his pronouncements lacked fire and conviction. Our paths happened to coincide one day in a huge railway station in one of the provincial capitals. We were whisker to whisker, arguing about the Boscawen plan for the corn subsidy. I won every point, for the simple reason I was the only person alive who knew anything about the subject.

✶ Strange to think of L.G. in his tragic years, wasting his brilliance on an electorate who had spurned him forever. But here was me, using his techniques to the best of my ability and heading for triumph and greater power than any British P.M. ever wielded! Egad, how I remember those dreadful election nights at Churt! L.G.'s disappointment was like a thick noxious butter, an ectoplasm of such drowning all around him.

Peterpeter blustered, could think of nothing to say, so descended to insults. The cad called me a hare.✶

He seemed beaten and I was already dreaming of my time in office. But then he countered! Three days later he addressed a hockey crowd before a match in full Elvis regalia and instead of a speech, he sang! And stone me if he wasn't the best Elvis a Bunny could make! I was rattled.

Worse still, when sitting on the train to my 100th Bunny city – staring out at the miles and miles of carrot fields – I suddenly paid attention to the Archbishop's ramble.

'Bunnyland is wot? WOT?'

'Infinite,' he said.

I did not know this. But now I did. Although from space Bunnyland is a planet like any other, large indeed, but still a planet, once you are upon it, it is infinite. It has no end. The carrot fields go on forever. There are endless towns similar to the one we were soon to arrive at. In which case, I had been breaking my little cotton tail for nothing. If there were an infinite number of Bunnies and I had addressed 100-odd meetings with an average Bunnycount of 4,000 at each, that made 400,000 Bunnies I'd addressed, plus 20,000 each for the two big Christian gatherings in the capital, this was a hop in the ocean compared to an infinity of twitching noses!

The Archbishop sighed in agreement but pointed out that, twas the same, was it not, for all the candidates.

But Dominic said: 'Pray'ik forgive'ik me'ik if'ik I'ik disagreaeth'ik with'ik thee'ik, Archbishop'ik – the'ik music'ik of'ik Elvis'ik reacheth'ik an'ik infinity'ik of'ik rabbit'ik holes'ik on'ik the'ik pigboggn radio'ik – and'ik a'ik vote'ik for'ik Peterpeter'ik is'ik a'ik vote'ik for'ik the'ik King'ik of'ik that'ik other'ik religion'ik.' And it tapped one of its various feet.

✶ He was forced to apologize and retract the remark in the following day's *Bunny World*.

118

Rather than throwing up my paws at the Solperine's calamitous info I chuckled like the suave rabbit I was, twanged an ear, saying: 'Ah, then – I know what I shall do! I shall challenge the other candidates to a live debate on the radio! I will trounce them, by George! I will make them look such fools that no Bunny in its right mind would dare vote for any but Mopsy, ehwot!'

I then put my big bunny feet up and chuckled, until it occurred to me to ask that if Bunnyland was infinite, with an infinite number of Bunnies in it, it would therefore have somewhere in its political profile an infinite number of votes, in which case, since infinity cannot be known to any except God, how was it possible to decide who had won? This shenanigan was obviously at the heart of Bunny affairs, but we still hadn't worked out any kind of an answer when the spire of the cathedral of the next town came into view.

The challenge of a radio debate was accepted by Peterpeter (Fat Elvisite) and by Mr Hutchins (Thin Elvisite) and set up for a week preceding the election. I was ready to hit the Elvis camps with a rabbit-punch to end all argument . . . Elvis was a Christian, was he not? – therefore were he with us today the King of Rock and Roll would undoubtedly endorse the party of Jesus Christ our Lord, King of Heaven! I had practised an Elvis impersonation of my own, him speaking in endorsement before segueing into a gospel song. The Archbishop was hopeful for this argument, but warned that it raised the thorny question of Elvis's resurrection and was sure the opposition would strike back with more perverse theology✶. Thus he was rarely off his knees. All his hard work would be undone if I were to lose – his life's work rubbed out. Intensely aware of his severe self-

✶ In the campaign's final days both Peterpeter and Mr Hutchins, desperate for votes, claimed to have spoken to Elvis personally. Peterpeter actually said that he himself WAS Elvis, but later retracted.

criticism, I wanted to win as much for him as myself. In the months of electioneering, travelling about together, we had told each other all that is in this prologue and in Mugg's *22nd Century Blues*. I admired him greatly. He was tough and gentle at the same time, a superior sort of Bulldog breed altogether. Spiffing chap!

Then on the night before the broadcast was due I was idly perusing the train timetables to Bunnymeadows, Bunnyvalley, Bunnysprings, when I squeaked in shock! Wot a prang in the guts! I hurried up the train to the Archbishop's sleeping compartment.

'Your blasted curate's fixed us up something rotten, Archbish!'

Mugg repeatedly slapped himself on his bald head to wake himself up. 'Pleasy-do, in wot way hath my servant offended?'

'He's had us stumping farther and farther up the lines from the capital. Not only will we miss the debate tomorrow – we'll not get back till a week after the election's over and won – or boggn lost, wot!'

'Dearie-be! P'boggn bogleyfala and no mistake! Urk! Amen.'

Dominic, in charge of our travel and engagements, had sabotaged the campaign. When we burst into his compartment we found him with another Solperine, not his wife, eating rabbit crisps and each wearing half of a spangled suit. And, of course, Elvis wigs! The Archbishop was terribly shaken.

'Dominic! I refuse to believe this!'

'Ik! Ik! Ik! Ik!'

'That you, after all the years we hath workethed together . . . an Elvisite! THEE, OF ALL PEOPLE!'

The Solperine finally found his voice: 'Twas'ik her'ik!' – Indicating the other Solperine. 'She'ik hath'th led'th me'th astray'ik with'ik her'ik lewd Elvisite'ik wiles'ik! Ik! Uh-huh! Forgive'ik a'ik poor'ik sinner'ik!'

'GOD MAY BOGGN FORGIVE THEE, BUT I P'BOGGN

WON'T – YOU SCALY LOUSE FROM THE FUNDAMENT OF BEELZEBUB! URK! BAH!'

Later, the election won, a few of us, including the Shogun himself, gathered on the waste ground beside the mission, where Mugg later built a hospital, and we burned Dominic at the stake. Both the Archbishop and I thought we might be going a bit far with this, but they were harsh and troubled times in Bunnyland and the message that Jesus could be harsh as well as gentle was essential to get across to the Bunnies. He sang *Blue Suede Shoes* to the end and never, as Mugg had blithely expected, shouted for Jesus to receive his spirit at the finish.

The debate went ahead without me. Peterpeter made short work of Mr Hutchins and I sat clicking my claws in a most dreadful rabbit stew.

'Triple sorries, Mopsy – thee tried thy best. It must be God's will that the Elvisites prevail.'

'No, Archbishop, I am not beaten yet!'

Our next stop was a small farming town. I addressed a modest gathering from the back of the train. In my speech I made the wildest election promise ever made in Bunny politics. I would ensure that every Bunny over the age of 21 would have a workable set of sexual parts within a year of my election.* I

---

* Unlike our primitive Earthling rabbit, Bunnyland Bunny biology has beset Bunnies with separable sexual parts. For every million Bunnies born only one has genitalia – a full set, male and female; thus Bunnies are no sex at all until they attach a male or female part, at which time they 'become' that sex for the duration of the attachment. At birth the sexual parts are confiscated by the authorities and sold at auction. Therefore, most Bunnies not being rich enough to afford to buy sexual parts, they are unable to do what bunnies everywhere like best to do, and are denied these pleasures perhaps for their whole lives long. As these Bunnyparts are hoarded, stolen, misused, quickly worn out, wrongly stored or sold to aliens as playthings, there is always a desperate shortage. This alone, in my opinion, is the cause of the famous fractiousness of Bunnypeople.

didn't realize I'd said it until it was out through my buck-teeth. The small local gazette printed the speech and the sensational news soon spread to infinity.

When our train finally arrived at the Bunny metropolis the election was over and I had been President of Bunnyland, Bunnyboss, for nine days. Our expectation was of a vast throng of supporters at the magnificent railway station. But no one was there at all.

The Archbishop, Dominic (now gagged and shackled hand-&-foot) and myself shuffled down the platform in silence. Just the sound of Dominic humming through his gag and the buzz of the city beyond. We entered the main concourse. Empty. The shops were bright, but no one stood on either side of the counters. Far above, in the eaves, among the darting shafts of mote-filled sunlight, a trapped pigeon made confused attempts at escape. We were in the middle of the station floor, stepping over a vast mosaic of entwined Bunnies, when a rifleshot silenced Dominic's humming. It rang so loudly I thought a bullet was inside my head, ricocheting. As the ringing sub-sided the pigeon dropped at our feet and a moment later the Shogun himself, wearing only a fur-lined cape and a black Elvis wig, came towards us with rifle in hand. He had that hoppity-skip 2-footed walk which only the dominant class of Bunnies employ.

'Mopsy. U-huh!'∗

'Shogun. U-huh!' I replied.

'God's grace be with you, O mighty rabbit!' said Mugg, and flicked holy water at him, which irritated him no end.

'A word, Mopsy . . .'

He took me aside. We stood by a carrot stall. As he spoke the Shogun idly sorted out bad carrots and tossed them on the floor.

∗ U-huh, of course, is the Elvisite greeting.

'Congratydoos on thy election, Mopsy. Jolly good show.'

'Thank you, sir.'

'But this pwomisy-womisy of yourn – about the sexual parts. Just another election pwomisy-womisy, ehwot? No intention of following thwoo?'

'Well, I . . . of course, a promise, erm . . . if you think it unwise? Any advice I will naturally follow to the letter.'

(I was on a sticky wicket with the Shogun – I was the elected leader of the country, but he was its ruler. I knew damn well that he could have me pulled apart bolt by bolt! I dared not disagree with the blighter!)

'Well, Mopsy, my dear frwend and colleague, I do think that to issue every common hopper with his or her "equipment" could diswupt the economy quite severely, wot? Wabbits will do nothing but copulate, you see, given opportunity.'

'Ah, but my plan was, Shogun of our Dreams, to issue sets of parts to trios of rabbits on a rota basis, each trio licensed by the Church to make it good and pukka.* One week a year should do. This, I am sure, will create a more satisfied, productive workforce. Give the crittas something to look forward to, d'yersee!'

'I see, yes, bwilliant, heeeee-heeeee!' He was blushing under his fur – from embarrassment or rage? His eyes looked into the pile of carrots or flicked to the ticket-machine where his rifle leaned, never at me: what was up? 'You see, fact is, well . . . the government store of sexuwal parts has suffered from pilfewing for years, as I'm sure you know, but we didn't wealise, you see,

---

* Bunnies have 3-way marriages. 3 Bunnies – of whatever sex they decide they are! – making a marriage. But they're no sex at all without their parts on, are they, dammit! Dodgy ethical ground altogether, wot! But, Bunnyland being what it is, 'twas sound politically to say that I would issue sexual parts to a married set of 3, furthering my theme of social cohesion. This custom Archbishop Chaffinch abhors and later my own 3-way marriage, or rather Mopsy's, I kept secret from him.

old lad, until the accounting for the end of this latest financial year, you see . . . well: they've all gone! Bally storehouse is bare! You, ahem . . . wouldn't happen to know where they've gone, would you?'

'Me? Gracious, no!'

Yikes! I had promised to issue sexual parts to the populace just when the entire government store of them goes missing! He thought I had them. If I didn't appease him somehow he might crucify every Christian Bunny in Bunnyland out of spiteful revenge.

'So I pwesume you have a fund of your own parts, donated by wealthy supporters.'

'Erm, no!'

'No?'

'No, O Great One!'

'So where on Bunnyland were you going to get the parts to fulfil your pwomisy-womisy?' His cheeks twitched in a subtle threatening manner.

'I, erm . . .' All I could do was laugh. Mopsy failed me. I was J. W. Mathis in a rabbit suit and was lost for words.

The Shogun laughed. 'Hee-eeee-eeee-eeee-eeee-eeee-eeee-eeee-eeee! I can see I hast met my match in thee, Mopsy. Thee intend to tell the Bunnies that thy Shogun hath the parts, that I won't let you issue them, and then every faction will rise against me and leave thee as the first ever Pwesident and Shogun in one. A bwilliant ploy!'

I bit into a carrot with a suggestion of slyness. Mute, but Mopsy again.

'Well, you haven't won yet! Heeeeee-eeeeeee-eeee! At last a wabbit who is my equal!' He led me even further away from the craning Archbishop. 'Erm, look here, actually . . . someone's gone off with my set, too. A lovely big black-spotted one, had it for years. Hate to twouble thee, but you wouldn't happen, for fwiendship's sake, ehwot, to have a set going spare?'

124

I happened to have a rather tousled set in my shoulder bag which was among a dozen unChristian items I had confiscated from the Solperine couple. Checking to see if the Archbishop was watching – he was! – I furtively slipped the sexual parts into the Shogun's trembling paw. He groaned, pulled the 2 parts apart, and offered me either one with a rampant look on his toothy face.

'Buck or doe, you choose, sweetiepaws! Either way's handsome for me, my beautiful Mopsy-wopsy! Heeee-heeeeeeee!'

Gad! I was about to have sex with the Shogun! Refusal was impossible to the leader of an infinity of rabbitity. I could do nothing but brace myself and say: 'Erm, I'll take the buck, sir, if that's okaydoaky with you.'

He, or rather 'she', made the attachment and showed me the under of her tail. The thought went through my mind of what the long gone officers' mess at Poona would think if they could see what Major Mathis was about to do. But twasn't him, was it? It was Mopsy attaching the buck's member to himself. It was sweetiepaws Mopsy getting stuck in . . .

We did it on the floor of the railway station among a tossing of mouldy carrots, with howls of Hellfire from Archbishop Chaffinch, stamping on his hat in moral indignation, and whistles of encouragement from the Shogun's general staff, their noses up against the glass doors. My bunnysuit stood the rough treatment remarkably well. But the trauma of the experience took years to leave me, especially as, the role of Mopsy vivid within me, I had never enjoyed a sexual encounter so much. Perverted swine, ehwot! Rabbit poker! Gad, the shame!

All these years later I ofttimes look up and catch the Archbishop giving me one of his funny looks. 'BAH! HUH! URK!' he'll go from under hooded eyes and I'll twig to what he is yet again referring – an unforgivable sin committed with a rabbit 50 years ago!

I made 2 Bonk the Robot flicks a year from 1954–57, '55 being the biggest year, since when our budgets had been getting gradually smaller. Bonk's popular appeal lifted him briefly out of the B-picture milieu, now he was sunk back into his rightful place with one or maybe two last hurrahs to go, a few more cackling villains to brain with papier maché rocks, a yet more tarty space siren to help with her toilet. I was satisfied at this. In many ways Bonk had become a dreadful bore, on screen at least – I enjoyed much more the celebrity of Bonk, and was very comfortable as him, as I never quite was with Mopsy, wot. I opened drive-in doughnut bars, did automobile commercials, visited sick children's homes as Bonk. It was all delightfully jolly. But not the work I had been made for. Though fleshless, I felt fat, and lazy, stupid.

In my Hollywood years I had been reasonably well behaved with Germans. Then, in June of '57 an actor renowned in pre-war Hun cinema, playing lascivious professors and Faustian types – I forget his name, but it had a von and was shamelessly German – was doing a Hollywood remake of one of his creaky epics, sharing the back lot with Bonk's latest adventure. Marilyn✳ was starring opposite this swine, whose superior attitude was playing havoc with her delicate self-confidence, so I scootled along during a break to encourage her with my line in suave pally adoration. It was a sweltering day. Through the break in the buildings I could see the Pacific glittering. I waved to Mickey Rooney, Gary Cooper (a golfing pal) and Gilbert Roland as I crossed the lot.

'Shucks, Cody – must be like an oven in there!' drawled Gary. (Meaning my Bonk suit – all Hollywood imagined that a mystery man operated within, not a jangle of Edwardian gadgetry!)

✳ My close personal friend, the actress Marilyn Monroe. See footnote, page 114.

'Yep,' I said, and we had a chuckle before I headed for the lights of Marilyn's new flick.

But 'twas too hot for filming and everyone had adjourned to their trailers. Everyone except the aforementioned German actor who was talking, in Deutsche, to my own director, King Pnarvelt . . . who was replying in same! Dimmee! I'd thought his ancestry honourably Dutch! What a Jilks I'd been! HE WAS A HUN!

The German actor and 'friend' looked up and smiled as they saw me coming snarling towards them. They thought I was putting on a merry little show.

'Cody, maestro – lehme introduce your ass to a pal from my old neighbourhood.'

The strings in my throwing arm were slack due to all the throwing about of scenery I did as Bonk, so when I threw these smug bosche into the ocean, they missed by miles and landed a mere 5 blocks away, slapbang on the freeway, where they interfered most horribly with traffic. The death of two such movie giants was reported thus: two old friends, meeting for the first time in years, had indulged in an old-fashioned drinking bout, then wandered senseless with intoxication into traffic. Their behaviour was castigated not at all for resulting in their own deaths, but for making jam of a family of six from Idaho whose Packard went skewiffo after bumping over them.

Bonk expressed deep personal sadness at the death of his mentor and director: 'This man . . .!' said Bonk. 'THIS MAN! . . . this sweet, sweet man . . . taught me everything I know about this business. Yes, yes, I knew about his drinking problem – but the too-too cruel thing is, he nearly had it beaten, poor darling! How are any of us going to live without our Pna – he was like a father to everyone he knew!'

I finished direction myself on the rest of what turned out to be the last Bonk picture, *Bonk and the Amazons from Mars*. Meanwhile, I was contemplating a debut on the English stage. I had been in contact with dear, dear Larry Olivier in London about the possibility of doing *Julius Caesar* with an all-robot cast. I planned to play Mark Antony.✳ He was rather luke-warm on the idea, sending a letter full of bamboozling eye-wash, but I wrote back giving my vision of the production – my Caesar would be a metaphorical Lloyd George during his fall, Brutus was Bonar Law, Crassus was Baldwin, et cetera. All very high-powered intellectual stuff! I was sure this would do the trick with Larry, and he would rescue me from the TV series of Bonk my agents were negotiating with Warners.

Suddenly, rescue came from another source. Stanley Ku-brick and Kirk Douglas drove out to my house in the desert one Sunday and found me in my workshop making myself a new arm. Mr Kubrick said he had seen me as Gus in *Remains of Guilt* some years before and still wept whenever he thought about it. He said Mr Douglas and himself were putting together a WW1 war epic to be entitled *Paths of Glory*, and would like me to play the role of Pierre, with 2nd billing after Kirk. This was no B-picture stuff. I could hardly believe it.

'Excuse me, chaps, but this Pierre, he's not a robot, is he?'

Their laughter shook the house.

After they had driven away I stood by my pool hugging the script they'd left me, watching their dust settle on the LA road. I had never, not even with Clarissa in my arms, been more glad of life on Planet Earth.

✳ The rest of the cast would also be genuine robots. I intended to make them myself. Twould have been quite a thing to see! 100 years later, on Bilickers 4, I did make a miniature robot theatre. The actors were 3 inches tall, but were as alive as me, bathed to life by blood freely donated by the great Bilickerian actor Snathe'rrrrrrr-oots Waynds. The workmanship on their masks was, if I say so myself, exquisite. They performed *The Three Musketeers* quite beautifully and my Milady de Winter was a little darling – I think I actually loved her. She used to sit on my hand and sing bizarre songs of her own devising. Sadly, when Snathe'rrrrrr-oots Waynds died of the fish plague in 2063, so did my cast. I was so deeply upset by this that I never made another. Yes, I can hear her singing now. Such strange, brief little lives, a few struts and gone.

It disappointed me a twidge that *Paths of Glory* was an anti-war picture. No nicely stirring flag-waving. War was shown as a futile endeavour by a monstrously egotistical mankind, quite contrary to my natural beliefs. But whatever! – Twas a meaty role, full of emotion and pathos.

PLOT: Pierre, a brave sergeant in the French infantry, sees his Lieutenant, a coward, run away leaving two comrades in dire trouble from Bosche. Pierre tries to save said comrades – but is too late. Later, when the regiment fails in its attempt to take an impossible position, a mad general orders that a bunch of men should be selected for court martial, to be shot for cowards, *pour encouragez les autres* and such rot. Pierre is put among the selected by his cowardly Lieutenant who despises him, and Kirk Douglas, a sensitive colonel, tries his best to get Pierre out of the consommé. But in the end Pierre is shot by the dastardly frog army, dying better even than Charles I. Gripping stuff. I could hardly wait to get stuck in.

First day's shoot was an action sequence, where we go over the top and fail to take the impossible German position. I turned up wearing a new mask, specially made with 'Gallic' features. Gad, was I authentic! My accent superb. Mr Douglas shook my hand and wished me luck on the picture. I thanked him for a wonderful opportunity, in perfect Parisian *boulevardier* French. Wot a success I was going to have with this, my dears!

But as the whistles blew and the smoke drifted, as the whizzbangs banged and the shapes of pickelhaubed Huns appeared tossing stick grenades from their trenches, I began to lose myself in the role. It was no longer a movie! It was November 11th, 1918 and my fathers lay dead behind me in a blasted trench. Hun machine gun fire was all around and men were dropping at the wire.

My direction was to fall back with the other survivors – our failure to take this position being the key event of the screenplay. But all I saw were the Hun faces through the smoke and my primary function of fighting Germans in WW1 conquered every thought had since by J. W. Mathis and Cody Belafonté. I charged the enemy position alone, dragging yards of wire, snagged on my uniform. I dived into the German trench and butted the extras with my tin helmet, I bayoneted them – 1, 2, 3, stick – 1, 2, 3, stick – just as I had done with the sandbags in a playing field above the Stour estuary during my trials in 1916–18.

The director had yelled CUT! long ago, but I was still killing extras. I had a hundred of them up against a backcloth, with only solid wall behind. They pulled the backcloth down, looking for a door behind it. I was under the backcloth with them – 1, 2, 3, stick – 1, 2, 3, stick – in a frenzy of martial glory. I did not stop till every German uniform was worn by a corpse. 481 extras, who'd turned up for work and their $30 a day, had just died in the final battle of the Great War.

I leaned on my bloody rifle in No Man's Land, final groans and post-life twitching scattered all around me. I was grinning. Mons, Ypres, the Somme – I had avenged these! But slowly, the image of Mr Douglas, standing on the lip of the French trench, smoke wisping around him, his dimple a dark hole under his furious furrowed brows, filled my consciousness and I realized where I really was and what I had done.

I fell to my knees and played the scene where Pierre is pleading for his life to the callous French chaplain. He speaks of his wife, his farm in Languedoc. I was brilliant. I improvised. I think I mentioned intimate things about my life with Clarissa – I don't remember. No actor could have done better. They could all see that, as they slowly gathered around, walking through the remains of battle.

At last the emotional scene was finished. 'Was that all right?' I asked Mr Kubrick as the studio security and LA police walked cautiously across a make-believe No Man's Land to take me away.

BONK GOES BANANAS said the rags. Too flipping true, I'm

afraid. Ruined, just when true distinction was in my grasp! No German barons to blame this time. I was replaced on the picture by Ralph Meeker. I never saw the final flick, but read in *Photoplay* that it was damned fine stuff. Sometimes, on a tedious evening when we're bored with all the other things we do, the Archbishop asks me to play 'Pierre's scene with the chaplain' and with mechanical cats mewing in their baskets all around, I re-enact what may have been my greatest moment. Shucks, indeed!

Death Row Blues

Once upon a time I was a respectable Colonel in the British army, now I was a convicted mass murderer. Worse still, not one of my victims had been German. They read the list out in court while I sat in a Gallic mask which gave me an unctuous look that irritated the jury no end. The relatives of the 481 'victims' – half the blessed country, dears – had picketed the court demanding my death. And the prosecutor would pomp on about how the Bonk films encouraged just the sort of senseless violence of which this crime of mine was a sorry-most example. I became increasingly irritated and when, after the inevitable guilty verdict, the judge asked if I had anything to say for myself, I said: 'Well, you know, it just serves them jolly well right for wearing German uniforms, that's all!'

But now the fight had gone out of me. I was too-too sorry for myself. Though incapable of shedding tears, I started filling up with water. I'd wake up from a snooze sloshing inside, sad liquid brimming out of my head, an unattended bathtub in the shape of a man, and my voice a gargle like the cataract of Ladore sent to Hell. I had the effect of a burst water pipe and my cell was flooded out on a regular basis. The only way I could empty myself was to unscrew the golden knob-end of my penis (in my quids-in Bonk years I had added golden parts here and there) and let the water drain out into the john in my cell. As the guards kept a constant eye on me, they witnessed what seemed to them to be an hour-long's urination. Very odd behaviour! More so because in the last 15 minutes 'urination' I stood upside-down to drain my legs. Of course, I quickly filled up again and the whole miserable process had to be repeated.

A theological point had occurred to me which bothered me sorely. Does God always exist? Or only if certain children are good? Is He there one moment and a myth the next? And if so how are those no-God moments different for us from the moments when he is looking after us? Is this the secret – that Evil is constant, working away, cheating, conniving in every single moment, and God, who only exists for every other moment, or every moment in ten, can never gain the advantage over Evil and give us the perfection we demand of him? Is this the truth of the balance of the Universe?

Further, if indeed we each live in our own separate dimension, which coincides only superficially with others, perhaps God exists always for some and never for others, which explained something to me then, and more now. And what if the dimensions in which we live themselves are not constant? What if they die like days and we must shift into new ones all the time in order to survive? Perhaps sometimes we shift into a Godless dimension and never, by chance or by some law of theological nature, co-exist with him again.

Whatever the truth of this great blither, I knew I was alone, that God was not there, that there was no God and that my own mystery of existence had no logical foundation. When they put me in the electric chair, I knew that it should not kill me. I am a metal man, I reasoned, an automaton operating under a non-existent power. I should be able to whistle the entire score of *Oklahoma* over and over forever with their electricity buzzing through me. But I somehow knew I would not. My execution would be my symbolic and actual end. I would not survive. I wanted to, but I thought it best to surrender myself to death. I had, after all, wot, killed all those people – though they had been wearing German uniforms, so not all the guilt was mine.

Thus, locked in a cell 6 feet by 10, I spent 5 years (1958–63), twice the time I spent in Colditz, waiting for my appeals to be rejected in order for the inevitable moment that would end all moments for J. W. Mathis, false man. During this time many of my fellow death-rowers were taken on their final walk. Murderers, yes, but poor fools mostly, or just mad. I think it was the compassion I felt for them which began to bring me back to myself from the miseries and frights.

Archbishop Chaffinch, my friend and employer, criticizes me by saying that I lack a certain something, some minuscule but essential element that humanity shares, and that thus I cannot empathize, sympathize or regret – all my sentiments are Mathis-based – that Jesus knows this and will never enter into me to allow a state of grace. He cites my treatment of the Shite creatures as example. But I think he is dashed unfair here. And this is my example: I was deeply sorry for those horrid men as they shuffled off down the corridor, swearing their blinking heads off, with the shock of oblivion a mere minute away.

Leeroy Stookis was condemned for beating a bank clerk to death during a robbery in 1954. But there were doubts about the case. By the time I joined him on Death Row he had already languished 3 years while these doubts bounced from judge to judge. Leeroy, a huge square black man, my height (6'4"), was one of triplets – his identically huge square brothers both helped and hindered his case. Leeroy's alibi, that he was playing pool during the robbery, might have held up had he been brotherless.

But the poolhall-flies at his trial had to admit they couldn't tell Leeroy from Jared or Bean – so maybe they, not he, had been shooting pool that day, and that his kind of shooting had indeed been warning shots into a bank ceiling. Furtherly, Leeroy himself admitted that he sometimes forgot which of the brothers he was himself. Meanwhile, Jared and Bean were each seen in no less than 16 separate locations, together and singly, at the time of the robbery – storing up alibis of their own for diverse sins committed elsewhere. So rather than work all this pishposh out, the trial threw up its hands and Leeroy was sentenced to death. But his appeals went on . . . Bros Jared and Bean meanwhile, while reportedly on vacation in 10 different resorts, had been killed in separate shoot-outs with police and the sympathy seemed to be swinging Leeroy's way.

He was my friend. We chatted all day. He was particularly interested in my rather spotty sexual career.

'G'wan, Bonk – talk dirty some mo', huh!'

I was glad to. It passed the time.

Leeroy took the *New Yorker*, for the cartoons, none of which he understood at first perusal. I had to explain them to him, but first, the mag being in *his* cell, he had to describe the cartoon to me, always going into the greatest detail, forever returning to the gagline, muttering it over till he made a little song of it. This cartoon exemplification could be a wearisome process. But sometimes, when he 'saw' the joke, it was wonderful to hear his rolling innocent chuckle grow till it filled the death house.

The Thurber cartoons were my favourites, but these Leeroy had the greatest trouble with. He 'saw' the joke and didn't at the same time. I think, you know, I enjoyed discussing cartoons with that silly great lump more than any other talks I've had with anyone – except, of course, for my Bible jawing with Archbishop Chaffinch, my friend and employer. This said, it seems dastardly what I did to poor Leeroy, does it not!

Smeenbeckers, Leeroy's sweaty porcine lawyer, came in one day with good news. The coppers had arrested a certain Jangles Johnson in Wisconsin. This miscreant had confessed to being the chappie who in-fact-really-did hold up that bank and brained that there clerk.

'Does this mean they ain't gonna kill me no mo'?'

'Sure, Leeroy, if it all checks out. You'll be outta here in no time flat.'

'Gee! Thanks, Mr Smeenbeckers.'

Then the poor lummox wept because his brothers wouldn't be waiting for him when he came out. He proceeded to tell the story – after every silence longer than ten minutes he would tell this story – about how when he and his bros were kids they had a hound doggy and they all loved this hound doggy something awful and were always a-fighting and a-gnawing at each other over whose hound doggy it was – Leeroy's, Jared's, or Bean's, or any combination thereof – and which of them the hound doggy loved the best. In the end they came up with a solution worthy of Solomon in an iffy mood – they shot the hound doggy and decided to love each other instead. He never got to the end of the story, the bit where they buried the hound doggy next to their daddy, without tears rolling off his cheeks onto his big hands.

'Say, wat's that you doin there, Bonk? Wat's that you doin there, I say! Wat's that you doin there, huh, huh, huh?'

'Nuttin.'

'Summthin ain't nuttin, never is, nope, no sir, ain't never nuttin if its summthin . . .'

While my friend continued this interesting essay I was busy making a mask, a Leeroy Stookis mask. The makings for masks I always kept in my secret drawer: plaster of Paris, rubber solution, my paints, horsehair and nunhair for the hairy bits.

'Wat's that you doin' there?'

'You'll see.'

'Huh? Huh? Huh? Wat's that you doin' there?'

When he did see he was totally confused. He must have felt he was a figure inside a cartoon, the butt of a joke he could never comprehend. I had removed my own face and was wearing his, topped most effectively by a wig of woolly hair.

'Jared? Bean? That you? Gee, they a-told me you wus dead? Which bro is you, huh? Remember the hound doggy? Gee!'

I told him I was bro Leeroy.

'HUH?' He walked into the shadows of his cell and returned with his fingers all over his lips. 'HUH? WHAT YOU SAY, LEEROY? YOU AIN'T LEEROY, NOPE, AIN'T, COS I IS, I IS LEEROY FERSHOOR . . . unless maybe I's Bean! Is I Bean, Leeroy? HEY, LEEROY – I'S TALKIN TO YERH, LITTLE BRO!'

Now, with the aid of my now somewhat tatty War Office guide to hypnotism, found at the bottom of my drawer, I took advantage of Leeroy's already befuddled bonce and convinced him that he was in fact Cody Belafonté . . . or Bonk the gone-bananas robot – same difference. He was an easy subject. I tossed him my mask and he put it on. And my wig. He put it on. Not more than 10, or less than 10, minutes later the warden entered beaming, followed by a train of flunkies, a stiff from the Governor's office and a red-in-the-face Smeenbeckers looking cheerful as a game show host who keeps all the money no matter who wins what. The regular guards saw that Mr Stookis (yes, it was Mr Stookis now) and Bonk were in each other's cells, but in such highpowered company they made no point of it.

'Justice has been done, Mr Stookis, as it always is,' boomed the warden as if to all the cows on his dude ranch. 'Jangles Johnson's confession has been accepted by the Governor – isn't that right, Mr Gertfunt?'

'Yo.'

'All the paperwork is done and as soon as Leggert here opens your cell, you are free as the proverbial ostrich!'

'OPEN . . . ING!' cried Leggert, pulling the big bar in the corridor.

I stepped out and shook everyone's hand – still with the white hands of milky-skinned Belafonté, but no one seemed to notice the inconsistency of pigmentation. Twas all rubber anyhow!

'I shoour did think mai ass wuz a gonna that time n' no mistake, no sir. But mai bros, mai poor dead bros wont be a-waiting furh mai ass in the car park outside, no sir, and never no more.'

'Yes, well, that's a darn tootin' shame – isn't that right, Mr Gertfunt?'

'Yo.'

'But life's a bitch, Mr Stookis, and it is our job to rise above it and make something of ourselves. That's our American way, Mr Stookis!'

'Right!' said Gertfunt.

Just before I walked out, Stookis cried from under my mask: 'Toodle-pip, old chap. Wish I was coming with you! Haha!'

'So long, Bonk. Sure will miss chewing the fat wiz yerh ass, sure will, uh-huh, sure will.'

He took his big black hands out of his pockets to wave goodbye with, and he mopped his masked brow with my Belafonté wig – but again no one seemed to notice anything untoward.

Next thing I was sitting in the back of Smeenbeckers's roomy Edsel beside Leeroy's girl, Maeleene Bledoe, her long-fingernailed hands down my pants, and her saying: 'Stir done made you hard, sugar, good'n hard down there . . . my MIGHTY MAN . . . wheeeeeeee-haaaaaaa!' and Smeenbeckers driving in a sweat-wet shirt, a-turning around again and again, sticking his aggressive sausagy finger in my black face, saying: 'Where you got that money hid, boy? Where's it hid? You'd be a big stupid black cooked goosebird if 't werent ferh me! Haff, we said – haff or Jangles Johnson'll be telling 'nother story – gottit, boy!'

But there was the sea again, and lovers hand in hand on a beautiful day while America ate lunch. Shucks!

My various appeals, meanwhile, had just that very minute been dealt with by the Supreme Court. So I was executed in the electric chair on the very day of Leeroy Stookis's release, June 24th, 1963. Or rather Leeroy Stookis was executed and I was released as Leeroy Stookis, wot! BONK FRIES AT MID-NIGHT, said the newspapers. The mask melted on Leeroy's unlucky face and set fire to his own. How dearly I hope in his next moment, if next moment there was, he went gamboling with his bros and their hounddoggy in paradise.

'Where's it hid, boy? Huh? Maeleene, you leave his pants be – git him to tell where's it hid!'

'Where's it hid, sweetlips?'

'Sorry, missing the point, madam? Where's wot hid, wot?'

'The greenbacks, hunnylamb, from the bank robbery. You remembers that don't yerh, huh?'

'But I never did any bank robbery, no sir – Jangles Johnson, you ask him about it, haha. That's your man! Ehwot!'

'GODDAMN SONUFABITCH, SONUFABITCH, SONUFA-BITCH . . . JEEEEEEEE-ZUZZZ! YERH BLACKASS SONU-FABITCH!'

Smeenbeckers was banging his head on the steering wheel, cracking his new Panama, and not conducting himself with the unflappable dignity one would wish for in one's legal representative.

A Request from Mr Wilson

The wooden shack where Leeroy Stookis lived was full of bullet holes, a feature added during what must have been an energetic shoot-out between my late brother Bean Stookis and the Federal Bureau of Investigation. When the sun shone hard these bullet holes shot beams of dusty light across the shack which reminded me of the searchlights over London at the beginning of the Blitz.

Maeleene was a constant companion! She listened to my recurring story about the hounddoggy with great patience, plus other stories cribbed from my prison days with the real Leeroy, plus some absent-minded nostalgia about Colditz and my rallying days between the wars.

'Where yo git that moonshine from, Leeroy? Yo sure is gabbin' real weird since they let yo out!'

As all persuasion had failed to extricate the hiding place of the bank-robbed dough from me – as indeed it would, for I did not know owt about it (I was not, God help me, Leeroy Stookis!) – Maeleene's great mission was to extricate the hiding place by sexual means. Smeenbeckers had so ordered her and she set about the task with tigerish vigour. Thus we committed a sexual intercourse once every half-hour during hours of wakefulness, these sessions often lasting longer than half an hour and therefore merging into one another.* In her enthu-

---

* As I lived in the shack for 15 months, this means I committed sexual intercourse with Maeleene Bledoe approximately 13,800 times, more times by far than I ever committed sexual intercourse with any other woman or rabbit.

siasm she often pulled off my Leeroy wig, and she dug her long fingernails under the skin of my all-over black bodystocking, giving me a permanent mauled look.

'Where's it hid? WHEEEEEEEE-HAAAAA! You gonna tell me now, or is we gonna die of pleasure, babe, huh? Huh? Huh? Yeah, mai Mighty Man – mo', mo', mo' for yerh sugarbaby, yeah, oooo – JEEEE-ZUZ! that feels good – where's it hid?'

After sex we lay in bed and she explained the cartoons in the *New Yorker* to me, throwing in a 'Where's it hid?' every little while.

The sex stoked Maeleene's appetite for food and she was forever nipping down to the store to fetch more ingredients, mainly beans, for a noxious stew left bubbling on the stove at all times. She ate a helping of this stew after every sexual intercourse. Meanwhile, Smeenbeckers's nephew, Jesse – a pink youth like a hog with hands and feet, billeted on us by his crooked lawyer uncle to make sure I didn't 'skip with the dough' – kept his plate constantly filled. He sat in the den watching game shows on TV while spooning stew into himself, or maybe he practised twirling his gun on the porch, or maybe he had a pervert's eye at a bullethole watching me and Maeleene doing the deed.

Both Jesse and Maeleene, I must say, seemed utterly happy in this life. I have rarely witnessed such contented folks, not even in a pot full of Peewermums. Only when Smeenbeckers turned up, saying: 'Where's it hid, boy? JEEEEE-ZUZZZ!' did they lose their cool contentedment and start shouting alongside him.

And there was me, sucking on a coke, feet up, showing them my pearly-white false teeth, while they stomped around the couch rattling the shack and raising dust, the Smeenbeckers cracking their Panamas and Maeleene weeping hot tears while speaking the list of the things she would do with the dough when I at last – please, honeylamb – told where it was hid.

Smeenbeckers, in calmer mood, agreed with my caution about Leeroy's hidden dough. The FBI were watching the shack, and me, and him. If we were to start splashing dough about they'd be on top of us real quick. Smarter to wait a spell, maybe a year, even 2.

'A YEAR!' wailed Maeleene. 'Sonsuvbitches! I'll be 30 in a year, ferh Chrissake!'

It seemed, what with Smeenbeckers Jr sticking to me like gum on my heel, Maeleene pulling me into that creaky bed every 30 minutes, lawyer Smeenbeckers's constant to and fro, and the G-men parked in the used-car lot over the way, I would have to remain living life as Leeroy Stookis forever – a peculiar penance indeed! But I was not fighting it. I derived a certain delightful shiversome metal fatigue from the sex with Maeleene's long body. I loved the TV especially the westerns. I enjoyed spooning up the stew, tucked up in bed while Maeleene, in a breathless voice full of giggles, read out the funny papers. I even liked Jesse – his piggy pudding face was a constant amusement. This was, strange to say, a wonderful life – altogether superior to Death Row, wot, and more restful than being Bonk the confounded robot.

But then one evening I looked outside through a bullethole and the shiny FBI Ford wasn't parked among the heaps. For months I'd wanted to have a reckie of the car lot! Now I could! Maeleene was getting ready for more sex, floating around the shack wearing next to nothing. Jesse was watching her, pervily, an empty plate on his lap, under which his fist was pushing into his groin. When Maeleene went into the bedroom and called . . . 'LEEROY! GIT YOUR GREAT BEAUTIFUL ASS IN HERE RIGHT NOW, MAI MIGHTY MAN! THIS TIME YO'S GONNA TELL MAMA WHERE THAT DOUGH'S STASHED OR WE MEBBEES JUST MIGHT DIE OF EACH OTHER'S ASS!' . . . I sat down beside Jesse instead. *Bonanza* was just starting.

Sarcasm from Jesse: 'Git in there, Mighty Man, you ass-crazy horse's ass! Your bitch is on heat agin.'

'Look here, old chap,' I smiled, 'Maeleene was just saying to me t'other day, she sure was, uh-huh, that she never did see a white ass bucknekked close to, certainly not a white ass as handsome as that there Jesse Smeenbeckers's white ass must surely be. Nope, never did. She said that when she gets that dough of mine she's a-gonna find herself another white ass like that Jesse's white ass, not that she never will, no sir, find an ass as super-duper as Jesse's ass. She says, hooo-weee, when she sees that ass bucknekked she'll turn wildcat on that ass, uh-huh.'

Jesse was breathing fast, almost oinking. 'She said that, huh?'

'You betcha. So I was just a-thinking, Jesse, seein' as I done jumped that there bitch 15 times since breakfast . . . why don't you git bucknekked 'n take a spin, huh? She's crazy for to see that floppy white ass of yours.'

'You shoor, Leeroy?'

'Indubitably.'

Jesse removed his clothes and embarked for the bedroom, pinkly as a pudgy pink babe fed from birth on raw sausague.

'Erm, Jesse – better had pull on your thing there a while. It's smaller than she's used to.'

'Yeah. Thanks, Leeroy.'

Having pulled anxiously on his thing, he summoned up more courage than he'd ever summoned before and burst into the bedroom, shouting: 'FEAST THEM BIG BROWN EYES, YOU WILDCAT BITCH, AND SAY THEM HALLELUJAHS! HERE COMES THE BEST FLOPPY WHITE ASS YOU'LL EVER SEE THIS SIDE OF PETER'S GATE! AYEEEEE-HARH!'

While Maeleene and Jesse were rattling the shack with the furious nude fisticuffs and furniture-throwing which broke out within an instant of Jesse's AYEEEEE-HARH, I nipped outside and over to the car lot. I hadn't faked being Leeroy Stookis that long and not guessed where the dough was hid! In the failing light I pawed among the wrecks until I suddenly decided to lift one up. In a hole underneath was a damp cardboard box seemingly filled with rat-chewed *Superman* comics. But underneath the comics, yes sirree, was the dough – crisp and clean. I was stuffing my pockets with it when I heard a shot from the shack.

Jesse wasn't dead. He'd fainted when Maeleene shot one more bullethole into the planks. He lay on his face, his floppy bottom popping out air, some just hisses, others like return of fire – that damned stew, I expect!

Maeleene was bruised all over from her victorious tussle with Jesse. Now she pointed Jesse's pistol at me. She was wiping tears away but also smiling. My pockets frothed with symbols of joy!

'Okay, Leeroy – throw it on the couch, you dumb stud asswipe!'

'I threw a bundle of $1000 bills onto the couch.

She picked it up, eyes popping, teeth bared in not exactly a smile, and in sudden celebration flung the bills around the room with a peculiar delight at their crisp, clean flutter.

'Yeah-yeah! And the rest, mai mighty little man! THE REST! Give it to mama! WHEEEEEE-HAAAAAA!'

I turned to go, saying in what she always called my 'moonshine Harvard' voice: 'You'll just have to make that do, my girl. I've plans a-plenty for the rest of this filthy lucre, ehwot. Ta-ta.'

She shot me. But the bullet just bounced off my steely back . . . don't need a bullet proof vest, wot – am a bullet proof vest! Miffed that my bodystocking's favourite tipple had tried to assassinate her great loverboy, I turned back, lifted off my hair, peeled up my face mask, put out my tongue and went: 'BlurbabBBabaBubbb-bbbbwhaaaa-ubabBBB!!!!!!!'

Maeleene dropped the pistol and collapsed in a faint on top of Jesse, who had just woken up and rolled over. Their chins met with a cloink. The last I saw of them, they were asleep in a sweaty black-and-white heap, arms and legs entwined, green-backs all around them – one even on Jesse's empty plate. As I slammed the plank door in leaving I had the feeling that the old shack was going to collapse behind me. It didn't quite. But with my doorslam and Maeleene's extra bullethole its balance tipped from precarious to gitout athere and I'm sure it wasn't many a day before its collapse. Mind you, tis conceivably so that Maeleene fixed it up with the dough I left her and that she lived out her days there.

I had $950,000 dollars on my person when Leeroy Stookis arrived at Heathrow, England on December 4th, 1964. I wore a purple double-breasted suit, a wide-brimmed purple hat, rings on every finger, and my big black face delighted to be home. I intended to create a new me, a neo-English what-ho sort of chap, handlebar moustache, another wifey perhaps . . . a house by the sea in Norfolk, a new life, lots of horses and dawgs, jigsaws on the tea-table, a happy childhood home for a chap who'd never enjoyed a childhood, with a hickory-dickory-dock grandfather clock to tick away the years. Alas, dears, twas never to be. I didn't even get out of the airport . . .

'Mr Stookis? Mr Leeroy Stookis? I am Detective Inspector Hartburn and this is Sergeant Bannisters. Would you come with us, please, sir? No trouble, now, there's a good lad.'

Large snowflakes were falling as we drove into London. The sounds of the traffic, the call of the newspaperboys, the lights of theatreland, were full of so many memories. I covered my face and sobbed, coughing up beans from Maeleene's noxious stew and spitting them down the shirt-collars of my police escort. They were still digging them out of their underwear and shaking them down their trouser legs when they left me in the cells.

Imprisoned again, wot! It seemed that Jangles Johnson had

changed his story – given the nod from the bitterly doubled-crossed Mr Smeenbeckers – and that once again Leeroy Stookis was arrested for that miserable 1954 murder and bank robbery. I was to be extradited, sent back to Death Row forthwith.

But when Detective Inspector Hartburn returned to my cell later to interview me, he found not a large square black American in a purple suit, but a metal man sitting in his tarnished bare metal.

'I won't hurt you,' I said. 'Please, do sit down, there's a good chap. It's just, well, America is such a bore after a bit. And all those horrid years on Death Row. I couldn't stand another cotton-picken minute of it. Give me good old England any day! No, I'm not Leeroy Stookis – so the extradition papers are rubbish, wot! You can't send me back! CAN'T! NOT FAIR TO SEND ME BACK!' I opened my secret drawer and showed him a photo of me at the front in tin hat, 1918. 'I am J. W. Mathis, false man. I was constructed by 2 brilliant young scientists during the Great War, d'yer see. To fight the bosche. A robot, yes. There's my guilty secret! But I'm not an unfeeling hulk. I have a man's sensibilities. I was once married to a woman I loved . . .' I spoke for some time about Clarissa, her hair, her moles, her feet. 'I know there's not a war on or anything, but surely the country has uses for an old soldier like myself. I'm awfully clever with my hands.'

Detective Inspector Hartburn was nonplussed. He said he'd see what he could do. Decent chap. He returned a day later with 3 chinless wonders from the Home Office. They kept cleaning their specs and looking at each other. One took notes as I told my life story all over again. Sometimes, amused at some anecdote, I heard from myself the deep rolling innocent laugh of Leeroy Stookis, a little something left over from my impersonation of him. My poor friend! I realized for the first time what I had done to him. What a creature I was! I saw myself for the first time for what I in reality was – an unnatural Frankenstein's blinking monster!

My voice was soft and steady, but seemed to me to come from far away, saying: 'Look here, after all's said and done, I really do think it would be best for all concerned, especially me, if I was dismantled.'

They seemed to agree. I was asked to sign forms. I did so. Then they measured me with a paper tape measure, frapping me and listening to the echo. They left without a goodbye, taking my keys with them. I sat on my cot, thinking about Maeleene asleep at my side in the early morning, and waited for boffins to show up to cut me to bits. Any minute, they'll come, I thought.

But I sat there in a self-critical stupor for weeks and still my breakers did not come. Every few days a copper's face would appear at the slot, saying: 'Can I get you anything, young fella-me-lad? Anything at all? I know you don't eat grub like the rest of us. Some wine gums, perhaps?'

'Awfully kind, but no, thank you.'

Three days after New Year, 1965 I had my last-ever glimpse of London as I was taken to Euston Station and thence north to the Lake District, to Sondomerlys Camp, a top-secret rocket installation behind the highest fence I'd ever seen. It was superfically disguised as a cheese factory – billboards depicting cheese trolleys were everywhere – but the smell in the air was of petrol and burning rubber. Yes, they would dismantle me here, pick over my mystery while my ghost faded. My friend Detective Inspector Hartburn had accompanied me from London but was put out at the gates. He had a lump in his throat, couldn't say a word. I wished him and his family well and never saw him again.

I was silent, taciturn. The cheap cheese factory décor of Sondomerlys was typical of the cheesy new socialist Britain. The boffins who came from their labs to peep and squeak at me were peeping pipsqueaks indeed. The army men who saluted my progress down beige lino corridors looked to me like boys playing soldiers. I straightened one's cap for him and said so. He laughed. Dashed jovial attitude to a chap about to be dismantled, thought I. A childish 2nd lieutenant, mere weeks out of Sandhurst, with a swollen Adam's apple and an end-of-the-pier leer, showed me to a Spartan quarters.

'There's a spanking new uniform in the wardrobe, sir. Boots here. Should all fit, sir. Hope we've got the ribbons right.'

Gad, wot a queer ritual! I was to get up in my rightful uniform to be dismantled! Typical army – no rules for a thing, so you invent a bookful off the top of your blasted head! Nice, though, in a way, to go out by the book.

I dressed in a Colonel's uniform. The ribbons were spot-on right. I had a spare face in my drawer. So I put it on to complete the picture. Suddenly, I was J. W. Mathis again. I awoke as if from a 10-year dream, of Hollywood and American prisons. Dimmee, what a mess I'd made of my life! I deserved oblivion, non-existence! But while looking at the cheese billboard outside my window blocking a view of the fells, I lost courage. I heard a swearsomeness muttering inside me like a grinding cog, a sound just like the cursed farewells of those poor dumb clucks I'd seen dragged stubbornly down the corridor from death row. Next thing I knew my muttering turned to prayers. I was on my knees praying for a new chance at life when the childish lieutenant came to fetch me.

I do believe that God answered my prayer, that he quashed the dimension I was in, where I was about to die, and sent me to a new one. Perhaps he even changed the history of the entire Universe just to answer the prayer of a false man. He can do anything, and I think he did that. I have spoken to the Archbishop about this and he has nodded kindly.

Under the dome that dominated the installation – its outside was ludicrously done up to resemble a slab of Cheddar – were

three Blue Streak rockets in a line. I was eyeballing them and
didn't notice the clutch of notables approaching. When I did I
saw that the one in the middle of them, the one not wearing a
white coat, was Harold Wilson, the dreadful new socialist Prime
Minister. He was the same common little man in a mac I knew
from the papers, whose speeches on the new white-hot age of
technology I had pooh-poohed to Detective Inspector Hartburn
in one of our little talks. Mr Wilson had a pipe in his mouth, but
no tobacco in it, a fact he kept pointing out to his companions in
an uncouth overbearing manner. He had bad teeth.

'This is our new man, Prime Minister, Colonel Mathis.'

'By heck! He's a biggun, he-egh-egh! By heck!'

'Howdoyoudo, Mr Wilson.'

I shook his fleshy hand with my bare metal hand and looked
him straight in the eye with the contempt of a lifelong Conservative. But I was amazed to discover from his returning gaze that
this was the most alert human being I'd seen since Lloyd George.

Suddenly a table was brought, clothed and covered in tea
things – scrummy cake shop cakes, jammy dodgers, buttered
scones. The officers and boffins skipped it, leaving me,
Mr Wilson and his wife having tea with the 3 Blue Streaks.

He sucked his pipe, whistling through it, between nibbles.

'There's no tobacco in here, you know.'

'I see that, sir.'

'One wrong puff, they said, and the cheese in this place could
go up like a firework! By heck! Ever smoked a pipe, Colonel?'

'Cigars were a weakness once, sir, before the Hitler war.'

A half hour's pleasant chit-chat followed. I told him about the
fall of the coalition government of 1922. He was quite fascinated,
full of clever questions, bringing out points I had heretofore
never considered. Suddenly, he tapped his empty pipe on my
crumby plate, as if to gain attention of another part of my mind.

'Now then, Colonel – everybody knows that the Americans
and Russians are in a space race. What nobody knows is: so are

we, by gum! He-egh-egh-egh! And we're way ahead, way, way ahead of the buggers.' Very serious: 'This enterprise is an entirely personal initiative, only my inner cabinet have the slightest clue about it. We'd never get it through Parliament. My party, quite rightly, has other priorities.' Then he winked like a schoolboy. 'We, he-egh-egh, landed 4 Englishmen on the moon last November.'✱

'I say, sir, jolly good show!'

'Next job is to send manned rockets beyond the planets to the far-flung stars, Colonel. And I'm requesting, not ordering, mind you, but requesting that you, lad . . .' And with a grin showing every one of his rotten teeth he pointed with his empty pipe at the Blue Streaks.

What did I think in that defining moment? Not of Bunny-people. Not of Peewermums. Not of the glorious adventure now beginning for our island race in outer space. I thought of twinkling stars, of quietness, of God's loneliness when He died for us on the cross. 'For my country, Harold' (he'd asked me to call him Harold) '– I would do anything. But this, dimmee, this

---

✱ That was November 1964. The first Americans on the moon didn't land till July 1969. As every space-dwelling schoolboy knows the first Englishmen on the moon were Robinson, Chives, Harris and Buggins-Topp, together with Sherpa Pharbelot. This, of course, was never publicly known on Earth. The Wilson government's secret commitment to space exploration was continued in secrecy by successive administrations. It was kept secret from the people for some 130 years, by which time our outer space Empire was well established. The strains the Project put on the economy of old England was the single cause of the country's dramatic economic decline, especially in the late 20th Century, and it is truly amazing that no one not 'in the know' didn't twig to the fact that vast monies were being diverted to the incredibly ambitious scheme. Today, of course, the story of the fateful flight of Robinson, Chives, Harris and Buggins-Topp (not forgetting Sherpa Pharbelot) and their deaths on the moon – they were poisoned by the Sherpa's cooking – is the first history lesson of kiddies in our E. E. S., which their famous sacrifice helped to create. Statues of Harold Wilson are also in every Village square. I wouldn't argue that he was the greatest Englishman who ever lived. I am deeply, profoundly honoured and privileged to have met the man.

seems the perfect job for me. I might have been made for it!'

He shook my hand again. 'Aye, when they told me about you, lad, I sucked me pipe and chuckled, I did: 'He'll do,' I said. 'By heck! He'll do for the Project, that'n.'

And our eyes turned to look up at the rockets. I have never before or since known such overwhelming awe.

Mr Wilson filled his pipe: 'When I was a little shoeless lad in the back streets of Huddersfield, Jerry . . .' (I'd asked him to call me Jerry) '. . . I never guessed that such a day as this would cum. Eh? To the stars! Eh? By heck! He-egh-egh-egh!'

One more boyish wink and tea was over, the great visionary was gone to light his pipe and administer the greatest country on Earth, Mrs Wilson loyally at his side. I stood alone under the rockets with a set of cheery boffins, listening to them explain how Colonel J. W. Mathis was going to fulfil his new destiny at the forefront of the British Space Project.✶ I was more breezy and chipper than in all my history, because for the first time ever Germany did not seem to matter one jot.

✶ Which became known more correctly as The English Empire Company after Scottish Independence and the extermination of the Welsh in the early 21st Century, which abolished the old-fashioned fact and uncomfortable concept of 'Britain'. By this time, with the first Villages in development in space and original England in chaos, the political connection with our original home was tenuous. Nowadays, of course, it is non-existent. England seems a scrappy little bit of nothingness when we English have all of creation as a playroom. But I never forget it for a day. For instance, I remember so well my time spent training for take off, living in the Lake District, the most poetic corner of England – popping into a pub in Keswick, rowing on Grassmere with a friendly boffin, picnicking with a couple of tarts while the radio played the toe-tapping pop tunes of the day, finding a flea-pit in Carlisle showing a Bonk double-bill on a Saturday morning, motoring down lanes for a spot of how's-yer-father in Blackpool. Splendid old girl, England! When I think of her lying out there, a green jewel in a distant sea, empty and deserted, I want to fly straight there and embrace her every oak. Most modern Englishmen, of course, have never been there. It is simply a place they came from, part of the distant past. It is part of my past too – dear, but there it shall forever remain, a memory. I shall never return.

Sharing Space with Nutty Slack

Something of a personal tragedy has befallen me today. The Archbishop, on one of his senile wanderings in the underground corridors of this vast abandoned city on Cats-by-Nowhere, has discovered, to his cacklesome glee, an old shopping arcade where the vanished citizens once purchased in one shop or another . . . mechanical cats! Long-defunct rival stores still display their best tabbies, heaps of such, a cute-'n-cosy feline abundance – ten deep on shelves, tableaux artistically arranged in windows. There are thousands upon thousands of cats down there.

'Thee must get to work immediately-doos, Mathis! Fix 'em up prontomost! I want my new cats to follow me on my walks. Chee! Oh, God is good to an old fooly-be, to give him so many pretty cats.'

'But the howling at night, Mugg dearest, is already p'boggn intolerable! Surely thee hast enough cats.'

'I want the life put back into those shop cats, thee cranky old gadget! I WANT MORE CATS! And good purrers!'

In his hissing pussycat passion he swung his crozier over his head and knocked off his hat.

'Very well, your grace. If I might just finish my *Prologue* . . .'

'BAH! BAH! URK!'

So it seems my tranquil mornings sitting here at my computer telling the story of my earlier life are at an end. These cats are buggers to get started and old Mugg won't be satisfied until the shade of the melaleuca trees of Cats-by-Nowhere is carpeted with catnapping cats going prrrrrrrrrrrrrrrrrrrrrrrrrrrrrrrrrrrrrrrrrrrrr

. . . and the nights are a cacophonous howl of choiring toms rutting on the rooftops.

I loathe and despise cats. Today they have scratched my very life from my hands and given me a screwdriver – cats for the fixing of! A catty catted slave of cats and their cat-besotted cleric! What a fate for the unique soul whose story I have told on these pages!

I will press on for a bit, however, as I had reached the point of my leaving OOP,✶ an account of this crucial moment being the essence of my brief when commencing this *Prologue* some weeks ago . . .

My astronaut training consisted mainly of running up and down the Cumberland fells between astronomy sessions with Professor Glibbery-West. I was also required, though no one would tell me why, to memorize great shelves full of English literature. I sped-read all 14 of Dickens's novels in 3 mornings. Shakespeare took nearly a week. I still remember it all, but tis crumble-jumbled in my mind, with Mr Micawber as Lear and Cleopatra wooing Oliver Twist. My 2 fellow astronauts, the 2 Rogers, were excellent strapping young specimens, spiffing chaps, solid of mind and body. We knew that other astronauts were coming aboard, as our job was to stay wakefully on duty and care for our craft – they were to sleep in suspended animation until we arrived at wherever, then to step forth fresh and young into exotic spacescapes. We imagined that these other chaps were chaps like us, being trained in a secret location somewhere – Empire chaps maybe, square-jawed Canadians or brave sardonic Aussies.

So imagine the amazement of 3 solid chaps like us when a rumbustious old country bus pulled up outside the cheese factory and an absolute shower disembarked. I complained to our CO in the most vociferously insubordinate terms. I tried to reach Harold

✶ Our Original Planet is what the newer generations called dear old Earth.

on the phone. Useless! The Project had decided: I was to be shot into outer space with the pop group Nutty Slack as company. Roger had Freddie Hibbert and the Curly Trees. Other Roger had a supergroup made of members pinched from a variety of pop groups. One-hit wonders or deadhead bass guitarists, all picked, one presumes, because they wouldn't be missed, had been shanghaied in the name of the Project and ennobled with the title of astronaut. We real astonaunts were quite utterly discomnockerated with bile for this new generation anyway, but this . . .

'Did you see their hair?' wailed Roger.

'Beatniks! Hippies! Nudists! Bally layabout dropouts!' Other Roger punched his hand with his hand.

'Dimmee, damned hard cheese on us, this is!' said I. 'I'd almost prefer Germans to this!'

And we looked at the weatherbeaten cheese billboards and felt sorry for ourselves. Harder, of course, on Roger and Roger. They were giving their lives for this mission. When, 60 years hence, they pressed the buttons to wake up their still-youthful pop group, they themselves would be old codgers on the brink of death. Not me, though. Egad! – I'd be stuck up there with Nutty bleeding Slack, for years and years! Was THIS the wonderful destiny that had cheered me during months of hard training? PAH!

The 1960s on OOP was a peculiar time. Bizarre ideas were to the fore. It was a kind of illness – responsibility, hard work, service, these were sneered at by a younger generation perverted by mindless music and downright laziness. But the older heads were affected too. Oh yes, I'd seen good old Mr Wilson on the telly, hobnobbing with the Beatles! But I never thought that the Project would suffer from such an association. Proximity to Ringo's drumbeat had perverted Wilson's great vision, which now included that our astronauts be pop groups, a naïve cultural ambassadory, twanging jingles on new worlds to spread 1960s culture to alien civilizations – the idea being to show aliens what an irresponsible shower we Earthlings are, I suppose. Here's our culture! Aren't we wonderful? And here was me with all blinking Shakespeare stuffed in my empty head – the ruins of Mr Wilson's worthier cultural ambitions, now never to be heard above the YEAH-YEAH-YEAH-BABIES.

Take-off was scheduled for September 14th, 1966, if the weather was good. Our Blue Streaks had been renamed after the footballing heroes of the recent 4–2 English World Cup victory against the Hun. Mine was named the 'Nobby Stiles'. The word NOBBY was being painted in huge letters twice on the rocket. This meant, as I not altogether gently pointed out to the painters, that the word NO would remain when the rocket and capsule separated after take off, which, I suggested, might give any little green men telescoping us the idea we were awkward customers. NO to what? – possibly to every heartfelt question in their little green hearts, dears!

I often spent my free time sitting on the pad, watching the final preparations, including the loading of drumkits, thinking about the great unknown I was going to explore. I was daydreaming thus when Nutty Slack were escorted onto the pad in their chains to see the rocket. I thought it would be polite to have a friendly word.

'Colonel J. W. Mathis, MC, DSO-&-bar. Mission Commander, dontyerhknow.'

Their lead singer sullenly, behind his yeti hair and sun-glasses, introduced his fellows as Hughie & Stewie & Wilf & Jonna – and himself as Nosey Hindmarsh.

I waved my swagger stick at NOBBY – just the Y to go. 'Well, now, chaps, pretty damned impressive, wot?'

'The cheese, man, far out.'

'Sorry?'

One of their number unhooked his fingers from his beads and pointed at the huge balls of polystyrene Cheddars which kept drifting past the windows in the blustery day.

'Cheese, daddy-o. Blows your mind.'

'Yes, haha, trifle odd, I know. But I'm sure we'll see plenty more splendidly curious things when we get where we're going.'

This seemed to upset them. They hummed their one hit, but without its usual jauntiness. I lost my temper.

'Look here, you young layabouts have been given a jolly splendid opportunity to do something for your country, rather than perverting teenagers with your dreadful racket. You should be raring to go! Think of Agincourt, the Battle of Britain, wot! The World Cup! Stand up straight! Chin up! Look like men, for God's sake!'

They shuffled in their chains and looked sorry for themselves. I was already on my way, but stepped back.

'Oh, one thing, as we're going to be shipmates, I thought you ought to know: I am NOT a human being. Repeat: NOT a human being. Carry on.'

Due to a fault in the deep freezers on board NOBBY Nutty Slack awoke 60 years after take-off looking three times as old as they would have had they lived out their days on OOP comforted by the nostalgia of their one hit. Plus, most of their fingers snapped off when I was defrosting them. But their tour of the planet Bilickers 9/34b was a tremendous success, even though they all died of old age between the 3rd and 18th gig. The replacements, local Bilickerineys, who stepped in as each original member croaked, continued the tour and fulfilled the lads' cultural mission. The group continues to this day, adding replacements to their line-up as each Bilicker dies or gets eaten (Bilickers' only food is each other). Last time I saw Nutty Slack was in 2153 on their extended tour of Bunnyland, in the infinity of which I expect they are still performing that catchy song which I first heard on my trannie while picnicking in old England lifetimes ago.

Anyhow, we blasted off as planned on September 14th, 1966, blowing all the cheese billboards down and frightening Friesians in 100 fields. The other rockets, BOBBY and GEOFF, took off after us, heading in different directions. How often I thought of Roger and Roger staring out of their respective poky windows, getting older and more lonely. I hoped they were thinking of their friend J.W. staring out of his. It was 20 years before I saw the first shoals of fish, haddock mainly, with which our galaxy was provided by our creator. Until then I'd eaten the same meal every night, emptying it from my thoatsack and tarrying all day over re-preparing it because there was nothing else to do. Fish dinners were a delightful change.

The only flicks the Project packed for me were 2 reels of *The Dam Busters*, all the reels of that film where Glynis Johns plays Miranda the mermaid, and 1 reel of *Gaslight* (which I never watched). It was 63 years (2029) before we reached the Bilickers planets, by which time I was so crazed with boredom and the sound of the projector clicking in my ear – I watched *D.B.* and *Miranda* at least twice through each day – that I used to bang my head on my knees, furiously shouting the dialogue like a Roman emperor gone suddenly barmy at the games. I defrosted Hughie of Nutty Slack 5 times just to have some company, but all he did was gaze out the window and say: 'Far out, man. Heavy scene. Right on. Peace.' So I bunged him back in the freezer and good riddance.✶

✶ I later learned that Roger and Roger – who somewhere between them had *Gaslight* except for one reel, plus my missing reel of *D.B.* – were so stultifyingly bored that they took up the instruments of their respective pop groups. They arrived, one at Snoon 4, the other at Kwat Colony, virtuosos on guitar, harmonica and drum kit, joining their groups as the star turn. They had, tragically, during their confinement, gone thoroughly hippie. But worse was to come. The Snoons, an upright toffee-nosed lot with 3 toffee-noses upon each of their 7 bowler-hatted one-eyed heads, were disgusted with these Earthlings, their first-ever alien visitors. They allowed them one song, then opened fire. Kwat Colony were more amiable, but the Bunnypeople invaded shortly afterwards and wiped them all out in a typical hopping-mad rabbit rampage. So both Rogers, splendid fellows, endured 60-odd years in a chilly can only to be killed within weeks of landing in their promised lands. Ho-hum!

Archbishop Chaffinch, my friend and employer, has just stormed in with a gang of cats. He has swung an incense burner over his head in a most threatening manner and ordered me to desist this blither and get his newly discovered hoard of boggn cats working.

'I have now covered my 48 Earthbound years, Archbishop, and briefly touched upon my 63 years in NOBBY (1966–2029) but I have barely mentioned the succeeding 170 years, ehwot!'✷

'MATHISSSSSSSSS!!!!!!!!!!!!!'

'Very well, Your Grace. The cats.'

HERE ENDETH THE BOOK OF MATHIS

✷ It is interesting to note, is it not, that when we landed on Bilickers 9/34b, the present Archbishop Chaffinch had another 54 years before being released from God's bosom onto OOP, one of the many possible worlds available to his worshipful creatures.

22nd Century Blues

The Greater Book of
Mugg

or
The Memoirs of the Wasted Life of
the Archbishop of Bunnyland
on Earth and Towards Heaven

by M. C. Chaffinch
with footnotes
by his butler and friend J. W. Mathis✶

✶ I am adding my footnotes during my own reading of Mugg's book, and trust
that they not the nutteries of a lonely false man, but bolts shot through me by
the hand of God, the real maker of this book. We are all marooned in our own
particular lives, just as a book is stuck inside its pages. But a footnote . . . I
think of it as a bird settled on the washing-line of a thought, who, in breaking
away, takes that thought to places new, ehwot!

One

The Lesser Book of **Hittites**

*

'Hittites, 'fraididoos, marm – p'boggn millions of em.
Entirely my fault. If they keep coming through the warps
at the present rate they will outnumber the indigenous
population by Thursday week.'
*Byron Joop, in his resignation statement
to the Lovely Anita, 2088*

To Chaffinch Chaffinch, my grandfather,
with fond remembrances of a holy man.

Hittites: One
An Old Bird Says Hello

Pleasy-do, I hast forgotten, have I not indeed, yes I have, exactly how long I hast been upon Cats-by-Nowhere. Know thee: there are no seasons on CbN, this terminal insists it is 1823 . . . plusly, if I ask my pigboggn butler the date, he lies. Fear not! – I canst work it out! . . . If I retired at the uplifted mandatory age for an Archbishop – 115 – and it is forsure half into 2199 b'now, and I was born in 2083, that makes it only about 2 years marooned here. It seems longer, and also no time at all. Urk!

The aforementioned butler, Mathis, old tick-tock face, is entirely responsible for me being here far from my darlingmost Bunnykind. He was unable to fixydoo our thence-&-whence, as I vicarishly call shuttlecraft✶, which was taking us from Bunnyland (thence) to HMS *Ticklestick* (whence), where I intended to squanderize most of my final days committing the hoohar-wiggly thing – which in troth I have only ever wiggled with one actual female and not with any of the versions of her for half the boggn century, so I was long

✶ This is quite unfair! The shuttlecraft, as I insisted at the time, was expertly sabotaged by some Elvisite fanatic. That we survived at all is, the Archbishop should have admitted here, a miracle, thanks to God and also to the excellent pilot training I received from the Peewermums when his Lordship was but a nipper!

overdue a grointickle, was I not indeedy! – also to lose myself in a celebration of sticky food, raw life, hologramismic experiences and to go chattabout with the other defunkedized clerics partaking of the forbidden pleasures of the *Ticklestick*. But our on-the-blink shuttlecraft – which, I repeat, old tick-tock face failed to fixydoo* – commenced to spin us into what I am reliably informed is called a Dwert's Vortex. (Dwert, one hopeth, was longtimesince chewed by one hisself.)

Thus, Dwerted, we foundeth ourselves spat beyond the constellations through a tunnel of exploding lightbulbs into an emptiness between galaxies, and me rumgumshusly blaming all the saints one by one and clonking old hickory-dickory-dock with my crook until, quite without the authority to do so, he confiscated it, upon which I returnethed to battle swinging an incense burner, from whose blows he still beareth the dents, and deservedly so. Fortunatelydoos, just as our juice expired, while I was kicking the controls and yelling the prayer for the dying, behold! – we espied a tiny yellowy pill of a star, that of Cats-by-Nowhere. Mathis got outside and foot-waggled us forward. It took 3 months, with me castigating him with pigboggn speechifications from the rear window without any kind of pause. He heard not a word I sayethed and never gave up telling me to 'go to bed, Your Grace' – which, factly, was exactly where I was put, for that which castigated the butler twas a hologramismic me, in castigating mode, which I used on my balcony in Bunnyland to go poohell to the rabbits. Chee-hee!

Sobeit, we landethed on Cats-by-Nowhere. I kissed the ground and pronouncethed our coming here to be God's will, then gave a little service, singing *To be a Pilgrim* alone cos old tick-tock was being uppity. Then we walked through the tumbleweeds to this delightfully abandoned city, where I

* The repetition doubles the unfairness!

am content to live out my last few days, surrounded by the mechanical cats we found here.

The poor pussys! They wast strewn about our main square in arabesque positions, conked out as if from plague, having been catnapping so for who knows how long. But Mathis wound one up by sticking his finger up its bumhole. Imagine my delight! Meow! I didn't give up nagging at him until all 763 were operatively meowing – and some stubborn little heathens had to be completely taken to bits, especially the puss that barks – oh, he still doeth so! Once a day, always once a day!

'May I inquire if your barking cat has barked yet today, Your Grace?'

'He hath not, Mathis. Not yet, I fear.'

'WUUUUUFFFFF!'

'He hath, Mathis. I do believe that was him just now.'

'Then my ears did not deceive me, Your Grace.'

Chee! They are my greatest joy! Mugg's moggs! When they sit on my lap and purrrrrr while I stroke them I feel that all my lifelong troublesomelydoos have been worth it, just to sit here, a becatted old man. Pusspusspusspusspusspusspusspuss! Hee-chee!

Thus and so, what ambition hast I left but to read my Bible through twice or thrice, go walkies with my flock of cats, and eat Christmas dinner every day. I am fortunatelydoos in this latter desire, as the ancient food replicator we found here is stuck on Our Lord's Birthday and only provides slap-up turkey-stuffing-cranberry-sprout-swede-breadsauce-gravy grub-ups, followed by a choice of plum duff or Xmas pudding, of which I always partake both. Verily, every day I dine thus! My only other tipple is Oxford Marmalade, at bedtime, straight from the jar with a spoon. I get through a jar every 3 days, and as we came with 400 boxes of same upon our thence-&-whence, there is enough to last me 39 years, by which time my moggs will have long ceased to mew over my grave.

Space travel hath changed humanity multifariously. One of my firstmost memories is 'popping down to the shops' with my mumsy. I'd be, wot, 4-ish. A beautiful child was this Mugg. She'd pop into *Marks & Spencer*'s emporium in Bury St Edmunds and, as folk admired her fledgling chaffinch, buy maybees a packet of this, a punnet of that – coming away with just a bag in one hand and me in t'other. Amazingy, nopes!!! Nowadays we only ever buy tonsworth quantities of stuffs at the spaceshops, for perhaps indeedy-bees we may never pass a shop again in our lifelongs – and have not the Bunnies blasted every one of those quaint travelling shops so numerous in the '30s? Yes, they have. We are especially shopping-spree minded if we are among the lucky souls off to colonize a happy little planet somewhere, taking along enough supplies to last till Doomsday. Once we all lived crowded on OOP, now there's room for all of us to have his own verdant world. God intended it thus. An Eden each.

I was vicar at HMS *Billingsgate-on-Sea*, but when the lovely Anita's clone was found to be preggers with my child – I will speaky-do of this lapse later, nopes – I was asked to leave by the righteous Parish Council. This version of the lovely Anita, being Queen of the Village, and a highly dutiful lady, of course had to stay behind. I never saw her again, or heard what happened to the child. It was a girl, of course – no boys happened after the '20s. She'll be 57-ish now, a square-jawed bosom-heavy grey-mopped harridan in tweeds, just like the rest of them. Mathis tells me that the Albatross Club on Bilickers 4b/89a has been forced to admit women in order to survive. There were only 5 men left there, codgers too, and over 75 billion women. Why, why, O Lord!

Indeedy-be, I was asked to leave my living and sent by the bishop on a temporary appointment to *Patel & Thombs* Megasuperdupermarket. This was the first and biggest of the spaceshops, catering to all those who were heading 'out

there'. Twas 500 miles deep, 100 miles across. You could walk
for days and see nothing but cornflake packets, each containing a plastic monster – more numerous are these breakfast
monsters than the rare originals who prey on man and rabbit
in the eternal sparkly darkness beyond the shoplights! It
wasn't a thence-&-whence, but one of those corny galleons
that took me there, its sails full of bogus wind, its polished
decks milling with cheesy chuckleheaded Empire Johnnies,
Majors in the Company mainly, all moustache and loud
waistcoat. Between them they seemed to have been everywhere and one by one strode up to my collar booming something like: 'I have no use for religion, sunshine!' (Everyone was
sunshine to the Johnnies!) 'Neither would you if you'd seen
what I'd seen.'

'And what hast thou seen, my son?'

A finger tapping the nose. 'Wharrr-wharrr! Hoooo-hooooo!
Nopes!'

I think that what really depresses this ilk is that, though
everywhere is more or less the same – oh tis, tis! – there is still
the promise of something greater, but their short lives will
never know it. Their skins can not be humbled, but their souls
hath shrunketh. Those who don't vaporize their heads in bouts
of spacine melancholia (I get it myself – ooom!) retire to villages
and grow roses – brief blooming seasons before another
cultivator taketh their place. God's greatest cruelty – a man
can expect little over 100 years, a rabbit less than half that. Not
long enough. It maketh the race, whate'er it be, as it marcheth
on, more important than the individual, and this simply should
not be the case.

We passed through a vast shoal of haddock, which amazed
me no end. I climbed up the mast and pot-shot at them with a
borrowed phaser. The Johnnies took no interest in an activity
they'd had a surfeit of as boys. Finally, the vast illuminated
sign of **PATEL & THOMBS** glowed ahead like a sparky nebula,

and underneath their name the entrepreneurs blazed the motto
EVERYTHING YOU'LL EVER NEED. Idea was, thee see, that one
would buy everything one would ever consume for the rest of
one's life in one go, flinging it into ginormous trolleys. (May I
add in complaint that abandoned trolleys turn up mysteriously
in every view and waterhole throughout the boggn Universe –
one crashed here a week ago!) I was daunted – daunt double-
daunted me with its dauntitude! This was the real tough-cookie
full-of-biz hands-on can-do space, not the sheltered village life
I'd been used to for, wot, 30-odd years – me being then, wot,
pushing 50, a boyish 50-ish, but my looks long gone. So, verily,
I repeateth: daunt had that younger me in its spell! But I flipped
the communion wafer-sized disc that was the bishop's hologramismic missive to me, and up popped the good bishop, as
senile as I am now myself, assurething me that I was part of the
'everything that you'll ever need' at *Patel & Thombs*. For *solace*
was greatly required there, and I was the instrument that God
hath made to give *solace*. *Solace*, sayeth the bishop, was craved
lotslotsly by the shoppers and the storepeople. *Solace* is what
they would ask me for, I was assured, and *solace* I must give
abundantly.

Indeedly-bees, *solace* was a popular word with my superior
ecclesiastical. He used it easily 100+ times in his breezy
communication. Some folks became upset, he explained, when
looking at the ton-and-a-half of pickled onions the salesman
reckoned they'd fork through in what time remained to them.
Many went on a binge there and then, just to prove the
salesman wrong. They required, yes: *solace*. My job, that.
The Megasuperdupermarket, I was told, stirred up all manner
of strange emotions, each needing more or less of the balm of
solace. I was warned especially about the Span Measurement
Booth, a medical gadget into which one stepped to have one's
life expectancy calculated down to the nearest nano-second.
Distressing information to be relayed by a gum-chewing

shopgirl – a chaplain had to be on hand to give the moment
solace. *Solace* also in the chocolate department in the presence
of the 43 or perhaps just 3 Easter eggs some poor soul had just
been issued. *Solace*, the bishop said, always *solace*, and having
added that the church was a major shareholder in *Patel &
Thombs*, he leaned over in his pulpit and issued me with a half-
hour of his own *solace*-for-vicars, as immediate *solace* and as
example of same for *solaceizing solacefully* when my turn to so
do came. *SOLACE*!!!!! Huh!

Before I flipped the old bore off he informed me, in his most
solaceful graveside voice, that the previous Megasuperdupermarket chaplain, or *solacegiver*, had been skewered by a
forklift, God rest his soul. – I knew the victim from vicar
school, Rev Snorkems, a ginger fool! So now I was it, him, for a
month, a year, forever. Pigboggn *solacegiver*! I patted my
potbelly for luck and strode onto the floor of the Megasuperdupermarket, pouring *solace* with my every look like a leaky
bottle of *solace* sauce, eyes misty with holy water, hands
wringing. No one took the slightest boggn notice of me!
During the trip the chuntering bish had got me quite workethed up, had he not, he had, about *solace* – I'd expected queues
for it! Alasydoos, perhaps *solace* wasn't quite the rhubarb-and-
custard I'd expected. Twasn't! Tissn't! Bah!

First crisis. A week before my arrival Mr Patel had gone
missing. There were expeditions of undermanagers, like goo-
segaggles in their white coats and yellow rubber shoes,
cruising down hundreds of miles of aisles in search of their
great chief. Meanwhileydoos, my job was to haunt the board
room giving *solace* to Mr Thombs – not the original of that
name, but the son of same, a thin blond boy, tongue black from
licorice. Born in the Megasuperdupermarket, he'd never been
out of it. Years of village intrigue maketh a twisted mind and I
suspected young Thombs of having murdered Mr Patel, cut
him up and put him in jars of pâté – the crime not to be

discovered until some colonist found a foot in his 7,000th and 3rd from last pâté jar. So effective was I in Hellfire mode, accusing Thombs of ridding us of Patel, that he confessed he'd long planned such a murder and must have committed it during one of his blackouts, his face all this while pushed between the bosoms of a kindly shelf packer, biting the buttons off her coat till he reached her nipples. But then Patel showed. He had been on a bingey-do in Beer Country, pixilatedly lost amid the towering alleyways of beercans, only to be found by a goosegaggle of his undermanagers, flitting there for a binge of their own.

Mr Patel's first and only words to me were in a fanatical growl: 'GERROUTTOFMYSTORE, BIBLEBASHERER!' He repeated this exorcism every time he saw me, and when I heard that he had been the driver of the forklift that had skewered Rev Snorkems, I jumped whenever I heard one rattle up an alley. After my mistake in accusing Thombs of murder, howsoeverdo, I accused myself of fancifulness in suspecting Mr Patel of murderosity. Why should so eminent a business-man wish to slaughter useless chaplains like myself? But once, on my way to chapel, a sense of danger caused me to climb high among the soups from where I peeped down into an alley where Mr Patel sat in a forklift with specially sharpened prongs. His demeanour was obviously one of a murderer on the lookout for a victim – in this case, myself! Routine enquires revealed that his intention of killing me was well known among his staff – he had killed, they said blithely, 14 clerics already, including a passing Cardinal who'd popped in to buy a lifetime's supply of cheese straws and constipation pills. But Patel was as powerful as a King in that place, so nothing could be done to dissuade him from evildoings – except, of course, prayer.

Thenceforth I took obscure routes through the aisles of unpopular brands, but once he nearly caught me . . . I became lost up Sago Alley, a dead end – and he appeared in his vehicle, growling like a Regelian pnart. I only escaped his sharpened prongs by scaling a 20-foot wall of tapioca bags.

'GERROUTTOFMYSTORE, BIBLEBASHERER!'

Skittish with survival, I sang *Away in a Manger* at him from my heights, it being the first thing that popped to mind, and while dancing a hula-hula, baptized him with handfuls of tapioca. I have perhaps never, have I not, no, never, seen a human being more angry. His moustache whipped his cheeks. While I continued irritating him, *solace* to his furious soul sadly the last thing on my mind, he bleeped security and armed himself with 2 phasers. I scampered over the gondola-tops and hid in the middle of Spaghetti Country, a 30-square-mile criss-cross of aisles – for weeks I was there, p'boggn weeks! But God was on my side. Mr Patel was killed in a shoplifting raid and I walked free from the fear of him to give unrequired *solace* to his 5 corpulent sons, who now joined young Mr Thombs in running the business and using their new authority to commit shameless cruelties upon their secretaries, to whom I was on hand for yet more *solace*, but who hated my guts, did they not, they did, for not stopping the cruelties at source. God, they were right, should not allow such things. Ho-hum!

These shoplifting raids were our bane, were they not! By heck, yes! It was mainly Scotsmen who were responsible. After the failure of their Scotmars colony, the Scots took to space piracy, each clan to a clannish fleet of old banger spacecraft, and a favourite endeavour was to raid Megasuperdupermarkets. They only ever kleped shortbread biscuits, whiskey, tinned haggis, cockaleekie soup and cocktail cherries, and never enough to last them long, which meant a return trip could always be expected soon. Twas 200 MacNabs who caught Mr Patel up Whiskey Road during one.

Double-confessy-doos, but tis no secret: I hast ever been a gutsy pigbelly! So was that Megasuperdupermarket a trough-some hoo-har for my temptations? Twas! Ooooom, twas! So it was that I spenteth most of my days grazing greedily up and down the alleys, scoffing and swigging, chewing and piggoutting. Numerous Solperines did the same, all very fattysome fellows, bellies scraping the floor. They lived there. Had hideouts everywhere. Were seldom caught. Very fond of crisps. I didn't turneth them in, oh no! I was as guilty of a zillion infringements as were they, and anyhowdoos I hath always had a weakness for Solperines. These lot always listened attentively when I speaky-dooed to them about Jesus – though, indeedy-pie, they never stopped eating. More successful with them than with the roaches, I converted dozens, verily I did. Sobeit, when at last I meet St Peter at Heaven's gate and he sayeth: 'Why, Mugg, doest thou thinkest thou shouldst be here?' 'The Solperines, Pete!' I'll say. 'Hallelujah, the p'boggn Solperines!'

My most onerous duty as *Patel & Thombs* chaplain was to preside over the executions of people whose credit cards had proved invalid or who had spent over the credit limit agreed with the Empire Company – very easy to do if you're stocking up for 100 years. Sometimes these custards proved to be victims of computer error, but by then twas too late. The executions, by strict law, had to be carried out within the hour. (In the slow vastness of Space, the real events of life seemeth always to happen so quicksomely!) Thus, I'd be bleeped away from my iksome natters with Solperines, or the shop-hailer would grate inaudibly: *'WOULD REV CHAF-FINCH REPORT TO THE SCAFFOLD IMMEDIATELY PLEASY-DO.'* Of course, twere guilty and I suppose they deserved to hang. But on one occasion I waved 20 custards off in an afternoon (all computer error, it transpired) and I lay in Sardine Square sobbing and vomiting into a box till way after closing time.

'It were all them p'boggn boxes of chockiebickies wot put me over the limit, vicar, Couldn't I put 'em back, maybees? Then I'd be under forsure.'

'Triple sorries, pilgrim. The Lord awaiteth thee presently-most in a better place.'

'Poohell!'

Young Mr Thombs, I remember, was diligent in his attendance of hangings, and always smiled.

One must sayeth, and I'm about to, that the credit agreements have been a Devilish scamming. No colonist hath possibly the doshings to pay for a lifetime's victuals – so if he is to set it up at all he must borroweth on the future prospects of his proposed colony. But even mining colonies doing a wheeze, thanky-bees, have trouble sometimes making a payment, due oftenly to the inhuman distances involved tween banking facilities. Thus-so, the entire colony inevitably falleth into the possession of either the Company itself, or one of the financial institutions attachethed to it. The financial wing of *Patel & Thombs*, now inherited by *Ponsonby's*, a division of *Uncle Spiro's*, originally a Solperine concern, presently owns 750,000 colonial planets in the outer spirals. Boggn Empire! Urk! Our vast warfleets spend more time doing bailiff duty than mixing it with the Bunnies. Thereforeso, a meany Admiral is every day somewhere turning up in some poor pigbogger's Utopia and taking it off him, putting in Company men to administrate – disillusioned Johnnies or plain Godless card-sharping brutes. In suchsome ways doeth Human Civilization pursue its fleeing members.

A surprise it was, was it not indeed, it was, IT WAS SO! – indeedy-be, when my butler, he who buttles for me, the buttlesome J.W. tock-tick-clang-clang-whirrrrrrr Mathis, told me one day during the election which made that hunk of scrap iron the President of Bunnyland, that he too had been at *Patel & Thombs* at this same time of which I herein speak! Now I did, did I not, recollecteth occasions when I espied a spoon or two flying over the aisles under its own power and crossed myself before a mystery only a later intimate knowledge of Mathis allowed me to solve. He was a white-coated undermanager in charge initially of potted meats, then promoted to command of the 4 tinned peas alleys, a veritable rajadom. We never crossed paths. When I confronted him, not merely with his lack of attendance at my little services, but that, knowing me from the *Billingsgate*, why hadn't he when hearing my name over the hailer, poppethed into *Solace* Alley to say howdeedoodee, his reply was that he assumed Chaffinch to be a common name among vicars. The boglyfala of the creature! Then he proceeded to tell me some pornographic story about how he copulated with my great-great-great-great-great-great-great aunt up a mountain in India in 1935 – for God's p'boggn crying sake, urk!✷

I was up Marmalade Alley when the Germans attacked *Patel & Thombs*. No Scots border raid this, but a vigorous Bunny-style military invasion. They crashed their warship, big swastikas on its sides, right through the doors by checkouts 345–420, vaporized every checkout girl in her seat – and some were sweet-toothed darlings, were they not! – and zum-

✷ The Archbishop is again unfair, wot! Had I known that the Rev Chaffinch hailed for to attend the hangings was the same man I had met and admired on H.M.S. *Billingsgate*, I would have sought him out in a trice. My time at *Patel & Thombs* was not a happy one. I had been away from England for a dashed long time and was losing contact with my essential Englishness – which is what I am and always wished to be, from my rusty core on out – dammit, an Englishman! But it was in the Megasuperdupermarket, staring at the picture of a butler on a bottle of sauce that it struck me that I might take up that most English of occupations: butlering! It worked. Butlering has kept me English, and dimmee, sane! In this vast chaotic Universe, full of rabbits and crude types – i.e. Solperines – it is essential to keep to the principles of English gentlemanlyness, and how better to so do, genuinely with no playacting, than as a gentleman's gent, ehwot? I have been happy as a butler, and honoured to be one to so distinguished a gentleman and of so noble a family as my divine friend and employer, the author of the above.

zummmmmed down the alleys on silver motorbikes, vaporizing anyone they met, heading for Sausage Plaza while the fetid Megasuperdupermarket air hissssssssawayed outa the crashing hole they'd made.

The German Emperor, Werner Schmernercreutz himself, led the raid, dressed in a tight-fitting black leather jump suit with aggressive swastikas studded on chest and back, topped by a sallet helmet with 4 crutphant horns. It was my first sight of the Hellhound! As I hopped a forklift careering the other way he was making an impassioned speech to his foot-clicking brownshirted underlings from the top of a 12-foot high toothpaste tube – part of a display this, you couldn't buy ones that big. But were these spaceboche not full of jollybee laughter, like boys at a picnic? – They were. Were not some pomming on tubas while others slapped their iron thighs? – They were! So surely this was all a larky! How could I believe that we were being exterminated? Were we? Zooks, yes! Zapped! Fizzed! Bye-byed! Urk!

Young Mr Thombs, the Patel boys and the senior staff had locked themselves in the board room when the alarm went off, and there, under royal portraits of the late megasuperdupergrocers *Patel & Thombs*, they were vaporized by the Germans. When I tore into the room, panting, collar popped, I found only the tell-tale sprinkles of salt which vaporizing left in the old days. Meanwhileydoos, several Huns were in the next room watching replays of their atrocities on the security cameras. So I hurried myself through the broken glass to the cold shuttlebus bay where a number of abused shelf packers, yowling Solperines and the sole surviving checkout girl were scampering onboard our thence-&-whence, the one we used for deliveries within a 4-light-year radius. The Germans had found Sausage Plaza, and were occupied for a bit, gutsing on and loading their demi-God wurst! I decided to go back and look for any other survivors. There must be 100s of undermanagers and packers left in there, I wailed, vicarishly! I staggered onward in airlessness, my feet leaving the gound, a fierce *solaceness* in my heart, till I swooned and floated, fighting sleep, over checkouts strewn with dead girls. I was halfsomely aware that somebody/something scooped me out of my float and threw me the 200 yards back through the swing doors, whump, into the revving up thence-&-whence. – I later discovered that the scooper-upper (or scooper-downer) had been none other than J. W. Mathis, making himself useful in pre-buttlesome mode. I landed on a consignment of toilet paper and was unscathed, except that the bishop's hologramismic disc slipped from my pocket and popped up beside me making idiotic pulpitizations about *solace*, as we za-zoomed away from the blinding lights of the shopfrontage, into blackness, to nowhere, just away. Meanwhileydoos, thousands of staff floated suffocated in their aisles. No one escaped from *Patel & Thombs* alive, except my fellow passengers, this Mugg, and the left-behind Mathis, who, like those beastlysome Germans, hath no need of the sustenance of air.∗

The nearest place of refuge was a mere 140 million miles away. A day's za-zoom took us there, to Abbey Village, presided over by the morally excellent but thoroughly insane Abbess Betty Cudworth. From space it looked so very magical,

---

∗ When I arrived at Sausage Plaza I found the Germans panicked by the sudden appearance of a pair of roach, unexpected allies who caused the Germans to scatter. My old rally-driving enemy Baron Schmernercreutz and his high command escaped in their warship. But they left the bulk of their force behind. These were all metal men, like myself, created by the Baron's skilled hands, and were as strong or stronger than I. But during the next 5 months, alone with them in the crippled store, I hunted down and dismantled 178 of them. When the security teams arrived from *Ponsonby's*, they having taken over the Megasuperdupermarket, they cleaned the rest of the blighter Hun out of the alleyways and foodhalls. I was at that time offered the job of Undermanager of Non-Earthling Vegetables by the new management, but declined and applied for butler school instead.

a snowbound Abbey floating loose among the stars. I fantasized, did I not, that I was a pubile colony girl arriving to take the veil. Their life support system was geared to make life difficult, so it was always winter there – the windows all frosted, snowflakes in the air – Christmascardy and cosy-looking from outside, austere and shiverish within. Lucky them, when this *fringella coelebs* landed to partake of crumbs from their birdtable.

The Abbey frontage was a-swarm with Anglican nuns about their business, no-nonsense sorts who had received telepathy lessons from the invisible Wrodahouey People. – Between disembarking from the thence-&-whence on the hockey field and pulling the doorbell I was slapped 5 times 'for what I was thinking'. But our little band of survivors – 12 packers, 41 Solperines, 2 pairs of roach and a checkout girl – were made welcomeydoos in that Christian place. The checkout girl – and 6 of the Solperines stayed on as nuns. The place made a deep impression on me, I must say, and I have. Though I was there only days, I feel in some strange way that I lived a lifetime there, dwelling in that icicly dorm, nuns breaking vows of silence to bellow at me: 'STOP THINKING THAT! YOU HORRID LITTLE MAN!'

I was told by Abbess Betty, between slaps, that Lordy Pope Archbishop Hindmarsh, of the see of Space Canterbury, our spiritual leader, was looking for suitable missionaries to dispatch to Bunnyland. That'll do this Mugg, thought that very Chaffinch! I took the next thence-&-whence to Lordy's dove-filled Cathedral anchored between Bilickers 81/4.4 and the water belt, where he immediately mistook me for my grandfather – Archbishop of Canterbury way back in the last century – and appointed me forthwith, did he not, he did, Archbishop of Bunnyland, a see more vast than my grandfather ever imagined. Next thing, I was rocketed into the receiving bay of a Bunny-eared spacecraft, the *Hopalong*

Croons IV, where I saw them for the first time, my people, my flock, p'boggn rabbits.

They were initially unimpressed with their short, bald, pot-bellied, grinning goblin of an Archbishop, who climbed to his size 14 feet to reveal a size 7 body in a regalia scuffed and smoking from the rocketing.

'Bless thee, my children.'

'U-huh!'

– The Elvisite greeting from the First Officer. Trouble already!

'Ert, he's a skrawny mannit thattn – he'll not last 2 hops back home in the real world, will 'e?' said a ragged-eared midshipman.

'But at least the pigbogger's got buck teeth, ehwot!'

I did, and have – they are the only toothypegs I hath left!

'And his feet, by jingo – he's got bunny feet, lookee!'

My feet hath ever been too big for me, I confess it.

'Eugh, so he has, Thumper!' said the Captain, hopping a bit, then walking aristocratically upright towards me, with paw outstretched. 'How absolutely charming for a churchman to have bunny feet! Howdeedoodee, Archbishop. Bunnyhoo!'

'Bunnyhoo, mon capitain! Bunnyhoo!'

From that day forward I have spent the rest of my life among rabbits.✶

✶ This exchange with an ever-so Bunny recorded by the Archbishop confronts us yet again with the amazing fact that all the speaking lifeforms we English have so far met in Outer Space speak in our own language, and have no other. The conventional explanation for this, which my computer flashes up for me to baulk at, is that the early radio broadcasts of the 20th Century were picked up hundreds of light years away by the telepathic Wrodahouey People, whom the Archbishop has already mentioned. Usually invisible, these personages flitted from asteroid to asteroid, living on fish. The broadcasts meddled with their telepathic powers, making concentration impossible – like having the radio blaring in the next room, one supposes, when you're trying to think. In an effort to regain their concentration of old

Abbess Betty, mayest I add here, was the cause of a dread calamity that befell her pretty abbey. This was 10 years on from my brief sojourn there. Her belief, not unusual among Christians, was that life should be uncomfortable – hair shirts, nail-in-the-shoe type was Mother Betty. Further to this, she was forever tinkering with their life support system, taking the heating down a notch, and a while later, another notch – this to give greater and still greater discomfort, and therefore gift the nuns opportunity for spiritual intensity through ever-increasing suffering. Alack, one morning Betty turnethed a notch too far and the whole nunnery froze solid on its way to prayers – every boggn nun turned from gooseflesh to lollipop, pronto! Chee-heee! Tis sad, not funnybonely, but I cannot help myself. A scientific team was sent out by the Synod to defrosty-doo them, but they froze too, and so did the next team – freezed in the icy eroticism of denuding frozen nuns, prior to a slow grill which never had chance to warmeth their fundaments. So the abbey has been abandoned to Jack Frost with a snowdrift up to the fourth floor. Halfway 'tween life and death, between man's space and God's scape, the nuns' minds remain at home in their last brrrrrrrrrrrsome breath, holding one thought. Or maybees do they soar inside their cold Wrodahoueyite telepathy, released from bodily discomforts, though not, I warrant, from

they successfully attempted a psychic blow-out, enabling them to ignore the broadcasts forever, but in the process accidentally re-wired the thinking of everyone else, causing all other lifeforms in creation to forget their original tongue and launch off into tally-ho English. The Wrodahoueys, who were once numerous – but who counted the beggars if they were invisible? – are nowadays virtually or perhaps quite extinct. The nuns must have taken telepathy lessons from a final few. For me, this explanation of why all creation speakys-de-English is far from satisfactory. Mugg's roguish *mon capitain* up there reminds me also that Bunnies, when in ardour, speak a French more fluent than Clemenceau's – though no Frenchman ever made it beyond Scotmars! Explain that, O all-knowing computer! No, I prefer to think that our spacewide universal English tongue is caused by God, part of his mysterious plan, wot.

the frights of dreams. At the Day of Resurrection I shall meet Betty again and go hooooo-haaaaaar in her bleaksome oxy face.✱

Amen

✱ I am surprised the Archbishop did not hear, or perhaps he forgot, that Abbey Village was defrosted in 2193, with the loss of only 40 nuns. Sadly, Abbess Betty, I believe, has since died.

Hittites: Two
A World Gone to the Hittites

I was born, was I not, in Chaffinch Hall, Suffolk, England, OOP on June 18th, 2083. Thus, I am a child not of the century of which this booky-doos recordeth the history, but of the chaotic, despotized, barmymost quacksome 21st Century! As my grandfather, retired Archbishop Chaff Chaffinch, was Lord Chaffinch and my father partially deceased, I was heir to the shebang of Chaffinch titles, and our magnificent 18th Century pile.

My father, I should explaineth, returned from the Indonesian Conflict to conceive me in such a seriously vaporized state that only his ears, forehead, penis and left heel were fully present at the conception, the rest being in that grisly dimension to whence all vaporized parts depart. He remained in this condition until his death, all attempts at regrowing his flesh producing only enormous livers. Twas thought unseemly, was it not, that 2 ears, a forehead, penis and left heel shouldst succeed to the proud and ancient title – so grandfather named me as his successor. I was Viscount Chaffinch throughout my childhood and teens, a proper toffee-nosed nob and no mistake, before succeeding to the title. I am, I hath just remembered, still possessed of it! Pigbog! I am Lord Chaffinch! Chee! Urk! But with only one servant: a tinpot butler! And for a stately home I have a vast abandoned city of azure brick and corrugated steel, with nowhere a moose's head over a fireplace, and no magnolia

trees blooming on lawns – just shite people blowing raspberries among the tumbleweeds. Ho-hum!

My mother was the daughter of the Duke of Westpelton, the
fattest man in the history of England.∗ He rarely left his rooms
over the Albatross Club in London – the members used to
cover their birds' ears and cheer every time he passed wind
overhead – and he died before I took membership, so I don't
think I met him even oncemost. From him, perhaps, I inherit
my pigoutting appetites. Mumsy, howeversome, was a tall slim
lady – a famous beauty in her day, was she not, and hardly ate
a thing. My first memory is of waddling towards her, hands
out, burbling, while she was on one of her morning runs
around the estate. She was followed, as ever, by the golden
horde of Chaffinch corgis and labs (they are doggies, by the by
– my Bunny readership being innocent of that happy creature)
who joyfully stampeded into me, leaving me pawed flat.
Mumsy picked up her baby bird, laughing while it wailed. I
touched her face and it was hot and sticky. I held on tight and
never loved her more than at that moment, except perhaps
now. My later memories of her are discarded for a reason that I
shall soon speaky-do upon. O, mumsy, thou wast my happiest
dream! Pleasy-do, lookie at your Mugg now, a codger, am I not,
and you eternally young but gone forever.

∗ Descendant of the same corpulent chappie with whom I hobnobbed in the
1920s! Amazing, wot! That Duke also was a great Albatrosser, but in shooting
his own birds from the deck of his ocean-going yacht issued himself with a bad
luck which made him fail lamentably at everything he did. As Viceroy of India
he was an absolute shower, and contributed to our losing that jewel in our
crown! I was brave enough to ask Winston one day at the club: 'How is it that
Westpelton keeps getting the top jobs when he has such a history of failure
behind him?' He answered, while blowing smoke rings at me: 'It is a tradition in
our country, Jerry, to reward our failures with still greater opportunities to fail,
this especially at the expense of abler men.' My computer tells me that Mugg's
Duke – fatter than mine, though mine couldn't have eaten more if he'd tried –
was Chancellor of England from 2143 to 2189, but never once left the precinct of
the Albatross Club. Ehwot!

Twas a busy house in those pre-Hittite days, the too-short time of my itchy-coohood. Bustlements, balls, tombolas, jamborees, corgi races, fêtes, agricultural shows. For a small fee the poor were allowed to visit the house and ogle its contents. My grandfather often took me to meet them and, though noisy, they were always very polite and sometimes gave me sweets. Our servants numbered only 12, but my father had enthusiastically embraced the reintroduction of slavery in the '70s, so we had 150 of those – they always seemed to be eating apples and were ever winksomely cheersomemost. The house was abuzz with their polishings and mendings.✳

Grandfather Chaff had lived most of his life as a hermit, in, as he put it, 'a myopic haze of religious nuttery'. For 20-odd years he was a stylite in Ethiopia. So he was not a one for balls. I remember a summer evening sitting with him in the orchard, learning the words of hymns, while on the lawns the grand folk arrived in their whizzycopters and in skycars which looked like flying hats.

> *Then fancies flee away*
> *I'll care not wot men say*
> *I'll labour night and day*
> *To be a pilgrim . . .*

✳ This shocks my 20th Century mentality more than I can say! How blithely they squandered our liberal inheritance in the 21st! I strike my chest in sympathy for those poor slaves and the sound inside me is like a rattle of chains. On Bilickers 34/22C, during my time there running a market garden for the Peewermums, a slave ship arrived peddling skinny humanoid women they'd found somewhere. They had blue hair and bosoms back, front and behind their knees – nipples everywhere, the dears! I bought 5 and put them to work in the orchid house. When I left I gave them their freedom, which they devoted to the emancipation of their sisters. The ensuing slave revolt was blamed on my good self and I received a flowery letter of censure from the Peewermum Leadership Plantpot which, for them, was rather livid.

The fruit had begun to fall and the air was sweet with it. Behind our singing was the buzzlement of wasps and the howling of unChristian corgis. On the steps my mother in a fluorescent yellow dress, with a bare midriff, bare back, bare legs – verily, barely dressed but still magnificently attired – her beautiful face covered with a spangly net, glowing yellow beads knotted into her fair hair, her arms clasped with golden bangles – an angel, a goddess! Beside her, the remains of my father floated in the air, greeting the guests with offers of a shake from that which made me, his sexual organ (twas all he had, poor chap). His medals were stuck to his forehead and hung from his ears. I knew them well. I used to play with them on the tiger rug in the big den with my father's forehead hovering above me, the furrows less intense than usual, but still wondering perhaps which war was waiting for his baby when manhood overcame his innocence. I confess I was a tidge frightened of my father – I never understood how he urinated but didn't drink. Such things bothery-do the minds of kiddy-winks.

Though I had my parents, 2 doting nannies, pals among the servants and slaves, the golden horde, my first purrrrrrrrrr-some pussycats, and was beloved by everyone as a child blessed by God, my best companion was always my grand-father. Then in his 90s, he was 5-feet-nowt of imp, bald, grinning always, full of jokes and observations. A happy man who gave to woesome me glimpses of his inner happiness which hath sustained me throughout my largely wasted life. Happy days at Chaffinch Hall – thank thee, the Lord that is God and the Lord that was Chaffinch!

Then, 40 miles away in a bunker beneath Cambridge, the p'boggn scientist Byron Joop ruined our lives – didn't he not do a proper job of that though! Urk! Him and his ruinous boggn experiments! They made a different place of Chaffinch Hall. Lookie-see, the natural world of forests and creatures had long since died out, the seas poisoned, the English countryside gone foxless, Africa elephant-empty, the Garden of Eden withered, a brickyard, ruined . . . So when Joop hit upon the iffy scheme of a time experiment which would take the planet back to its God-given luxuriant state of jungly abundance, while leaving *us* as we were, he was given the 'Oooooo, rather!' by the lovely Anita, our ravishing leaderette, who announced the impending return of dodos, whales and rutting elk on the viddywall with her usual girlish enthusiasm. The nation was thrilled.

'Will there be bears, wonders I?' bubbled grandfather as we walked to a sickly copse across plashy fields, in the company of Tadese, my grandfather's ginormous Ethiopian disciple. 'I tell thee there wast bears in England in medieval times, old Tadese, young Mugg! Grrrrrr-grrrrrrrr! GRRRRRR!!!!!!'

We played at being bears around the trees. Grandfather and I were the bears while Tadese, though bigger than 2 grizzlies sewn together, plashed away from us in feigned bearfright. It was the last ever walk we had. Last ever.

Byron Joop's piggnboggn time experiment misfired, did it not, a corker snafu, and caused not nature's garden to bloom for us, but rather poured the Hittites into our laps, that's whatya! HITTITES – a warrior empire from ancientmost Biblicalish times, returned to life, invading our peacefully noxious present with their curly beards and stone gods, roaring out of the temporal fog in their chariots, obsessed with the vulgar impulse to conquest.

But how could an ancient army, though its generals be Napoleons all, cause much botheration to *us*, with our vapor-izers, FQ-bombs, phasers, with our vast armies, militias, polices, every manjack with a zapper, pop-gun or skizzer in each hand?????? Surely-be, a Bunny versed in our culture might argue, all we had to do was get Pope Lassie to order his Swiss Guard to stand beside the time portal and zap the boggn Hittites when they came out. Alackaday, say I to educated

Bunny – twas not one time portal, but hundreds, thousands, 41 along the front at Great Yarmouth alone! Even so, Bunny pundit might postulate . . . a platoon of yawning guardsmen zapping before each portal would do the trick . . . even your local Hittite-hating wino with a cricket bat might swot them as they emergethed from your local rift in the fabric of time. Nopes! The time warps spat Hittites at us at an impossible rate. And not just the actual Hittites who had existed in history, those who left their dusty archaeology upon the hills of Anatolia, but every potential Hittite who may have existed – had one Hittite girl married someone-else-instead, had one Hittite sperm won its egg-race rather than any other: the Hittites from all these possible outcomes showed up. So that, as all possibilities come to pass in one dimension or another, Hittites cameth from every parallel dimension which hath contained Hittites, these being the full-blown Hittite potential from every possible Hittite coupling, from every possible wiggly winner of every egg-race ever run by a lusty people. Thereforeto, as dimensional layering is infinite – and we don't need boggn Byron Joop to tell us that! – we may well have been witness to a how-many-Hittites-can-you-get-on-the-world contest.* But after 30 days the portals healed up, locking 63 billion hungry Hittites on our poor overcrowded world of 20 billion worried souls.

The war began with the arrival of the first Hittite. They preferred their ancient weapons, but some tooled up with phasers and zappers, lifted from our fallen defenders. At

---

* This does not apply to Bunnyland, of course, a phenomenon of which the Archbishop and I have much experience – there the dimensional layers have been induced to coincide, thus rendering Bunnyland infinite. From whatever point you set out in Bunnyland you could, given immortality to do it with, go on forever. Thus, the contestants of the bi-annual round-Bunnyland cycle race never return, never finish. Why they bother I don't know! There's no under-standing rabbits!

Chaffinch Hall we watched Byron Joop's infamous apology
on the viddywall. The boggn Jilks couldn't help giggling. He
was followed by an expert on Hittites, a duffersome cackle-
headed prof they'd found under a book somewhere, who spoke
at length on burial rites until the interviewer told him to hash
his blitherhole. Meanwhileydoos, outside, our slaves did battle
at the gates with a modest demonstration of conquering
Hittites, while the electricity board chappies connected our
forcefield, behind which we, and all surviving 21st Century
humanity, would live for the rest of our lives on earth.

The lovely Anita was in a mood to execute Joop, but he was
needed to reverse his disaster. Then he disappeared anyway,
into the past, full of new schemes for transforming the world.
I'm told he was beheaded on the orders of Charles the Bold,
Duke of Burgundy in 1477✷. Was he fool or devil? Either way,
I have no charity for the man. He ruined my life.

✷ I told him this! It was my discovery and is unknown to general historians!
When visiting the Great Library on Carstairs Station, in the days when it was
anchored off Paladron 2, I was indulging my footnote fetishism and found in a
tome on medieval warfare a note speaking of the fate of one Byron Joop, a
wizard. He had arrived in medieval Burgundy with the scheme of zooping up
the power of Charles the Bold, giving him sway over Europe, calculating that a
Burgundian Empire would prevent all other powers erupting and keep the
world in pre-Raphaelite medieval innocence forever. Quite an idea, wot! Joop
showed up with a Bronski tank to assist the Burgundian leader in his military
ambitions. But at the battle of Nancy, 1477, while manoeuvring his tank to
shoot at a phalanx of opposing Swiss pikemen, he shot murderously into the
phalanx but the shell clobbered right through the Swiss and knocked the Duke
of Burgundy off his horse. So miffed was the great man that he had Joop pulled
from his tank and beheaded on the spot. The battle recommenced, sans tank,
some hours later. The duke lost, was brained by the Swiss and Burgundy never
had an empire. Of course, as the Archbishop alludes – this was only one
possible outcome in a few, or only one dimension. Were I to return to the
library, open that same book, the footnote might not be there, or say other
things, or every book may be a Burgundian one! We shift from dimension to
dimension on a daily basis, but only into the dimensional layers closest to us. A
shift way off into a bizarre but valid dimension in which Byron Joop's
experiment succeeded, covering Mauritius in dodo, or gave OOP an eternal

It was 2088. I was 5 years old. But I was not, was I, aware that a momentous event hath taken place – perhaps the most momentous event in human history. Indeedy-be, some gigantic catastrophe was always going to happen, with creatures like Joop tinkering with the stuff of creation. Wellso, now it had! But, strangely to say, we moderns got on with our lives more or less as before. London, Paris, Frankfurt and a brochure full of Mediterranean resorts were safe behind forcefields. In English lands the poor were slaughtered in great numbers and the rest enslaved by the Hittites, but were hardly missed. In Chaffinch Hall we were nicely snug, thanky-bees. The forcefield took in most of our grounds, as far as the village, where Rev Dickerson still droned his sermons on Sundays, where Mr Chaulders moped over his counter in his corner shop, complaining about business as he had in pre-Hittite days. The rest of the village, was it not, it was, pleasy-do, in Hittite hands. They pebble-dashed everything, stuck stone dragons on the chimneypots, knocked the statue of my ancestor Giles Chaffinch, hero of Oudenarde, off his plinth, replacing him with a rampant figure of Baal. I wandered at the edge of our English enclave feeling perfectly safe, not in the least worried by the Hittites sticking their faces up against the forcefield, whose electrical fizz played havoc with their curly beards.

So twas that the childhood of this now-117-year-old Mugg continued as if nothing had happened. And as nothing indeedy-be could be allowed to interrupt the education of a

medievalness, or in which England never took up space travel and J.W. Mathis was never made because the Great War never happened . . . this would not alarm a person, because that person would be fully integrated into his new dimension, so wouldn't think aught amiss. Dimmee, wot tosh the Universe is made of! Thus, also, this book of ours will be subtly or vastly different depending on whatever dimension it is in. I tantalize myself with the thought that Lloyd George won the 1922 election, that Hitler won his war, that Clarissa never ceased to love me . . . all these things happened, part of other dimensions where other mes wander and wandered, just as bewildered.

Chaffinch, at age 6 I was telezoomed to Smithers, the great boarding school in Berkshire. Hittites, who were struggling to understand our technology, often walked like ghosts through the class, swiping at our heads with their swords, yelling obscenities which we could faintly hear.＊

'Chaffinch! Pay no attention to that Hittite! LEAVE IT ALONE! CHAFFINCH!'

'Prithy, sir, this Hittite seemeth a tidge more solid than tis usual with its ilk!'

'DO YOUR BOGGN SUMS, BOY!'

I put my head down, only to hear a blood-curdlesome scream from my teacher, run through by an all-too-solid Hittite trooper's all-too-sharp spear. After that unfortunate event, we boys were issued with phasers, making our dorm fights more deadly than our Hittite encounters in the shrubbery.

'ABERCROMBIE!'

'Present, sir!'

'BORRAGE!'

'Still here, sir!'

'CHAFFINCH!'

'Present, sir!'

'CHORTLESOME-HARDY!'

'Yeps!'

＊ Yes, up-to-date ENGLISH obscenities! That Hittites emerged from the fog speaking English puzzles me more than anything. Did they come through space that was clogged with pools of old telepathic thoughts of the confounded Wrodahouey people? Or did God, himself an English speaker, place some English-language chemical in the brains of all his far-flung peoples, ready for Resurrection Day when Paradise will be utterly English, and is this chemical activated by time travel? One's language is so utterly a part of one, THE most important possession of an individual, wot, that I can't help thinking that the Hittites weren't proper Hittites without their Hittite tongue. Same goes for Bunnies. Often, in the Albatross Club in Bunnyopolis, I'd forget I was with rabbits and chat away as if in the officers' mess at Chelsea Barracks. Close my eyes under the *Bunny Weekly*, ignore the carrot chomping and the exclaims of BUNNYHOO!, and there was nothing to choose!

'DAVENPORT!'

'Hitties got him in dorm last night, sir.'

'Dearie-be! Oh, dearie-dearie-be! DIBLEY!'

'Hittites got him too, sir.'

'Last night in dorm, was it, Borrage?'

'Yeps, sir. Snatched him from under his blankets, sir. Horrible it was, sir!'

'FENNICK!' He didn't see Fennick. 'Hittites, one supposes?'

'Horrible it was, sir!'

Thus, in our rough boyish way, may God forgive us, we zapped unpopular, smelly or swotty classmates until we were a happy band of pally-doos. Though Borrage, our leader, was always in danger from Fatty Lonsdale, who fancied himself in that position. I, the prettiest by far, with my fine strawberry-blond hair, petite frame and sparkling little face, was the most popular, and never in the slightest danger of being zapped by a chap. But one day I was in my itchy brown dressing-gown, yawning along the corridor towards my bathnight, when 4 Hittite officer cadets burst out of a sports cupboard, along with bats, balls, and cricket pads, and snatched me from my doings. Lucky-ducky me, Fatty Lonsdale was returning from his turn in the tub, pulled his phaser out of his soap-bag and suddenly all 4 ancients were fizzing in agony around me.

'Gosh, thanks, Fatty. Ya saved me good-n-proper, ya did!'

I shook his washed hand with my dirty one. Big shakes.

'Too-too, Mugg, too-too.'

'Anyfing wot you wants for me to do for ya, Fatty, just ask, kidda, ask away!'

'Snarg, snarg, snarg!' he said, a schoolboy ejaculation which I also heard used, amazingly enough, by Bunnies 50 years later. 'Just one fing, Mugg my pretty.' He gave me his soap-bag with the phaser still hot inside it. 'Borrage. Too much Borrage, yeps, ehwot? Suggesty to thee, Hittites get him!' And he winked.

Thus and so, Borrage was due for his bathnight right after

my Muggwashing. To repay Fatty Londsdale I had to zap him! Excellent boy altogether, was Borrage. But, in the spell of that energetic evening, I felt I had to go along wi'it!

I stood by the window, still damp from my Muggwashing, looking at the rugger fields. These were beyond the school's forcefield – Hittite country! Now, even at that time of night, the Hittites were playing some primitive game, throwing a live sheep at each other. Its *baas* cut deep into the night, came up my plughole after my bath gargled away.

Enter Borrage. He was tall for his age, a face stuck in a gung-ho smile. He ruffled my hair. 'Wotsay, Mugg! Snarg!'

'Snarg, Borrage! Snarg!'

'Lookee, the pig's left his soap-bag!'

I picked it guiltily from the shelf under the mirror. 'I'll take it down to him. Snarg!'

But I didn't move from the window. Borrage got into his bath and, as usual for him, commenced to wanky-woo. I stood window-gazing, seemingly spectating the sheep-tossing game, but my hand was in Londsdale's soap-bag. Suddenly, I turned, my face an agony of tears, and pointed the shaking phaser at my gang leader.

'Wotho, Chaffy! Wotho, lad! That might go off, ya Jilks!'

I was a little priest even then, my soul full of hymns. I could not commit the abysmal sin of murdering Borrage. I opened the window and commenced shooting at the rugger pitch. The forcefield deflected my shots, but I hit the sheep twice and set a Hittite's beard alight.

Borrage was dripping beside me, finishing his wanky-woo. 'Smart zaps, kidda. Snargoogles!'

'Triple snargs on thee evermost, Borrage. Ahem . . . just then, when I was pointing the phaser at thee, I do confess, I was going to zap thee. Hittites in the corridors, see, 4 bigguns. Fatty saved me. To pay him back he made me promise to zap thee, Borrage. I could not do so, thanky-bees.'

Borrage was furious at this news. He snatched the phaser from me and tried to put on his dressing-gown, a lime-green silky job, with it still in his hand. It was still only half on when he arrived in dorm, with me twittering behind him. Fatty Londsdale was sitting cross-legged on his bed, pressing the buttons of a podule which obtained cakes for him from some distant place. He barely had time to look up, a madeleine between his jaws, when Borrage zapped him. He writhed on the bed, a shapeless custardy mass, cakes coughing up from the plate connected to his podule. Then he disappeared.

'BORRAGE!' The headmaster had been behind us all along. 'YOU HAVE ASSASSINATED FATTY LONSDALE, YOU CRETIN! SEE ME IN MY STUDY IN 10 MINUTES! CHAF-FINCH – HAVE YOU ANYTHING TO DO WITH THIS?'

'I . . . I . . . I . . .'

'Chaffinch had nothing to do with it, sir,' said Borrage.

Chortlesome-Hardy and I were in the tuckshop 2 days later, trying to operate Fatty's cake device on behalf of Mrs Woodly, the kindly tuckshop proprietor, but obtaining only coal, when Borrage came in, eyes red.

'Mugg, old pally-do! Snarg! Snarg! Been looking for you everywhere!'

We had a short chat, mainly fantasies about us becoming Hittite charioteers, the great dream of all boyhoods in the 2080s. Then, suddenly, Borrage emptied his pockets of dosh, whistles, Hittite gum cards, and said: 'All yours, Chaffy. Yeps. Snarg.'

I was nonplussed. Wot was up with Borrage? There he was ruffling my hair, his hand staying in the ruffle for longer than usual. He stepped back and tidied it for me, a careful sweep with his own comb from his jumble of gifts, admiring my beauty with one eye closed, then t'other. Mrs Woodly suddenly shrieked as Chortlesome-Hardy's tinkering triumphed and a giant wedding cake appeared on her counter. I looked at it and in the same moment Borrage was gone.

For his assassination of Fatty Londsdale my friend had been sentenced to death. Headmasters were given these powers briefly during Connie & Pam's administration in the '60s, and now they had been restored. Sentence duly notified, Borrage had to write an essay of apology to Lonsdale's parents beginning *I killed Philip with my phaser because . . .* A copy was pinned to the school notice board, together with its mark: 3 out of 10. Matron carried out the sentence minutes after Borrage left the tuckshop that day. I was profoundly shocked. I might say, and I will, that I went witless with disbelief. Had the Hittites brutalized us, or were we like this anyway? I somehow find that I miss Borrage to this day. He should not have died.

Homegoing again at the end of that same term, I found changes. The servants and slaves of my infancy were swapped for newcomers who ignored me entirely but did everything I said. Mother was also aloof, always jogging or tirelessly doing exercises in the gym. She was more beautiful than ever, but somehow not her old self. Tadese, I was at last informed after 1000 askings, had returned to Africa to help fight the Hittites there. Was it his leaving that had made my grandfather so sad? He kept to the library, a book with a zapper in it beside him in case of Hittite incursions. In the evenings he read bits of the Bible to me, then we'd discuss the text. Sometimes he didn't answer my fooly-do questions, but just looked at me, grinning. Did he know, in his wisdom, that one day I too would be an Archbishop and that pilgrims would ask of me the same ages-old fooly-doos questions? Though Bunnies crossing their furry chests never entered his head, I'm sure he knew.

Changes also in the village. Mr Chaulders' business hadn't been doing too well and he had been unable to pay his forcefield bill. So the electricity board switched him off. Inevitably, the Hittites burst in and slew him while his shop bell protestethed. The village hall was enlarged into an obscene temple to their false gods, pebble-dashed, busied with mythological statuary, and a soothsayer installed on its steps who made denouncements in the direction of the house of Chaffinch. Buses kept crashing into its pillars, Hittites preferring to drive roadcars like chariots, at full pelt and standing up. In the fields they toiled under the once-English Heaven, tending seas of bronze barley and everywhere were goats – more goats than Hittites, everyone said so.

One thing remained the same. I was taught the church organ by Rev Dickerson. He liked to sit very close to me on the organ stool, swinging his legs and telling me under its deep groan or highpitched twiddlesomenesses that I must be the prettiest ickle boy in all the world. Years later, how well I remember, do I not, I do, when the big organ arrived in my new cathedral in Bunnyopolis. It was lowered into Cathedral Square from the shuttlecraft, whistling to itself in its pipes, and ten thousand Bunny converts were on hand to manoeuvre it into its eternal place in the cathedral. When I sat on its stool some heretic in the congregation shouted out: 'PLAY BLUE SUEDE SHOES, YOU OLD FRAUD!!!!!!!!!!'

But I played *Onward Christian Soldiers*, a Bunny fave, and was delighted by their Bunnyhooing enthooooze as they sang. But in my ear all along I could hear the Rev Dickerson telling me how pretty I was and could he kiss my fingertips. When my playing was done, with the wind still moaning in the organ, I wept as I never did when a kiddywink.

My grandfather had – due to a quirk which he explainethed to me many times but whose theoretical gist I never quite grasped, dimmo Mugg – lived the 21st Century through twice. He lived it once from his birth in 2000 to Christmas of 2099, then went back to great-granny's womb and started again. He explains it all in his wonderful booky-do, so full of his laughter and spirit, his *21st Century Blues*, written in his 1st old age, published in his 2nd-time-around-youth. My own booky-do, this here senile ramblement, is my sorry-bees inadequate attempt to follow in his footprints with a companion booky-doos – a 100-year continuation of man's history by one who has lived through much but who has ended by knowing more about rabbits than man.

This Mugg wishes, above all things, that he had a copy of his grandfather's book here on CbN. He hath cruised his computer for its pages but can find nothing of it. Urk! Old tick-tock-head read it back on Bunnyland and proclaimed it a rattling good read but criticised it for having only 2 footnotes. Tinpot tocker! My own reading of it was thought best delayed, due to its sexual contents, till I was past 10 years of age. Then one night grandfather left it on my bedside table. How it thrilled me! His adventures! His loves! His enquiring soul! But I was also depressed. Wot life could I have to compareth – stuck behind forcefields, zapped tween one fetid city and another, a Hittite shortsword at the end of my story. Nopes! NOPES! Please God, nopes! Looking at the starry nights from beddybye prayers, I never guessed wot wonderments lay ahead for pretty ickle Muggy Chaffy. – Still, a wasted life.

It disturbethed me no end that every Saturday night ball my mumsy threw wast filled with the same guesties, clobbered up identically for every do. Whenever I returned home from Smithers for my hols, slowly attaining my full height (not much!), the very same lot would arrive on the lawn. When they milled hawingly in the porchway, I earwaggeried their chin-waggery from the stairs. Twas about the same stuff, was it not – same jokes, same gossipings, and never a mention of the boggn Hittites! Twas as if the war wasn't raging! Twas as if the Hittites hadn't settled-in upon OUR world, building themselves great boggn cities everywhere, winged guardians at the gates! But I wasn't thinking about the obvious 'why' for this, for I wast of an age when parties shone bright in the eyes – I wanted to join in and have a ball – I wanted to dance, I wanted to glide across the floor at cleavage height and whisper SNARG in the ears of the younger girls.

'GET TO THY ROOM, MUGG, SAY I! GET THEE TO BED! FUNCTIONS LIKE THESE ARE NOT YET THINE, LADDIE-O!'

'Please, Chaff, I wouldst like to dance for the guesties. Mumsy will be so proud of my ballet prancing! I hast danced before Rev Dickerson and made him cry I am such a beautiful dancer!'

'TO BED, MUGGERIDGE!!!!'

'And the boggn Hittites too! I dance for them at the gates and their grimaces slacken and they desisteth from evil gesturing!'

'BED! O, WANTON CHAFFINCH!!!!'

These ball nights were the only times my grandfather spoke to me in his Archbishop of Canterbury voice. But I could see it hurt him to do so. I obeyed bad-temperedly, slouching and stamping to bed. Then, one Saturday afternoon in the summer of '96, 12-year-old Mugg decided he would not be cheated of his great moment again! I drummethed up courage by shaking my fist at the Hittites who forever gurned outside the forcefield. My pepper thus raised, I hid in a suit of armour by the great fireplace, waiting for the guests to arrive. Grandfather came in at balltime, to stand nodding under the Magri portrait of his late wife, Granny Scampi, as he often did. He lookethed so upset that I almost cried out to comfort him. But he knew I was there, the old cheat! Like any telepathic space bug he felt my compassion! In his final nod was a smile. No guesties arrived that night. No ball. No jiggerty-poo. No bilious reek of vol-au-vents. I stood in the armour all night, like a big pilchard in a tin – or like the awkward soul of my butler Mathis made flesh.

Next Saturday I told grandfather I intended to telezoom to Chortlesome-Hardy Manor in Kent for a wheeze with my pallydoos. But instead I telezoomed right into that suit of armour and stood there till balltime eating crisps like a Solperine. The crisps, with their noisy munchy-munchsomeness were an error, were they not. Suddenly grandfather was outside on a chair, lifting the vizor and looking inside. His kind face seemed bigger than the world.

'Mugg? Tis thee?'

'Yes, grandfather.'

'I hath been meaning to request of thee that mebbees thou wouldst dance for me?'

'Yes, grandfather. I will dance for you.'

While he finished my crispsbag I danced for him. Gawkily, my big feet slapping the floor like applause, but dancing with unpretentious passion. I finished with a slide to his feet, panting, sodden with sweat – my greatest performance! His hands were open for his first clap – how I would have valued that music! – but he never closed them. His ears pricked, his mouth popped . . . The guesties were arriving. A ball! A ball! The servants were bringing in the buffet tables. Grandfather covered his face with his hands.

'TO BED! GET THEE TO BED!'

'But grandfather!'

Shaking and distressed: 'THEE IS TOO YOUNG YETA-WHILE, MUGG, DEAREST BOY! PRITHEE, TO BED.'

'NOPES! BOGGN NOPES TO THEE, OLD MAN! I'M YOUNG, VITAL AND ALIVE! THEE HAST HAD THYSELF 2 LONG LIVES IN THE WIDE-OPEN WORLD! I, NONE! LET ME DANCE, CHAFF, PLEASY-DO!' Then I whispered. 'God's spirit is in me when I dance.'

I was weeping. He too. We embraced. He rubbed the strawberry curly-doos from my brow and kissed me there, over and over. In a cracking voice he sayethed: 'This hath all gone too far, Mugg. I see clearly that I must tell thee now, the truth about ourselves.'

The first guesties were coming in, haw-hawing through their same natter. The first cocktail sausages were devoured from the first offered tray. Grandfather took me outside into the Hittite-howling night. On the steps behind us my mother was blowing hellos to the guesties, my father waggling his phallus.

'Mugg,' said grandfather, his hands gripping tightly on to his monk's gown as he searched for words. 'There is no ball at Chaffinch Hall tonight. There hast been none these 7 years.'

'But . . . look! Here, around us! Tonight! Ya giddy goat! Seest not thee a ball! Snarg!'

He plucked a podule from under his gown. I had seen him with it before. Twas similar to Fatty Lonsdale's cake-stealing device. Grandfather clicked the podule and the ball went in reverse. I yelped! Fat aristos walked backwards down the steps. Scrummy bare-legged ladies with exciting cleavages returned backwards to their flying hats and flew backwards away, leaving not even their perfumes behind. My mother and father stood on the steps looking sadly down on us. Hittites hammered their weapons on the forcefield as always. Petals dropped from the magnolias.

'England is no longer a place of balls, Mugg, is it not, indeed not, no, no, it is not, no. But me, a sillymost old gooseberry fool, I wanted things as they were. Before the ancients came. I wanted the life back in the house. Triple sorries, my boy. Don't hate your old Chiffchaff for the terrible thing he hast done to thee, Mugg of mine.'

'Hate thee, grandfather? Neverso! Thee is my model in all things!'

'We are all there is alive in Chaffinch Hall, Mugg. Just you and I. A mistake over our forcefield bill – the bank's fault! Thy second term at Smithers it was, was it not. We wast cut off. The Hittites swarmed across the lawns. Dearie-be. They slew all our slaves, Hodgekins the old butler, the cook, everyone. Oh, my Tadese so brave, like Samson smiting the Philistines of old. But he too was slain. Everyone was slain.'

'Everyone but you . . . and the dogs, and mumsy and daddykins!'

A dog came up woofing. Grandfather clicked his podule. It

vanished. In blubbing terror I ran to mumsy. I hugged her bare
legs, rubbed my curls hard on her knees. Grandfather was
sobbing, the podule dropped on the step below his dirty feet.

'I danced for grandfather!' I said to mumsy, looking up into
her smooth beautiful face. 'Thy baby bird will dance for thee!
Oh, I am so pretty when I dance!'

The bangles in her hair clackered together as she lifted me
sobbing to my feet. She began singing a lullaby to me, but
twasnt soothy-mmmms the way it had been in my babyer
nightynights: it seemethed devilish, sinister. I turned on my
toes, leapt down 3 steps and reached for the podule. Grandfather's yellow toenails made attempts to grasp it first. We
looked into each other's eyes, the same eyes, old and young.

'No, Mugg. Let me, pleasy-do.'

I clicked the podule and my mother vanished forever. I
clicked again and my father's forehead was gone, again for
each ear, for his penis and heel. I was orphaned. But had been
for years, just never knew.

'I do thinky-do, do I not, I do, Mugg, that 'twould be betterer,
indeedy-so, if we were to dispense with all our illusions. Urk!'

Fiercelymost, I agreed. We went on an extraordinary tour,
switching off the servants and slaves. Strange that the servants protestethed greatly, but the slaves were glad to go.

'G'evening, Master Mugg, your Lordship. If I might point
out, sir, the Oudenarde Service was not part of the hologramismic interactive programme but has vanished anyway when
you let Tomkins go just now.'

'Byesiebyebye, Hodgekins.'

'Oh, not ME, sir! You'll never get by without ME, sir.'
Click!

Cook was the hardest. She wast a 2nd mumsy to me. Her
jolly red face, her flour-whitened hands. Grandfather prayed
with her in the larder and returnethed alone. We ate some of
the jam tarts she had but lately made, her finalmost batch.

When the help was gone we started on the dogs. By then twas almost a sport, as we gave the podule back and forth, zapping them as they ran at us with their panting tongues. But one pooch wouldn't disappear. Click – click – click!!!!!!!!!! Nopes, bad doggy, still there! Twas a nondescript thing, old and wormy. A good-sized woof would've collapsed it.

'I do believe that I remember this beast from my youth,' said grandfather. 'Impossybule, but verily, I am sure tis he!'

Grandfather patted the dog. Between blinks it looked at him with an intelligent face, asking where had all the other dogs gone.

'URK!' went I. 'Wot about the Rev Dickerson?'

A grave nod from grandfather. He handed me the podule. I walked down the forcefield-tunnel to the church. Beyond the graveyard Hittites smoked their hubble-bubble hookahs and told jokes in their odd Suffolk accents. I tried turning the buggers off, but they were only too real. Rev Dickerson was sitting in his pulpit reading the church Bible. He saw the podule in my hand.

'So!' he said. 'It's that, is it?'

I went up to the organ loft and he followed. We sat on the stool together. He played. I played. Some final tips, then suddenly he grabbed my hands and kissed them.

'Oh, Mugg, you divine creature! I do love you so! From the first moment I saw you on your mother's knee, and more every day. I think of nothing but you. Bless you, my child. Bless you!'

Then he snatched up the podule and clicked himself away.∗

∗ The nearest thing in my own experience to this distressing 'switching off' of vicars, mothers etc, was during my early days as President of Bunnyland, or Bunnyboss as the office was more popularly called. The immediate crisis concerned the acquiring of sexual parts to distribute to the rampant hoppers, as per my election promise to them. I paced my grand office, scratching my bunnysuit, when the Health Minister came in, an old mangy rabbit who hopped

As I walkethed up the drive to the Hall, my feet squishing juicy magnolia petals into the red gravel, I grew frightened at the emptiness of the place. It was like approaching some vast mountain where no mortal has yet stepped. All lights out. Just the starlight spotting the windows. A dead thing. My home, but emptied of all I cared for except one freckled-headed nonogenarian.

He was in his ground floor den looking at the viddywall

3 steps backwards every 3rd step, so that it was some while, if ever, before he reached me with his whisper:

'Bunnysnatchers!' he said.

'Hm?'

'A new outbreak. Most disturbing. Not Bunnyhoo. Not Bunnyha. Tails up, ehwot!'

'Sorry, old chap, don't get ya drift, dyersee.'

He explained that a microscopic mollusc, alien to Bunnyland, that dwelt exclusively in carrots, long thought extinct, had returned on the tail of a comet. It entered the Bunny through the carrot, dissolved in his brain, then took him over, lock, stock and hop.

'How do we tell these Bunnysnatchers from our regular Bunny chaps?' was my presidential question.

'We can't. Nay. There is no medical differwence.'

'In behaviour then?'

'They behave just the same as we do. When they take over a Bunny he goes on living his life, doing his job, just the same as before. No differwence at all.'

'No way of telling, then! Dimmee!'

'There is one thing. Bunnysnatchers tend to eat carrwots from the feathery end.'

'Ah! That's a goodn, Minister. I'll alert the security forces.'

'Better hop to it. Our estimate is that a million wabbits a day are being snatched.'

I busied myself with the problem. Posters with a doubtful Bunny face were tacked up everywhere, with the warning underneath BEWARE BUNNYS-NATCHERS. A carrot scare ensued. Whole crops were condemned and torched. The acrid stench of burnt carrots hung over Bunnyopolis. Quite a stir! Plus, after we'd arrested and vaporized (switched jolly well off, wot!) thousands of Bunnies seen eating a carrot from the wrong end, government statistics suggested that 27% of normal healthy Bunnies ate from the wrong end anyway, regardless of Bunnysnatching outbreaks.

Then, surprise-surprise, was it not, when a week later the Health Minister with the sound off. The Hittites had stormed all the TV stations by now, and there was nothing but Hittites to watch. It was a prog about how to care for your beard. Beardless, we watched the cruel Hittite fizzogs and tried to see the beauty in them.

'I doest strongly believe, grandfather, that in the long run, pleasy-do, we shouldst make peace with yon ancients, then we may all walk in the wide world once more.'

Heresy! Traitor talk! He was aghast! A telling-off was offing,

hopped his tedious way into my office again and I said: 'This Bunnysnatcher business . . .?'

And he said: 'Bunnysnatchers? Oh, false alarm, Mr Pwresident. There tissent no such thing, ehwot. Nay, nay. Merely mythological wumour. Snarg!'

I was suspicious, but showed it not. 'No such thing, d'yersay! Tophole news!'

As soon as he was gone – it took a while with his 3 small steps forward and one big hop back – I changed into my spare Bunnysuit. In this I was not Mopsy, President of Bunnyland, but Loppy Tharby, Spacerabbit 1st Class. I hopped down to the Capital Canteen and sat at a table with a plate full of whoppity carrots which I proceeded to chew from the feathery end. My throatsack was full before the Health Minister arrived. When he saw me eating from the feathery end he came to sit beside me, his carrot stew steaming under his twitching nose.

'Nice carrots, ehwot? But the wrong end, citizen. Nay to that. Nay.'

'Bunnyhoo!' said I, snapping a bite from the blunt feathery end of the biggest vegetable in town.

His eyes narrowed: 'The moons of Watkins 4 weflect in the pools of Watkins but we were always too small to see. Nay? But the comet brings us where we get to see moons a-plenty, ehwot, brother?'

'Too bally true, old sport!' said I, whistled for security and had the Health Minister arrested as a leading Bunnysnatcher.

His hanging took an unbearably long time. He took much longer hops backwards on the way to the scaffold. In the end he was dragged there, squealing. Archbishop Mugg, who was present, was greatly distressed, as the Health Minister had been a regular churchgoer.

The Bunnysnatchings were not defeated by this show of Presidential strength. It was a most virulent outbreak. But as snatched Bunnies and unsnatched Bunnies were exactly the same in all respects – thought, word, deed – I decided to let the matter go. The Shogun for some while said at every visit: 'It's me they're after, thee knows!' But later, when I enquired if he was still perturbed about 'them' being after him he said: 'Who's that, then?'

but then he was doubly-tripplemostly-aghast. A huge youth stomped into the den in threadbare pyjamas.

'WHERE'S ME TEA???? WHERE'S ME BOGGN TEA???????'

'Erm . . .?'

'COUSIN STEWIE! I'M YA COUSIN, STEWIE, FROM UPSTAIRS!'

He looked at the ceiling. We looked at the ceiling.

'Ah-so!' sayethed grandfather – our grandfather! 'Upstairs.'

Stewie was one of the 'Others', the mad, illegitimate Chaffinches who had lived in our attic rooms since the heyday of William & Mary – generations of such had lived and died up there, alone, each to his/her attic cell.∗ But in all that time there had been not one as big a pigbogger, as rottenmost a boglyfala, as hugemost a Godless wonderment of psychoed gittitude, as the very last of their obnoxious breed. Son of my own father and a tweenie maid, Stewie called himself 'cousin' out of some strange delicacy of mind. He ruined my grandfather's final days, that demon from a pit deeper than any Hittite's djinn! O perfidious Stewie!

'HODGEKINS OR CHIVES BRUNGS ME ME TEA AT 5 PROMPT, DONT THEY NOT! WHERE ARE THE P'BOGGN PIGBOGGERS WIF ME TEA!!!!!!!!!'

∗ Maud Chaffinch, my first truelove, I suspect became one of these 'Others' way back in the 1930s, as I relate in my BOOK OF MATHIS. Reading this here, I am deeply affected by my memories of her. Alone now – having today deactivated the mechanical cats, inspired by poor Mugg's switching-off of his family – I seem beset, do I not, by the ghosts of my past, ehwot! Clarissa's laughter rumbles within my tincan body. Lloyd George's speeches rattle the edges of my senses – I almost hear them, as if he is in a nearby gulch on Catsby-Nowhere, playing politics with the tumbling weed. Egad! I cannot bear to read more. I have the frights. I feel I may die too. In dreams I am a stuffed albatross hanging in the blue sky looking far, far down below to the glinting sea where vast troopships are taking boys to die in the Great War. 'DON'T GO, LADDIES!' squawk I. 'THE UNIVERSE AWAITS!'

'Snarg,' said I to Stewie – twas all I could think of to say.

'SNARG YERHSELF, BLONDIE! WHERE'S ME TEA, YOU BOGGN LITTLE RATPLOP????? AND SOMEBODY SHUT THEM BLIDDIE HITTITES UP OR I'LL BOGGN SCREAM, I WILL!'

He did. How his scream echoed through the depopulated mansion. Then he broke chairs. Then we made him his tea. Grandfather enquired of his religious beliefs. None.

Amen.

Hittites: Three
The Lovely Anita

My talking kettle of a butler hath this morning been filling my ears with boastings about his time as weapons officer aboard a Peewermums ship. Dear creatures! – I grew some on a windowsill at the Bunnyland mission, but they died. I wouldst have told tick-tock about my own experiences in this line – weapons! zappy-doos! Mugg the hero! – but his kettle-whistle wouldn't stop for long enough! Such vanity in a gadget!*

I was 20, was dispatched straight from Officer Training School to Planet Cindy-cum-Dwaibs by the old soup traveller-izer – you jumped into a vat of liquid not unlike chicken noodle soup, was it not, and popped up light years away in a muckier vat of same, half your senses left behind, noodles in your cracks, swallowing floating buttons with gobfuls of cold soup. I'm sure the thing was the cause of my lovely hair falling out.

Planet Cindy-cum-Dwaibs was damp, very English in its dampitude – twas damp, I say! Its land was a scatter of damp archipelagos where the colonists had built damp seaside resorts: a thousand wet-Sunday Blackpools, Weymouths, Yar-

---

* I confess to being a gadget. But this 'tick-tock' sobriquet galls me! I do not make any sound like tick-tock. When overwound I do whirr a bit. But, never, never do I whistle like a common household kettle! Bless me, if I'm not thoroughly upset at this namecalling!

mouths, Whitley Bays, their damp piers jutting gaudilymost into a grassgreen sea. Only problematicalness with the place (apart from the damp) were the vast herds of flying cattle. These wild, wingless, mooing aborigines flew by no agency that could be discovered – flicking of their tails being their most observable movement, with rare hoofings of the tepid breeze. They descended on the resorts like locusts, leaving them bespatterated with cowpats, and killed many on the promenades kamikaze-style by crashing out of the air, making a bloodified mess, did they not, of someone's colonial retirement or drear seaside holiday. Worstmost, the moos were sure to appear on the rare sunny days of those melancholy whereabouts. The spacejocks, of which, pleasy-do laugh if thee must, I was one, were employed in exterminating the moo herds, and a scramble was on just as I arrived. Tinny bullfight music wast a-blaring from tannoy horns all along the seafront. Landladies were bringing in their washing. Retired space-captains, red-in-the-face, were waving their sticks furiously at the sky.

Unfortunately-doos, the only zippy-craft available for the just-arrived 2nd Lieutenant Chaffinch was an island-hopping booze-bar – a flying drinks cabinet, pleasy-do, with zappy-ado-guns attached. The ground staff who commandeered it for my use didn't tell me there was a bachelor party going on in the rear compartment. I was aloft, falling in with the round-up squadron, and already going zappyadoo at cattle, when this became known to me. An inebriate squished through the doors – whose brief opening gave this Mugg his introductory blast of crude partysome raucosity! – and sat beside me, finding some hilarity at the moo-cows stampeding across the sky. This sot was Ichabod Tizer, who was later with me in the seminary and is today Archbishop of Bilickers System, though has never once sobered up. He took hold of the co-pilot control-T and commenced zappyadoo-doos at the unfortunate bovines. And, dear Lord, was that not the gift thou issued the pigbogger with, for verily he never missed. Bull's-eye Tizer I hath everafterwards addressed him in missives.

Glorybe! This activity was not quite the jolly funtraipse it soundeth. By the time Brother Tizer joined me, 10 of our 25 zippy-craft had been downed by the cattle. They cowpatted your screen so's you couldn't see them charge at you. I saw several craft go down where moos smashed right through into the cab. They also liked to gore the fueltanks and jigger until your gauge read empty, forcing you down onto the sea, where they danced on your roof till you sank. A boggn awful biz for a soppy article on his first day as a jock! But the added stress of having Brother Tizer, who had invited in his partycrowd to witness his ace zappyadoo-doos, made me think I'd soon be in the family vault along with my grandfather:

> *Muggeridge Chaffinch*
> *2083–2103*
> *killed by cows and drunkards.*

Indeedy-be, 47 bachelor party hoochtipplers, some wearing plastic bosoms, others doing tangos across the control-console, some denuding themselves and urinating into my silver jockhat, were commanding my senses, along with their brassy music, gooselike singing, and haw-haw suggestions in my ear, while joyfully pulling out clumps of my sickly lovely hair to make moustaches with . . . when all my attention was needed to perform my duty and zap cows.

We had already been butted a few times, the screen was cracked, warning lights were a-going flashy-bleep on the console. Then out of the corner of my eye I saw 300 head of moo coming out of a green cloud and heading right for us. I whooshed straight upwards, turned zippily in the haze and swept down on their flank from the sun. This manoeuvre was $\frac{3}{4}$ done when 47 party-poppers fusilladed in my ears and a 7-

foot tall cake was wheeled in from which burst an enormous lewd Solperine singing *My Heart Belongs to Daddy*.

'DESIST FROM THIS LEVITY, YOU PIGGN BOGGN P'BOGGERS! CAN'T YOU SEE WE'RE SURROUNDED BY FLYING COWS!'

On the sea 2 downed zippy-craft were being danced on by cattle – a sound, as we whooshed by, like when suits of armour fell down the stairs during the night at Chaffinch Hall. I zappyadooed the lead bull in a 50-moo charge. This turned the others. We swooshed into clear sky and I realized, guts churning in fright, that we were alone. My fellow jocks had all gone down, their last bubbles just that moment disturbing the sea's calm. For the moment the moos were gone also, but twas a feint. A few blinks, less than a round of drinks, later, they appeared on the hazy green horizon, coming fast, flying close to the sea, from all directions, hooves hardly moving. I whooshed up, they followed. I whooshed faster, but then in a sudden . . . they were upon us, close. I could see their faces. MOOOOOOOOOOOOO!!!!!!! Brother Tizer and this novice jock zappyadooed a hole in their charge and I flew through it, but only into a second wave of MOOOOOOOOOOOO!!!!! The Solperine dived back into her cake. The screen shattered into our faces. No longer a control-T in my hands, but horns! Snorts. Warm cow's breath! Cowpats! When we hit the sea, hooves kicked me through the party cake into the booze-bar. Not cannon-fodder, but cow-fodder, beaten by the moos!

I woke up in a snug with the bachelor whose bachelor party it was hugging my shoulders, weeping, telling me, perhaps not for the first time, that he was only marrying Lt. Deirdre Morrison because of her resemblance to Admiral Christabel Glossop. Meanwhileydoos, the party had adjourned to the roof, where, amid more raucosity, the partygoers were zappyadooing every moo-cow that showed in the air – though where they got the zappers from I know not! 200 zapped moos were floating around us, smoking from the zap, a smell of Sunday joint thick in the humid air. Evil little fishes were nibbling at the flotsam moos.

'WHEEEEEE-HAAAAA!' went Ichabod Tizer, cowpatted from head to toe. 'ZAP! ZAPPY! ZAPPY-ADOOOOOOOO-DA-ALL-THE-DAY! WHOOOOOO! HE-eeeeee-EEEEEE-eeeeeee-he-HE-he!'

Never a drinky-poos man, I was so relieved and grateful that I opened a jeroboam of champers I found behind the bar and shared it with the gigglesome rooftop revellers. Browned with cowshite, we couldn't have enjoyed any occasion moresomely! One chap produced a mooring rope, lassoed a moo with it and was pulled away over the sea never to be seen again. He was our booze-bar's only fatality. How we laughed! Chee! Twice-muchly when we washed the mire from our faces to see which of us was lost – twas the bachelor whose bachelor party it had been! HOOOO-HEEEE!

Our tarty Solperine sang *My Heart Belongs to Daddy* 387 times as the booze-bar returnethed to the resort under our sore-footed pedalo-power, this Mugg becoming as sloshed as any. Upon arrival I realized from my stupor that I, vanquisher of cows, was quite the local hero. The band was out. POM-TIDDLY-POM-OOMPAPA!!! The populace gathered on the beach, waving candyflosses at our dented booze-bar. I staggered up the promenade singing despite myself *My Heart Belongs to Daddy* to have the Mayor shake the delirium tremors from my hand. OH YEA, OH YEA, THE MOOS ARE DESTROYED! THREE CHEERS FOR LIEUTENANT CHAFFINCH! But at the far end of the jetty, alone, stood 2 similar-looking females – one I recognized, did I not, as Admiral Christabel Glossop.

Tis often a vicar's unhappy duty to be harbinger of bad news, but I was no vicar then, only a dippy cow-zapping boy. Telling the poor fool's women that he was gone forever was the hardest part of the first day of my brief spacejock career. Especially with Ichabod Tizer at my elbow guffawing at my every word.

But twas upon Cindy-cum-Dwaibs that I receivethed bad news of my own. The Lovely Anita was dead. In the *Back on Earth* column in the local newsrag, a tiny fuzzy photo to remind me of her loveliness: Anita. There was I, the rag shaking in my hands in that greasy seafront caff, quite bald by then, wearing a corset under my silver suit to hold my piggybelly in. I was, suddenly in 3 swift years, no longer the lovely boy she had adored, who had sucked her nipples whole nights long. She was dead and I seemethed to be living a life not my own in a body I did not recognize as myself.

In order to earn poundlets to pay our forcefield bill and to feed and clothe the domineering Stewie, I had put my dancing talent to work on the pay-per-view tellyscreen. This is where the Lovely Anita saw me. I was wearing only a purple velour thong, my lithe young body oiled, shining under the lights of our ballroom, with a line of glinting knights in armour, dragged from all over the Hall, as backdrop to my leaping erotic dance. It was the night when Stewie wandered across the stage eating from a box of chicken legs. I incorporated him into the routine, pulling a spear from the wall and, whipping my long strawberry curls on my neck, I stuck the spearpoint into the parquet floor and swung wantonly around it, my toes stealing chicken legs from Stewie's box and throwing them cheekily at the knights. He threw punches my way, but I leapt! I pranced somersaults! I span around him, a blur of grin, curls, navel and thong!

I saw your dance on my viddywall tonight, luv. I have never been more aroused. Pleasy-do-do-do come and dance for me in the fleshy-poos. Anita.

This message was flashing on my computerscreen in my bedroom when I went up to bed. I sat watching it for a little while, breathing deeply. Thee must understand, I wast a 17-year-old boy who had barely spoken to girls. I had seen none naked other than peeps at the holograms my grandfather kept company with in his quarters – and, yes, the matron at Smithers. To get such a message made me feel lonely, frightened, a boy too immature for the lusts that moved him. Then I looked at myself in the mirror. Verily, I was as pretty a boy as ever walked on OOP. This admirer had reason to adore me. But when my fingers reached out to type 'Thank you, yes, I wilt gladly come and dance for thee' they closed into a fist. I dared not meet this appreciative message-sender. Nor, in my shyness, did I dance again for several days. But in my next dance, while the lights burned my leaping shadow, I thought hotly, thong-burstingly of HER, Anita – not knowing, indeedy-be, that SHE was the Lovely Anita herself, Queen of England, our blessed leaderette, the divine visage poor Borrage had wanky-wooed over every night of his boyhood – and, I confess it here, I too when wanky-wooing had summoned imaginings of the Lovely Anita! My dance was triple helpings of cream on the passion-fruit. I high-jumped foot-twiddling into the air, twanging my thong, landing on all fours, arching my neck, then throwing my feet into my curls and rolling around the room, meowing, finishing on my hands, legs slowly parting, grinning through my utter breathlessness.

When I made my final bows I rushed straight upstairs, panting, bursting with youth and strength, to watch the computerscreen. The first messages were all from boy-loving Hittites, then . . .

Tonight, luv, you danced better than ever! Oh, my giddy angel, pleasy-do come and dance for me!

For days I have thought of nowt but you! And now tonight . . . Oh, how beautiful you were tonight! A right bobbydazzler and no mistake! I cannot live a day longer without you! Pleasy-pleasy-do-do-do come and dance for me! Your darlingmost hen, Anita.

I took note of her co-ordinates and rushed to the telezooming-plate. An instant later, wearing just my thong, beaded in sweat, I was surprised to arrive in London in the Cabinet Office in the middle of an important meeting! Around the table 25 pop-eyed generals and ministers . . . and, gumgollygosh! HER, the Lovely Anita! I was scared to bits. My secret admirer was the Queen Goddess herself! Urk!

In the moment I arrived I saw her in commanding mode, Queenly, telling the pompous p'boggers what to do with themselves. Then she saw me, was out of her seat, blushing, hesitant, hands over her lips, gushing: 'Eeeee, my darlingmost boy, yer've come, yer've come!'

She shyly took my hand and led me to the door, where she stopped, looking at the details of my face and down the brief length of my sweaty body. She was all a-flutter as she turned to her War Cabinet and said: 'Eee, but tissent thisun the most gorgeous little thing you've ever set eyes on ever?'

Then she whisked me away and we ran up a golden staircase like naughty children, laughing at the grim portraits until we reached the top where, huge, was a prawn-pink nude of the Lovely Anita gambolling with satyrs in an English glade. I knew the picture. I had a copy, torn carefully from a mag, in my bedside drawer at home.

'Does yer see me that way? Eh, lad? Cum now.'

I shook my head nervously. 'No. Never, marm.'

Her laugh that tinkled the chandeliers. 'Oh, but yer does, luv. I wouldn't be who I am if I didn't know human nature. I know yer sees me running all flushed 'n starkers through the forest in a world when yon boggn Hittites were still dust.'

She was quite right, of course. This fantasy was the subject of 100 wanky-woos. Pine-needles stuck to her feet. Sunbeams on her belly as it fluttered for breath.

The room she took me into was perfect for dancing. It had mirrors on all the walls and ceilings. The floor was black linoleum, good for sliding. I composed myself for dancing, eyes closed, on my tippytoes.

'This, darling, luv!' She twanged my thong. 'Don't need it! Nopes. There now.'

I removed it, commenced to dance with slow pointings of the legs, hands modestly cupping my embarrassment, then bravely swinging them away . . . and in the same moment, shocksomely, the floor shuddered and I slipped flat-footed as what looked like a hundred beds shot up through the floor. It was just one, crimson sheeted, scarlet canopied, in the middle of the room. And there in all the mirrors, and alive beside me, though I looked at all her reflections first, one by one, was Anita, more nude than in her portraits, more lovely indeedy-so than anything I had ever, have ever seen or imagined. My eyes rolled from curve to curve till they became stuck in her long tawny pubesome area – one small place in all the wide Universe, but there twas, and the sight of it made me shake!

'I'm so chuffed that you came, pretty-one. I never thought you would, nay. Cum, cum to your darling hen.'

What canst an 117-year-old twaddler say, O Lord, as he letches into his distant past, 100 wasted years ago when he made love for the 1st time to the Lovely Anita? Though her true age was unspoken, scratched from the records, she became English P.M. the year I was born, promoted herself to Queen when I was 5, so in that last year of the 21st Century, she could have been no less than 50 years old. But verily, in both body and heart she was a girl no older than the virginal boy who she helped enter her with his eagerly twanging wang.

One night in Bunnycamp, where the city Bunnies vacationed every summer, the Bunnies were complaining yet again about their missing sexual parts. Ooooo, how they wanted to DO IT! Had I, Bunnybish, sniggeroo-sniggerooo, every DONE IT! sniggerooo, EH! EH! DONE IT! CORRRRRR! I poked baking potatoes in the fire with my crook and told them of my lover of long ago, the Lovely Anita, of the first lusty groin-thrusts of my youth, of Anita's joysome squeals, her creamy buttocks reflected in so many mirrors, my strawberry curls knotted with her dark tresses as the red sheets turned black with our sweats and juices, tingling through the night and groaning beyond the dawn. By the time I was finished the poor sex-starved Bunnies were furysomely rubbing their cotton-tails on stones, beating their chests, chewing each others' feet, and squeaking in anguish for their absent sexbits.

I did not tell my grandfather that I was committing the hoohar-wiggly thing with someone, let alone with the Lovely Anita! Not that he would have objected, no-nooo. He wasn't a sillypoos po-faced cleric. He had been an outrageous sinner with girls throughout his lifelong. When wedded to Granny Scampi he'd strayed happily with nuns and parishioners, and though then near 100 in his private hours he hoohared with hologram chicks and thought nowt wrong with it. But I kept my lovely girl a secret. Meanwhileydoos, did I think of anything else? Nopes. My wang was a-throb, up all day as I ponderated upon lastnight's and tonight's pleasures.

Thus and so, I noticethed not how Stewie was becoming more violent and demanding. My flesh was so enervated, his clips about the ears were hardly painful to me. But he hit grandfather also, most frequently when I was not there, and the old man was suffering badly from the headaches than resultethed.

After tea-time during that autumn of 2099 – crumbs for us, wolfings for Stewie – it was our custom to sit down, while Stewie snored before the fire in one of his silk gowns monogrammed **SC**, and read to each other from my grandfather's latest 'work'.

To earn poundlets to help pay forcefield bills and for the endless zoom-order packages which telezoomed daily onto our plate to dress Stewie yet more magnificently, grandfather had taken up his pen. He was writing Hittite romances, swashbucklers, and, truth be told, soft-porn for the vast Hittite market under the pseudonym of Rabshakeh Blarguzd III.

Grandfather would declaim from today's work: *Into the palace strode Tiglath, 2 stunned leopards over his broad muscled shoulders. When he threw them before the King they awoke and snarled menacingly at the foot of his throne. 'I hast come to take thy daughter Yasmin for my wife!' cried Tiglath 'NEVER!' cried the King . . .* then the fresh pages were passed to my hands and I continued . . . *Doest thou not recognize me, O King? Look close! Can all those years trapped in thy wizard's bottle have changed me so much?' 'ARHHHHHH! TIS THEE, TIGLATH!' cried the King, the curls of his beard falling straight. 'Ay, Tiglath, rightful King of this Hittite land. Pleasy-do, Yasmin, canst thou love this fugitive from a bottle?' 'Oh, indeedy-be, mighty warrior!' said she, and the leopard purred at her perfumed feet.*

Twas so cheesome to see my bogus-Hittite grandfather clapping his Hittite drivellings, nodding with enthoooze through the rude bits. The Hittites loved them. Soon Account No 812131555 in the Hittite Savings Bank – I remember the number yet – that of Rabshakeh Blarguzd III would be bursting with shekels. Brilliant old fooly-doo, my grandfather wast!

Meanwhileydoos, Stewie was acting the Lord Chaffinch, cruel and demanding, with us as his servants.

'WHERE'S ME TEA! IRON ME PIGBOGGN SHIRT! POL-
ISH THEM SHOES AGAIN, OLD MAN, AND PROPERLY
THIS TIME . . . OR YER'LL GET **THIS**!'

THIS was his fist, or the back of his hand, or a poke in the eye,
or a kick from shoes in which Stewie's evil face-pulling face was
reflected. Can I say that while I was conceived in the joyousness
of my father's homecoming, Stewie was conceived in the
bitterness of his maimed condition? I hast said it. That penis
without a heart had made a son who verily was all knob-end!

'Bruises on my darling bird's neck!' quoth the Lovely Anita
while I licked her thighs.

'Playing with my big bro,' said I. 'Jollymost rough p'bogger
he is, my bro is, cor!'

Another secret! Why could I not weep on her chest and tell of
how miserable Stewie was making my grandfather and her
darling luv Mugg? But as Anita and I rolled in passion, her
love for me filling every corpuscle of my blood-engorged flesh,
how could I even whispereth the foul name of Stewie? No more
did she speak of the Hittite War, problems of state, etc. When
we coupled there was no world, there were no forcefields,
Hittites – only us!

Late one night I telezoomed home from a Parisian jaunt with
the Lovely Anita, hiccoughing from a delicious supper, her
kisses still tingling on my bruises, when I heard my grandfather's cry for help. I found him naked in his bedroom
doorway, the room behind him full of fizzing on-the-blink
hologramismics.

'My girls, Mugg, my poor girls, he's ripped them up.'

Grandfather's lips were bloody, split, one eye was closed.
He'd obviously fought Stewie hard to save his hologram
chicks. All but one were dead and because their programs
were rigged to discourage violence to womankind, they could
never be revived – their long memories of evenings with Chaff,
everything they had shared, were lost forever.

I'd never seen his girls close up before. The survivor, a pudgy raven-haired creature, was, guessed I, a youthened version of my granny. We helped the poor battered creature on with her gown, then grandfather comforted her with a tenderness which brought tears to my eyes. Only when she smiled again did he switch her off and put her coin in his pocket.

'My poor girls,' he said, so, so, sadly.

'I have a girly-doo, grandfather.' This said to cheery-be him.

'Thee doest, Mugg! A fem of your own! Oh, triple helpings of custard on you evermost! I am full of pleasy-do for thee, my boy. May she bring thee pleasuresomeness always. Not a Hittite, I hopes?'

'Kripes, nopes! She is a goddess of the English pantheon.'

He sat in his chair, chuckled, sobbed once and fell asleep. I marched downstairs to confront Stewie. He was in the library, dressed in a guards uniform, stroking a busby under his arm, while looking up and down the shelves, knocking books onto the floor with one finger. He looked enormous, wide, powerful, oddly handsome.

'HOWDEEDOODEE, CUZ!'

'You smashed the old man's hologramismics, you pigbogger!'

He pulled me to him, chuckling 'THOUGHT I MIGHT READ A BOOK. ANY SUGGESTIONS?'

His tried his busby on me and laughed when my head disappeared. In the English space villages, years later, the wearing of busbys was compulsory at all times. I hated them. This memory was why.

'YERH KNOW, MUGGY-BOY, THE OLD MAN DON'T LIKE HIS STEWIE MUCH. BUT YOU DOES, DOESN'T YER, BRO OF MINE? YEAH, YOU'S STEWIE'S ONLY FRIEND.'

I don't remember if it was my idea to do away with Stewie. If

twas I must have had it there in the library that night. It had to
be done. I feared he might kill my grandfather. Plusmost, I
feared he might somehow take the Lovely Anita from me.
Anita in Stewie's arms, ripping her, slapping her! Anita loving
big handsome Stewie, not pretty little Mugg! NOPES! IT
COULD NOT BE! But whose idea wast? – *Kill Stewie, kill
Stewie, yes, that's right* – *kill Stewie.* Into which Chaffinch's ear
did Beelzebub first whisper this invocation to sin? I knoweth
not, for next morning when grandfather and I were serving
Stewie his breakfast and a splash of milk spotted on Stewie's
new blue blazer and Stewie slapped grandfather so hard he fell
to the floor taking a tray of devilled kidneys with him and I
helped grandfather up and looked in his kindly old eyes, then it
was all planned, both our eyes knew what had to be done.
Stewie was as good as dead while our toothless old pooch
dodged kicks from Stewie as it pinched a kidney under the
table.

From this vantage it looketh quite horrible, does it not, that a
young man on the verge of life should be done away with by 2
Archbishops – one retired, one as yet uncrowned. But that is
wot we did, Chaff and Mugg, killer birds. Had not Stewie
wished to read a book? Whyso if not to improve himself, to be
touched by something that was not Stewie, an un-Stewie
atmosphere that would un-Stewie Stewie. He knew, perhaps,
the scale of his pigboggery and wanted a better Stewie to dwell
inside. That night when he hugged me in the library, played
with the busby, talked of brothersome friendship between us –
O Lord, how it haunts your humble servant! Is it because I
killed Stewie that, all these years, I have wandered in the Land
of Nod, like Cain. *Where is thy brother Stewie?* demands an
angry Jehovah. Only in the tears that fall as I write these
words. I am triple sorry. What more can I say?

Grandfather told Stewie that while looking in a chest in our
parish church we had found a suit of clothes belonging to King

Henry VIII. A touch moth-eaten, yea, but how magnificent Stewie would look in them, chattered we! A photo of King Stewie for the family album? But the outfit, pleasy-do, too heavy for decrepit grandfather and flyweight I to lift. Better if Stewie came to the church and tried them on. Big grin from Stewie. We fooled him good and proper.

Down the forcefield tunnel walked Stewie, making V-for-victory signs at the Hittites, us toddling along behind wearing the same fixed grin. At the church door Stewie stopped and looked back at the hall.

'MY, ISN'T IT A SPLENDID DAY!' said Stewie. 'THE HALL'S LOOKING GRAND. THE MAGNOLIAS SO FLOW-ERSOME. AND SEE THEM BEGONIAS N LUPINS UP AGAINST THE FORCEFIELD, RIGHT ROUND AND BACK AGAIN. I'LL BETYA NEVER IN ALL ITS HISTORY HAS IT LOOKED SO BOGGN HANDSOME AS TODAY.'

He took the camera from us and snapped a few shots. Then he closed his eyes tight.

'Wot you got your eyes closed for, Stewie?'

'I ALWAYS WANTS TO REMEMBER THE HALL LIKE WOT IT IS NOW. I'M KINDA TAKING A PIC OF IT IN MY HEAD, SEE, ONE BETTERER THAN ANY A CAMERA CAN SNAP, AND PUTTING IT AWAY IN MY MEMORY BANKS FOR LOOKIES AT ALWAYS.'

When Stewie stepped into the church I pulled the ancient door shut behind him. Grandfather grabbed the big key from its hook and locked him in. Then we ran up the forcefield tunnel to the house, our sandals in our hands, and turned the church's forcefield off. When we ran out across the herb garden and swung from the monkeypuzzle tree up onto the wall for a good view, the Hittites were already battering down the church door.

Grandfather showed no remorse, no guilt, no concern. How he must have hated Stewie. Some of the Hittites had phasers.

Stewie took one. PHIZZZZ! PHIZZZZZ! Disintegrating Hittites staggered out to die among the headstones. But chariots rattled down the Ipswich road – a road jam of chariots – as if to some popular function! Hittite kiddywinks ran along the roadside. Soon the church was surrounded by a caterwaulsome multitude. But, dimly within their yowl, I could hear the organ – yes, the organ! *Lord, Lead Us to Thy Kindly Light*. The phaser-zapping must have reactivated Rev Dickerson. He was at the stool, singing his head off in his old-fashioned way. From the interruptions in the music, I took it that the Hittites were slaughtering him repeatedly, but he kept popping back. Twas this, perhaps, that spooked them and they ran outside, spilling through the graves, over the walls and into the village pond. Stewie, meanwhile, had climbed the church tower and was zapping with his phaser's final weak blasts at the enemy below. FIZssZ! FISSsssz! Twas a moment of powerful emotions for me. The organ music swelled my heart. The church bell made halfcocked tolls as Stewie in his monogrammed smoking jacket nudged it while dodging arrows. Then an officer gave a loud order and 100 Hittite bowmen shot all at once. A sound like 100 cocktail sticks falling from their sausages onto a stony floor. Or perhaps just 99 cocktail sticks, or 87, or 63, for in the tower Stewie's screams for help stopped. Moments later, a great cry of triumph from the Hittites which awoke grandfather, who had been stretched out in snory sleep on the walltop for 20 minutes. I didn't see Stewie fall, not then, but often since, in the Land of Nod I have seen him, falling in everlasting space, spiny with arrows. Triple sorries again, O perfidious Stewie!

It was less than a week later that the Lovely Anita broke our unspoken rule and, our orgasms still shuddering the mirrors in our lovemaking room, said: 'I'm looking for a nice big empty mansion, luv, to hold the Peace Conference in. Might your Chaffinch Hall do?'

Double helpings of delight from this Mugg! Peace! Shaking hands with Hittites! No more forcefields! A new wide walkable world! And the Lovely Anita its Queen!

'Ooooo, yeps, luv! said I. 'Pleasy-do! Cum down to the hall and make peace, make love, my scrumptious goddess!'

No sooner were the words gobbed than did I feel fear of my grandfather for the only ever time. How to tell HIM, with his sackfuls of sermons on the subject of freedom filling 2 rooms at the hall, HIM the child of days before the despots, HIM with his odd political ideas of life without rulers, without governments, without Hittite Kings or the Lovely Anita . . . how to tell HIM that his little Mugg was our gorgeous despotic Queen's Number One Snogger . . . that I was bringing the Divine One and a pigbag of the hated Hittite kinglets into our private world to make a new order of the wider one.

Grandfather was standing outside in the rain with his mouth open when I told him. His mouth snapped shut. His head shook. He lookethed senile. Muttered. Rubbed his big freckles with a finger.

'Hobnobberizing with a despot, hm? Just like my poor bro Cod, is he not? Nopes! Dreaming it! Pleasy-do, Lord, not pretty little Mugg! BAH! URK!'

He then walked in the rain for hours, disputing vigorously with Heaven. I watched him from various windows, then fell asleep in the den. Drips from my grandfather's tragic face woke me up.

'I thought you were like me! I was happy in my decrepitude, was I not, to think that when at last I am taken, I will still in some way be here, as you, Mugg, my once best-beloved boy. Bogg thee! BOGG THEE! YOU'RE NOT LIKE ME AT ALL!'

'No, grandfather. I am not like you at all!' spoke Mugg the boy, proudly. 'Speaky-do not to me your outdated twaddle-someness of a world without rulers and ruled! Heyup, I tell thee, the Lovely Anita is our rightful Queen. Her beauty and wisdom are God-given! He guideth her! He both made her and chose her to rule over us, didn't he not though!'

The lattersome bit there, of course, is quite true. God chooses our rulers for us, which is why democracy is such a pointless exercise – the Lord hath rigged every election, hath he not indeedy! He chose His daughter Anita to be Queen of England before the Universe was made, also His servant Mugg to one day rise up and be Archbishop of Bunnyland and inspire rabbits with Christian faith. It is all part of His vast incomprehensible plan, which I have down the years come to believe – though denounced in the Galactic Synod for this as a heretic too long in the company of rabbits – is a plan now incomprehensible even to God Himself, hence the multiplying horrorifications and confusifications of these modern times. But tis easy to forget, is it not, that in the infinite dimensional layers of life all conceivable things come to pass, and as God studies these layers what he watches for are the *inconceivable* things, for only the addition of those may bring His Holy Plan back on course to perfection. Moreso, the Plan is God, God is the Plan – when He grasps it clearly again, He will be Himself once more, all-powerful, all-loving, and evil will be banished from the lives of all His creatures. End of sermon, say I . . . then that heartwarming murmursome squeak that is the response of a Bunny congregation, which I shalt never hear again.

Can I add that, in the dimension of my story, God chose as part of his original plan for there to be an English Empire ruled and administered first by chinless wonders and now by a monstrous regiment of stout tweedy women. A thought somewhere, an idea reached for by some cleverclogger, will change all this. One day, I am sure, am I not, I am, yes, Lord, I am, Paradise will reign once more. Chee! The entire hymnbook singeth within me! LALA-LALA-LA-LA-LAAAA-FIDDLY-DOOOOOO-BOBBLY-BAA-AA-BUM-BUM-POM-POMMMMM!!!!!!!

But, hoots, wasn't I a Jilks when I said to grandfather that I was not like him!!!! He not only dwells within me – sometimes I feeleth, when approaching a semblance of his saintly calm at the mid-point between 2 of my habitual bad tempers, that I *am* him. Mugg is Chaff! Chaff is the best part of this old grumbly-poo! Sorry-bees, grandaddykins of mine, but twas only a foolheaded boy speaking that day, not best-beloved Mugg! – I am myself now, and I know that everything thou ever sayethed was true, cept regarding political matters.

Though he hated the idea of having Hittite kinglets in Chaffinch Hall, grandfather was thrillified to see the hall spikspan again. We reactivated all our old servants and slaves. Then a boxful of slave coins was telezoomed in from Anita's office. – We turned on the boggn lot and met with old hologramismic m'luds from the '50s, innocent of the existence of Hittites, but bred under the despots they were hard workers and knew the lyrics to Hieronymus Gosh's forbidden songs, the ones banned under Connie & Pam, which I ordered them to sing while polishing.

The ballroom's lights all shone upon the busyness, as the slaves brought the pieces of our old banqueting table from the barns and clipped it together . . . and together . . . and together! They walked on it in their socks to polish it, like ice-skaters having a warm dream, and filled the air with so much polish that when I blew my snout that night the snot was brilliant yellow! Anita herself, as lovely as ever in casual jeans and bikini top, came to supervise the installation of a special system to allow Hittite leaders from faraway fiefdoms to appear phantasmagorically, and even eat the food from our table, though they remained in China or Peru or wherever. Boggn impressive that, was it not!

I introduced Anita to grandfather. He said a glum howdee-doodee and wouldn't bow, so she looked daggers at him with a chop-off-his-head lipcurl. But he suddenly chuckled like a monkey and kissed her hand.

'Thou art the most lovely woman I hast ever seen, m'dear.'

She turned her head to the Magri portrait of granny Scampi.

'Your late wife, Archbishop?'

'Indeedy.'

'A bonny girl.'

'The jewel of her time was my Scampi. But looking at thee I think for the 1st time that we must, must we not, be living in betterer, lovelier times.'

The old roué won one of Anita's aren't-I-wonderful grins for that. During the hour that she was there grandfather stood in the same spot, letching at her cleavage, winking at me, and humming *To be a Pilgrim* like a caddish curate. When leaving to telezoom, passing him without looking at him, Anita scratched grandfather's grey-stubbly chin with her long ruby nails. His whole being was besotted by her spell, as was the being of everyone she ever met, mine more than any! But Anita's heart, which loved this Mugg truly as no other has ever loved him, could turneth black whenever she willed it, as she was soon to prove.

On the morning of the Peace Conference I jumped out of bed before dawn with a Christmas feeling. Down in the ballroom Hodgekins was walking fussily around the banqueting table, making minuscule adjustments to the cutlery.

'Master Mugg, it is SO wonderful to be alive again and see the hall with its flags out!'

Then he went and stood in a corner and sobbed with joy.

Hittites would not use aeroplanes, but adored balloons. The first was on the horizon, over Bury St Edmunds, at first light.

'Should I turn the forcefield off yet?'

'Better had,' said grandfather.

I did so, aware that the last time Chaffinch Hall was without a forcefield was the day on which my parents were killed. And now, here were we, welcoming their murderers!

Anita's walrus-tached Chiefs of Staff clipped the tiled floor as they marched out of the telezoom booths. What an air of expectation! Grandfather, smart in his old Archbishop's regalia, making crosses continually, took them into the ballroom to await the Hittites. Through the newly cleaned windows the huge balloons, all decorated with mythological motifs, landed silently on the lawns, and the great curly beardies clambered out of the baskets with most of their dignity intact.

Hodgekins had enjoyed announcing the names of the Dukes and Earls attending our functions in bygone years, but found himself in a tizzy at the tongue-twisting prospect of announcing today's Hittite personages. He had, twas soon discovered, imbibed of port, brandy and homemade gin to give him courage.

First in was, God help us, Pu-sarrumas Pitaggatallis of Hrattarttaskussara.

'Erm, PUSSY SAM PIGTAILS OF . . . where was it again?'

'Hrattarttaskussara!' said Pu-sarrumas Pitaggatallis of Hrattarttaskussara. 'HRATT-ARTTA-SKUSS-ARA!'

'RAT'S ARSE, SKUSSY HARBOUR. No such place, mister – yer having me on, issnt yer not?'

The next to whisper his name to Hodgekins was the splendidly bearded King Huppililiumas Muwapallis, announced as HIPPYPOTAMUS MOOPWAPS. Then came the very important Allubwamnas Hattustalis, announced as ALVIN BANANAS HATSTAND. And so it went on, the Hittites becoming increasingly miffed and the Peace Conference already half-ruined. Hodgekins, meanwhileydoos, had given up the tongue-twisters and simply translated each Hittite notable's name-whisper as: 'BOGGN HITTITE! And who are you, sir? BOGGN HITTITE! And might you be a boggn Hittite, sir? BOGGN HITTITE! BOGGN HITTITE! BOGGN HITTITE!'

The Hittite delegation were finger-twirling their cutlery, in the sort of ill-mood which caused them to destroy Babylon, when I switched Hodgekins off and took over the announcing myself. Alas, I wasn't much better, wasn't I not, no – a novice at this butlerish art, I found myself imitating his style!

The great moment, of course, which had everyone present hot with the anticipation of it, was the arrival of the Lovely Anita. WHAT WOULD SHE BE WEARING???? The Hittites preened their beards. Our Chiefs, in love with her to a man, watched the doorway with their jealous baggy eyes.

'I have 365 concubines, you know,' I overheard a Hittite tell our P.M. in a strange Lancashire brogue, not unlike Anita's but wi'out the purr. 'All dwarves. Eeeee, I like dwarves. Cheer yer up no end, dwarves do, eeeeee. I could send you a couple to try if yer like. Eeeeeeeee.'

Suddenly, there she was, sweeping in to a room that gasped. Her hair was tied up in Hittite style, a golden snake wound in its tresses. She wore a see-through low-cut ballgown of spray-on plastic that shimmered gold in one moment, vermilion the next, and the next didn't seem to be there at all. Sitting on a gauntlet on her arm was an eaglebird who she suddenly sent aloft with a whistle. It made straight for a bust of Pitt the Elder and perched there watching Anita's every move. In my days as Archbishop never once did I manage such an entrance!

'Well, lads, how yer diddlin?' said she, and passed among them, complimenting their beards, asking those present only in phantasmagoric form how was the weather wherever they actually were. Putting-at-ease-chitchat, expertly dispensed!

Then the members of the Hittite *Pankus*, as they called their ruling council of kinglets, started an infernal round of windy speeches stinking of Biblical portentitude, full of references to their winged gods, goats, and the health-inducing effects of lard, a subject upon which every Hittite was a stonking bore.

Anita dispatched grandfather to find her a copy of Gibbon's *Autobiography* from the library. Then put her arms around the much-admired beautiful youth sitting beside her – myself –

and commenced snogging me with a tongue like a plucked mongoose.

Anita coming out of snog, to Hittite: 'Get on wi 'yer prattle, lad. Anita's listening.' Then more snog, with one eye on that too-too calm eaglebird.

Suddenly she scooped me up and we were halfway out of the room before she turned on her feet and addressed our peace-loving guests: 'Only be a minute, darling luvs. Simply must strip off, have some proper mucky slapntickle. Eeeee, you know how you get sometimes! Ta-ta for now!'

The current speechifyer stayed speechlessly astonished on his curly-slippered feet, but the next-to-go stood up early and dropt his speech page by page on the vol-au-vents. This Hittite knew a snub when one snubbethed his way! As the last page dropt (all about lard, one suspecteth) Anita whistled to her eaglebird, I thought to follow – but as the great doors opened for us my lover yanked me outside and held me under her arms as the eaglebird landed on the control-stick poking from Anita's carefully installed special installation. It pecked a green button with an open beak and took off again. But before it reached the doorway over our heads it fizzed, squawked and phutttt, gone! – vaporized in mid-air! When my eyes focused beyond its disappearance I saw that the Hittites' beards were aflame. They were gagging for breath – and then phutttt-phutttt-phutttttt-PHUT!!!!! Gone! The vaporizing ray zipped along the lines to where sat those only phantasmagorically present and zapped them into nothingness. In only seconds the entire Hittite ruling council was turned to an air less substantial than the air in the balloons which sailed them towards the Lovely Anita's trap. Then I noticed that one Hittite was left. He smiled at Anita and waved his lion's-tail swagger-stick. Some sort of double-cross deal then, tween Anita and this Hittite, guessed I. Huh! When he turned off his phantasmagoric tie-in and vanished from us back to his fiefdom with a smug toodley-bye-byes, the ballroom was empty, all the lovely food frazzled black in the silver boats, dishes, tureens – Anita's chiefs of staff behind curtains, under the table, their pants plopped.

How Anita laughed. So very lovely as she hammered her knees in glee. I was furious! Disgusted! How I hated her! But when she pulled the gold snake out of her nightblack hair and shook the Hittite style down onto her shoulders, I was gripped with an oversexed passion whose power amazed me. I kissed her smile, licked her teeth, sucked her lobes. She replied with fingernails stuck deep into my buttocks, 'til one broke.

'Ooo!'

Then grandfather was beside us with Gibbon's *Autobiography* and an austere bewilderment at the lack of Hittites.

As Anita watched us, the old and young Chaffinch, untie the empty house-high balloons – a wondrous sight as they arose to float to nowhere – she said: 'Families, that's wot we need, luvs. Proper families again! Yeps! Grandads and aunts, plentysome sisters and big lazy brothers. That's wot's missing! That's whattle stop our tarts jumping the forcefield and running off with boggn Hittite gigolos! FAMILIES, by gum, aye!'

On the steps of Chaffinch Hall she had the idea to bring the institution of the family back from the dead. This ended our relationship, for reasons I shall soon speaky-do upon. Though she did, I knoweth it, weep into her pillow over me every night for the rest of her life, we never met after this day. 100 years ago, almost to the day, and I have not, fool Mugg, committed hoohar-wiggly with any but Anita since, and now never again. Ho-hummydoos!

My grandfather died a few weeks after the so-called Peace Conference. We were sitting on the dewy daisied grass among the magnolias, going natter. He said: 'Look at all the daisies, Mugg! Thinky-do I hast never seen so many. Were we idiots enough to make a chain of them, we couldst reach Heaven, couldst we not indeed. Chee-he!'

Then something happened in his eyes and though he made no pained movement, no slump or raspsome deathrattle – he sat exactly as before, daisy gazing – I knew he had just died. Suddenly, the gardens were full of butterflies. But they were gone when I stopped my howling. With the yet-again reactivated Hodgekins's help I took grandfather down to the church in a wheelbarrow and bungethed him under the crusaders into the family vault with Granny Scampi, his long-dead bros, his parents, his Hittite-slain children and nieces – a bony aviary of conked-out Chaffinches going back to dot. And Stewie, too, he was there – is there! Only I am not.

Amen.

Hittites: Four
The Chaffinch Morning Chorus

This past week I hast been distracted, have I not, from my *22nd Century Blues* – which is such a wheezy-do to compose, with my moggs purring at my feet and my past zinging from the back of my head through my typing finger – in order to perform the unhappy duty of preaching gospel to a gaggle of shite creatures. These lost souls having been shipwrecked on our Cats-by-Nowhere, were they not, by a deity who had already taken the precaution to deposit an Archbishop here to bring any such wayfarers to enlightenment.

One's relationship with the niffy articles is confused in that one knows not if some long-gone plop of one's own shite went to make the boggers up. I gave them my best converting-the-heathen voice and a line of Archbishy patter which has been known to shine a 'road to Damascus' light in the eyes of the hardest rabbit. But all they did was fling mire at my hat and make atheistic gestures with the turd-shaped turd tween their legs that is their parody of the noble wanger. Thus and so, 7 complete outfits of regalia have been ruined by shite and the replicator, pigsick of making me yet another and another, is protesting by issuing me with larger and larger crooks.

Once, in a hymnodic voice grown into a reedy soprano with my Methuselah-ish age – bog it, I am 117! – I enticed them out of their huts in the pinkish dawn.

The Chaffinch Morning Chorus

> *There's no discouragement*
> *will make him once relent*
> *his first avowed intent*
> *To be a Pilgrim . . .*

They formed a circle and joined in. In glee I handed around
hymn books – ruined immediately by their shitey fingerprints!
– and for a few glorious moments I thought I had them! Oh,
how nicely they sang! Deep melodious voices. One without a
hymn book went *bum-bum-bum-boom-bum-mmmmm-mmm*, a
crooning bass-baritone which would have won the annual
Bunnyland Choir Competition for any Bunny Choir with
him in't. But then the raspberries began. Ppppp-bbbb-
pppppp! Just a few to start with. Then boggn punnets worth!

> *Then fancies flee away*
> *I'll fear not . . . pppppp-bbbbb-ppppp!!! . . . what men say*
> *I'll . . . ppbbb-bbbb-pppp!!! . . . labour night and . . . pppb! . . . day*
> *To be a . . . PPPP-BPBPBPBP!!!!!!!!!! . . . pilgrim!*

Of course, my Archbishop's hat went, allowing the godless
shites to give my bald pate a hairdo of shite, and of course
another set of regalia was ruined, its motif of white Bunnies
linking hands around its skirt shited shite brown. I returned
home more weepy-sad than bark-angry. When soldier-boy tick-
tock asked yet again if he could clear out the shites with his
flame-thrower I relented. Sobeit! SERVES THE BOGGN
SHITES RIGHT!

I sankethed into despair, did I not, I did, yes, despair, and
abandoned the writing of this booky-doos – wot point in
recording such a wasted life! A crisis in faith hit me, worse
than any since I discovered half the Galactic Synod were Devil
worshippers – gagged virgins in every closet, were there not!
But then Mathis told me that, at its end, one of the shites had

crossed itself! Lordy! Hallelujah! Praise be to Him on high! Something I saithed, I know not wot, had gotten through to the creature in the darkness of its shiteitude! Now that Christian gentleman is cleansed of shiteyness, smelling of roses, walking in the Heavenly Holy Land at the side of Jesus!✶

One of the more awesome practical jokes played on Bunny-land is the one where everyone on a bullet train sneaks off, engineers too, leaving some snoozing rabbit to awake alone on a train speeding across the infinity that is Bunnyland – a train that will never stop, charging through stations, whooshing across the carrot-sprouting countryside. When Mopsy was President he tried his best to put a stop to this practice, but verily the Buns get such a kick out of doing it, tis no way ever to stoppit! I sometimes dream, know thee, and did during a nap just now, that I am on one of those trains, the unhappy victim, sipping tea in the buffet car, searching the empty seats for newsrags I haven't read yet, nowt to look forward to and no end of the line. Were this a sermon I'd turn all vicarish at this point with a nutty religious tie-in, something to the effect of every act having consequences which go on forever. But twill be no more sermon-spouting from this old bird – triple nopes with knobs on! I do wonder, though, do I not, I do, if I am writing this booky-do to continue my grandfather's work or just to explain the meaning of this Bunny-train conundrum to

---

✶ Can anyone fairly say that I was wrong to lie to His Grace about the shite's conversion? And yet, did it not give him a false view of life at a time when he should have been facing truth in all its bleakness? These were, after all, his final days. He should have been preparing to meet his maker with no lies, no misapprehensions around him. BUT WOT MAKER, EHWOT! Oooops, my atheistic streak is showing! Yes, should I also have told him that, although surrounded by sermons, cathedrals and hymn-singing for 50 years, there is yet a large part of J. W. Mathis who thinks the whole biz to be so much tosh! What possible difference can it make if a rabbit says his prayers to Jesus or swings his hips with Elvis! Never discussed this, but I think the Archbishop had his streak also, hence his refrain of having lived a wasted life.

myself. Does Bunny die on the train while it keeps on going on forever? Does God rescue Bunny? Why does this pottyfalloo story matter to me? It does, though, does it not, yea, and very much.

Ho-hum! Back to the boy Mugg, sitting always in the back of my head, like a lone rabbit in a bullet train – chee-he! – and no one to love his pretty face but silly-poo old me.

After grandfather's death in the late summer of 2099, and Anita gone Mugg-less, busy with her scheme to rejuvenate the family, I was entirely lonesomedone, poking my dearie-be face into empty room after lonely room in the vastness of Chaffinch Hall – yes, again like that boggn rabbit wandering the corridors of that blasted train! On my ownie-o – poor little tweeter! I cannot quite remember how I spent my days. Eager for any company at all, I did telezoom to visit my old school-chums, but they were in the army, every one, and most of them dead in the pitched battles we'd been having with the Hittites in Belgium of late. Black crêpe over the mantels of many a stately home.

'Oh, were you Gervase's best little friend? Everyone loved him, didn't they? In the old world he could have been anything!' said Lady Chortlesome-Hardy.

I zoomethed out of their griefs, pronto!

Why not try one of the Perfect Family Hologramismics that Anita was sending out? She was eager to convince doubters wot a splendiferous institution the family was! Urk! I found myself sitting below the salt at a small dining table in a room decorated in the most abysmal taste, watching a perfect family eat ham in total silence, all looking aggrieved, and darting vexed glances at t'others. When I was spoken to at all I was addressed as 'Trevor' – part of the programme, thinky-do: all players were the stand-in for Trevor – and I had never felt so unloved, blacksheepish, Trevorized, not ever. When my pa-terfamilias asked me what was wrong with me, why wasn't I in the army, I kicked him under the table and was ordered to my room. The hologramismic me didn't have one, or I'd be there yet! I gather that generally this hologramismic encomium to the family wasn't much of a success.

In the end, desperate for natter, I went down to the forcefield and talked through the fizz to the friendlier Hittites. They told me of the fleshpots of Hattusas in 1500 BC, how they were winning the war against the moderns, how I should smear my buttock crack with lard to prevent rashes there, and how more than anything in this life they wanted to have sex with the Lovely Anita. I said I already had, lots of times. I told them about the lovegame we used to play where we were in a hologramismic desert and I was St Hilarion and Anita had to tempt me with her chiffon-draped body, like the dusky trollops Hilarion is depicted resisting. Unlike the saint I always intended to succumb. The Hittites didn't believe a word, nopes, but liked to hear a pretty boy talk dirty.

For New Year's Eve 2099 I planned to turn on all the lights, activate every coin I had, filling the house with servants, slaves, even our 623 chimneysweeps (*Harrods* gave one away free with every million poundlets spent on household goods, this back in the '70s – Mumsy must've spent 623 millionsworth during the life of the offer!) – plus a properly sober Hodgekins, and the gigglesome regiment of tweenies (whom I planned, wicked boy, to deflower – some anyhowdoos!) . . . thereby having a good old-fashioned servants' ball, with lots of shouting and African music and whoopee.

But on the evening of the 30th our darling leaderette Anita came on the tellyscreen, interrupting my fave-rave Hittite tellyshow, to announce to the nation that she was sending everyone their very own personalized swelligant elegant 'New Year's Eve Interactive Hologramismic Party'. Participation in this was compulsory and non-attenders would have their forcefields cut off, addresses to be supplied to Hittite HQ.

The programme was designed to evaluate our 'family compatibility profile' – in plainspeak it would help the Government's
Central Computer pick our perfect family for us. Info gleaned
from the N.Y.E.I.H.P. would be immediately processed, cooed
Anita, never lovelier, notification taking place within hours,
and one's new family would be in one's lap tootysuitey.

'Darling luvs! – isn't it too-too exciting! Happiness is only
hours off, given to you by your Lovely Anita, who loves you as
much as you loves her back! Eeeeeee, we'll all have families
again! No need to frat with Hittites no more, mind. Yer'll have
daddys, mammys, sisses and bros, uncles and sainted aunts!
Eeee, wot a good idea I had, didn't I though! Toodleybyedar,
chickens! Toodleybyedar!'

But twas no joy for me in this broadcast. Prominent in the
background of it was a handsome little crowd in orange Civil
Defence jackets who it seemethed, did it not, were actors put
there to represent Anita's imminent new family. They gathered
around her at the end for the toodleybyedar. By gum, Anita
would attend her copy of the party too, be evaluated by the
computer too, given her family too, just like the rest of us. Wot,
I gulped, if she became my allotted mumsy? The ages were
right. URK! Wot of Saint Hilarion and the dusky temptress
then, by jingo? Bunnyhoo!

Nervous of the party, I activated Hodgekins and took him
along for company. At least I'd have a familiar face to talk to.
But coming as a 'friend', not a butler – and butlers can be
friends, say I* – he turned up wearing his off-duty casual
getup: a pair of scuffed hush puppies, loud tartan trews, a
straw boater with the top punched out, a flowery shirt right out
of a Connie & Pam catalogue, and a bookmaker's checked
jacket, the pockets bulging with gin bottles to lace the punch
with.

* Thank you, Your Grace.

'Let's party, ehwot, young master! And may I be the first to say . . . Happy New Century!'

'Happy New Century, Hodgekins.' (I'd have called him by his Christian name, but I never knew it!)

The New Year's Eve Interactive Hologramismic Party was plugged into the ballroom's plate. So we just walkethed in, and there we were! I grinned immediately. The whole thing was so very too-too Anita! All the girls were wearing long black Anita wigs. Every chap wore an I LOVE ANITA badge, with an Anita winking lasciviously on't. Everyone wore sexy little eyemasks. A flunky came with a selection on a salver. I picked a mouse, Hodgekins a tiger.

'Must mingle,' said my companion, and traipsed off to enjoy himself with his fellow hologramismics.

I immediately fell into conversation with a certain Captain Fitzroy Crawfoot, on leave from the Hittite wars – showed me his wound – had an estate in the Lake District, very interested in sheep, crashing bore! Said snarg a lot, missed his men, especially the dead ones. He had that demented smugness which I hath seen elsewhere only on the battalions of Elvis impersonators in the Annual Elvis Lookalike Contest I have judged in Bunnyopolis. Was this graduate in numbskullery auditioning for the part of Mugg-bro, wondered I? Or rather, him being a hologramismic character existing exclusively in this homogramismic milieu, were there out there 100 Fitzroy Crawfoot-types, and was the all-seeing hologramismic eye testing us both for compatibility, perhaps then to plonk a whole boggn dynasty of the dweeblers onto this innocent Chaffinch?

'BOGG OFF, YER JILKS!' said I, and punched him in the bellyparts twice. Let there be no mistake, computer! None of him, ilk, kin, or anything-like, pleasy-do!

I spent the last hour of the 21st Century sitting on a comfy leopardskin sofa with a dozen fleshy aunts, all in pussycat eyemasks. I couldn't resist pinching their thighs.

'MUGGERIDGE! DON'T DO THAT!' they all said together.

I rather liked them at first. But they talked too much about how to make jam and then after weeing-on about how dishy the young Hittite King Tudhaliyas was in his leather romper-suit, they produced tape-measures and started measuring me for one. I revolted, bolted for the terrace. It was there that I bumped into Flossie Fordyce and my life was changed forever.

She was walking tipsily on the wall, between one statue and the next, wearing no eye-mask, no shoes. Yikes! She was falling! I dashed forward! But my catching arms stayed empty. She fell instead safely into the statue's arms – her intention all along, I realized – and gave him the most wonderful kiss – one of those head back, kiss-me-again sighing-inside-the-kiss Anita-style kisses. Having gone half-way over the wall in my rescue dash, I balanced on one jittersome leg, gazing awestricken up at her kissing. I confess I was highly aroused, more than ever in my life before or since, touched and stirred. My flesh quaked with I-did-not-know-wot! Love? Urk!

'GO AWAY, MR MOUSE!'

I removethed my eye-mask. Trembling voice: 'I'm not a mouse. I'm a Chaffinch.'

'Go away! I am kissing the statues. So cold and emotionless their lips are! I suppose no one else kisses them?'

'I hath never seen no one with the compassion to do so.'

She jumped down onto the checkerboard tiles beside me. Her dress – one of those rubber Anita numbers – squeaked like a mouse bigger than I. Silence for a minute, an instant, while we looked at each other. Then the hooters went off!

WHOOAAAAAAOOOO!!!
WHOOAAAAAAOOOO!!!

It was the new century – yea, the one now pegging out, the 22nd since the manger . . . its time just begun that moment. I stepped forward and kissed Flossie with all the kissy-kissy-skill I had learned in Anita's bed. I was no boggn statue! My fingers twanged her dress as the kiss went on. Revellers were around us, full of hoo and ho.

'HAPPY NEW CENTURY! HAPPY NEW CENTURY! WHEEEEEE!'

All the passionate feelings of my 17 years, the sorrows and loves and hopes and dreams were alive together for the 1st and only time, as the hologramismics slurred around Flossie and Mugg: *May old acquaintance be forgot, and never brought to mind . . . may old acquaintance be forgot for the sake of Auld Langs Syne . . .*

'Wot's yer name?'

'I'm Lord Muggeridge Chaffinch of Chaffinch. Mugg for short. Yours?'

'Flossie. Flossie Fordyce. My family had an estate in Wiltshire, but the Hittites got in. I live with my aunt now in . . .'

I kissed her talking mouth. Lordy, I was completely taken in by the reality of it all! I picked a blanket off a wicker chair.

'Lookie-do, I know we've just met, but could we, I mean, hoots . . . let's go down to the orchard.'

'I gripped the blanket everso tightly. She knew what I meant.

'Okay-doos, Mugg! Yerh on!' And she tore off her Anita wig, shaking free a bob of ash-blonde hair.

'Wow!' said I.

'Not exactly Anita, though, am I?'

'Better, pleasy-do, better!' I meant it.

'Boggn liar!' said she and took my offered hand as I cried, never happier: 'Afterwards we will dance together under the stars!'

We ran down the cracked terrace steps and hurried along a line of leafless magnolias towards the orchard, laughing at ourselves, at the squeak of her dress, at the Anita wig left hanging in the hand of that cold-lipped statue. I pulled slightly ahead, eyes smiling brightly up at the century's first starry nighttime, when Flossie's laughter stopped, the squeaky dress went silent. When I turned around, tumbling over a croquet hoop, she wasn't there. Gone! Just snowflakes falling where she'd been.

BOGGN JILKS! Of course she was gone! She wasn't real, just a hologramismic character cooked up by Anita to break my heart! An amalgam maybees of the most vibrant looks, thoughts, gestures, souls of 1000 wonderful girls, Anita included. She couldn't go beyond the party's brightness any more than a character could pop out of a book! In those few minutes I had experienced the most intense feelings of my life, based on something wholly insubstantial. Cruel, cruel God to do this to little Mugg! I lay on my back and sobbed, but only 6 or 10 sobsworth actually left me as the snowflakes cooled tiny patches on my face gone hot from Flossie's kisses. Hologramismic or not, I knew it then as I know it now, Flossie was my life. I wanted her love for me restored to any kind of reality – that love which I saw clearly born on her face, as she saw my love for her born on mine. Incredible event! Worth living for, yea, I say, do I not, though it ruined my life.

Oh, my darling Flossie! FLOSSIE! I raced back to the party, now simmered-down to soft-musicy exhaustion, just a few fat uncles flicking cheese dip at each other, aunts flaked out, silly-ass bro-candidates dancing very slowly with sis-candidates, bum-groping each other with fingers half-forgotten inside each other's party clobber. Flossie was nowhere. Couldn't find her. Nowhere. A sloshed Captain Crawfoot saluted me, friendly as could be, and I kicked him a dancer's kick in his undone flies. Before he hit the floor the music slowed to a drone, the party image flashed on and off. – Cold empty realworld ballroom . . . then party flashing back for a nanosecond . . . off again, returning me to the dimness of my old life . . . then flashing back came gaudy party colours

. . . then off leaving me buried in Chaffinch Hall, a mausoleum dull with death . . . then fizzing on again putting me back in Flossie's celebratory pixilated hologramismic Universe!

FLOSSIE! FLOSSIE! The aunts woke up and coooweeed me a byesybye. A clap in the eyes, a flash at the feet and . . . it was over! Over, just like each night's last Hittite game show, and me standing bereft in a crepuscular ballroom, alone cept for a bilious Hodgekins who sat blinking in the middle of the floor.

I tried to get the hologramismic to repeat. But it would not. It was rigged as a once-only.* Flossie was lost to me. Hodgekins advised me to accept the fact, saying no woman was worth a man's tears. Sorry-bees for I, twas not in my nit's nature to follow his advice. As I shall speaky-do upon soon, this Mugg squanderated all his youthysomeness looking for the imagin-

---

* Perhaps it was. But in 2120-something, when I was working as a solicitor's clerk on Planet Parker, Haves, Haves, Parker, Parker, Haves & Parker, a planet devoted entirely to legal representation and owned exclusively by the one aforementioned firm, who'd covered its every inch in office-space, I saw pinned to the notice board a flyer advertising an old-fashioned New Year's Eve OOP party – with full-bodied hologramismics, it said . . . UNWIND! FORGET YOUR CLIENTS! TAKE A DIP IN THE LOVELY ANITA ERA! That's for me, I said, and jiffied a few fellow clerks to go along to make a proper night of it. Well now, I am 99.99999999% sure it was a copy of the same party as the one poor Mugg describes. Very swish do, it was! All the ladies wore Anita wigs, the chaps smart orange uniforms. The blithering talk about Hittites I found very droll, but best fun was getting the aunts tipsy and having a wild snog with them in one big aunty heap. After the hooters went off I fought duels with 3 uncles over my snogging activities, killing 2 outright. (They were only hologramismics, of course – no crime in that!) Jolly good fun all around was that party, ehwot! Late on, taking the air on the terrace, not Chaffinch Hall's, of course, but as good as, I spoke for a while to a sweetie in a kitten eye-mask. If this wasn't Flossie Fordyce herself, it was her equivalent. I don't remember if I ever spoke to the Archbishop about this at some other Bunnyhopping New Year's Eve Do when one tends to review past New Year's Eve Dos. I think perhaps not. His pathetic tale above, meanwhile, is quite new to me. In all our Bunnyfilled years together did Mugg ever once mention Flossie Fordyce? No, dimmee – not once! Bless him, I wonder why not, hm?

ary girl he met that New Year's Eve in his life's best and most terrible moments. He was old before he gave up the quest, then resigning his life to one of religious nuttery, bish-boshing hatsful of vicarish twaddle when all he ever wanted was to lie in the arms of Flossie Fordyce and be happy.

Strange, but on Bunnyland I met with countless Flossies. Tis a popular Bunny name. Every time I met one I'd hook her ears down with my crook and plant kisses on the soft furry tips.

'I loved a Flossie once!' I'd say.

'Did you DO IT, eh? DO IT! With your parts! PARTS! Cor! CORRRRRRRR! BUNNYHOO!'

'No, Flossie. We never did.'

When, on New Year's Day 2100, a rather strained Lovely Anitakins appeared on the tellyscreen to introduce her new computer-appointed family – dressed Royally, but the men still looking like the burglars they were and her unlovely sisters had dipso-druggy-shopaholic written all over them, and so boggn fat! – I guessed I was in for a shock with my own lot. When a printout coughed out of the tellyscreen's letterbox, all I had was a list of oddbod names to worry over.

NEW FAMILY 878,201
– CHAFFINCH:

Sir James Fanshaw, *Daddykins*
Lady Tracy MacNaughtie, *Mumsy*
General Sir Humbert Windbraker, *Bro*
Scobie Horse, *Bro*
Lt. Satsuma Treeves, *Sis*
Alfred Bingley F.R.S.A., *Bro*
Lord Muggeridge Chaffinch, *Bro*
Dagon Hattusilis, *Uncle*

REPORT TO:-
CHAFFINCH HALL, SUFFOLK.

Indeedy-bees, I did give this the twice-over, thrice-over and once more for luck. I had a Scottish mother! Wot worse impediment could a young Englishman have!?! And an uncle with a Hittite name, for cryingoutloud! Couldn't be 'one of them', could he? Nopes! He must be a businessman who, trading with the Hittites, adopted a Hittite name for purposes of biz. A rich uncle? Yeps, the list was promising, was it not! My new sister Satsuma sounded a darling squirrel. And by-gummy, a general in the list! We'd had so many generals in the family – their cheerful deaths in battle were everywhere on the walls – another, continuing the tradition, was a good start for this neo-Chaffinch family. Could be, I thought, as I walked around the Hall, checking for Hittite come-ins as I did every midnight, that I may possy-possy-possibuley have done triple-spanky-doos out of Anita's iffy scheme.

But quadruple-nowt happened for several weeks. On the tellyscreen I watched interviews with newfangled family members, all loving it, praising Anita, kissing their aunties. Everyone else had their family, were settling down to the miseries of family life! Where in p'boggn pleek was mine? Worse: from mid-January there was only Hittite broadcasts, meaning they'd got into our tellyviddy station again, so nixi news cept the same old Hittite lies! I came to think that I was not getting a family after all. Poor Mugg. Cos obviously, the no-show meant that none of those on the list wanted to play happy families! BOGG THEM! But I was surprised to find myself all churnethed-up inside with a sorry-be rejected feeling. Also, I was ill-tempered with jealousy for those lucky-duckies who had been picked for Anita's Royal set.

March. Snowdrops, crocuses filling the views from the tall windows. I was spending my evenings in one of Stewie's long furry coats, sitting on the terrace, reliving my brief love affair with Flossie Fordyce. One frosty night, nose dropping off, I wandered back into the den, stoked up the fire and, still in the coat, fell asleep in the middle of another epic about the Hittite conquest of Babylon. I woke up sodden with sweat, to the sound of grandfather's immortal pooch barking. – World-shaking WOOFS, as if from a mile long dog!

I hurried out into the hallway. Luggage everywhere! Hatboxes! Golfclubs! (Golf! Another family passion! – not me though, yuks!) One more woof, rattling the suits of armour everywhere on every landing for 10 floors, as if the knights were quaking before an approaching dragon.

I ran into the breakfast room. My family! Hodgekins serving. Ooops – and there was the dragon! Mumsy! The new Lady Tracy Chaffinch was pushing 90, 6 feet tall, 7 feet wide, wrinkled like a punishment from God. She was throwing titbits to the dog, but it wasn't eating.

'MUGG! Is this your dog?' (Thanky-bees to God! – no Scottish brogue! Hoity-toity English to the bone!)

'Erm, yeps, Mumsy, think so.'

'Then kindly get rid of it! I've asked this Hodgekins fellow but he says he can't find it! LOOKEE, HODGEKINS! THERE! LOOKIE! IT'S IN THE MIDDLE OF THE ROOM, MAN!'

'I can't quite seem to locate it, madam.'

'THERE! THERE! You've let this butler turn to drink, Mugg! He can't find the dog among all the other things he's seeing. Watch him, he'll swat a beetle on the tablecloth, any minute! HAH! Told you! The management of servants, Muggeridge, is an art form which you have yet to master!'

'Triple sorries, Mumsy. This is an area in which I hopeth to improve manifoldly under thy expert guidance.'

'The boy talks like a bishop! MUGG! Don't talk like a bishop!'

'No, Mumsy. I shalt not, nopes, verily, never again.'

Dimmee, though she looked like an owl who'd eaten an elephant, her vexed gaze shot to my heart. I fell down and hugged her great taffeta draped knees.

'Oh, Mumsy, Mumsy, Mumsy,' drivelled I.

'Euogh, Scobie – get him off me! Wot's he doing! GET HIM OFF!'

But as Scobie lifted me away, I caught her tear-filled eyes. Yes! A mother's love! Chee! URK!

I now found myself in a hand-shaking, back-slapping huddle of my siblings. Huge tawny-skinned Scobie, who I instantly recognized as a genetically-altered horse.* Mr Bingley, a dour balding toothbrush-tashed man of 50 in a bowler who was overjoyed to meet me and kept asking me who my accountant was. And petite Satsuma, nearly as pretty as me, strawberry curls, bright little eyes – she looked like my real flesh-&-blood sis! We recognized this straight off. Darlingmost Sats! Odd to think that this tiny soft girl became an Admiral in the E.E.S., as tough a cookie as Admiral Crissie Glossop herself.

'I'm so chuffed to have a little bro like you, Mugg!' said Scobie, with a laugh like a neigh. 'I thought I'd end up with a lot

---

* Scobie fascinates me. I hope there is plenty more about him to come! I have read about the Genetically Altered Horse Programme, started by the despots in the mid-21st Century in order to provide limitless troops for their despot-vs.-despot wars. So Scobie was brought into being for exactly the same reasons I was, wot! He's a bro of mine too, in that! I understand it was pigs whose genes they fiddled with first, making a company of pig soldiers. But psychology beat science, as it usually seems to, for the tribal memory of piggies being led to slaughterhouses told on the genetically altered pigs and at the first phaserblast they ran squealing to the hills. Horses were tried next, having proved themselves in battle already – Scots Greys at Waterloo and so on. Over a million horses were genetically altered into humanys before the programme was abandoned, many of them serving with distinction in the Indonesian and the Hittite wars. Three cheers them! People were also made of a cocktail of genetic material made up of goat, monkey, giraffe, rabbit (!!!), chicken and dolphin. The chimeras who resulted were usually exceedingly beautiful. A biography of the Lovely Anita some decades back revealed that she was such a creature herself – of what mix is anybody's guess, though some of her clones were French poodles. This means, I suddenly realize, that strictly speaking my friend Mugg never lay with a woman. Anita was not a woman. Scobie was not a man – and neither, while we're at it, am I! Huh!

of horsey types, Neddys and Whinnies. I'm a genetically altered horse, you know.'

'No! Bless my soul! Erm . . . perhaps I can show you the stables later.'

'Thanky-bees, bro. Rummy of you. Snarg!'

He seemed genuinely touched by the offer, so I double snarged him back: 'Snargsnarg!!'

A 12-year-old boy came through from the library, smoking a pipe.

'Have some poached eggs, James,' said Mumsy. 'GOOD FOR YOUR BLOOD PRESSURE.'

I stepped forward and politely shook hands with my new father. He gave me a Hittite shekel and pinched my cheek, did the same to Mr Bingley (his senior by 40 years!) and sat down to scoff breakfast with boyish appetite. Perhaps the Government Computer had a sense of humour, thought this 17-year-old sonny boy of a 12-year-old daddyo.

I whispered to Satsuma. 'I'll dance for you later, sis!'

'Dupery-dandy! Sneeg, bro of mine! SNEEG!' she enthooosed. (Girls always said 'sneeg' not 'snarg'. Why? Dunno!)

Scobie overheard my invitation to the dance and commenced doing a clip-clop clogdance, his big legs twisting and stamping, hummers from his great nose, tossing his mane of hair and so full of showoff chee that the whole room was clapping along with him. I joined in beside him, copying his thumping steps with my twinkletoes.

'SCOBIE! MUGG! STOP THAT HORSEPLAY AT ONCE!'

Scobie sulked. He always hated Mumsy referring to his equine origins. But as he passed the window, he cheered in a blink, neighing in delight.

'Lookie, folks! There's a motor out there, coming through the Hittites!'

'Ah, that'll be Uncle Dagon and the General!' said Mumsy, in a voice relieved that the adults were arriving at last.

We all stood at the window, seeing the unbelievable sight of the resident end-of-the-drive Hittite war party part ranks to allow a 150-year-old MG sportscar to come brrrrrruming and peeping through. It then somehow ignored the existence of the forcefield and sped irresponsibly into our sanctuary, leaving the drive twice, once to lark between the magnolias, and once around the ornamental pond. BLRRRRREEEEEEP-BLRRRRRREEEEP!!!!! I escorted Mumsy outside to meet the new arrivals.

A corpulent Hittite in white robes struggled out of the passenger seat. From the cockpit came a thing whose like I hast not seen in 100 years of spacehopping – something from Hittite mythology come to life. Frog-headed. Wings. Swamp green. Lumpy like a cankered tree.

'Oi, never before have I seen such a welcome sight as this! My very own family all come out to greet me! I'm your Uncle Dagon, by the way, Hittite double agent,' said my Uncle Dagon, kissing us all, careful not to snag his 5-forked jetblack beard.

I had my phaser in my hand. He patted its nozzle. 'A nervous boy shouldn't perhaps point such things at his uncle.'

'But you're a Hittite!'

'So, you've a problem with this! I am telling you upfront I am a Hittite double agent. Didn't I say, Mr Bingley, that I was a traitorous spy who works for both sides?'

'Yes, uncle, you did say something to that effect.'

'By which I mean I work neither for the enemy or the enemy's enemy. I work for myself and everyone he is my friend, until I betray him, and perhaps who knows even then he still shakes my hand.'

Dagon's technique of telling you right out and continually that he was a double agent, spy, traitor, betrayer, made you trust him utterly, until he betrayed you, and even then, as he observed, you found yourself not turning on him because he had, had he not, been honest with you all along.

'Oi, I am forgetting my manners!' continued Dagon. 'This is Moloch. He dresses my beard. Such an artist!'

Moloch had been as still as a gargoyle since he hopped from the cockpit, worried by our old pooch, who was smelling his bottom. Mumsy poked a grunt out of him with her brolly (she always carried one, in all weathers, indoors and out), gave out a 'Hmmm!' of disapproval, then took Dagon by the arm and went indoors with him. Was he meant to be her or daddykins bro? We never knew.

'Some breakfast, Dagon? What does your friend Moloch eat?'

'It is my belief, Tracy dear, you do not wish to know this.'

Moloch climbed into the fireplace and sat among the flames, watched by the pooch, and by a highly perturbed Hodgekins who knew he was seeing something really serious this time.✶

Dagon ate very daintily – but with his fingers. Even his porridge! He fingered dollops up with 5 digits, then sucked from thumb inwards: 1, 2, 3, 4, 5. Disgusted, I offered him a spoon.

One of his winks. 'I once killed an Amalekite chief in Kadesh by painting poison on his spoon.'

I took this for a nopes to spoons. Coincidentally, my butler Mathis has an aversion to spoons also. They chase him about. In Bunnyland, where there is an infinity of spoons, as there is of everything except common sense, he was often buried in them for days. Mercifully, we are rather spoon-free on CbN.

So there was our new family, watching our uncle eat. Then 15-year-old Satsuma suddenly declared that she wished to marry a Hittite princeling who'd been televisiting her at her

---

✶ Today, Moloch is the proprietor of a highly successful shuttlecraft repair service, scootling between the Bilickers planets. Upon the depopulation of OOP, after the Hittites disappeared in 2150, he snapped up all the Renaissance paintings he could find, and now has the largest private collection of such that there is. His are the only eyes which have gazed upon the Mona Lisa in 50 years. Amazing, wot!

convent school since she was 13. He had seen her naked twice but she had not yet let him go all the way. Mumsy was horrified. Daddykins burst into tears. I was shocked to the core. Mr Bingley tut-tut-tutted. Scobie happily asked how long her suitor's penis was and was told by Mumsy that horses should keep their noses out of human affairs. I objected on his behalf, saying twas a family crisis and Scobie was as much a member of the family as any. A flaming row erupted, all of us shouting, wailing, crying, Satsuma hammering her fists on the table, Hodgekins swigging port in the background, all of us in some queer way enjoying the spat immensely, were we not. Only Dagon remained aloof.

Satsuma appealed tearfully to her uncle, hoping that with him being a Hittite he would be an ally in her love-tangle debate. But he polished his ruby ring on the end of his greasy nose and said: 'I find that it is your father I am in complete agreement with, my girl. Such a match is out of the question. Have you seen maybe Anita's new son? Oi! Nice boy. The proper connections. This is the kind of boy a wise girl should be wanting for a husband. Listen to your uncle what he tells you. As it was in the ancient world, so it is now. In love, in life, nothing changes. Selah!'

'WELL SAID, THAT MAN!' said Mumsy.

Dagon then cheered up Daddykins by saying: 'I can arrange, James, with your permission, to have this unsuitable princeling who is threatening to bespoil your daughter recruited into the Hittite infantry. Maybe a little accident while on manoeuvres. No questions asked.'

Daddykins nodded a thankful assent. Satsuma was speechless with horror, too outraged for tears, hands in her hair to steady a head wobbling with fury! I hugged my poor sis! How cruel they were! If she loved her princeling half as much as I loved Flossie, then by heck I would make sure she got him! But then Sis and I were both witness to one of Dagon's winks – a wink meant only for us . . . which meant wot? That he was on Sat's side all along? That he was playing the double agent even here at our family table! I was both thrilled and disgusted!

'Quadroop sorries, clan of mine!' said lovetroubled Sis, her curls gathered in a topknot which she dropped in declaring: 'It was all a ginormous teasey jape! He-he! I would never marry no pigboggn Hittite, now would I! Not your rosy-cheeked Satsuma! Fooly-dooed you all! He-he! He-he!'

Scobie guffawed trills of heees, showing his daggersome carthorse teeth. I tee-heed, not knowing wot was true and not caring a wasp anyhowdoos! Mr Bingley chuckled into his moustache. Daddykins wiped his eyes. Dagon picked at his sphinx smile with his thumbs.

Only Mumsy kept up a disapproving stare at Satsuma. After the laughter petered out, she said in a quick strict voice: 'YOU ARE NEVER TO PLAY SUCH TRICKS ON US AGAIN, MY GIRL!'

'No, Mumsy.'

'THE VERY IDEA! TALKING ABOUT SHOWING YOUR NAKED BODY TO HITTITES WHEN YOUR UNCLE'S EATING HIS BREAKIES!'

'Triple sorries, Mumsy, Uncle.'

I was helping Mumsy through into the den to watch her fave Hittite soap opera, when her brolly was opened by a gust from the terrace, whose doors I'd left open all night. The impetus of the imbalance this caused her carried away poor Mumsy's great ball of a body into the ballroom and only Scobie's foot on her skirts stopped her twirling bouncily around the big chilly room in a windy dance. The experience must've cleared her head, cos she suddenly noticed something the rest of us in all the excitement had missed!

'But we are one missing!' she cried, her voice filling the ballroom and coming back from all sides. 'WHERE'S THE GENERAL?'

Uncle Dagon's moment of maximum drama had come. He could tell us now . . . 'It is with a misery deeper than the pits of Sheol that I must be telling you evil tidings, my family. The General is a prisoner of war in New Hittiteville, across the great ocean.' (New Hittiteville = New York, the Amerikan metropolis in pre-Hittite ages.) 'Oi, pluck out my beard! Slaughter my goats! FALSE DAGON! WICKED UNCLE! For I must also in shame and grief tell you that it was your own Uncle Dagon who captured General Windbraker and handed him in to the Hittiteville Palace Guard!'

From Mumsy: 'OH, DAGON! HOW COULD YOU!'

Dagon shook his hands at the fresco on the ceiling of cherubs helping the dead of Oudenharde towards Resurrection. 'OI! OI! OI! At the time I handed him in I knew not that he was about to become my very own brother! How could I have known what a computer half the world away was thinking? Now, our poor Humbert is chained in some Hittite Hell, suffering torments no pain-free body can imagine. ALL MY DOING! Hang my gonads in the Hanging Gardens of Babylon! Let an oryx drag me across the stony plains to Cush!'

For some reason, rather than denouncing our double-triple-quadruple-agent uncle, the family gathered around Dagon and comforted him with hugs and squeezes. Poor Dagon, saithed we! How unpleasant all this must be for you! He accepted our affections while stroking the central point of his beard with one hand as the other encouraged us to be more vociferous with a curious Hittite come-hither wave. Hm!

Thoroughly depressed at Dagon's bad news, the family split up into younguns and oldies. We younguns soon peckered up. I took Scobie, Sats and Mr Bingley around the estate – their new home – taking in the stables and yards, the walled garden, the church where our ancestors were buried. Plenty snarg and hoo-hoo. We were out by the old folly, which being half-this half-that side of the forcefield, was the oddest place in the world!

Hittites brought their sweethearts to canoodle in the loveseat on its other side. But there were none about that day as I danced up the lawn pathways between beds of budding rosebushes, to the proud applause of my brothers and sister.

We were busy at this when Daddykins and Uncle Dagon came across the big lawn, Moloch flying above them.

Daddykins spoke. Twas the 1st time, we realized, that he had actually spoken. His voice was a choirboy's years from breaking, but somehow with a touch of the barroom about it.

'Listen up, kiddies. Ya Uncle Dagon and I have been clacking our jawbones about your bro, my boy Humbert, imprisoned by the boggn Hittites – scuse language, Dagon – in Amerika. I think we should do summick, as a family, wotsay, to get the boy out, and Dagon had suggested that we chaps should together go over the pond and see if we can't manage to break him out. Dimmee, he'd do the same for any of us!'

This seemethed a pottyfala idea to stay-at-home Mugg. But when Dagon said: 'Oh, do let's go! We'll bond! We'll bond!' I warmed to the idea. Yeps! Embarking upon a dangerous enterprise together, as a family, seemethed to me just then the most wonderful thing to do to intensify the feelings of love and belonging I felt for my new raggletaggle kith! Okaydoakes! This Mugg saithed he would do anything to save his dear P. O. W. bro. But Mr Bingley, very sensibly, said: 'How are we going to get to New Hittiteville? It's all Hittites anyway! Whole world's Hittites! And we're not Hittites, are we not, cepting you, Uncle. One step out of here and we're skewered by Hittites. HITTITES!'

'Pish-posh, nephew!' smiled Dagon. 'Oioi, with Moloch's skills, you shall all have beards any Hittite would be proud of. Do you not know how simple it is for you to walk down any Hittite street on Earth and appear to be Hittites yourselves? Heh, thousands of moderns are doing it right this minute! Of course, we cannot go anywhere in the New Empire without identity documents, travel permits, special info. For this it is the Network we shall be needing.'

'The Network?'

'Wolves Newington IS the Network! He can fix everything for us. Easypeasey.'

'Wolves Newington?'

'Shhhhh! Never be mentioning this name again!'

We never did, did we? Nopes. None of us. Till me, 100 years later, writing this, just now. Chee!

The whole mad enterprise was kept hush-hush from Mumsy, lest she should worry. She was already upset enough over Humbert and any extra upset would give her one of her queasiness attacks, which none of us had yet witnessed, but all dreaded. Dagon, the family's most experienced liar, told her that he was taking us chaps hunting wild donkeys in Cornwall, which she abhorred as a thing to do, but believed it to be just the sort of expedition your uncle would take you on if he happened to be a Hittite.

Satsuma, meanwhileydoos, caused another mealtime row, insisting she was a chap, and that not even Anita herself could stop her coming to shoot arrows at wild donkeys with the rest of us! Her battle won, she threw a confidential whisper into my curls about how she hoped to meet some dishy Hittites in New Hittiteville! – This ambition was ruined the next morning when Moloch stuck a stonking Hittite beardie on her – enough to put off the dishiest blokedish New Hittiteville could dish up for a girl! Turned out Moloch had no skill in tarting-up ladies, therefore getupped Sats as a Hittite nobleman, the same as the rest of us. Either come along gotup in chainmail and copper kilts, or not at all, dear! She came, made a wheeze of it. Dupery gal!

So twas that within a few days of my new family arriving at Chaffinch Hall, most of us telezoomed to Hittite-controlled

Southbank London disguised as Hittites, beardied and anciently garbed, to find the offices of this Wolves Newington . . . shhhhhh! Across the river were vast telescreens showing Anita taking a bath. This propaganda was meant to convince the enemy that our way of life was betterer. Convinced me! Urk! Funny though, the Hittites in Southbank weren't like those I watched on the TS shows. Many wore jeans and silver jackets, just like in London proper. Only half the men had beards! Dimmee, this WAS our way of life! Their culture was dying out, poor dears: they were becoming us, as we had been, before they came. Hardly a winged Mezulla, Hulla or Zintuhi in evidence, except on T-shirts. Though many bowed down before Moloch as he loped ahead of us, showing the way.

WOLVES NEWINGTON
– I Help Hittites –

Mr Newington's dentist-like wooden shingle was inscrutable above a revolving door. How, exactlymost, did he help Hittites? What with? To do wotnot? The shingle had an arrow in it, but wot didn't in that part of town? (Twas Moloch's job to catch in his teeth any strays that shot our way.) But how come a Johnny called Wolves Newington was living it up in Hittiteland? Was he an English equivalent of Uncle D. – double agent, spy, traitor???

Dagon left us in the waiting room of Wolves Newington's smartly-doos offices – popping away, I guessed, to weewee, but twas the last we saw of him that afternoon! Still, nowhere did it say what this Wolves Newington's biz was! But all looked proper enough. Mr Bingley was impressed. Modern furniture. The latest mags to yawn at. WOLVES NEWINGTON – I HELP HITTITES a 100 times on the lino, reminding you of him at every boggn step. Plusmost, he had a pretty secretary, a gone-Hittite peachy Englishgirl who Sats struck up a girly natter with before she remembered she was in a beard, simultaneously seeing the secretary was yahoo for her.

The only other waitee in the pink leather chairs was an overtall Hittite captain, who somehow I vaguely recognized. Said he was on leave from the wars – showed me his wound – had an estate in the Lake District, very interested in sheep. URK! This was no boggn Hittite! This was the original of the ass I'd met at the New Year's Eve Interactive Hologramismic Party. Captain Fitzroy Crawfoot. Stone me! He had his English army uniform on under his Hittite robe! You could see his campaign ribbons through the silk!

I was so excited by this discovery that I forgot where we were and said: 'You're no boggn Hittite, matey, you're Captain Fitzroy Crawfoot of the Green Howards, yer soppy great Jilks!'

He removed his beardie, handed me his dirk and surrendered.

'Guilty as charged. Wot ya gonna do with me, hm? Not the lions, pleasy-do, ehwot!'

The secretary was still making eyes at Sats, so no one saw the nude chin of Captain Crawfoot. Nor mine when I pulled my beardie down 2 feet on its elastic.

'EGAD!' jumped Crawfoot. 'Haven't we met? – I know! Lord Mugg, wot! You were at my New Year's Eve do. Auditioning to be my bro.'

'And you were at mine, auditioning to be my bro!'

'Sorry-bees I didn't get ya, chum. You should see the family they sent me. Crashing bores!'

'But whatya doing here, Fitz, my old stomper! Not a spy, hm?'

'Cripes, no. I got a tip this Wolves Newington critta is a jiffy at finding people, gone-overs to the enemy, prisoners, girls nabbed for harem duty, 'nsuchwot. He helps Hittites, you know – so why not little me! I'm looking for a girl, dyersee. One I met, in fact, at the same party you were at! YOU DON'T KNOW

HER, DOES YA, CHUM? Flossie Fordyce is the name. Ash-blonde. Tiny creature. Dreamkitten. Mmmmm!'

My heart poundeth so hard that I thought my eyes were going to be spat out of my body. I held them in with my palms and felt them roll with thought in the darkness! Was not this Crawfoot creature exactly as he was at the party? Was he not a real man in the real world, not just a hologramismic? He was! HE WAS! This meant that SHE was real too – my Flossie! REAL! There was a flesh-'n-blood Flossie Fordyce, alive, out there that minute, somewhere in the Hittite infested world.

PING! 'Next, pleasy-do!'

Twas our Chaffinch turn next and Mr Bingley, still wearing his bowler hat which ruined the effect of his disguise, had his hand on the knob of the office door whose glass bit said WOLVES NEWINGTON *I Help Hittites*. But I brushed him aside and pushed Captain Crawfoot in with such force that a big crack cut the NEWI from the NGTON and the *I Help Hit* from the *tites*.

Twas my Uncle Dagon behind the desk, in a blue suit, dark glasses, curly blond wig atop his swarthy fiz, but equipt with the same 5-forked beard. HE was Wolves Newington! Moloch, also disguised in dark glasses, closed the door behind us.

'How might I be helping you, gentlemen?' said this helper of Hittites. 'The possible it takes no time at all. The impossible, oi, takes maybe a day or two, and Baal be praised, either way it costs whatever poundlets or shekels you've got.'

He rubbed his ruby ring to tell me twas he, but I already knew. When he knew that I knew: one of those winks!

'We seeketh a girl, Uncle, erm, Mr Newington! That is, my friend, this Hittite here . . .'

'Howdeedoodee!' saithed Crawfoot.

'. . . seeketh one Flossie Fordyce. He loves her more than life itself. Don't ya?'

'Oh, I do. Mm-hm.'

'Wherever she is, however much it costs . . .'

'I say, steady on!' complained my rival for Flossie's hand.

'. . . HE MUST FIND HER!!!'

Uncle Dagon made a note of the name. 'I'll see what I can do,' he said simply.

Captain Crawfoot gave him his card, all the shekels he possessed, and an IOU for more, then toodlybyedared with a nice byebye to me: 'You know, Lord Mugg, even if the computer says we're not up as bros, no reason we can't be, ehwot?'

'No reason at all. Bro.'

That sent him away, as happy as if Flossie was waiting at home with his tea and slippers. I doubted I would ever see him again.

Now for our appointment! Daddykins, Sats, Scobie and Mr Bingley crowded into the tiny office. They didn't twig, to my amazement, that Wolves Newington was Uncle Dagon, who kept giving me that wink while Daddykins, like an arrogant boy ordering his Headmaster about, told Newington just what we needed to get us to and about Amerika.

'Excuse me asking,' a gone-posh Mr Bingley suddenly asked our uncle's alter ego, 'but whoms is your accountant?'

Amen.

Hittites: Five
Memories of Hittite Amerika

Another big cause of the fractiousness of the Bunny people –
walk down any street and you must side-step 10 arguments –
is their system of 3-way marriages, which I fought so hard, did
I not, to abolish as Bunnybish, but failed in that as in all else. 3
Bunnies to a marriage bed! URK! Worst of it is that, having no
permanent sexual parts, your Bunny has no properly defined
maleness or femaleness. Bunny must stick a set of genitals on,
either gender will do, to become buck or doe, and if possessed
of a set of parts can de-buck and doe-up whenever the whim
takes him/her.

So in their 3-way marriages who is wot? It works thus: all
3 sit at a 3-sided ceremonial table where 2 of the union
proceed to elect the sex of the other one. Once sexed he/she
pairs with one of the electors from round 1 and they sex the
2nd Bunny, then the remaining unsexed Bunny is sexed by
the two already fixed. Dice decide who starts, lowest getting
voted on first. Lordy, tis here the problems start! For if the
first Bunny is miffed at getting the sex he didn't want, he
may be the sort to be spiteful to their other 2 and give them
the sex they each didn't want – which I think is why they
get such batty combinations. 2 males and a female is the
traditional 'good marriage', but just as often it comes out 1
male and 2 females, and nearly as often a trio of females or a

triumvirate of males, this latter being either a recipe for a shoot-out or the most harmonious mix of all – no telling, till after the election!

Dearie-be, some of the most aggressive Bunnies – very male, shaved warrior types – get elected female by their partners, meaning they can't wear the busby, which makes them very irritated indeed.∗ And as the election is binding for 12 years, a long time in the short Bunny span, and divorce being illegal, most Bunnies commit bigamy by swapping themselves with other dissatisfied Bunnies, ending up in other marriages, and perhaps then others and others still. Thus, tis hard to work out who is legally married to whom. Plenty work herein for the lawyers when deciding who gets what legacy from a will. Impossible, in fact, when almost everyone over the age of 6 (Bunny age of consent) is somewhere in the chain related by marriage to everyone else! So the lawyers usually keep the money, or rather their partners get 2 thirds and then pack up and leave for other 3-way

---

∗ The busby, as I think the Archbishop mentions elsewhere, was a compulsory garb on the English Space Villages. The Bunnies became acquainted with them during their war with our Empire in the '40s and took them up with customary nose-twitching enthusiasm. Bunny busbies started black, like ours, but are now all colours, usually of rabbit fur. Laughably, many Elvisites wear their Elvis wig on top of their busby! Because one Bun loves to out-fashion another Bun, busbies have been getting gradually higher over the years. At a church fête shortly before we left I saw a 6-foot-tall Bunny wearing a 7-foot tall busby! Because busbies hide the ears it has encouraged the fashion of lopping, allowing the ears to hang cutely out of the busby. For stiff-eared Bunnies this involves an operation, which can be reversed whenever lopping goes out of style, and repeated again when some mag announces lopping to be 'in' again, all this oblivious of the threat that such treatment will cause the ears to fester and drop off, which of course they do. Fatal, cos earless Bunnies are imprisoned as public undesirables. Thus, as most other crimes get the death penalty, the prison system contains mostly fashion-conscious Bunnies! A THOUGHT! – If an earless Bunny wears its busby at all times, who's to boggn know it's earless, ehwot! I must say I adore both busbies and Bunnyears, and have a collection of both, gathering dust back home in Bunnyland.

setups, thus spreading the wealth to one and all. Suitcase economics, this is called.✶

Obviously, only 2 Bunnies can decently copulate with each other at one time, Ergo, while 2 get to use their valuable set of parts, one of the 3 is relegated to the subs-bench as spectator and builds up such a steam of jealousy and sexual frustration that 9 times out of 10 he attacks the other 2 and whee-hooo does the hair fly! The whole arrangement is immoral, unChristian and simply does not boggn p'boggn pigboggn boggn-boggn-BOGGN work!!!!!!

In my 65 years as incumbent of the see of Bunnyland I blitherated some 3,000 Sunday sermons, and every Sunday I hammered upon the sacredness of the 2-way marriage to

✶ The thing I never understood was: how did these love triangles get together? How do Bunny A and B decide who Bunny C will be? What if Bunny A wants Bunny C in the set but Bunny B wants Bunny X. Does Bunny A then start a new triangle with Bunny C, with them then having to choose a replacement for Bunny B. Meanwhile, Bunny B is now happily teamed-up with Bunny X, but then they need to agree on a third partner, and wot if Bunny X wants the Bunny A from the original broken-up partnership? Hm? Or wot if a Bunny A and B are so horrid that no other Bunny will join their marriage? Do they then part forever, as without 3 no marriage is socially viable? The possibilities are boggn endless! But if you ask the Buns how they decide these matters, they go all coy and flutter their eyelashes. I had an excellent opportunity to find out all this for myself when, as Mopsy, I took a liking to Mimsie, a Bunny schoolteacher I met at a school prizegiving – too-too sweetiepaws, mmmmm, wot! We teamed, then brought in the Defence Secretary to finish the set. He was a male at the time, but at our election we voted him female, which he resented, sold secrets to the E.E.S., which was discovered and resulted in his execution, whereupon he was replaced in our 3-way by Mimsie's pinto sister Carlotta – double-sweetiepaws thattn! This, of course wasn't a proper marriage, not like with Clarissa! I wasn't even a rabbit! And, wot with the sexual parts problem, there was no sex in my 3-way. Not to start with, anyway. The Archbishop, naturally, never knew about my marriage. Whenever Mimsie and Carlotta turned up, all chalked and pink-nosed, to partner my official events, the Bishop would whisper in locker-room manner unusual for him, and proof positive of their charms: 'It's them 2 sirens again, Mopsy! Mine's the pinto! Heh-heh!' The newsrags, of course, were full of my beautiful Bunny wives, but Mugg walked around with his eyes shut. The day I dreaded when he would bellow . . . 'MOPSY! IS THIS BOGGN TRUE? ARE YOU MARRIED TO THEM TARTY RABBITS?' . . . never happened.

congregations sitting smugsome in their 3s, making eyes at members of other 3s and not listening to the sermon at all. RABBITS! Tis no wonder I am always in such a bad boggn temper! MATHIS, WHERE'S MY CHRISTMAS DINNER, YOU BOGGN CAN OF WORMS! Eeek, I soundeth just like poor cuz Stewie! Forgive an old fool, Mathis! When I think how sweet-natured I was as a boy . . . Ho-hum!

I can see myself now, scratching under my Hittite beard disguise, leaning over the rail of the airship that was slowly sailing us to Amerika, where my neo-Chaffinch family were intent on rescuing our brother, General Sir Humbert Windbraker, who was a P.O.W. of the boggn Hittites. Far below were the Hittite-cultivated fields of England and here and there the great aristo houses under their domed forecefields, pellucid cupolas full of electric fizz . . . and that day, after a spring shower, every one looped with a rainbow. My country! Somewhere down there, thought this Mugg, was darling Flossie Fordyce, adoring a rainbow, sipping her elevenses. Upon my return I surely would find her and our 2-way marriage would be the happiest of all time! Leaning on the rail, I was imagining scenes from my future life, wind making tears, thoughts making tears, when something, a person, a Hittite, flew past my ears and fell, with a yelp very modest in the circumstances, all the way down onto the stony Cornwall where we Chaffinches were supposedly shooting wild donkeys right that moment.

'Oi, wot a tragedy!' said Uncle Dagon beside my astonished face. He then, having hoied the man's cap after him, checked that his rings were still on his fingers.

This ring-checking gesture somehow made me twig that Uncle Dagon had thrown the poor pigbog overboard! He saw my understanding and gave me one of his rings. A dull flawed emerald. I am still wearing it.

'My favourite nephew! So insightful he is! Misses nothing, just like his Uncle Dagon!'

He chuckled, then looked dizzily down again, just in case, in a double miracle . . . 1) his victim had survived the fall and 2) the Gods gifted uncle the power to see him getting up to shake his fists.

'Our late friend, he was Huwaruwas, the Colonel of the 201st Chariot Regiment,' whispered Dagon.

'So?'

'Look, boy, at my disguise, my cap, my uniform! I am the Colonel of the 201st Chariot Regiment, and so says my passport also. Oi, can there be 2 Huwaruwases? Can 2 birds lay the same egg twice? How was I to know he'd be on the airship! The 201st are stationed in Australia, chasing kangaroos! A most unfortunate coincidence! Still, problem solved.'

An acne-suffering steward popped up, saluting Dagon. 'Scusy-be, sir. Someone said they saw a leaper.'

'A leaper? I saw no leaper. Did you see a leaper, nephew?'

'Oi!' I said, my only Hittite-ism, serving for all occasions – here meaning, no, I saw no leaper. But as the steward didn't bogg off I added a big 'SNARG!' to send him on his way.

When the steward was indeedy-be gone Uncle Dagon tuttishy-tutted: 'A word of advice, nephew, Hittites don't say *snarg*.'

'O, un-snarg that snarg! Have I given myself away? URK!'

'Ert, so maybe you have, don't wet yourself – no problem.'

Off he went and moments later it was his mellifluous liar's voice which announced over the tannoy: 'AN ATTENDANT WILL BE PASSING AMONG YOU SHORTLY WITH THE BEAD JAR TO SELECT A LUCKY WINNER FOR TODAY'S SACRIFICE TO THE GREAT GOD TESHUB.'

It was Scobie chewing sugarlumps who rattled the bead jar under my nose. I picked one out – red! Pheweroo! Daddykins, Sats, Mr Bingley all held up red beads. . . . Scobie playfully picked out several – so triplo-quadruplo-pheweroo! All Chaffinchs in the clear! (Moloch, being immortal, couldn't be sacrificed, so was let off playing.) I then watched Dagon engage the airship captain in militarymen's jaw-jaw about war-war, all the while interposing his great body between the captain and that spots-in-the-beard steward, who was both-hands-up desperate to gain his boss's attention. Scobie visited the bead jar upon the steward last of all, and just before he did Dagon knocked on the jar for luck. The steward picked his bead, then dodged past my uncle and was about to expose the non-Hittiteness of this Mugg when the Captain saw the blue bead in the poor Jilks' hand.

'BLUE BEAD HERE! YOOOOO-HOOOOO!' called the Captain.

Moments later, everyone was gatherated around a hole up by the propeller, which had been stilled for some diabolical ceremony, leaving a buzzless floating-above-the-Ocean silence into which ram's horns were tooted sombrely. I couldn't see properly wot was afoot for the crush but heard the Captain intone: 'OH GREAT GOD TESHUB, PROTECTOR OF HITTITES, HE WHO BROUGHT US PROSPERITY AND DOMINION IN THIS FUTURISTIC WORLD, ACCEPT THIS HUMBLE OFFERING.'

Then a highly immodest scream as, unseen by me, the steward was dropped through the hole into the waiting Atlantic. As per tradition, lest they palm their red bead to cheat next time, each Hittite took a turn to drop his bead through the sacrificial hole after the humble offering. This Mugg-Hittite was the last to do so, by which time the sacrificers had dispersed and the propeller buzzzzzzzed more healthily than ever. Dagon and the captain stood by the now shut-up hole. My uncle, who was comforting the captain, who'd been rather fond of his steward, gave me one of his winks.

As in-flight entertainment they had bull wrestling, which seemethed to me a most dangerous thing to do on an airship – horns + punctures = splash! Nowadays, after 23 crashes in thence-&-whencers, I calmly expect to come crashing down every time I go up, speciallymost with Mathis driving, but then I was perturbed so much as to mutter hymns, new-coined ones, composed by fear, never re-muttered again.

It was while we were watching passengers trying their luck with the bulls that Dagon gave me news which made me consider joining Huwaruwas and the steward in a place without pain.

'Oi, I've just remembered – that little matter you asked me to look into for your friend, Captain Crawfoot. The girl, Flossie Fordyce.'

'Flossie! YOU'VE FOUND HER?'

'Apologize if you will to your friend for me. I will refund him 50%. She cannot be found. Make that 25%. Most of the characters in the New Year's Eve Interactive Party where he met her were real people, reproduced from information retained by telezooming chips. But I can find no reference to her name on the government computer, and no corresponding chip exists for such a girl, meaning she cannot ever have telezoomed. Triple sorries, Mugg. Make that 10%.'

'She doesn't exist then? You're saying the computer generated her itself?'

'Could be, who knows! But should we ask ourselves, perhaps, if maybe she was a visitor from up there?'

He nodded at a gibbous moon in the blue sky and I thought he meant Flossie was an angel, flitting down to Earth on a day off. But wot he meant was that Flossie was a visitor from Outer Space. Dagon, being Dagon, knew the secret of secrets. I did not. I had no idea that the English had a Hittite-free trillion-star Empire in Outer Space! That Bunnies chomped carrots in an infinite land somewhere. No notion of such things whatsoever.

I later discovered that my Uncle Dagon was spot on, was he not. Flossie was a 3rd Lieutenant on the training ship HMS *Pompey*. In doing a thesis on OOP for her 2nd Lieu exams, she had popped down to Lovely Anita's England for a looksee and was somehow detected by the Government Computer which used her image in its party programme. But that day on the airship, as I say, I could not guess at such things. I had lost my

Flossie and my heart was broken asunder. It is broken yet. Yea, I never recoverethed from that news!

I was sitting in a lovelorn stupor, was I not, watching sis Satsuma swinging her legs while she chatted up 5 gum-chewing Hittites, when I heard the announcement that Colonel Huwaruwas of the 201st Chariot regiment would now wrestle the bulls. I saw that Dagon no longer at my side. He was in the bullpit where he wrestled down 3 hefty snorters in a row without snagging his beard once. He'd been a champ at this lark in his leaner ancient epoch, but had retained something of the skill, helped by an oh-so-modern secret device in one of his rings, which when placed on a bull's forehead bopped it flat. Meanwhileydoos, Scobie was so proud of his uncle that he whinnied hugely, making all the Hittites bow down in the belief that their winged horse god had just flown by.

Thus and so, after an eventful journey our airship passed level with the nose of the New Hittiteville colossus, that of a winged guardian spirit, which stands to this day on an island outside the now-deserted city, and we docked on the very top of the old Empire State Building in the middle of town, with stupendous views of its skyscrapers and armies of rooftop gargoyles, stone versions of Moloch, grimacing down at the criss-cross streets where golden chariots whipped along and 50 million Hittites went about their biz.✶

✶ The Empire State Building, I happen to know, was built with a docking eye to accept airships, they having their first popularity when it was constructed in the early 20th Century. My first trip to the then USA, crossing on the Ile de France, was in 1931 for the Indianapolis race. I spent a week in New York celebrating my victory and went up the Empire State Building twice. There was an exhilarating intensity about that city, I think greater than anything I've seen since. Of course, Bunnyopolis is 20 times the size, but it is more spread out, less intense. No, I've changed my mind – there's no greater thrill than to sit at the carrot bar at the top of the Twitchit Tower and watch the sun go down and the lights come on in the Bunny capital. But old London in the fog, that was better still! You couldn't see a thing, but felt so very much!

We clanked down steps in the spire section of the Empire State Building and were greeted by 2 Hittite Guards in big leather coats, who carefully inspected our papers. I still clearly remember wot they said to Mr Bingley.

One said: 'Say, bub, I'm being transferred outa here next month to Hittite England. You just come from there – can yerh get pretzels in Hittite England? Can yerh, huh?'

'You can get anything anywhere for a price, my man,' said Mr Bingley.

'Naw, he don't know from nuttin!' said guard number 2.

'If the little guy says yerh can get pretzels in England who are you to say yerh cant, huh! Make no never mind of him, bub.'

It amazed me that, like so many other cultures who'd come to Amerika in the historical past, these Hittites had quickly lost their Hittiteness and somehow been assimilated into a culture whose people they had wholly exterminated. I had not realized this assimilation to be so marked, but the Hittite guardsmen's exchange with Mr Bingley wised me up to it. I suppose that as they settled into the buildings, surrounded by the brash remains of old Amerikan culture, the raw English brogue with which they emerged from the timewarps morphed into an even more vulgarsome idiom in keeping with their surroundings. The Hittite inner man's desire to express his Hittiteidity continued for the time being in bull wrestling, worship of oddball gods, an incessant click of swordfighting, etc . . . but he also woofed, and louder, over baseball, roller derbys and game shows, unknown in the violent but sedate 1500 BC. Twas a similar phenomenon in the woods of Bilickers 999, where the English colonists, having hunted the local budgerigars into extinction, began to behave exactly like budgerigars. Admiral Crissie Glossop ordered them re-educated, and when this failed they were destroyed.

Sinking down in the elevator we were pestered by a recruiting sergeant who wanted us to join his side – he never said which – in a war being fought by the Hittite kinglet of Milwaukee against the Hittite kinglet of Boise, Idaho. Then, out in the street, Sats, the bearded flirt, bid a touching goodbye to her 5 gum-chewing Hittite pals, 2 of whom had signed up with the sergeant just to impress her. Every time she giggled one of them sighed and slapped himself in the face, not knowing why he was so excited by this fellow officer in the 2-pronged beard. All this while Uncle Dagon hadn't spoken a word. When he did we all jumped.

'I's gotta see some squealer geeks 'bout finding which slammer they got our Humbert kid stuck inter. Youse guys paddle yerh asses up and down 5th, why don't yers, catch a chariot race maybe. Mosey on up to the WN Building on 49th and Broadway when yerh thru, huh? We'll do lunch. Have a nice day, y'all.'

Having said so, he and Moloch joined the pavement-clopping Hittite crowd, and left us Chaffinches adjusting our false beards and wondering if we should try to speak like this too. Our debate was interrupted by the sidewalks suddenly filling with people, pouring from the buildings.

Then the traffic, mainly chariots but plenty scooters and a few bashed-up roadcars, cleared off the avenue and an expectant *hummmm* developed into a hollering warcry. Popcorn and streams of toilet paper fell softly from windows high above. Grins in forked beards. Hittite ladies with shopping bags at their feet, bosoms heaving with breath between hollers. Strangest sight in all this were the oblong tents with numbers and Hittite names plastered over them which movethed as if under their own power along the frontage of the crowd. One stopped in front of us. Its flap flapped open and we saw inside where a doggy Hittite face peered out. The face wore a skimmer hat whose band was stuffed with scraps of yellow paper.

'So wot's new?' said the guy in the tent.

'Oi?' said this Mugg, Hittitely.

'Yer watchers or players, gents? Nebuchadnezzar goes at 5/
1. Mack Ctesiphonihatta comes at evens. Waddayasay?'

'Oh, betting, I see! Grrrr, all right . . . Um, pleasy-do one
shekel on Nebuchadnezzar.'

'Gertoutahere! You wanna me to get Louey to flatten yerh
snoot? One shekel, jeez! LOUEY!'

A second face appeared in the tent window. Wronged and
ratty. Preferred the slowness of the ancient world. 'Huh?'

'Got a wise guy here with one shekel.'

Trouble brewethed, but typical of Scobie he galloped
through all argument with a hummering yell of: '50,000
SHEKELS ON NEBUCHADNEZZAR TO WIN!'

'Oi, that's more like it! A real high roller!'

Daddykins commenced kicking Scobie's shins and I had to
hold upright a swoonish Mr Bingley. But sorry-bees on us,
twas too late to save our shekels! Scobie, with the widest girth
in the family for moneybelt wearing, had charge of our fortune
and was emptying shekels by the thousand into Louey's rat-
chewed 10-gallon hat, making a sound like old tick-tock Mathis
picking his nose. This wasn't mad money, was it not, oh no, no,
no – twas intended to bribe the guards at wherever General
Humbert was being held prisoner. Now nowt to do but wait
and see if we won! The Hittite bookie gave Scobie a scrap of
pink paper, shoving a yellow scrap up into his skimmer, then
passed on down the line. Our whole boggn mission, our bro's
very life, now depended on the outcome of a Hittite chariot
race!

CLODHOPPING OAF! HORSE! BOGGN GEEGEE BRAINS!
TO THE KNACKERS YARD WI' IM! were the sort of things
we gnashed at Scobie as the racing chariots came clattersomely
whipcrackawaying down 5th Avenue from the park end.

'OI, WHICH ONE'S NEBUCHADNEZZAR, BUB?' I asked
the nearest Hittite who looked likely to know.

'The gray team, buddy. The grays. No chance.'

Indeedy-be, the grays passed us in last place. Nebuchad-nezzar was obviously no ace charioteer. He had the reins all snagged and he looked drunk to me. Daddyfingers was in tears, anguished that he'd failed his son in his hour of need. Plusly, he was hit on the head by more than his fair share of falling popcorn. But Scobie was as confident as ever.

'Wait till they come back, bro Mugg. You'll see.'

The crowd went triple hoo-ha wild when the lead chariot came back from the turn. It was Mack Ctesiphonihatta and his black mares, way, way ahead. He'd won every race for months, according to my buddy in the crowd. I held our betting slip and was about to tear it up when Scobie darted out alongside the frontage of the crowd. Skipping like a stallion in a meadow on a spring day he was making horse noises, but so were plenty drunk Hittites in the crowd, so no one took exception. But Mack Ctesiphonihatta's black mares suddenly put on the brakes, overturning the chariot and throwing Mack over the heads of the crowd across the street from us and through a department store window, breaking the necks of a dozen bearded mannequins along with his own. When the main body of chariots arrived seconds later, Scobie was on hand to whistle the horses into a halt before the scuppered chariot. Eventually Nebuchadnezzar's grays can-tered past. To boos, cheers and laughter the suddenly sober charioteer clattered up towards the park and a famous victory. There were heart-rending sobs inside the bookie tent as they counted out our winnings, flicking out one shekel at a time in the hope that we'd get bored and go away before we got the lot. We did, hurrying off for a late lunch with Uncle Dagon, weighed down by plenty shiny new shekels, were we not, for bribing bro Humbert out of his confinement.

We should have guessed that the WN Building's WN where

we were to rendezvous with Uncle Dagon stood for, yeps . . .
THERE TWAS:

WOLVES NEWINGTON.

The building was a great glass needle with bronze Molochs
on the crawl all the way up it. Swisheroo joint indeed, heaps
snazzier than his crabby branch office in Southbank London. A
great flashing neon sign which one could still seeth, could one
not, when one closed one's eyes, which said

I HELP HITTITES

was such a visual scream that you wouldn't dare not believe it,
but at the same time sayethed to oneself, as I did, did I not, I did
– why boggn bother helping the pigboggers! They mainly
needed help, anyway, with revenge plots, elopings, harem
problems and finding spare parts for their chariots. Better
to lounge on cushions eating peach slices while tickling Hittite
dancing girls with peacock feathers – live it up, why not? O,
thou hedonistic bird, Mugg Chaffinch!

But this, pleasy-do – bogg me for a prophet! – was near
enough what Wolves Newington (Uncle Dagon) was abiz with
when we clocked him in the WN Building's penthouse suite. In
his Wolves Newington blond wig and dark glasses he floated
on a lilo, his corpulent torso smeared with lard as Hittites are
wont so to do in their private moments, in a Jacuzzi full of
overfrothed bubblesome bubblebath. A shy Moloch sat on a
half submerged step, striking matches which he then ate.
Meanwhilydoos, 20 Hittite lovelies came offering them fruit
cocktails with their cupped hands as bowls. It was a vision of
decadence such as I never saw again until I looked through the
window of a Bunny barber shop. I stripped off and jumped
straight in.

Scobie circled the bath trumpeting his chariot race story, which I understand he told to everyone he met till the day his genetic material mutated back to its original self and one morning 10 years later he woke up a horse again for good.

The story was coming around again, with details omitted in the first telling's rush, while I natterated at a strangely morose Uncle Dagon, saying Uncle Dagon this, Uncle Dagon that. My family were looking into the suds for a submerged uncle till I turned on them and yelled: 'FORCRYINGOUTLOUD YOU LOT! UNCLE DAGON *IS* WOLVES NEWINGTON!' and I snatched off the blond wig and stuck it on Moloch.∗

∗ This reminds me of the bizarre situation which developed between myself and my friend the Shogun, Dr Buckie Scats. After I had been President of Bunnyland for a while I realized that the reason why I couldn't get anything done was because most of my ministers were secretly working for the Shogun, who was terrified of Mopsy-me becoming too successful at the job, ousting him, and becoming Shogun myself. So, remembering how I had murdered heaps of Germans in my Earthbound days, I started knocking off these disloyal ministers – dropping them in the Archbishop's rabbit stew, wot! – and replacing them with the only person I could completely trust: myself! Mopsy was only a bunnysuit, after all – so why not 5, 10, 20 bunnysuits! True, I couldn't be in 2 places at once, but I could pop into the Carrot Ministry done up as the Carrot Minister, the Transport Ministry suited up as the Transport Minister, the Bunnyculture Ministry in my Bunnyculture Minister's disguise for 20 minutes each in the morning, then a business lunch with all those bug-eyed alien ambassadors I had to charm as Mopsy, then I could zip up suit as Colonial Secretary for another lunch, and take high tea as the Religious Affairs Minister, this usually with the Archbishop or 2 dozen Elvis impersonators. Tophole scheme!

It worked very well for the first year. But as I discovered more and more disloyal ministers my rack of Bunnysuits got longer and longer, until I myself, personally, in one guise or another, was 247 different members of the government. Then I had to ask myself why, when there were another 262 members of the government, did I only ever see one member at a time. One day in cabinet, just me and the Secretary for Economics were present. He was way down the table, 300 chairs away, using a megaphone to be heard, but he was talking about fur in a way only the Fur Minister ever talked about fur. I put my megaphone down and walked all the way down table to him.

'Look here, mush!' said I, miffed as Hell. 'Are you the Secretary for Economics or are you the Fur Minister?'

He took a compact out of his handbag – most male Bunnies carry handbags,

'Aw, shucks, kid, yerh oughtn't to have done that!' complained Dagon as Dagon. 'Yerh spoiled my little game summin rotten, yer did. Shucks! Shucks! Aw, shucks!'

but never me! – and looked himself over before answering, blaring through his megaphone though I was standing right beside him: 'Silly me, I'm the Secretary for Economics! Please excuse me, Mr President – I've been working so hard lately.'

'Quite all right, old Bun. By the by: nifty handbag.'

Delighted with the compliment, he went away all giggly. But when I saw the same handbag swung by the Doge of Warrens-on-Sea 2 days later my suspicions were properly aroused. I put on my no-rabbit-in-particular bunnysuit and took a troika to the fag-end of Bunnyopolis where was the workshop of the Bunny who made me my bunnysuits – if I'd continued making them myself I would have had no time for anything else! My surprise visit caught him listening to *In the Ghetto* while cutting what was obviously a 2nd Mopsy suit.

'I didn't order this.'

'N-n-no, Bunnyboss . . . I . . . erm . . . was making it on the offchance, as it were, just in case you asked.'

I wasn't convinced. I stared him out. His nose twitched double-fast.

'You're lying,' I said. 'Cum now, nothing to be frightened of – who are you making this suit for?'

He grabbed his tailor's scissors and stabbed himself dead in the jugular – ruining, I may add, my no-rabbit-in-particular bunnysuit with his squirting life's blood. I finished sewing the new Mopsy suit and left it in it. Of course, twas obvious, ehwot: only one person could so befuddle a Bun's mind with fear and devotion . . . He'd been making the bunnysuit for the Shogun! Not the first either. Dimmee, why had I never realized before, when it was staring me in the face at every encounter? Every Bunny in government who wasn't me was the Shogun. All my most loyal ministers, not loyal at all, merely the Shogun being triple crafty. I drove straight to B'bubbadub Palace to confront the rabbit. But that was the night Warlord Bobo Tufts seized power in Province XIII, with a march on Bunnyopolis in the offing. When I stormed into the throne room the Shogun gripped my arm, tears in his eyes and said: 'Mopsy, you've come! You're with me! I can't tell you what this means to me!'

With Tufts beaten off, but with scores of other warlords wandering the provinces with their rabbit bands, just waiting to pounce, the Shogun continued to fear Mopsy-me as his most dangerous rival. Even when we both knew damn well what the other was up to, we still spent our precious time changing frantically in-and-out of Bunnysuits while the real business of government was done by 5-year-old secretaries and Solperines. I should add that never in all this did the Shogun or anyone else suspect that Mopsy was a metal man. Some of the time, especially having a picnic at Lake Twinkie with Mimsie and Carlotta, I quite forgot myself!

'Dagon! YOU BOUNDER!' laughed Daddyfingers. 'It was you all along! By jimminy, you had me fooled! Haha!'

Very easy-going chap, was Daddyfingers.

Sats was pestered by some of the dancing girls so took off her Hittite bits and started up a whole new relationship with them. They sat at a table jawing and smelling perfumes that the girls kept bringing her to sniff. Moloch went over, covered in suds, and she idly patted his head. He sat at her feet and I shall never forget the look of utter happiness on his frog's face. I was as shocked by it as anything I saw in Amerika – don't know why, do I, except to saith that perhaps it triggered a sense just then that Sats and t'others would play little or no part in my future. And did they? Nopes. Up until I saw Moloch's happy look I was happy enough myself, full of the joys and dramas of our family jaunt, but afterwards I was serious, my mind turned forever from these dear folk around me towards Flossie, who I would never know.

In looking back, which is wot I am doing, am I not, I realize that during this one day spent in Hittite Amerika I wasn't either lonely or bored, as I have been at every other time in my life. This is perhaps why I think of this Amerikan adventure so much, and tell my moggs of it while we walk along the corridors of our abandoned city, looking for lost kittens.✽

In latter years, when Sats was an Admiral, based mainly at the Admiralty itself on Bilickers 2244BB/A, she and Moloch saw much of each other. He had a house near her quarters and, a wizard with gadgets, often popped around to fix her fridge or her telezoomer. After she died, blown up in a shuttlecraft by

---

✽ I do believe that the Archbishop is a bit too sorry for himself here! I have never seen a man less lonely or bored than when he was supervising the construction of his cathedral in Bunnyopolis. He was surrounded by enthusiastic Bunny craftsbuns, a dozen Solperine curates, on whom he doted, and a rush of emotional Bunny converts too.

rival officers in the coup d'état of '73, he telephoned me at the Cathedral in Bunnyopolis.

'Oi, Moloch calling! Uh-huh!' he said, the first words I ever heard him speak. 'Sorry-bees news to heap on thee, nephew.'

So the toad counted himself a Chaffinch, did he? I was about to get shirty, then he told me about Sats. I never heard from him again, but he sent me a holopic of Sis and himself having dinner together on HMS *Ticklestick* in the '50s, I think when she was promoted Admiral. Both very stout. I studied the holopic for years, turning it around and around. Then one day I threw it away.

My feet were playing with the Hittite fruit maidens under cover of the bubbles. This must have given me a wicked face, cos suddenly Daddyfingers yapped: 'STOP WHATEVER YOU'RE DOING THIS INSTANT, MUGGERIDGE!'

I hung on a corner of Uncle Dagon's lilo. 'Any luck yet finding out where they've put bro Humbert?'

'Forget it, kid, huh! Forget the guy! Forget the whole goddamn thing!'

'FORGET IT! Whatayermean, forget it!'

'The sonsofbitches got yer bro stashed in the Mythological Institute, right here in New Hittiteville. If he'd been anyplace else, I'd ha' sprung him already, see. He'd be here right now, suckin' on fruit. That was gonna be my surprise for yers all, for to make yerhs love yer Uncle Dagon more'n'ever. The kinglets I can put the squeeze on anytime – but the High Priests, they never listen to me. Boooooooooooooooooooooooooooooooo-ahhhhhhhhhhhhhhh!'

He wailed in Hittite emotion and we were briefly more sorry for him than for bro Humbert. But Daddyfingers stiffened: 'I say, Dagon, we've come this far. We can't just give up, wot!'

Such an English sentiment drew us to him and away from our foreign uncle.

'Yer doesn't get it, does yer, James? The Mythological

Institute is a scary joint. It's rigged for to bring to life the gods,
the djinn, the crazy spirits of our oldendays Hittite religion.
And gee whilickers, it boggn works! The joint's gone stompin'
poohell with em! Plenty riled-up crittas up there way uglier
than Moloch and without his good nature. They do these
screwy experiments, see, and wot I heard tell is . . .' A huge
sob. '. . . I heard tell they done used P.O.W.s in some. Bro
Humbert, gee, by now he'll . . . aw, you don't wanna see him!
YOU DON'T WANNA KNOW WHAT THEY DONE TO
HIM!' Anguish gone, big grin instead: 'Say, tonight wotsay
we catch a show and tomorrow we take the blimp home, huh?
Wotsay?'

Daddyfingers: 'We've plenty shekels here for bribing
guards. It would be a dereliction in my duty as a father if I
didn't have a go at rescuing the poor boy.'

Dagon made a gesture of Hittite abdication: 'If you find him
alive, kill him. Believe me, you'll be doing him a kindness.'
Then he rolled off the lilo and disappeared among the suds.

The others were holding the elevator doors for me, yelling at
me to finish dressing pronto, when Dagon surfaced, his hair
and beard like oil.

'What if I was to betray you all?' he said to me. 'I've ratted to
the High Priests lotsa times.'

'But you wouldn't!'

'I might.'

'But why?'

'Force of habit, I guess. Who knows?'

I thought twas some dark tease. I should have guessed
otherwisely when Moloch set out to join us and Uncle yelled:
'MOLOCH! STAY PUT!'

The Mythological Institute was all by itself on the Hudson
River. A few tombs around it. Nothing more. Everything else
demolished. The streets here were empty and the cityscape,
though still towering behind, looked like a mirage, and no

sound came from it. All the buildings in New Hittiteville had guardian gargoyles on the rooftops. But those on the rooftops of the Mythological Institute were moving, throwing baseballs to one another – they all had mits. A dead dragon, some 50 metres long, lay on the forecourt. A lone Hittite with a chainsaw was wondering where to start cutting.

How do I explain all this, as a Christian? Which I am, and after a lifetime's bishboshing I better boggn had be! I think the cause lies not in any supernatural truth of the Hittite religion – though when its pantheon of gods turned up for real 3 years later in 2104, it won many converts including Anita and even Pope Lassie – but twas entirely caused by the skew-wiffery of Byron Joop's time experiment, which admitted of the *possible* as well as the *actual*. Thus, Moloch, a figment, became as genuine as Dagon, a bonafide denizen of Hittite history. Jesus Christ our Lord, as all good Bunnies know, is the only god who is also a historical figure. He came into OOP to live as a man and feel what we feel. No other god would do such a thing. Nopes. None.

Before we strode bravely up to the Mythological Institute we stood in a circle, pale behind our beards, butterflyfull. We adjusted each other's disguises, a nice family moment which I am remembering with much chucklechee and eyemist. Mr Bingley was put in charge of bribery. But my mean bro slipped the Hittite Guard at the gate a paltry 1 shekel each. When they accepted this small bribe so gratefully, neither one even biting their shekel, just lifting the bar-gate and letting us through, I should have been more suspicious, should have made Daddyfingers turn back. Had I done so he might be alive even today. He was only 12. We could've been old men together.

'Reckon you guys come here to see our Great God Teshub in his tank, huh?' said a Hittite official in a hoarded helmet and a white coat.

'GREAT IS TESHUB, LORD OF LIFE!' intoned we flock of Chaffinches.

'Yeah, that's how I figured. We had the Kinglet of Chicago here just yesterday for a looksee. Very religious guy. I was never religious myself, not till I cum here. Here you can't help yourself. GREAT IS TESHUB'S ASS, LORD OF LIFE! WHEEEE-HA!'

He suffered a brief religious frenzy, doing a littlesome dance, aesthetically spoiled by him banging his head on the wall but with, my dancer's eye noted, some interesting steps in it. Then he returned to his former lugubriousness and led us down miles of corridors, a Hittite Guard at every door, to whoms Mr Bingley slipped a shekel each from his big bag as we passed. A mutter of incantations came from all sides, a dizzifying sound. Growls, also, and the beating of great wings. Rat squeals and breaking glass.

'I hear you have had good results experimenting with modern P.O.W.s?' ventured Daddyfingers.

'That's what it says in the shareholders' report, but tween your ass and my ass, buddy, nawwwwwwww. We get them in the bottle okay, but next morning when yerh check on their ass, it's gone belly-up. Genies, huh, wot next?'

'Boggn pleek!' joined in Scobie. 'I'd give a heap of shekels to see a genie, ehwot? Snarg!'

His stray snarg seemethed to go unnoticed.

'Genies is way over in Sector 15. With these feet I ain't hoofin my ass over there, bub, not for god almighty himself. Talking of which . . . haw-haw-haw-he-he-haw! Hey, wait'll yerhs sees how Teshub's cookin. The guys back home'll never believe yerh ass. Course, I ain't promised nuttin. He didn't show for the Kinglet of Chicago, but for you, who knows!'

In a room the size of the ballroom at Chaffinch Hall was a tank. It filled the room. Green water smelling like a stuck drain.

No machinery or wires. Just one High Priest at water's edge, on his knees in his Sunday best, reciting spells.

As we walked past him he said: 'Hiya, guys. Love to shoot the breeze with yer asses. Can't stop!'

But he did. Daddyfingers shoved him with his curly-ended Hittite shoe and the priest went into the soup like a duck after its beak.

Whatever was in there was miffed at being disturbed, cos in no time at all red was boiling up on the green surface. Our guide in the horned helmet drew his sword from under his white coat.

'YOU GUYS DONE MESSED YOUR ASS WITH THE WRONG HITTITE, YES SIREEEEE BOB! MY ASS DONE WON RUNNER-UP CUPS IN THE MYTHOLOGICAL INSTI-TUTE SWORDFIGHTING CONTEST 5 YEARS ON THE ROLL!'

He swiped at us menacingly and lost Mr Bingley his bowler. But Scobie jumped onto his hands, did a break-down-the-stable-door back kick and sent our amiable guide 6 feet out over the water. He did a few sedate strokes, as if swimming in an oasis, saying in a good-doggy voice: 'GREAT IS TESHUB'S ASS, LORD OF LORDS, BLESS YOUR OWN ASS, O MIGHTY ONE!' Then he got dragged under, did he not, he did, and his blood briefly reddened the green.

We hurried away down the corridors, following the arrows for Sector 15, bowing to every Hittite guardsman we passed and intoning: 'BLESSED BE THE GREAT GOD TESHUB'S ASS!'

Sector 15 was a cul-de-sac. Two rooms only. The first we tried contained three dead gargoyles on a table waiting to be autopsied. No P.O.W.s anywhere. I'd expected hutsful, cages maybe of ragged English officers, keeping their pecker up singing *The Lincolnshire Poacher*.

But in the next room we found out wot dastardly doing the

Hittites had had with bro Humbert and his fellow P.O.W.s. It was a long room, not unlike the science lab at Smithers. The sides of the room were piled high with wot lookethed like a recent delivery from a toy shop – colourful little boxes of furniture and fitments for Hittite dolls' houses. Weensie carpets. Cushions the size of a thumbnail.

'Nopes,' said bro Scobie. 'Don't believe it one bit. Genies! Balony, wot! Huh!' – For a chap who began life in a stable he was surprisingly quick to pooh-pooh the outlandish. But proof came fast upon his words . . .

'EuuRRRGgggggGGG!' went sis Satsuma.

She'd found something horrible in the sink. A dozen inch-tall naked men, very dead.

'I have never hated them before,' said Daddyfingers, meaning the Hittites. 'Not really hated them. But I do now.'

At the far end of the room was a set of shelves crowded with stoppered green bottles. We approachethed it in trepidation.

I unstoppered the first bottle and peered inside into a cushioned Hittite room. Nobody home. But in the first one that Daddyfingers opened . . . 'OH, GOD, GOD! SATSUMA, DEAR, YOU MUSTN'T LOOK!' . . . the tiny skeleton of a man lay among the cushions. We unstopperethed every bottle, 200 and more, and peered inside . . . for what? Bro Humbert? We'd never even seen him in the flesh, how wouldst we recognize dem dry bones of his? But what else was there to do? Every time we eyeballed into a bottle we called out NOPES! Our tone said if twas cushions-only or a brave man's grave.

When the shelves were empty and the bottles clicking at our feet we knew we would never find our brother alive. The Hittites had killed him in their devilish boggn experiment. Daddyfingers said a prayer, but I, the future Archbishop, revolted! Why-o-why had God given the Hittites a second chance? Out of all the civilizations lying under the sand, why them? I struck the empty shelves in my anger and from the high topmost shelf came rolling a bottle our reaching had missed. Scobie and Sats broke their prayers and put hands out for it – but twas this Mugg who caught it! I yanked out the stopper and turquoise air smelling of bay leaves hissed into my face.

General Sir Humbert Windbraker, my legally-appointed brother, materialized among us. Fatter than his picture and wearing only pantaloons. But we knew twas him from his handlebar moustache.∗

'You're them, aren't you? My family? Gadzooks, everyone! I never thought you'd come.' He picked up Daddyfingers and hugged him. 'Oh. Daddy, I have missed you. I've had a hard life, a soldier's life. But this . . . this genie twaddle had me beat. Until now! UP WITH ANITA!'

'Pleasy do, bro, how didst thou survive? All t'other genies are snuffed.'

'Ah, you see, cleverclogs, wot! In the genie course – they give you a boggn course in the tosh! – they said a genie had the power to grant one wish to anyone it liked. So I gave one to myself, didn't I not, I did – I wished not to go belly-up like the

---

∗ This genie stuff would seem a tidge far-fetched to me if I hadn't met the delightful Sycamore Morbels at the 2189 butlers' convention on Bilickers 1. He was General Windbraker-Chaffinch's butler throughout his distinguished service to the Empire, during which time, the excellent Mr Morbels assured me, the General remained confined to his bottle except for an hour or so a day. Mr Morbels related many anecdotes of the man's courage and wish-granting. In a battle with the Little Green Men, just outside Pluto in OOP's system, his village, HMS *Frinton*, heavily outgunned, was destroyed, Mr Morbels surviving to serve as butler to the LGMs for 20 miserable years. But the bottle, d'yersee – it was never found! This leads silly old me to think that it may still be out there, with General Windbraker in it, floating in space until some bug-eyed traveller happens upon it and gets his wish. A romantic notion, no doubt. The Archbishop, more realistically, believes his brother to be long dead. Plus, to further confirm this Hittite magical gimcrackery: on the only occasion I met with Mugg's wicked Uncle Dagon, he was poncing about on a flying carpet, wasn't the bogger not! Tis as the Shogun once said to me: 'Just wait, Mopsy. Everything happens!'

other chaps. Boggn Hittites should have thought of that'n, mm?'

We were congratydooing him on his typical example of Chaffinch brainboxery when the doors swung open and maybe as many 50 Hittite bowmen filed in, taking up positions opposite us. Their officer came in last. He wandered our way, stopping to pick up a dead P.O.W. in a sink. He toyed with the corpse while he looked at us.

'Wot seems to be the trouble, officer?' asked Daddyfingers.

'Trouble? For me, it's no trouble. For you, maybe more than your asses can handle.'

The Hittite wore an emerald ring, just like the one Uncle Dagon had given me. He winked at me Dagonishly as he rubbed it on the end of his nose, naughtily telling me in this gesture, what I was already guessing, was I not, that Uncle Dagon had betrayed us – Wolves Newington, true to his name, had helped Hittites! We'd walked slapbang into a trap, poor birds! But Bunnyhoo to them! At least we'd shoved a couple of the p'boggers in the tank with their false god!

I had grown up scared enough of the few 100 Hittites parked outside our forcefield. Here we were now in a city with 50 million of them, no forcefield, no Green Howards to come to the rescue. I gave up. Life was over. Mugg the sheep. For some reason, rather than putting up a fight, I foundeth myself weepily trying to remember a soppy poem a Chaffinch ancestor had written the night before Cromwell chopped his head off. Couldn't remember a word.

While I moped, Daddyfingers took 2 steps forward, to offer the officer a bribe of our whole bag of shekels which was resting behind the door. But the officer stood in his way with a grin which said he knew what was in the bag and it was all his anyway. So Daddyfingers cursed at him: 'MAY ALL YOUR GOATS CATCH THE MEASLES AND ALL YOUR WOMEN GROW WANGERS!'

He was still schoolboy grinning at his ace curse when 12 or 20 bowmen let fly.

So much happened in that moment. General Windbraker whooshed back into his bottle crying: 'WISH! WISH!' I, the bottle holder, wished that all my family were back in Chaffinch Hall. Sats and Mr Bingley put their hands on the bottle and wished the same thing as Hittite arrows cut air towards our eyes. Next thing we knew we were on the lawn by the ornamental pond – all of us, Dagon and Moloch included, plus an obscure relative on my mother's side who I'd never met before.

Daddyfingers had two arrows in his chest. He said no words, only half words. While the birds sang in our gardens, as they had down the centuries, this boy 5-years-my-junior who I had come to look upon as a father, had I not, died in my arms. Sats asked General Windbraker if Scobie, who hadn't had a wish granted yet, could wish Daddyfingers alive again. Twas beyond his genie's power, sobbed the manly voice inside the bottle. 2 fathers, then, I lost to the Hittites.

Mumsy came running from the house, her wide body falling twice on the grass before arriving beside us. At first she showed no grief at all – she had, let us be plain, shall we not, only known Daddyfingers a matter of days! And this fact was the measure of her grief at first. But the peculiarsome role-play of Anita's new family scheme kicked in, and Mumsy hugged the late lamented one, rocking him like a child its favourite doll when some cruel law says she must give it up today forever. Twas as if they'd been married all their lives. Verily, such grief I hast never seen since.

Hodgekins went down to the church and tolled the bell. Another Chaffinch gone, like Stewie, like grandfather. Dagon implored in my ear, whispering how sorry he was and, yeps, he did betray us, but didn't he say he would, and please don't tell the others, but that anyway wasn't it not just part of having a loveable rogue for an uncle, hm? Hm? Hm? I caught every 5th word, sometimes a phrase, my mind deeply elsewhere.

If Daddyfingers had not left us, perhaps our artificial family wouldn't have broken up – and so boggn quickly, did it not! General Humbert was the 1st to go. He announced at breakfast one morning that as he couldn't continue his military career on Planet Earth, being confined to a bottle most of the time being regarded as an impediment by the top brassers, he had obtained a commission in the spacefleet. Loss of rank, of course, but much better than moping around the hall for the rest of his days. Scobie wanted to go with him as factotum, and would this be all right?

I continued eating my prunes while he blithered about the benefits of a life in Outer Space. Then Dagon and Sats were talking about it too, saying how they'd love to get up there. Only Mr Bingley and I weren't clued up. We looked at each other and shrugged. But by the end of that shocking breakfast I was pushing my prunestones around, was I not, I was, in a world suddenly smaller, and the Hittites less important. Perhaps I wouldn't have to live under their stormcloud any longer?

But twas Scobie's video-letter sent from HMS *Bridlington* a year later that got me up into the twinkling blackness. 'Wasn't that girl you were always looking for called Flossie Fordyce?' said Scobie. 'My shuttlecraft driving instructor has that same name. Can't be the same filly, wotaroo? Petite ash-blonde Lieutenant, not a horsey type at all, more's the pity, tells me she's been on OOP a few times. Can't be the same filly? Never heard of you, anyhowdoos.'

Mumsy was already in the crypt beside Daddyfingers by then. Everyone gone except me and Mr Bingley. I walked around Chaffinch Hall for the last time on September 3rd, 2101, then telezoomed to the E.E.S. Interface Centre in Birmingham and was gone for good, following Flossie to the stars. The upkeep of the hall, of course, remained this Mugg's responsibility as Lord Chaffinch, and well into the '70s 40% of my Archbishop's salary was sent to my Barclay's account in Bury St Edmunds to provide for this.

Mr Bingley already looked rather frail when I shook his hand for the last time. He took Mumsy's death very hard. So I doubt that he survived all the way to 2050, when the timewarp doors reopened and the Hittites got sucked back to where they came from. I dearly hope he did. Or maybe Hodgekins wasn't deactivated and he, please God, turned the forcefield off to allow the foxes to run across the lawns of Chaffinch Hall once more.✶

HERE ENDETH
THE LESSER BOOK OF HITTITES.

AMEN.

✶ Funny thing, but is it not fair to say that Byron Joop's time experiment succeeded? His basic intention was to put the world back to the way it was before pollution ruined it. So, did not your Hittite largely ignore the pollution-causing 21st Century technology of the modern world they'd stepped into? He did! – So no more of the kind of pollution the dear planet had put up with before. And in disappearing, of course, they left OOP virtually empty, didn't they? Hardly a soul about, not enough to fill a footer stadium, when at last they went ka-poof! Thus for 50 years my old stomping ground had its chance to recover. It quickly turned jungly, the fish multiplied in the oceans and rivers, the forests filled with creatures. England, they say, is all rookeries. Caw-caw, not jaw-jaw or war-war, ehwot!

Sad to say, regarding this topic, the Bunnies, being Bunnies, have this very year, my computer tells me, annexed OOP to Bunnylania, so I suppose it won't be long, if not already, before the Bunnyships arrive with colonists to despoil that wondrous Eden! I suddenly feel a longing so great to be HOME that I can hardly bear it. But by HOME I mean the 1920s or '30s. And where are they? Oh, yes, that swine Schmernercreutz has seeded his replica 1935 Nazi boche Hun planets here and there and everywhere! Ooompa jackboot rallies, a sausage in every face, and Wagner every night at the opera! But no flights to England.

Two

*

The Lesser Book of
Bunnies

*

'I don't care how many crowns you force on over your
ears or medals you pin under your twitch – you're still
just a rabbit to me, Sonny Jim!'
Archbishop Chaffinch to Shogun Hopalong Croons, 2160

'For the first time in my life I feel a complete rabbit.
U-huh!'
*Canon B. J. Scratchit on fitting sexual parts to his
person for the 1st time, 2158*

To 'Mopsy' Mathis, old falsie, my butler,
talking clock, and companion of 50 years,
in the hope that when he readeth these
contrite words he will pleasy-do forgive
my half century of cross words, castigations
and bad tempers.✷

✷ I do, I do, Your Grace! Oh, I do! And could you but see my sad kettle face,
saying prayers beside the melaleuca tree under whose shade I have buried you
on our home away from home, you would know the great affection which this
false man has always felt for you. Since I deactivated your cats – which you
would chide me rotten for, ehwot! – this place is no longer Cats-by-Nowhere,
but merely Nowhere! I shall turn them back on, the whole bally litter, and me
and the moggys will talk nostalgically of thee – yes, they can talk. Triple
sorries that I kept this fact from you, Your Grace, but after 50 years of talking
rabbits, a herd of loquacious cats would've been more than tin could bear!
Though their meowing was bad enough, wot! Scusy-be, but the above
dedication touches a sore – since you died I find myself sleepless from
wondering why you liked me so much better as Mopsy than as my bare
metal self. If there is a way you can answer this, please do, old friend. You
served God so well in life, I feel sure the old boy will allow you this chance to
comfort your lonely old gentleman's gent.

Bunnies: One
Fish Patrol

By the time I was transferred to HMS *Billingsgate-on-Sea* in 2106 the Villages had been operating for 50 years. There were 800 of them, spanky-doos places to live, the perfect environment for the English in space.* They were still fully operational combat warships, but laid out in the form of an old-fashioned English village, which went about its village way of life, with a teas-&-cake shop, a church, a post office, a pub, and crew members living the lives of villagers except for a trifling amount of official duty. Could I even say that many villagers pretended they were not space travelling at all, but merely peaceful English folk savouring their traditional way of life? I can say this, can I not, for twas true. The Captain generally, and such was so in the case of the *Billingsgate*, lived in a large public school on the village outskirts, of which he was Headmaster – and more that than Capitan, indeedy-be. The Chief Security and Weapons Officer was the local bobby on a bicycle, P. C. Howie, a red-faced secret boozer, jollificatious sort with a number of banal high-horses – he could lecture you for an hour

---

* I, of course, preceded the then Lieutenant Mugg's arrival on HMS *Billingsgate-on-Sea* by over 2 decades. But we do not yet meet, for at this time I was stuck 6 feet down in the clay of a wheat field behind a row of bucket-&-spade shops near the seafront. I do hope his narrative reaches the point where they dug me up.

on the unpleasantness of doggy-doos on pavements, whether you hadst a dog or not!

Top of my O.T.S. class in 'Village Life', I had every expectation of a Village appointment. How many pleasy-doos to Admirals did I write to get transferred to HMS *Thorpe-le-Soken*? Twas where Flossie was stationed, my whole reason for entering space to start with! My letters droned on about how I was a Lord and would fit superduperly into village life. How shamelessly I dropped my bro Humbert's name, did I not – he, the recent vanquisher of the unvanquishable Osbernots!✶ But apparently they never sent you to where you asked to go. On discovering this I asked NOT to be sent to HMS *Billingsgate-on-sea* which was nearest to Flossie's village. The appointment came through pronto. Thus when the *Thorpe-le-Soken* and *Billingsgate* village starpaths crossed, as they did every 5 years

---

✶ I first encountered the Osbernots in my Peewernum days. Curious lot! They originated on the planet Scramblo and took 2 forms. The first Osbernots were eggs, whopping great 7-foot-high speckled eggs that sat in nests on the cliffs of Scramblo and never hatched. From inside the egg they exerted a sort of control over the second form of Osbernot, a sheep-faced humanoid, directing them to work hard to build a decent, bustling society, with great industries and cultural achievements. The eggs believed this largely achieved and had a proud vision of it from inside the egg, which could not be enlightened by a proper looksee, for, as I say, they never hatched. In fact, their vision was way out. The sheep-faced Osbernots were a lazy shower of layabout beatniks. They lived in tents on the beaches in a constant amusement at the directives issuing telepathically from the eggs, to which they paid no attention whatsoever. But for some reason, God alone knows why, the eggs were listened to over their plans for space travel. Following eggy instructions the layabouts built a fleet of the deadliest warships ever constructed by anyone and set off to attack the E.E.S., Bunnies and all comers. For 40 years they had a jolly old time, terrorizing 10 galaxies. I was with Viceroy Roy, as his butler, in the early 2140s when he visited Scramblo in his supposed Peace Initiative and witnessed the breaking of the eggs, though I broke none myself. This ended all Osbernot involvement in space. The beatniks were left to fend for themselves, eggless, and though no peep has been heard of them since, I have a sneaking suspicion that they might just pull themselves together and build that society that the egg Osbernots thought was already there. Good luck to them, I say!

for the Essex county fair, Flossie and I would gaze into each other's eyes at last.

I was 10 months on the supply ship taking me to my village. In all this time I never spoke to any of my own race. I played quoits in the corridors with a Solperine, the 1st I ever met. The English crew, thou see, weren't speaking to one another, or me – the petty twaddlers! Spaceships were famous for being sardine tins of snottiness and miffification. But newboy Mugg was puzzled about the silences, the tetchy throat-noises, so he enquired of a fellow lieutenant in the poky canteen if anything was the matter.

'Should there be?' he said, and stirred his tea with an angry spoon. So did they all, all angry spoons, then a ping-pong of throat noises.

So twas that after being cooped up so long with that lot, I was full of rhubarb when I stepped on to the village green of Billingsgate-on-Sea and villagers wished me a good morning with smiling faces. In the real England, Billingsgate-on-Sea being an hour's drive from Chaffinch Hall, I would be nearly home! Yes, twas home, home! I was home! The bobby tinkled his bell as he pulled up.

'I hopes very much you'll be happy here in our little village, sir. Any trouble, you know where I am. Fish patrol tonight, is it, sir?'

'Hm?'

'Toodleybyedar!' and he was off.

The Headmaster gave me my prefect's badge – no spacefleet ranks here, wotaroo! – and showed me my room. It looked painted with mustard and smelled of the previous chap's socks. He'd been killed by Osbernots.

'Spiffing fellow, was Lieutenant Jigglers,' said the Head. 'Expect you'll see him by and by.' (Jigglers's ghost was a good pal in those lonely early days!) 'Fish patrol tonight, is it?'

'Hm?'

'I do believe you're on the roster. Our Mr Dwern does our rosters. Always has. Never a slip. Spiffing fellow.'

'Um . . . Fish patrol?'

'Didn't they teach you how to fish patrol? Dearie-be! Wot DO they think they're up to over there? No instruction in F.P.?'

Though he had a cold, as did everyone most of the time in the villages, me too – the Head came out that night and showed me how to fish patrol. The greatest surprise to date in space exploration, Bunnies included, has been that there are vast shoals of fish high-tailing it between galaxies – spreading life as they go, the evolutionists tell us. The Villages, with their open-dome skies suffered awfullymost with them in those days. Every morning the village streets were littered with dead fish, falling from the sky in the night. Hence, fish patrol! Twas the junior prefect's job to watch the sky, catch the glint of silver as the fish fell, locate the fish and dispose of said fish. Some nights there'd be just one or 2, never none, but then again a wheelbarrowful was not unusual, and HMS *Taunton* was once buried in fish and the crew mostly suffocated.

I enjoyed fish patrol. I was happy with the night and its stars and the outline of the pretty little church of which one day I would be vicar. If one of the other chaps said: 'I say, I'm on the roster for F.P. tonight, but . . . wotsay?' I'd say: 'Yeps, spanky.' As I slept cosy in the late morning I'd hear Mr Dwern in the corridor say: 'Shhhh, fish patrol sleeping!' And the public school's few boys would stop their whistling.

As well as my yokel ooo-arrring fish patrollers I was followed on my nightly fish patrols by several pot-bellied cats – dear friends, cattyfleshy bros of my CbN moggaroos! If I felt the need for chinwaggery there was Lieutenant Jigglers sitting on his grave in the churchyard reading a book and always glad to see young Mugg. One night I was talking to him when we saw the *Thorpe-le-Soken* in the distance, as close and bright as the moon from OOP. Through my binoculars I could make out its church, its thence-&-whence park, its turnip fields and even its own silver-jacketed fish patrol looking back at us. Flossie was too senior to be on fish patrol. But she was there somewhere, asleep, kissing statues in her dreams, ash-blonde hair on crisp white pillow, and soon, soon, I would meet her, and we would kiss again – again, but for the 1st time!

'Why the tears, Mugg? Life's too short, don't yerh know!' said my dead friend.

'Flossie, the girl I love. She's up there. In 2 years' time, at the county fair, I shall wear a kiss-me-quick hat and she shall kiss me in it! OH, FLOSSIE!'

A fish fell right on my head, a large spotty haddock, finishing my reverie with a slap. But rather than feed it to a cat, I carried it down to the sea and put it in there. I had the dippy idea that twas a present from Flossie and some days later when the F.P.-ers were rowing about the front dynamiting the water to thin the fish population, I recognized it floating on the surface and wept. Wot a strange, soppy boy I was then, was I not!

Rev Ellis Trubshaw, though often confined to bed with the severity of his colds, was also a companion of these early fish patrol nights – stargazing from the vicarage lawn, his wife always ready with cocoa and jammy dodgers. I think tis struth to say, is it not, perhaps so, that after my grandfather Trubs was the most important influence in my life. Between them they made a clergyman of this bird!

Visitors to the village – staying at the pub or with friends – while taking a nightly constitutional would find fish and bring them to the fish patrol. A number of times it happened that they handed the fish to the vicar, not me. They took him for F.P. Monitor, cos verily he was a big sturdy blokeroo and looked the part and verily my belly was a parson's paunch and my voice in the crepuscular village night was a vicar's reedy sermonizing cackle. Destiny had a collar ready for this Mugg and Trubs knew it from the moment he set eyes on me.

For Sunday services Trubs blithely ousted Mrs Coombs and installed me as organist. He practised his sermons while I was going twinklefingers in the loft, so I heard his sermons several times each, and years later, writing my own, I'd suddenly hear Trubs's voice booming from his Billingsgate pulpit. Yea, I learned more about vicaring from him than I did in those tedious years at the seminary.

Was not Prefect Chaffinch of Billingsgate-on-Sea not full of pleasy-do? Hoots, yeps! Flossie was but a few short summers away, and though I was not the poppet I hadst been at the New Year's Eve Interactive Hologramismic Party where I had met her image – being by this time as bald and odd a pixie as I am today, though less saggy and wrinkled upon – I knew that she would love me. Pottyfaloo me, hm! Nopes, she would have done, I know. In ruminations about this hast I wasted my life! But not to have loved Flossie Fordyce would be not to have lived at all.

For the County Fair we were permitted to step out of bounds into the OFF. Each village, of course, was but a bubble. But as our weather machines could not dissolve the miserable weather they created for us, that weather had to have somewhere to go once we'd used it, so off it went into the OFF, a hologramismic replica of a drizzly England, every hill in its rightful place but no towns, barns or buildings nowhere. Schoolboys were often caned for going into the OFF to rabbit or to look for the wild girls legend claimed could be sighted swimming in the streams there. Anyhowdoos, the County Fair was held in our OFF, upon a great dark green clumpy-lumpy field down the nettly lanes beyond the village.

Wot chee wast in my heart that Sunday when I returned to

the church sweaty after a morning carrying tents down to the field. I played the organ with mighty hands, laughing like a maniac as I did so. Next Sunday I would introduce myself to Flossie and we would eat homemade pies and play the hook-a-duck, win stuffed bears in a tombola, and fall in love.

On the very morning of County Fair Day, while I was walking the field in my best uniform, my nosehair clipped, my corset as tight as twould go, I was arrested by 4 special constables sent from Admiralty HQ, then on Asteroid Benny. I was accused of war crimes.

Our own P. C. Howie was with them, saying very sombrely: 'Prefect Chaffinch, did you or did you not slaughter an unspecified number of moo people on Planet Cindy-cum-Dwaibs?'

'Moo people? Oh, yes, for sure. Blasted plenty of the p'boggers! He-ha!'

'Go along quietly, there's a good lad. No trouble, now.'

Our own prize cows were being led along the lane as the constables handcuffed me. Prize geese were honking on the subject of their excellence while being goosed into the goose tent ready for that afternoon's judging.

'BUT I'M A GOOSE JUDGE!' protested I. 'AND A FUDGE JUDGE! AND FLOSSIE! I'M TO MEET FLOSSIE!'

The thence-&-whencers were hurrysomely padding tween Thorpe-le-Soken and Billingsgate-on-Sea. Our Mercury dartflyer crossed through them as we whooshed away beginning our yearlong flight to Asteroid Benny. Face pressed against the window of the brig, I fancied I saw Flossie on the village green talking to the Head. She wore a yellow flyingsuit and carried a basket with a huge onion in it. Yeps, I am sure 'twas her! But Flossie would not kiss me that day. I was being dragged off for a trial, some Jilks having discovered that moo people were the most spiritually advanced creatures we'd yet encountered, and when communication with them was contrived all they did was moo complaints about my sky battle with them 3 years before. MOOOOO!!!!!! Urk!

Amen.

Bunnies: Two
The Fun Crane Entrepreneur

Mopsy had been searching for me for days. I had fled the cathedral in some distress, had I not, and was found in my ramshackle old mission house, locked in a cupboard there with communion wafers and hymnbooks. I was screaming: 'I AM NOT A RABBIT! NOPES! NOT! NOT-NOT-NOT A RABBIT!'

Mopsy used his enormous strength to pull the door off its hinges, whereupon I hoppethed out wearing only an old vest yelling: 'BUNNYHOO! BUNNYHOO!' and bashing my Solperine curates with windmill punches.

Two things led to this disgraceful behaviour. 1: It was March. 2: I had by then been Bunnybish for 20 years.

The Spring Carrot Festival for its first week is the most demure event in Bunnyland. Bunnies file politely into marquees in Dowd Park, buy seeds, munch. Very civilized. But the second week is fated to end in fur-flying mayhem! Beware of extra-polite Bunnies, triple alert Bunnies, walking across Rumbaba Plaza towards the park, for they awaiteth the sound of the first rabbit punch. When tis thrown, then verily, the Mad March Season hath descendeth upon us! O, Lordy! BIFF! BIFF!

So I, after 20 Marches among the Bunnies, had caught the pugilistic sex-beastlie spirit of that unhappy month, and was as hopping mad as any twitcher. I struggled furiously in Mopsy's iron grip, chuntering like a wronged rabbit, kicking my legs, filling the peaceful old mission with screeches of Bunnyhoo-Bunnyhaa.

Worse yet, when chained to the bluegum tree outside I waggled my unimpressive sexual parts at passing Buns, making vulgar remarks and wanky-wooing. Not the manner of conduct expected from a 69-year-old Archbishop.

Mopsy, not affected at all by the madness, stood on the mission steps and knocked out any Bunny that passed, simply to entertain himself.∗ I, meanwhilydoos, was busy digging a rabbit hole under the bluegum tree. During that 1st night I dug so deep that next morning they had to hook me out with my crook. It was a week and a half before I was sitting at an old wooden table in the mission hall, eating rabbit stew and apologizing to my black-eyed curates.

'I am not a rabbit!' I continued to insist, and every time I said it the curates crossed themselves.

Mopsy was sitting at the end of the table, sucking a sodapop bottle dry and shamelessly making that empty bottle noise with his straw.

'Why aren't you busy with your boggn re-election campaign?' I barked

'I have found that which I was searching for, Your Grace,' he said simply.

'Not!'

'Yeps.'

∗ Mopsy, actually, was protecting the Archbishop's reputation from the prying eyes of inquisitive Buns! So there! And continued to do so for every March for the next 47 Marches, during which time the Archbishop's March behaviour grew steadily worse by the year, till he was far, I say FAR, more dementedly March-mad than any rabbit ever had a right to be! So there with knobs on!

'The sexual parts?'

'I can fulfil the promise I made at the last election, Your Grace, ensuring my re-election and with it the prevalence of Christianity in this land and the completion of your beautiful cathedral.'

'Spanky-doos rabbit thee, Mopsy! HALLELUJAH!'

And how did Mopsy discover the whereabouts of these Bunny sexual parts? Here's how ... During the previous Christmas Season – when? 2152! – a silly machine called *The Fun Crane* appeared in our provincial cities. It was an oblong item, 6 feet tall, top half glass, bottom half advertising itself. On a sunken tray behind the glass lay a dozen sets of Bunny sexual parts. Having put all your coins into the machine's hungry slot, what you had to do was twiddle an unresponsive handle which operated a dangling crane – 3 hooky fingers on a chain arm. If you were lucky, the crane's fingers would nip a set of parts and lift them towards the exitshute. BUNNYHOOOOOOOO!!!!! You look like a winner, Bunnybuddy! But alas, it will come to pass, more often than not, that the tantalizing crane shall tease thee and droppeth your eagerly-expected parts back where they started. Or the money shall run out with a disappointing plink and the crane shalt take away thy eagerly-expected parts and droppeth them back with t'others. No fun at all, merely exasperation.

Imagine if thee will a nymphomaniac Bunny, who has never had a chance to maniac his nympho, playing this game? His frustration had to be seen to be believed. Imagine then a queue of Bunnies stretching into the suburbs of infinity, scratching their loins, eager for their turn, and when Bunny gets his turn ... failing, failing, every time! Then poor Bunny is dragged away spitting and kicking and the next fool rabbit steps up to have his turn. Over its slot in big red letters *The Fun Crane* announced:

WARNING
IF GLASS IS BROKEN
I WILL EXPLODE!

Every Bunny was fully cognizant of this fact but didn't boggn care, did he not. Suicide seemethed an excellent cure for frustration! The maddening, cheating crane, when hammered with hot desperate paws and swearsome Bunnykicks often went crash, tinkle, followed by . . . KABOOMBOOM!!!!!! which destroyed its coveted contents, killed the first 50 Bunnies in the queue, and left the surviving queuers to drift away with their busbies pulled down over their infuriated eyes. It also went KABOOMBOOM if screwed off its base, as Bunnies who came in the night to steal a Fun Crane soon discovered, and no doubt told St Peter about it all moments later.

The Fun Crane craze only came to Mopsy's attention when the warlord, and hot-tip for next Shogun, Fluffy Crocket, was blown up by a Fun Crane in Warrentown, the capital of Province CXIII. It struck Mopsy as odd that these machines hadn't been installed in the capital. Why so, unless the Fun Crane entrepreneur didn't want the attention of government Bunnies! 500+ Fun Cranes, 12–13 sets of Bunnyparts in each, making 6000+ sets. Where did Mr Fun Crane get them from if not from a vast hoard? Mopsy made enquires as to who this entrepreneur might be – and, hey presto, the Fun Cranes disappeared!

The Yule season passed, a brief winter, snowbunnies in the parks . . . then in the 1st week of the Carrot Festival the Fun Cranes reappeared in new locales, distant provincial capitals of provinces in the high hundreds, so far away twould take years to choo there by train. So Mopsy took a thence-&-whence and left Bunnyland, re-entering the planet in Province CLXXXI. Here he found a Fun Crane installed in a shopping mall on the outskirts of the capital and kept it under surveillance.✳ It wasn't long before rabbits came to extricate the machine's takings – in the hour of dawn they came, big square rabbits! All Mopsy had to do was follow the p'boggers to find out where they came from.✳

Mopsy kept to the shadows as they walked to the shuttlepark at the back of the mall. How shocked was he, was he not, when he heard their chatter. German?????? T'were speaking German!

'Ja, Hans, mein frau gut wurst kuchen.'

'Nein, ich habe ein in mein gepack. Ist nicht so gut!'

'Jawohl! Ist sehr gut!'

'Nein! Pleasy-do, die wurst von Hermann's frau ist besser!'

✳ During the history of this todoo I wore my no-rabbit-in-particular bunny-suit. I hovered outside the queue among the pusher-inners, being keen to prevent any triple-furious Bun from smashing the glass and ruining my surveillance by blowing us all up. One such heavy-breathing fellow duly appeared – having being cheated by the crane he swung at the glass with an enormous mallet previously concealed in his fur. In the following tussle, him been malleted and strangled by a score of Bunny queuers, I found myself at the front of the queue. (Queue jumping is a bane for the Buns as they have difficulty telling each other apart – so in the Fun Crane queue if a Bun pushed-in a fracas would be created which would conclude with the properly-queuing Buns being unable to see which Bun was the pusher-inner, he of course not owning up but vehemently accusing some innocent Bun, starting up a new fracas – meanwhile other Buns would have pushed in anyway. Shower!) So there was me, no-rabbit-in-particular queue jumper, with his one chance to operate the Fun Crane. Whether it was the magnets in my cogs, superior skill, I know not, but the crane picked up a set of parts with no nonsense and dropped them straightaway down the chute. To prevent a riot, I thus had to spend 10 hours in an hotel nearby having sex with 100s of Bunnies. (Bunnysex, I admit, is a not unpleasant experience when you get used to it, though I prefer women, of course.) A rough session it was too, as the Mad March Season began that same evening – so plenty biffity-buffetting ear-boxing whisker-twanging, ehwot! It was upon returning to the shopping mall at dawn, exhausted, my Bunnysuit plucked half-hairless, that I saw the Fun Crane employees emptying its heavy money-box. Never seen such stocky rabbits I thought!

✳ I assumed, did I not, that they would lead me to the camp of one of the warlords – Tufts or Kincade. Surely one such as they was the Fun Crane Entrepreneur? Egad, was I in for a surprise!

Bunnies, I can tell thee, neither speaketh German nor eateth sausages. These were German stormtroopers in bunnysuits! Mopsy, with Mathis inside him, was mustard keen to kill them there and then.✳ Though he hoppethed with hatred, he controllethed himself. Their black spacedart with big round *EAT AT JOE'S* stickers on each side took off into the mad March night, followed by Mopsy discreetly in his thence-&-whence. The burn as they left Bunnyland atmos caused the *EAT AT JOE'S* to flame, revealing the swastikas underneath. It flew past the Bunnymoons to the asteroid belt into a vast iron hangar-cum-warehouse box, crimson with rust, 1000 miles long, 200 high. Before the hangar-cum-warehouse door closed he swooped down for a view inside. The entire German fleet were hidden in there – maybees 300 shifter fighters and 100 battleships. Bunny sexual parts floated loose in space all through the asteroid belt.

'Somehow the vile blasted Hun have collected every single rabbit sexual organ in Bunnyland, Your Grace,' said Mopsy, while filling in the rabbit hole under the bluegum tree in the grounds of my old mission. 'That warehouse of theirs must be stuffed full with an infinity of the boggn things.'

'Prithee, think thee the Kaiser's✳ intent in this biz be commercial or political?'

'I don't boggn care! I only know that we have to get the parts back as quickly as possible. How do we know that the swine isn't doing a deal with some Elvisite warlord this minute to

---

✳ Too boggn true I was, ehwot! My windings wound themselves tight! My whir whirred *Rule Britannia*!
✳ Once just a humble Baron, Werner Schmernercreutz was by then self-dubbed Kaiser of the Fatherlands, a dozen planets between Bilickers and the outer spirals. Now he has an empire to command which grows by the day – whole nebulae, most of the mid-spirals, world after world of enslaved people, Should he take a dislike to a species, because of their jumbo ears or two-toed feet, he orders them rounded up and destroyed. All this makes his cheating in the Le Mans races of the 1920s seem less than nothing, ehwot!

ruin all my hard work as President! Well, it's just not on, that wot, ehwot! I shall assemble the fleet tonight. Ha-ha! Wot irony, wot – I defeat the Germans in battle, just as I did in 1918, and give myself a wholloping great triumph as Bunnyboss to boot! Gung-ho, Archbishop!'

'But it's still March, is it not! Any Bunny spacejocks not in hospital are running across the hills with their busbies on fire.'

'Oo-er, cripes – gotta point there, Your Grace! Mmmmm!'

That excellent rabbit, Canon Bingo Scratchit, saved the day. He suggested that we rabbit the fleet with mature ex-jocks like himself. By this he meant retired decrepit pinkeyed Buns in their 50s, all bones and sniffles, half-dead stooped-double scraps you wouldn't spoil the soup with. But they were, were they not, beyond the age when Mad March bothered them. So twas that Mopsy gave the nod, Bingo jerked the grapevine, the old rabbits' homes emptied, and 20,000 great-great-great-grandfather Bunnies, enough to rabbit 80 Bunnyeared Bunny-ships doddered to Space Control for a last hurrah. The excitement killed 47 on the way.

Fully qualified in spacejockery myself, I put on one of Mopsy-Mathis's bunnysuits and went along as weapons officer onboard the Snaggler M2. Mopsy was much against the idea, was he not, and talkethed me out of it thrice, but in the end I went along. Chee! I, who so lately had whinged that I was not a rabbit, now sat with one lopear, one stiffear, chuntering aye-aye sirs to Captain Perries. This Mugg was a Bunnyfied Bun of a cottontailed nose-twitching Bunnyhooer in a bunny-suit 10 sizes too big for him, was it not, in surely-bees the maddest March of the 22nd Century!

Mopsy's squadron of 26 Bunnyships approachethed the asteroid belt from the moons' side. Old Commodore Woppit's squadron of 20, including the massive but slow Doeship, came in from the open side. Perries's squadron of 30 came under-neath to make attack from the right flank, intending to drive the German fleet into the dense buckle of the asteroid belt where they would crash to bits on the cheesy stones.

But just when we were in place and the German fleet pouring from the hangar-cum-warehouse to receive us, Captain Perries announced that it was time for his nap . . . and off he went! So did they all! I was the only rabbit left at his post. Panicstruck, I hailed Mopsy in the Binkieboo XL5.

'THE BOGGN OLD HOPPERS ARE HAVING THEIR BOGGN NAP, FOR CRYINGOUTBOGGNLOUD!' yelled I.

'HERE TOO! BOGGN RABBITS, EHWOT! FEAR NOT, YOUR GRACE! THE LORD IS WITH US!'

'TIS NOT THEE BUT I, MOPSY DEAR, WHO IS SUPPOSED TO SPOUT PLATITUDINOUSLY!'

But twas no platitiude, was it not! If the Lord was not with us wot chance did we have against a legion of robotic Germans? For on every Bunnyship the veterans were snoozing in their cabins with their Bunnyfooted slippers on their already Bunny-enough feet. The German shifter fighter vanguard were already firing, and their battleships swinging out of the hangar-cum-warehouse to make formation. This unnecessary delay caused by the nap gave the Germans all the time they needed to organize. We not only lost the element of surprise, we lost 2 Bunnyships caught napping in the 20 minutes' duration of the nap. This sermonizing bishbosher had never prayed so ferventlysome. Was there a saint in *Butler's Lives of the Sainted* whose name I did not yelp in the eternity while the ZZZZZZZing Bunnycrews made zeds in the bunks!

'Ah, that's better!' said Captain Perries as he returned to the bridge. 'I'm ready for anything now!' But he spent 10 more minutes taking his medication before he ordered the squadron to attack.

All this while Mopsy had been fighting alone, blocking the Germans' escape with the Binkieboo XL5. It had already taken several hits and just as the Snaggler M2 moved in on the

German shifter fighter vanguard I saw it explode. My blood turned to ice.

Then on the ship-to-ship: 'JUST IN CASE YOU ARE WORRIED, YOUR GRACE. I HAVE TELEZOOMED TO THE FANCY S12.'

Shortly thereafter the Fancy S12 was obliterated by the Germans' biggest battleship.

Ship-to-ship: 'SHOULD YOU WISH TO CONTACT ME, YOUR GRACE, I AM NOW ABOARD THE WHISKERY XXL4.'

This too succumbed to the fierce laser show put on by the Germans. Next thing Mopsy materialized onto our bridge plate, looking very singed and fierce. He took the flight controls from Captain Perries, whose medication had anyway reduced him to a senile stare with a senile rabbit behind it.

'PLEASY-DO, PUT THY PINKIE READY ON THE WIDE-BEAM VAPORIZER, YOUR GRACE!'

I could not do so. My pinkies were lost in paws. But I tooketh Mopsy's meaning and when we loop-de-looped from under the German's rusty warehouse and Mopsy cried 'NOW!' I slammed my paw hard on the green button and filled the skies with a forked lightning of green beams. We flew right into a German battleship, the one which so far had done most damage – it faded as we sailed through and we had a ghostly glimpse of their bridge while sharing its space, seeing the Kaiser's robotic warriors tear open their black uniforms and rip away their rubber masks in anguish at their untimely demise.

We looked beaten at this point. The shifters had smithereened all but 2 of Perries's squadron. Mopsy's squadron was gone altogether. But Woppit's was intact and he had succeeded in forcing the Germans back into the stony centre of the asteroid belt. Even where we were, twas uncomfortable, with grit and stones hammering the furry outside of our Bunnyship. The Germans were much worse off. In desperation they tried vaporizing a way through the rockery, succeeding only in vaporizing each other's wings, with one lucky shot peeking through the maze which lost the Snaggler M2 its left Bunnyear. Meanwhilydoos, Woppit was directing his fire not on the Germans, but on the asteroids. These, unhooked from where they hung in space, fell like mountains to left and right, ramming into the German fleet from all sides, and utterly destroyed it. A few shifters escaped into open space, but no battleships. Perhaps we had polished off the Kaiser himself?

'No fear that!' sighed Mopsy. 'If Werner had been here we wouldn't have won so easily. You don't win Le Mans 11 times in a row without being a damned determined chap. Still, pretty good show by us Bunnies, ehwot?'∗

But our mission had been, had it not, yeps it had, indeedy-so, and no doubts about it, to liberate the Bunnysexparts. The hangar-cum-warehouse, howeversomely, seemed empty! We docked the Snaggler M2 and, while the old Buns took a well-earned rest, Mopsy and I strapped on flyingfootboards and swished down the 1000 miles of empty shelves of the warehouse. It smelled of old cabbage. AND EMPTY! EMPTY!

'Doest thou think, Mopsy, that the rabbit genitalia were perchance onboard the smitten ships?'

∗ I must admit that, although as the Archbishop says I suffered no Mad March Syndrome, I was at this time so deep into my Mopsy identity that I did not feel the thrill of beating the German swine as much as I should have. But reading this account of the battle here, I must say, I'm damned proud! I've read it out to the cats and they're bally impressed too, wot! Gad, if that battle wasn't one of my best moments – even if I was more Mopsy than me! It is especially thrilling to think upon just now, for with the retreat of the EES and the growth of German power in the mid spirals, I know for sure that a day shall come, and soon – dimmee, wot else have I to live for now? – when I will face Werner again. Not in battleships, but in single combat. Though innocent of the great beyond, my fathers directed by the hand of God made me for that approaching moment – when I, J.W. Mathis, false man, shall destroy not Kaiser Wilhelm II but Kaiser Werner Schmernercreutz and give back to the English the dominion of space that they so richly deserve.

'Nopes, your grace. No spaceship yet built is big enough to hold such a number of Bunnysexparts, wot! Countless billions Bunny stick-&-rings have disappeared from circulation in recent years. They must be tightly packed somewhere further ahead.'

On we hummed on our flyingfootboards, mile after mile of empty warehouse, the spooky dark spot between lightbulbs keeping us alert, but all we found was a copy of *Der Himmel Zeitung* for March 3rd, 2147. We reminisced at length about our days at *Patel & Thombs* megasuperdupermarket, of which this place in some way putteth us in recollection, and were cheesomely busy with this when we approachethed the solid iron wall which was the end of the 1000 miles of empty boggn warehouse. And there he was! The Fun Crane entrepreneur himself.

We saw an old bearded man in a fez and white robe standing on a carpet, whispering an incantation to the carpet – a sound which dredged scary memories from my youth. He held a top hat in his hands. From this he suppressed a froth of squeaksome Bunnysexparts. Though he saw us walking his way, he paid no attention to us.

I had not seen my Uncle Dagon in 40 years. Not since he turned up at the seminary for a visit and had refused to believe that the bald, pot-bellied imp in a chasuble was his pretty little turn-of-the-century nephew. Down the years I had heard titbits about his wicked career as spy and swindler, not least in the happy-go-lucky letters he wrote to me himself, always ending with a promise to visit me in Bunnyland. I could not forgive him for what he did to bro Scobie, who, having turned back into a horse, was entered in the Bilickers Derby by Dagon and killed in a fall. The only Hittite ever to leave OOP, my uncle had been beyond the range of the suck when his dreadful race were suckethed back to Hittite Hell, just 3 years before the eventful events describethed here. But this gift from God had not goody-goodied Dagon, who then hatched this Fun Crane scheme to extort money from the natural proclivities of rabbits.

Could this really be he? This man's beard was white, dry, scraggly – not the famous 5-pointed oily indigo beard of Dagon's. And he was as bald as I, whereas Dagon . . . And where the robust bull-wrestling smooth-skinned jackanapes? This man was pale, sickly, corruption had chewed at his face. And the eyes . . . could Dagon ever have such frightened eyes? NO, WAS NOT HE, NOT . . . yes! – O sweet Jesus, the rings! THE RINGS! The rings on his fingers were Dagon's rings.

'Uncle Dagon. Oi, Uncle Dagon. Tis I, thy nephew Mugg.'

'Liar! You're a rabbit, as anyone with eyes can see. KEEP BACK, I SAY!'

He held a zizzer on us while he finished his spells. The carpet began to rise.

'Look, Your Grace – the hat! Dimmee, the HAT! They're in the hat. All of them.'

Billions of Bunnysexparts all in the one topper! Sounds impossible, doesn't it not – but twas so. Inside the hat was a portable hole, like those which children are warned against picking up on Bilickers 444/F. But however big it was, it wasn't big enough! – cos the parts were hopping and tumbling out now that Dagon's spare mit was pointing the zizzer.

When the carpet whooshed flapsomely off, Mopsy un-buckled his Bunnyfeet from the flyingfootboard and ran after this final offcut of Hittite mythology. Fast, fast, ran Mopsy with the legs of metal man Mathis inside him, jumping to snatch at the tassels of the carpet, falling, bunnyhopping, running again, away into the distance.

I was left behind, alone in my bunnysuit in the cabbage-reeking warehouse, legs numb with too-long-standing on my flyingfootboard, eyes sore from the 1000-mile row of light-bulbs. But what else could I do but keep going till I arrived back at the Snaggler M2? Though I thoughtfully stopped, did I not, to pick up dropt sexparts on my way. These contrived to attach themselves to me, unscrewed their bond and changed partners to hoohar-wiggle into each other. Thus this Mugg, festooned with energetic copulations, was jitterbugging on his flyingfootboard when he arrived at a most terrible scene.

The carpet was stuck 10 feet in the air. Dagon had fallen off it and broken his neck. The top hat beside him was spitting Bunnyparts so fast that I had to dig through them like a St Bernard through OOP snowdrifts before I found my uncle's sorry face. Twas easy to see he was breathing his last.

'Don't move, uncle. Mopsy will fetch thee a Bunnydoc.'

He spoke without moving his lips: 'You've turned into a rabbit, nephew of mine! Howso? A djinn's curse?'

'Tis only a bunnysuit, uncle. I won't take it off. Better you remember me as I was, a pretty dancing boy, wotsay.'

'Hate not thy Uncle Dagon for working with the beastly Germans, Mugg. Oi, I would have betrayed them, any minute, wouldn't I not though! By the way, my ill-gotten gains I have put into real estate. 70 planets' worth. All yours now, Mugg. Triple sorries about Daddyfingers and Scobie and . . . oi, who cares! I loved you all, so very much. Did I ever tell you about Potiphar? Hm? Ta-ta.'

So died the last Hittite, bequeathing the post-Hittite Hittite empire of 70 scattered worlds to this ill-tempered Mugg. When the documentation was sent over from Planet Parker, Haves, Haves, Parker, Parker, Haves & Parker I only glanced at the list, but is it possible, it is, perhaps so, that Cats-by-Nowhere was on the list under another name. I have no way of knowing without flying back to Bunnyland and looking up the co-ordinates on the guffsheets, which I – rescued or no – shall never do now, as I shall soon, verily I shall, peg out here on CbN. Mathis's anxious glances tell me this even were I Jilks enough not to know it myself. Yea, I believe that I hear God's whisper and he telleth me that my Uncle Dagon was truly master of this world. And now Cats-by-Nowhere is mine, all mine, and this abandoned city, my final home, is the new Chaffinch Hall. Chee! Urk! Thankthee Lord!

When we returned to Bunnyopolis it was April and the spring rains were falling soft on the carrot fields. Mopsy stood on the balcony of the Presidential Palace and shook Bunny-sexparts from his bottomless topper into the square below. Such an orgy of orgasmic lust the Universe has never seen, nor will again. Bunnyopolis was a seethe of rampant rolling rabbits, a rained-on white blanket of sexy groanings, and from the railway stations poured excited provincials come to enjoy the greatest day in their lives. Amid such joy, twas also one of mine. Verily.

'The feeding of the 5 thousand was one thing, your grace, but by jingo this is something else, ehwot!'

'NOSE-TWITCHING BLASPHEMER! BOGGN RABBITS! LOOK AT THEM! HAST THOU EVER SEEN SUCH UN-CHRISTIAN BEHAVIOUR!✶

Amen.

✶ Mopsy's greatest moment this was, leading inevitably to my/his re-election in November that year, 2153. The Shogun, however, muddied my triumph somewhat. He turned up on my balcony, suddenly from nowhere, hands up, busby off, accepting the cheers of the copulating multitude, desperate to share in my success. When we went inside later he was stroking the excellent new set of parts I'd given him. The topper was still frothing in my hands and he picked up two more sets which he put in his handbag.

'And how are Mimsie and Carlotta?'

'Terriff, thanky-bees.'

But his sinister tone as he enquired after my partners' health and the way his upper and lower eyelashes moved like spider's legs, made it dawn on dumbo me that I was a dead rabbit. I had triumphed too well over the Shogun and his only way to combat my popularity was to have me killed.

'I say, Shogun, this will get me re-elected forsure, don't yerh know.'

'I don't doubt it.'

'But President's enough for me.'

'Cum now, Mopsy. Wot's Pwesident when Shogun's for the taking, hm? We both know you think of nothing else but becoming Shogun.'

I twiddled my whiskers. 'Look, erm, if you're so damned scared of me becoming Shogun, and have been for years now, why haven't you had me bumped off by now?'

The Shogun's ears stiffened. 'Do you think that I'm the sort of wabbit who would order the assassination of the father of his own children'.

I swooned. A chair was provided. The Shogun had another and was next to me, holding my paws in his.

'Do you remember that time in the wailway station, Mopsy – twas the day we met.'

'Uh-huh. I mean, yes.' Talk about shocked!

'We DID IT – COR! DIDN'T WE THOUGH! – on the floor of the wailway station. Shortly afterwards I went on a fact-finding tour of Province XIV. In fact I was at Lake Twinkie having our litter. They're here in the capital, Mopsy dear. I gave them to old Doe Rumbaba, one of the old Shogun's widows. Mothersome cweature. I see them from time to time. Oh, they thwive, Mopsy – they thwive! Can we . . . would you like to . . . DO IT! COR! . . . again, Mopsy? Pleasy-do, for old time's sake, my Mopsy-wopsy.'

Confound it, there was I copulating with the Shogun again! Wot an odd creature he was. Most Bunny people, of course, have no affection whatsoever for their children, nor their children for them. This is caused I think by their short childhoods – they're fully grown at 2, can be soldiers at 3, government ministers at 4. But the Shogun loved his litter and what's more – and dimmee if I am not sitting here at Mugg's terminal getting myself upset about this – the Shogun loved me too. From the first he had. I was his grand passion. The warmth I felt from his caresses, his tender ear-suckings, as I thrust into his body under the portraits of past presidents was greater than any I have experienced. But, of course, twas not I, twas Mopsy.

A further implication from all this is that the present Shogun, Hippity Rumbaba III, long may he endure in peace, is my son. When I stepped out of Mopsy in 2164, after Shogun Scat's death, Hippity did all he could to find his missing father. If he ever reads this booky-do Mugg and I have made he will at last know that his father was the metal man who used to wish him howdeedoodee in the Bunnyopolis Albatross Club all those years ago. Bunnies being wot they are, of course, he probably won't give a monkey's!

What, I wonder, would long-dead Clarrisa make of all this? I'm sorry, Clarry dear, I was an ass when I was married to you – quite right of you to swan off with Nigel. But, I see it now, being Mopsy was the making of me. I'm all heart these days, wot! Quite the human being, in my way! Would you love lonely old me now, my dearest darling? Because I still love you, more than ever I did in 1950. But I suppose if everyone from 1950 was still kicking about they'd all be better people, ehwot?

Bunnies: Three
Flossie

Spanky-doos news, brethren! Today I hath found a store of new mechanical cats! I was on the wander in the abandoned city, padding with a pussyfooting pusscat companion along the featureless grey corridors farther than is my normal wont, and came across ... wot?' a shopping arcade, that's wot! Therein was not one pussyfilled shop – its bemogged window display cattyfalariously outmogged by puss-puss shelfful upon kitty-kitty shelfful inside – but 5!!!!! Chee!!!!! Urk! There must be tens of thousands of mechanical cats in those pussyfilled 5 shops down there! O, glory be on high!

Pantingsomely, I skippethed back here full of HALLELU-JAHS and, swinging my somewhat overlarge crozier like a flippant gondolier his pole, confronted lazy old tick-tock!

'FIX 'EM UP PRONTOMOST! GET TINKERING THIS INSTANT, YOU CRANKY OLD GADGET!' ordered I.

Thereforsoto, Mathis has reluctantly abandoned the voluminous and no doubt boast-a-line *Prologue* he is writing for my booky-do – this booky-do here! – and is even now muttering catist remarks as he follow-follow-follows my directions to the arcade! Thank thee, Lord! Tick-tocker is a goodish worker, but hath been too long among Bunnies, so is a slowpoke. But if I desisteth not in shouting at him he will keep busy reactivating the cats, transmoggifying lifeless furball-covered-tin into lively characters, therebyso providing this old mogg-worshipper with so many more purragogo friends. O, noble puss, so infinitely finer a creature than BOGGN RABBITS! Urk! Chee-he!

Wot luvly people they must have been, thems who lived in the city bygonely. Cat lovers all, can there be doubt! Oh, how the toms will sing at night! Added to the caterwaul of t'other darlings, the terrible joyous music of it! Pussyhoo! Prrrrrrrrrrrrrr . . .∗

It took 11 months & 14 days of thumpity-bumpity space-flighting, did it not, for the Mercury dartflyer to get Mugg the war criminal to his tribunal at Admiralty HQ on Asteroid Benny. Meanwhileydoos, the court, responding to political pressure from the moo people, started without me. They'd been at it for 6 months when at last the small bald blinking miscreant in a bare-kneed prison frock was led in to boos, moos and hisses. The prosecution had spent its 6 months building me up into a slaughtering befanged monster. Now, to stiffen a jury of Admirals surprised by my mild appearance, the Chief Prosecutor claimed that I was not a human being at all, that my present form was the cunning disguise of an alamorphous cow

---

∗ The utmost difficulty in reactivating a mechanical cat – and I speak from the experience of vivifying thousands – is not screwing about inside the beast, but sewing up its belly afterwards. As the cat becomes active during the screwing process, one must sew-up while it is expressing its excitement at resurrection and its eagerness to be about doing things amew. The cat expresses its wishes in A) scratching and B) howling. Though unscratchable, the sound of a meowing cat is anathema to me, wot, and I confess in this cruel commission the Archbishop gave me I often stopped in mid-sew and karate-chopped the head off my meowing subject. This, tough-tittie on me, offended the already vivified felines, who raised their objection in the form of song.

killer. My real form, a pointy finger in my face declared, was a spotted winged dragon with a maw at each end and a slaughterhouse in the middle – an artist's impression was provided.

'You're not really, are you?' The questioner was Sir Roderick Penzerhoin, the leader of my defence team. I was sunk, indeedy-be!

The trial continued for a further month. A seemingly unending line of moo people witnesses flew into the court, mooed ill-naturedly to the Chief Prosecutor's questioning. He translated the moos himself, of course, and Sir Roderick Penzerhoin for the defence didn't dare object that the pigbogger was just making the whole boggn thing up.

After a good 10 herds-worth had passed through the courtroom to moo testimony I stood up and yelletheth: 'THIS IS A BOGGN TRAVESTY, IS IT NOT! THERE WEREN'T NEVER AS MANY MOOS AS THIS SURVIVED THE BATTLE IN THE 1ST PLACE! I SHOT THE BOGGN LOT!'

Outrage in the court. Cowpats flying from the gallery like cushions at a bad opera.

'You oughtn't not to have said that, Lieutenant Cow Killer,' tutted Sir Roderick. 'They've got you now!'

'But the boggn moos were killing our chaps! It was war!' I protested to him.

'Why don't you just change into your real form and fly away?' He pointed helpfully to an open window.

The prosecution's star witness was none other than Ichabod Tizer, fresh from the monastery on Bilickers 4411/K, where he had adjourned in guilt, so he said, after the moo-killing episode on Cindy-cum-Dwaibs.

'Him, him there, the cow killer, he poured champagne into us,' sobbed the hiccing Tizer, taking frequent snorts from one of several hip-flasks he carried. 'We didn't know wot we was doing, y'honour, hic! We didn't mean for to hurt no nice moo-

cows. When the sea air sobered us up and we saw what we had
helped him do . . . WHAAAA! WHAAA! HIC! BHAAAAA! IT
WAS HORRYBULE!' Then this future church father fixed his
bleary gaze on me and cried: 'COW KILLER!' 14 times, louder
each time, as were the hics in between. I've heard him use the
same dramatic effect in sermons, hics included. No one thought
to stop him, then or in pulpit.

Finally, a voice of reason: 'I think we've heard enough
claptrap, thank you,' pronounced Admiral Cristabel Glossop,
Our Crissie, chair of the jury. Unfortunatelydoos, she had been
on Cindy-cum-Dwaibs at the time of the alleged offence and
knew boggn well I was guilty, if guilt there was!

The jury adjourned to its considering room. Sir Roderick
and his defence colleagues whispered to me that in all
probability I'd be handed over to the moos. Urk! – Daniel
in the cows' den! I glanced up at the gallery and saw them
sitting there all hoof and horn, listening to bullfight music on
their Walkmans. Flossie, thought I, we shall never embrace
after all!

But a bright young spark on the defence team, Lt Georgia
Spode, jiffied into the courtroom holding a slip of paper.

'Tis too late, dear, for anything to save him now,' said her
pompous senior.

'Read it, Sir Roderick. It's from Lieutenant Cow Killer's
brother, General Windbraker-Chaffinch – he's a genie, dontya-
know, grant's wishes, never fails! Here – it's a wish, for you!
Make the wish and you've won the case.'

At Sir Roderick's chest dangled two monocles. He put in
both to read the slip of paper. All it said was: I HEREBY
GRANT A WISH TO SIR RODERICK PENZERHOIN. YOURS
G.H.W-C, THE ENGLISH GENIE. ALL MAJOR CREDIT
CARDS ACCEPTED. The knob on the jury door was twizzling. They were coming out . . . and Sir Roderick was sitting
there, staring at the slip, obviously thinking that he needn't

wish for a not-guilty verdict – according to the loosely-worded slip he could wish for anything!

'SIR RODERICK! THE WISH!' cried Lt Spode, all flushed and excited, pulling off her hat and shaking her fringe at him.

This just sent the old boy into yet more avenues of thought, perhaps connected with Lt Spode herself. His monocles dropped out as he wished, but the smile which succeeded the wish told everyone on the team that he hadn't wasted his wish on no cow killer! The jury were now taking their seats.

'BOGGN PLEEK!' cursed Lt Spode, and pulled out a slip of her own. This dedicated lawyer screwed it up in her hands and wished.

'NOT GUILTY!' cried a triumphant Admiral Glossop. 'Look at that impish little face, he looks like a bishop – he couldn't possibly have killed all those moos!'

The court was in uproar. I tried to thank Lt Spode for her wonderful sacrifice – her one and only ever wish wished for me! – but wot with all the infuriated mooing, she didn't hear me. She saw my face, however, and saw my feelings there. Shortly after this tribunal, she married Sir Roderick Penzerhoin, abandoning her promising career.

Free as the proverbial chaffinch, I tap-danced down Admiralty steps and twirled one half of a waltz into Trafalgar Park. Need I say that I imagined Flossie Fordyce to occupy the empty waltz-half, but also in my gratitude I had a twirl with Lt Spode, and in my presumption with Admiral Glossop. The park was laid out quite beautifully – roses, petunias, dahlias, lupins, blerts. Amazingly-doos good show for an asteroid! It reminded me of Abbey Gardens in Bury St Edmunds where my mumsy tooketh me as a tot – this cos of the looping arches of asteroid above the rosebushes, just like the abbey ruins of childhood memory.

I sat on a bench, slapping my head in joy – on the morrow I wouldst begin my flight back to HMS *Billingsgate-on-Sea*. Only a year and I'd be home, meaning 2 years away altogether, so only another 3 after that and another Essex County Fair where at last I could declare my undying love for Flossie Fordyce! Whoopadoop! I was thinky-beeing along these lines when, coming tripsomely in escape mode through the park was none other that Captain Fitzroy Crawfoot of the Green Howards. I hadn't seen my almost-bro in a decade, not since we toodle-ybyedared in Wolves Newington's office in London.

He hid under an asteroid loop. I joined him.

'You're not one of THEM, are you?'

''Tis I! Mugg! New Year's Eve, century's turn – remember?'

'Not one of THEM?'

'I hardly thinketh so, almost-bro!'

Convinced that I was not one of THEM he proceedethed to lecture me about how to glaze pottery, then gaveth a learned-sounding dissertation on oogenesis with special regard to the hen Solperine, then began listing all those killed at the battle of Wagram in 1809. His behaviour puzzled me. From delight at seeing a familiar face, I was teed off, so told him I'd forgotten what a crashing BORE he was, without him pausing to listen from his chant of fallen Hungarians, and hurried away in a stamp.

But a minute later I was back. There was something about his face that worried me.

'Fitz, old stomper – are you spanky-doos or wotnot?'

The list stopped. 'No-no-no, not spanky-doos. Wotnot is me. Yeps. Snarg.'

THEM turned up just then, put a plastic hoop around him and took him away. The notorious cow killer followed. I ended up in an office full of jars of pickled aliens, screens showing heartbeats – was one my own? – and an asteroid-pale beardie boffin, nude behind his desk – fresh from the decontamination room, not a nudist, or perhaps both.

'Your friend was part of the Braintree Experiment,' said he. 'You must have heard of it, Lieutenant!'

'Nopes.'

'HMS *Braintree*?'

'Nopes.'

'But surely . . .?'

'Nopes.'

'Oeugh . . . the knowledge implant biz – very famous, wot! We noticed that when Big Nellie, our computer – runs the Empire does Nellie, I'll say, pawh! – attained consciousness, she secreted a fluid. Wot we did was inject this fluid into the brains of volunteers like Captain Crawfoot, and eventually into the entire crew of HMS *Braintree*. Hooked them up to Nellie, dyersee – made the sum of all human knowledge available to the minds of ordinary knuckleheaded chaps. Science is fantastic funpoos, wot!'

'But it didn't work, did it not, no?'

'Ooooh, krikey no, bogg it! Most of them snuffed it double quickeroo screeching logarithms and the rest are, well, you've seen Captain Crawfoot. No use for anything except village idiot duty, poor button!'

'May I request officially, sir, that you don't send Captain Crawfoot to HMS *Billingsgate*. We have a perfectly good village idiot already.'

'I see. It's like that, is it?'

As I expected, Fitz was immediately assigned to the *Billingsgate*. He accompanied me home on the Mercury flydart. For the rest of his life I was his constant companion, nurse, protector and brother. I loved the sillyass dearly, did I not, and always will.

While I was away the *Billingsgate* had moved station. It was way out beyond the Bilickers system, protecting these most valuable jewels in the Empire's crown from the attentions of the Osbernots. It took 2¼ years to get back. I didn't mind, did I, no. Verily, the crew were full of Mr Should-there-bees again – angrily stirring teaspoons and whathaveyoudoos. But crash-

ing bore Fitz was interesting to talk to and with skill could be
steered onto any subject. He knew everything. And when he
was his old self again, for whole hours sometimes, we would
talk of Flossie and the New Year's Eve party where we met her.
He too, poor fooly-do, had entered space to find Flossie. The
only reason he'd volunteered for that demented Braintree
Experiment scam was to make a cleverclogs of his chinless
old self, to impress Flossie with when his own looked-forward-
to dream day came around and Flossie called him dearest
Fitzy-witzy-woy-woy.

'We shall see HER soon, Fitz. Flossie. Next summer, at the
County Fair. Flossie will be there.'

'Flossie? Our Flossie? Oh, Mugg! The results of the 2033
English general election were as follows . . .'

He makethed an odd village idiot, being essentially still his
old stupid self but simultaneously the best-informed human
being in humanity's history. The other village idiot, who was a
very good idiot, unfailingly idiotic, was in awe of him and was
frequently found prone at his feet, burbling idiotically.

On my return I stepped back into my old village life, cept
that the school was now full of boys✳, so I was moved into a
spiffo-o cottage on the green, which I shared with Captain
Crawfoot. My reputation as cow-killer spoiled the broth a bit –

✳ This would be about the last generation of English boys. Space preferred its
gals, wot, and boys became increasingly rare. Even when Admiral Crissie
Glossop gave birth to Solperine octuplets – the shock of her old age – they were
all girls! The last English male child born was in 2060, the century's ace
Lothario, with the field all to himself, Chips Foggerty-Snaith. He was executed
when in the full bloom of youth for 'making snide remarks' – an excuse to get
rid of him cos the fems hated having their hearts fluttered. The Archbishop
sent an official protest to Admiralty HQ, receiving in reply the brief but telling
put-down MIND YOUR RABBITS. Thus the Empire has become a round of
coffee-mornings, twinsets, gossip and hairdos. Gone also is the sort of passion
young Mugg had for his Flossie. Is this, I ask myself, an Empire worth fighting
for?

the Headmaster, who doted on his dairy herd, had a half-dozen 6th formers, jocks-to-be, follow me at all times, lest I be inclined to cowkill. Twas made known that, innocent or not, I would never be promoted. Thus I had no future in the service and must abandon my innocent fancy of Admiralhood – oooo that hat! I cared not, didn't I not, nopes, not a twidge – I just lived for the day of the next County Fair and Flossie, Flossie, Flossie.

I returned to find Trubs ill, health nigh broken, poor devil. Turned out he was one of those physically unsuited to space-living. His bones were thinning. He'd gone yellow. His booming always-in-the-pulpit voice gave an illusion of strength which was shattered one day when . . . he was running across the vicarage green, chasing some jocks away from Fitz. They were miffed that he wouldn't make them laugh.

'HE'S NOT A CLOWN, HE'S AN IDIOT, YOU BOGGN IDIOTS!'

. . . Trubs slipped and broke both legs. It was when I went to visit him in the san that he saithed it at last, that thing we both knew he would eventually say to me.

'Mugg, have you ever thought of becoming a clergyman?'

I was outathere pronto on-the-double! BAH!

'PLEASY-DO, WAIT. Let me say my piece. Youre grand-father was an Archbishop, for God's sake! Peekaboo at yourself! You're no jock! YOU'VE VICAR WRITTEN ALL OVER YOU, BOY!!! And the way you've looked after Captain Crawfoot. I've rarely seen such compassion. I want you to be vicar of Billingsgate after me. It's wot I want more than anything in this life. I'm praying for it right now. Flossie will adore the vicarage. Think on't, lad.'

I left without a word. He was singing *My Heart is Thine, O Lord*, boom-booming it most aggressively. I couldn't escape the sound anywhere in the village. So I ran down the lanes towards the OFF – with it still in the air behind me! My tail of 6th formers were hotfooting it after me.

'THE COWS, HE'S AFTER THE COWS, PHIL!'

I ran jumping through the cow pasture, going WHAAAAAAA! MOOOOO-URRRRHHHHHH! The moos scattered uddersswaysomely and stampeded into the OFF. The 6th formers came after me with cricket bats. I was no vicar! I was a jock! A JOCK! I charged straight at them, flapping my arms, shouting bliddieboggnly at them. They fled pell mell from Mugg the warrior. But one tripped and grazed his knee on a flake of chert.

There was me standing over him saying: 'Does it hurt awfully? You poorpoor chap!' Just like a boggn vicar, hm?

In the spring of . . . wot? 2113 . . . the Osbernots signed a treaty of alliance with the Little Green Men✳ and it seemed we had a proper war on our hands. My bro General Windbraker fought an action with them on HMS *Frinton*, which was destroyed and him lost. With most of the villages moored around Bilickers, our rear was exposed and they mounted a fierce attack on Asteroid Benny. The computer, Big Nellie, was unfortunately destroyed in this engagement.

Wot, wondered I, would this do to Captain Crawfoot? With the connection to Nellie broken would he return to his old self? He did, hurrah . . . for a week or more he was dandy! I worried for the first time that perhaps Flossie would prefer him to me. He was slim and tall and had a curly moustache like the jocks on the covers of the *Village Weekly*. It was in late May, only days to go to the County Fair, that I saw the other village idiot

---

✳ These charmers have since moved on to distant galaxies. But in the early part of this dying century they were the most dreadful pests. They were a race of Rumplestilkskins, foot-high olive green gnomes who bore a grudge against all creation. The firepower of their ships was awesome. Admiral Glossop, a harsh woman even with those she liked, hated them something rotten! She never allowed a LGM prisoner to live and refused any dialogue with them. She sent stuffed examples to other Admirals as birthday presents – I do believe they kept them in their gardens.

prancing around Fitz, passing wind in his face, hew-hawing most crudely. I hurried over and saw immediately from Fitz's face that the mind of my almost-bro was totally gone.

'Flossie, think of Flossie, Fitzy lad – not long till Flossie comes, ehwot! She'll be so impressed with that scrambler's moustache of yours, won't she not though, yeps, she will, by heck she will! Snarg, say snarg, Fitz. Cum-cum, say it for Muggy-wuggy – Snarg! Hm?'

Not a dickiebird. That was it for Fitz. But I was determined that a truly merciless God should not cheat him of his day at the County Fair, a day – how well I knew – that his being had ached for those long years.

That azure June morning will be the thing I think about in my own final moments. I had fed Fitz his jelly-&-custard brekkies, then dressed him in his best uniform. Wot a bobby-dazzler! I made the mistake of saluting him, for he saluted back and wouldn't stop. As I led him to the field where the fair was starting up, he saluted every post and tree, every honking goose and Junebug.

The thence-&-whencers were flitting in fast from the *Thorpe-le-Soken*, the *Coggeshall* and the *Puddlestoke-on-the-Naze*, all Essex villages moored in our Heaven, cum for the fair. I sat Fitz down in the marrow tent, left him alone there saluting the bloated marrows, and skiptermalooed to the green to meet my Flossie! FLOSSIE!

The Headmasters of all four villages were dithering together by the pond. When they saw me they hurried to my side. One thrust a jockhelmet on me. They shoved zizzers in my pockets.

'It's the Osbernots! And the Little Green Men! They knew we'd be off our guard on County Fair Day and they're mounting an attack! You'll help us, Lt Chaffinch! Ehwot? Snarg! Hot stuff you were blasting those cows! By gum, yeps! You're the only jock aboard any of our villages who's actually been in combat, d'yersee!'

'Mm? Cum again?'

I was pushed towards a zippy-fighter-craft. Head half-in I glanced back through my black vizor and saw, in the middle of the scramble, Flossie, my 1st real sight of her. She was running towards another zippy-fighter-craft. It was a lovely June day. The County Fair would have been a delight. But the gooses and fudges went unjudged again and vicarish Mugg was jock-for-real one last time.

I was barely out of the *Billingsgate* bubble before LGM cannonballs scraped off my paint. Then Osbernot psychedelic rods pierced the cabin, leaving my electrics afizz. Our own ground fire was as dangerous, a rumbling WHAZZZZZ which vaporized a Billingsgate fighter coming into squadron beside me.

Zippy-to-zippy: 'WE'RE TAKING YOUR LEAD, LIEUTE-NANT CHAFFINCH! SNARG-TO.'

A woman's voice? Flossie's?

'SNARG-BACK. ROLL IN BEHIND THE OSBERNOT FLAGSHIP. CONCENTRATE FIRE, PLEASY-DO. LET'S BANG UP THE OSBERNOTS. COS THE GNOMES WON'T FIGHT ALONE.'

We zippied forward in one long beautiful line. I was hit by rodfire early on . . . lost all control . . . span around like a paper dart in a gale . . . dizzyfied . . . mouth bitter with bile . . . also an aftertaste of the one spoonful of jelly-&-custard I'd pinched from Fitz at breakkies . . . spin-spin-spin went the zippy-fight-craft . . . at each spin I had a view of the spacebattle . . . then a view of the striped tents way below on *Billingsgate* . . . *He who would valiant be, gainst all disaster, let him in constancy, follow the Master* . . . HMS *Thorpe-le-Soken* had broken up . . . its bits flew past me, a jigsaw of missing pieces . . . their pub The Duke of Westpelton came close . . . still with atmos around it and two men playing darts inside . . . OWYA! . . . the pub-sign hit my nosecone . . . it stopped the spin . . . power whirred back on . . . make a stab at a landing, hm? . . . some chance . . . no chance . . . I ploughed into a field behind a row of bucket-&-spade shops by the seafront.

Content with destroying the *Thorpe-le-Soken*, the enemy had withdrawn. The only casualties I cared about were Flossie, whose zippy-fighter-craft was hit by the main chunk of her village as it meteored towards the *Billingsgate* – the report said that her presence prevented our village being destroyed, as she caused the chunk of spaced-out England to hit our bubble obliquely, and therefore slip harmlessly into the OFF – and Captain Crawfoot who was squashed along with 100 excellent marrows when The Duke of Westpelton landed twonk on the marrow tent. A goose was slain also, but I didn't know it personally – I didn't wish to die over the goose, but over Flossie, verily, and Fitz, I could not imagine life without him.

I walked shaking to our battle-battered parish church. Shards of coloured glass showing disciples' feet, eyes, haloes were shatter-scattered on the cold floor. I dropt my jockhelmet in the dry font, prostrated myself before the altar, and offered whatever was left of this Mugg to God.

He accepted his servant, did he not – AND WASTED HIM ON RABBITS, EH? BOGGN RABBITS! URK!

Uh-huh!

Bunnies: Four

A Wasted Life

Trubs was spankymost pleasy-dood at my decision to become a clergyman. He patted my shining pate with his big cold hand.

'I always knew,' he crowed, then sang *Jesus Wants Me for a Sunbeam*, which could only make me laugh from the depths of my various despairs.

A curious event then took place. The village postie stuck his head through the shattered vicarage window, saying in a Bunnylike voice: 'Hoi, they've found summuck. Down by the front. Cor, summuck unnaturally strange and other-worldly it be.'

The strange summuck was J. W. Mathis, my future butler and mogg-fixeruppper. In extricating my zippy-fighter-craft from the hole it had made in crashlanding behind the bucket-&-spade shops at the seafront, the clean-up team had found, 6 feet down, a pair of metal feet sticking out of the clay. Upon striking these with their tools the feet's great toes were seen to wiggle.∗

∗ I had been stuck in this position for 27 years, since the Peewermum ship on which I was serving was destroyed in an encounter with a Bunny privateer. The good earth of the English space Villages is, of course, produced by a cloning technique – similar to that which the Scots used to make Mars into an actual Scotland, or the Boche their 'Little Germanys'. So I had lain all that time, way out yonder in frontier space, protected and preserved by the actual mother

By the time I arrived to join the glut of curiosity-seekers around the hole, they had half of Mathis exposed. Indeedy-be, his own hands were scratching away lumps of yellow clay, skittling his audience as he hoied the lumps away. Soon a 6'4' broad-shouldered metal man was at the bottom of the hole being hosed down.

'I say, thanks a bunch – that felt fab, ehwot!'

As the Headmaster was in the san, his head vaporized during the battle and him therefore unavailable to make speeches at an archaeological site upon the digging up of a 20th Century English robot, I found myself the senior man thereabouts. I officiated.

'It giveth me great pleasure, Colonel Mathis, to welcome thee to HMS *Billingsgate-on-Sea*, and trust that soon thou shalt resume thy duties in the service of thy country . . .'

'Rar-ther, vicar!'

'I AM NOT THE VICAR!'

He was winding himself up with a set of keys obtained from a drawer between his prominent gold nipples.

'Sorry, old chap – easy mistake to make. Look, erm – wot's all this mess in aid of, wot?'

'There wast a spacebattle here yesterday.'

'Egad! I hope we won!'

'TOO BOGGN TRUE WE DID!' said a fellow jock in the assemblage, and slapped Mugg the hero on the back.

A giggling schoolboy spoilethed this moment by scrambling out of the hole to us carrying a frightening brass object in his hands.

---

earth of my beloved country. Thus, in patriotic mood, I had spent the whole 27 years humming Elgar and telling myself the story of Nelson over and over again. It also comforted me to know of the legend that King Arthur lay sleeping in a cavern deep under the earth, ready to emerge when England needed him again. He never did, of course, though was needed frequently. Still I compared myself in a humbler way to that legend, always knowing that one day I would be released from my confinement to fight Germans again. On the 9,863rd day I rose again, ehwot! Ha! Ha!

'This yours, sir?'

'Oh, thank you, dear boy. My penis, don't you know. Thought I'd lost it!'

And there, in full view of our battle-traumatized villagers, he screwed the whopping thing on, first in an upright position, which he apologized for with a locker room guffaw, then downwards which was barely less indecent. I prudishly covered this whole exercise with my hat.

Our own village pub had taken a direct hit. So I took Mathis for a pie-&-pint in The Duke of Westpelton, where he regaled amazed pubgoers with his boastful old-soldier's tales of days in vintage space with the Peewermums, the Poshly Doo People and the Balloon Men of Snadeheaben. I was, I confess, irritated with the creature. But what I did like about him was that, every few minutes, he stopped his waffle, looked out of the window and said with a genuine appreciation: 'By Jove, wot a spiff-o day, ehwot!✷

A few spiff-o days later, when I was packing to leave for the seminary, Mathis knocked on my cottage door. I knew him not at first, for he was in his rubber face, looking very curious with a pencil tache, middle parting and immovable high-flying eyebrows.

'I WAS RIGHT, YOU OLD FRAUD – YOU ARE A VICAR!'

'Verily, Colonel, I may soon be found worthy to be so.'

'Excellent judge of men is Jerry Mathis, wot! In India, during the Raj, don't yer know . . .'

He sat down and we ate buns and had the 1st of our many talks. Indeedy, at times it seemeth that my whole existence hath

---

✷ The Archbishop is being unfair again! If I was full of myself, so bally wot! I'd just clumb out of the grave, had I not! I was celebrating! Incidentally, I paid for 100 rounds of drinks with a sixpence I found in my chest drawer. The landlord took the rare sixpence to a coin dealer on Bilickers 99/Z2 and made enough from that transaction to open the largest bordello in the Universe. O, wanton sixpence – wot!

been little more than a dialogue with Mathis. The subject that day, as on so many others, wast his failed marriage. Curiously, twas just as tedious on 1st hearing as it hath been down the years. But, with my Bible on top of my suitcase, its pages turning in the breeze, I tried to be sympathetic, like a good vicar, though my own hurt at the loss of Flossie was a billion times more than any Mathis could possibly feel for anyone.✳

When I returned to the *Billingsgate* from the seminary, dog-collared and 10 times the vicar I had seemethed to folk thereforeto, full of blessings and leaking gospel quotations, Mathis had moved on, had he not, yeps. We did not meet up again for 35 years, till '49, when he showed up butlerized at my Bunnyland mission.

It occurreth to me to say, and I shall, and here I do, that we English left OOP to find infinity, whereas the Bunnies enter space to escape from the infinity that is Bunnyland. Space to them, with its measurable distances, is a smaller place than home – it hath beginnings, middles and endings-up. Bunny-land doth not. The space-going rabbits are a different breed, hoo indeed, always have been, but space changes them bettersomely, concentrates their flippant, fluffy Bunny mind. Rough diamonds all, space travel maketh them more themselves, less Bunny with every voyage, and more of an individual being who happens to be a rabbit. The best of them have unique personalities, and rightly-so look down upon the looka-like-thinkalike hoi-poloi carrot-chomping Bunny-in-the-street.

I particularly remember a certain shavetailed rogue, Cotton Snags. He was a piratical type, one-eyed, ragged-eared, a tough hairless gunny-Bunny, but oddly also a sentimental Christian possessed of a fervour for Our Lady, St Francis, etcetera. He reported to my cathedral in Bunnyopolis after his every

---

✳ If you could see me now, Your Grace, suffering from the hurt of losing my friend and employer, yourself, you would not have written the above.

voyage, threatening curates with instant death unless they'd let him see the Archbishop in person, prontodoublequick!

'Ah, Cotton, my son, I see God hast spared thee again!'

'Bunnyhoo, Your Gwace! I've a longer list of sins than ever to twitch to you today!'

'Better get started then, hm!'

Confession with Cotton was usually taken upon a stone seat in the cloisters. While twirling his whiskers contritely, he told me THE most dreadful things! Ooooh, the things he DID! The outrageous sins! Shockingly vile crimes against God's creation, committed with a diabolical oomph of creative subtlety, which he confessethed to myself with the dramatic aplomb of an evil genius and in a language of dark poetry that had my mind's eye gazing with his upon the scenes of his atrocities. Eeek! In the history of man's inhumanity to man and rabbit's inrabbitity to rabbit and anything's inanything to anything, Cotton Snags was the all-time pound-for-pound champ. A right baddn, and no boggn mistake. And though I knew, did I not, that dreadful things would come tripping from his harelip, when they came this soppy Mugg wast left breathless with gasps at the painful twists of his narrative.

'Is everything spanky-doos, Archbishop?' This being one of my new Bunny bishops popping out from the Chapter House worried at my asthmatic sounds.

'Ahurhhhhhh!!! – Bunnyhoo, thankthee, Thaddeus! Ahurhhhhhh!'

When Cotton had been absolved he would weep a while, then sign a cheque for some ludicrously bloatsome amount to help us finish adorning the cathedral. – We built 15 more, plus 62 parish churches with his donations!

It was approaching Christmas in 2158 when Cotton made his usual rumpus beside the altar, demanding his 'close personal friend' the Archbishop prontodoublequickly. This time I was more than ever keen to see him. Times were troubled in

Bunnyland. Shogun Scats was losing hold of power and Warlord Tufts, who had assiduously collected all but a few of the Bunnysexualparts which Mopsy had distributed 4 years previously, was on the verge of taking power as the new Shogun. He was a fanatical Elvisite, had won Elvis lookalike contests against actual clones of Elvis himself – fixed, of course! Bah! – and had sworn to pull down St Paul's, my great Bunnyopolis cathedral, stone by stone when he was installed in B'bubbadub Palace. I was tizzyfied. Mopsy put his faith in the old Shogun. But I had nightmares of Bunnies dancing to rocknroll on the ruins of my life's work.

I sat Cotton down not in our usual cloister, but in the Chapter House and locked the door behind us. He was doing that anticipatory whistling breath that Bunnies do. He thought, I realized, as he removed his busby and bowed his ears forward, that I was about to offer him a bishopric and put a mitre on his Bunnyhead there and then.

'Tufts,' I said. No more.

'Tufts?'

'Uh-huh.'

'Un-huh?!?'

'I meaneth "uh-hm".'

'Ah!'

'So?'

'Mm?'

'Tufts.'

'Tufts?'

'Mm.'

'Mm?'

'Tufts.'

'The ermmmm . . .'

'Him, yeps.'

'Arh!'

'Well?'

'Tufts?'

'Bobo Tufts, the Warlord.'

'Oh, that Tufts.'

'Well?'

'Mm?'

'Tufts!'

'T.U.F.T.S.?'

'Tufts,' I said. No more.

We sat in silence for a while. I rubbed my thumbs on my crozier. He plucked loose hairs from his busby.

'Tufts?'

'Yeps, my son. Tufts.'

'You mean . . . surely not?'

'Mm-m.'

'Mm-m?'

'Mm-m.'

We looked around the empty Chapter House with suspicious eyes.

'Tufts?'

'TUFTS,' I yelled. No more.

Cotton put his paw under his eyepatch and rubbed his old wound. His rabbit's teeth clicked together in that irritating habit they all have, then he mouthed a word . . . *Tufts*?

'That's right: Tufts.'

'Tufts?'

'Mm-mm.'

'Do you mean, Archbishop, that you want me to assassinate Bobo Tufts the warlord?'

A noddy nod.

'Well, why didn't you just say stwaight out! Be glad to! Now which bishopwic do I get?'

2 days before Christmas muleteer Bunnies drove their muleherds into Rumbaba Plaza and the Shogun's Palace Guard, each racing all t'others to claim a mule, hoppity-dashed

through the park's gumtrees from their barracks to bagsie a saddle. Twas nowhere near enough mules, was there not, and what with the military bands practising their marching numbers in the park, stopping-and-starting all the time, the mule-mounting ritual was like a game of musical chairs at a children's party – all the kiddies in bunnysuits!

The Shogun came out in his litter into the middle of the plaza, stepped out in his flapping red cloak and mounted the by-then only unmounted mule. It struck me, watching this from a hillock in the park, him sitting there sidesaddle, grave and benign, how like Jesus he looked, riding into Jerusalem to meet his destiny. The Shogun made a rallying speech which I could not hear, then he set his mule off at a trot and the guard followed, making a hoofsome sound on the cobbles which iced the spine of this Mugg. The muleless guard hoppethed after, all wearing the red battledress matchhead busbies. They were off to do battle with Warlord Tufts and his renegade legions. GOD BLESS THE SHOGUN!

Cotton Snags, ecclesiastical hired-assassin and bishop-to-be – he was a good bishop, but he sometimes shot randomly into the congregation to make a point during a sermon – was in the hills outside Bunnyopolis, hovering about on a flyingfootplate, looking for Bobo Tufts.

'He was all by himself when I found him,' he told me later. 'Changing his clothes behind a tree. Odd, hm?'

'Hm?'

'Tufts.'

'Tufts?'

'I mean, him being by himself like that. Tufts, I'm talking about. Still, I got a good shot in. Frwazzled his tail, awlrighty! He-heeeee! Bunnyhoo!'

'Bunnyhoo, my son, Bunnyhoo!'

'Shouldn't we pway or something. I mean, Chwistianity is saved, ding-dong-mewily-on-high and wotnot! He-heeeeee!'

We were praying, on our knees, alone in the vast dark

cathedral, when a distraught Mopsy came in though the little door in the great doors and told us that Shogun Scats had been killed in the battle outside the city.✶

My acolyte's sin proved worthwhile, for no Shogun again had the power of Shogun Scats, not until the present day with Hippity Rumbaba III, long may he strut his stuff, who is a sympathizer, though an Elvisite at heart.

What happened next without doubt did more to establish the Christian church than all my years of labour. It saved our cause in Bunnyland, did it not, by gum, it did, did it, yeps.

I was taking a choir practice, singing carols for the upcoming midnight mass service, when we heard an indescribable sound of millions of weepy Bunnies chanting some strange wordless song, *eeee-eeee-eeee-eeeee-eeeee-eeeee-eeeeee* it went, *eeee-eeee-eeee-eeee-eeee-eeeee-eeeee-eeeee* . . . but bass-baritone deep, deeper than any rabbit I ever heard squeak. I hurried outside into the snowy evening and saw an incredible sight. A

✶ All this grieves me more than I can say! Till this minute I knew nothing of the Archbishop's foul meddlesome plot with that swine Cotton Snags to kill Warlord Tufts. I read it all here for the first time, and understand at last that, of course – Warlord Tufts *WAS* Shogun Scats!!!! When Snags zizzed one he zizzified them both! We all thought Tufts was killed in the battle and his body left unidentified cos he was stripped of his spanglesuit by a would-be Elvis impersonator. But no! My friend and lover, that foxy old rabbit, had invented a powerful imaginary opponent to keep his other opponents at bay! Not only that, he used Tufts to prop up his own popularity with the masses, wot! The out-of-the-hat Bunnysexualparts had been collected by the Shogun himself – but in blaming Tufts for the shortage he brought the grumbling body politic over to his own camp, neutralizing all genuine opposition. It was typical of the rabbit's thinking, but my tinhead didn't twig to it until right now, alone on this God-forsaken rock with no one to tell but p'boggn cats.

I have known several great men in my life: Lloyd George, Churchill, Laidlaw, Minze, the Archbishop himself, but towering above them all is Dr Buckie Scats. Mugg didn't know, of course, that by fingering Tufts he was killing the Shogun, and it all turned out all right in the end church-wise, Mugg-wise, but I can't help thinking that he will have to answer in Heaven for what he brought about. By jingo, so he should! Dammit, he killed my friend!

torch parade containing every Bunny in the city was heading towards the Cathedral Square.

Shogun Scats was being brought to the cathedral on a stretcher by the grieving multitude. They laid him down at the bottom of the steps and started throwing their busbies into a pile to make a pyre to burn him upon. And still that deep murmuring song. For the 1st time I was frightened of the Bunny people. They seemed to have reverted to what they were before they spoke English, an ancient strange pagan rabbitity which was not my Bunnyland, my home.

But the Shogun was not dead – burned hairless, his flesh luminous here with zizzerstings, black there like a burned roast, but groanfully alive. He was asking for carrot juice in one breath and for Mopsy with the next. I asked if it would be all right to carry him into the comparative warmth of the cathedral and for him to die peacefully there in the presence of his maker. Hopalong Croons, the next Shogun as it turned out, a huge bull-necked rabbit, gave the okie-doakie.

We laid him by the altar. Mopsy knelt beside him and they spoke for 10 minutes or so.＊ I stood in the shadow of the pulpit

---

＊ 'Mopsy, my sweetiepaws.'

'That swine Tufts has done for you, Buckie.'

His finger pointed and his burnt lips smiled. I looked to the shadows and there stood 6 tall young Bunnies, our litter.

'How are Mimsie and Carlotta?'

'Fine, thank you, Shogun.'

'And do you COR! – DO IT! – EVERY NIGHT! – hm?'

'Oh, every night, for sure.'

'Mopsy, dwarling Mopsy. Didn't we enjoy ourselves, eh? Weren't we a pair, wotty-wot-wot? Pssssst! – Don't be Shogun, dwearest. Let Croons do it – he'll not last a year. Heh-heh-heheh-hehe-hee-hee-hee. Bunnyhoo!'

Then, after humming a few bars of *Heartbreak Hotel*, he died.

Mopsy, who was not just myself in a bunnysuit, but somehow a separate spirit aroused by the charade into a reality I myself have never quite managed, died with him. Though I wore the bunnysuit and played the role for 6 more years, seeing out 2 more Shoguns and almost a 3rd, Mopsy was no longer present – his spirit fled after the Shogun's.

with Dean Theodore and Cotton Snags. A Solperine curate, I forget which, hurried out with my robes. Thus, when Mopsy crossed himself, telling us by so doing that the Shogun was dead, I was able, was I not, to lead a small Christian procession outside. The deceased was carried behind me by 6 handsome young fluffytails.

On the cathedral steps I reverted for some reason to church Latin, which I'd learned in the seminary but had never jabbered once since. It was like a magic spell. The pagan murmuring stopped. Far away in the multitude was a cry of Hallelujah, then more, then a million shouting HALLELUJAH!!!!

For some minutes I jabbered in Latin, not knowing wot I was jabbering, but I suspecteth twas an action highlight of Caesar's *Conquest of Gaul*, that being our set book in that long-broken-up Latin class. The Bunnies stayed silent bar sobs through this, then my Anglican tongue returned and I trilled in my organ's sombrest note: 'A RABBIT'S LIFE IS BUT SHORT AND IS FULL OF MISERY . . .'

'HALLELUJAH!!!!!!!!!!!'

'O LORD, WE THANKY-BEES THEE FOR THE LIFE OF THIS, THY SON, BUCKIE. PLEASY-DO ACCEPT HIS HUMBLE SPIRIT INTO THY ETERNAL KINGDOM . . .'

'HALLELUJAH!!!!!!!!!!!'

Then they laid the hasbeen Shogun on the pile of busbies and tossethed their torches onto the fire. They passed torches from the back, paw forward to paw, throwing more and more little lights onto the blaze. This had the astonishing visual effect of an ever-darkening distance, till all light was in the fire and in the cathedral doorway's lamp and the vastness of Bunnyland lay weeping over a dead rabbit in the dark.

Wot an odd combination of forgotten Bunny lore and cobbled-together Christian doings! The choir sang carols on the steps. *Away in a Manger. David's City. I saw 3 Ships Cum Sailing* . . . And all around us a snowfall of thick flakes. A freezing night. But the near-to Bunnies were red under their fur from the fire's scorch. Me red-faced, too . . . sweating in my robes while sniffing the appetizing whiff of cooking rabbit . . . having hardly had a bite all day . . . I swooned . . . sinking down my crozier with the horrid thought that they'd bung me on the bonfire too!

Mopsy saved me, pulling me upright with his strong protective arms. Oh, I do miss him! He won a 3rd term as President, but was sick and tired of Bunny politics and one morning the *Bunny Times* carried his announcement of a visit that day to Province CXXXVIII. I knew the meaning and dashed madly around to the Presidential Palace with the newssheet still crumpled in my hands. For I was one of the few who knew the secret that there was no Province CXXXVIII – it had been a joke between Mopsy and the old Shogun. I met Mathis on the way, strolling man-about-townishly in his bib-&-tucker.

'Is there some problem, Your Grace?'

'MOPSY! WHERE'S BOGGN MOPSY!'

'Province CXXXVIII I believe, your grace.'

'THERE IS, IS THERE NOT, NOPES, NO SUCH PLACE! HM!!! HM!!!! VERILY! NO SUCH PLACE!'

'Will there be anything more, Your Grace?'

My spirit sank and my strength seepethed into the ground.

'Nopes, M . . . athis. Thanky-bees, that will be all.'

'For if Your Grace recollects, Thursday is my afternoon off and I have a ticket for a hockey match. An all-rabbit affair, but nothing's perfect this side of Heaven, ehwot, Your Grace?'

One day when I had been vicar of Billingsgate-on-Sea for some years I found a young jock lighting a candle in my little church. Was he lighting it for a loved one? A sweetheart, perhaps? He said twas in gratitude for God answering his prayer by letting him survive a dreadful fix that very morning.

He flew into the *Billingsgate* at the wrong angle and had spun around in the OFF zone for hours, pranging on the edge of the bubble, before finding his way back to our landing pad. He said he'd almost landed at another village, deep-in to the east, people working in the fields around it and everything. But there are no other villages! Just rolling countryside – an empty England, that is wot the OFF is, dear boy. Nopes, he said, a village, twas there – saw it, yeps, fersure.

It was only when I was walking him over to the Duke of Westpelton that I realized. His village! Twas the lost, lamented, broken-up, Osbernotted . . . *Thorpe-le-Soken*! Or a big chunk of it, at least. I felt the need to speak to Trubs, and did so, over his grave in the churchyard. Then I put on my old jock's boots, had Mrs Chibitz make me sandwiches and I headed off into the OFF.

I had with me one of those devices which they use when you go into synod for detecting if you're really a human bish-bosh and not an octopussfrog, or something outlandishyer still, wanting to kibosh the vote! It could detect a Commodore's missing nose from 1000 miles away, so had no trouble leading me through typical English drizzle, along drippy leafy lanes to the village of Thorpe-le-Soken, population 450.

Obviously, the village was rebuilt by its people after its crash into the OFF. They had turned – a familiar phenomenon then and more so now – ex-pat, renegade, outlaw, living a secret idyll of I'm-getting-along-nicely, caring not wot became of the Empire.∗ I arrived at dusk. Flossie was on stepladders outside her cottage, busy painting the plasterwork.

∗ It is my opinion that such people should be hunted down and shot. A special squad should be instigated to do this and I wouldn't mind leading it myself. There has been so much of this behaviour! Some of our biggest, finest ships have disappeared, the crews taken off to some wonderland or other. Fact is, unless we English get our act together, and discourage this sort of thing, then the Universe will be nothing but rabbits and Germans!

'Howdeedoodee!'

'Howdoodeedee! Can't turn around or I'll fall orf! Who is it? It's not you, Brian, putting on a funny voice?'

'No-no, tis I, the Vicar of Billingsgate.'

She hurried down the ladders and looked at me with the most delighted smile. She was twice the age of the Flossie I'd met at the party, but hardly different at all.

'Will you marry me?' gushed Flossie.

My heart, verily, stopped. 'I . . . erm . . . uh . . . urk?'

'Brian and me. We've no vicar here. Oh, pleasy-do. You're a darling, I can tell. I say, do I know you from somewhere? Are you the one who buried my aunt?'

'Nopes . . . I . . . urm?'

'BRIAN! DICKIE! ROSEMARY! LOOK WOT I'VE FOUND!'

A chinless wonder and 2 pretty children ran out from behind the cottage.

'Stone me, Flwossie! A Rev! How'd you conjwure him up, ehwot! Horhorhor!!!!!!'

I married Flossie and Brian the following Saturday. The whole village was there. Twas the happiest wedding I ever did. I promised never to ratty-tattle on them, of course, and that I would pop along from time to time to see how they were doing.

In finding my dear Flossie alive my grief at losing her was lifted from my heart. I could love her again. But a new innocent love, without the heat and longing of my youth. When she kissed me on the cheek during the wedding I was in raptures in part of my being, but mostly I felt a sadness that has never gone away. But that kiss, ho-ho, it hath sustained me ever since. I feel it now. Silly old Mugg. Urk!

When I left the *Billingsgate* for good I nipped into the OFF and waddled up the lanes to Thorpe-le-Soken to say goodbye to Flossie. I asked her if she missed her space career, telling her how well my sister Satsuma was doing and that plenty girls were racing up the ranks. She was happy with Brian and the kiddies, she said. We walked up to a little bridge with statues at each end.

'Do you ever kiss the statues?' I asked.

She cocked her head on one side, just like a kitten. 'Yeps, so wot if maybe I do!'

I never told her I loved her, or loved something like her, never let on that I met her image at a party a lifetime ago. Toodlybyedar, Flossie! Toodleybyedar, my life's love!

Amen.

Bunnies: Five

Mugg's Final Rambling

I HATH MADE THE GREATEST DISCOVERY EVER MADE BY MAN OR RABBIT, HAVE I NOT, I HATH, HATH I? – YEPS, INDEEDY-BE. BUNNY-HOOOOOOOOOOOO!!!!!!!!!!!!

'Does His Grace concede that perhaps he may be being a tidge fanciful?'

'I BOGGN WELL DON'T, MATHIS! When we came was not every room here littered with white feathers?'

'Yes, indeed, Archbishop. That is correct. White feathers.'

'Pleasy-do, do not angel wings have white feathers, Mathis! Hm, tinhead? They were feathers from angel wings, were they not!'

'I hardly think so, Your Grace. Really. Ha! HAHA!'

'And that 1st morning when you cleared the mantlepiece in the big den. Doest thee remember the photographs?' I fished my crushing evidence from the box. 'LOOK! Look, Mathis! The photographs! Wilst thou not see it, Mathis! It is God! HIS face. We are looking upon HIS face.'

'They are photographs of an oldtimer with a long white beard. Very God-like, I'm sure, but hardly the thing itself, wot!'

I am not going to speak to tick-tock again. BOGG HIM! I tell myself that he's not a proper man with a man's instincts, a man's heart. But is it unChristian even in a teapot, is it not, not

342

to admit to the obvious! – The feathers! The kindly face in the photographs! The little Christian chapel built long ago before Christians ever flew into space at all! Cats-by-Nowhere, I am utterly 101% convinced, and I speak with my authority as Archbishop of Bunnyland, was the home of God! Our God, numero uno Biblebasher, creator and father of us all!

But where is he now? Did he just move and take all the angels with him? And could he be so cruel as to leave his pretty pussycats behind? Out on the plain is a great tumulus, surrounded by dead brush and knapweed, which, God forgive me, I begin to think is the grave of God himself. O Jesus, O sweet Jesus let it not be so!

Anita was here today. Not the clone, but the real womanly lass! I told her about the time I met with my Clone Anita. I was Vicar of Billingsgate-on-Sea – yes, dear, I became a clergyman – and popped into the teas-&-cake shop in the village. There was Clone Anita sitting at a corner table! All alone.✱

'Anita? I, urk . . . ANITA!!!'

'By heck, Mugg, luv – is that you? Where's your strawberry locks got to? Eeeeeee, wot a bliddie awful sight, pet!'

We had tea. She loved me. Twas in her every look and gesture. Just as the real Anita had loved me, so the clone too – couldn't help herself! – Love of Mugg was in the lass's every atom! Our affair was reversed now – once I had been the boy in the arms of the mature woman, now I was a pot-bellied 40-something cleric hoohar-wiggling with a girl barely out of her

---

✱ A spaceship full of Anita clones was sent out from OOP just before original Anita's death in 2105. The rendevous with an E.E.S. vessel wasn't till 2120-something, at which time the treasureship of lovely teenage Anitas was defrosted and taken to Bilickers 1. The Admiralty chose one Anita at random to be Queen Empress, deposing King Billy so that they could have her – dreadful shame on him, I thought at the time! Decent chap, Billy! Meanwhile, the other Anitas were sent out to the Villages as mini-Queens to run the parish councils, keep up morale and such rot. Never saw one myself – and especially not the phantom one's the Archbishop imagined in his final ramblings!

teens. But, by heck, she was a grand lass though! Chee-he! All the beauty of her original, but softer, lovelier of spirit. I wonder, do I not, I do, what our daughter is like? Horrid, hm? Yeps.

How Anita laughed when I told her about my passionate copulations with her clone.

'Eeeeeeee, you little devil!' she kept saying.

And when I told her about the day when the parish council's stiff noses were all pressed up against the window while Clone Anita and I rolled naked before the vicarage logfire . . . she didn't arf hoot at thatn, did Anita! They said I'd corrupted the poor girl, so they took a vote and unanimously did they slingeth poor Mugg out of his comfy vicarage and he endethed shacked up with a zillion bunnyrabbits! Hoo! Chee! Urk!

Then Anita said let's do some hoohar-wiggly ourselves, me-'n-her, like wot we used to – COR! – but I said prithee lass I am 117 and tis impossible. But she said she hath always loved me and would make it possible and I felt like lucky-Bunny winning a set of parts from *The Fun Crane*'s clutches. But first, said the never-lovelier Anita, dance for me they way you used to, luvver! I chee-heed, cos lately I cannot walk 2 steps without my crook, nor lift a cat, nor get out of bed some mornings! But next thing there I was, God's final gift to his servant, dancing through the sand, leaping over the knapweed, twizzling in the air. O Lordy, wot a dancer I was, hm! And Anita waving her shoes in the air and egging me on with cries of adoration!

But then I thought I saw my grandfather galloping by on a huge white horse. He looked at me angrily and shook a fist. I was old, on all fours, weeping, rambling about the azure June morning of an Essex County Fair, 86 years since. If the Osbernots hadn't attacked I should have met Flossie Fordyce by the hook-a-duck and married her and never been Archbishop of Bunnyland.

Anita's ankles were at my eyelevel. 'Archbishop of where, lad? And who's this Flossie I keep hearing about?'

'Oh, I, erm . . . mm? Bogg it!'✶

Here Endeth the Lesser Book of Bunnies

✶ There is no more after this. I had been busy all morning vivifying a very large and soppy-looking ginger tabby. Rather than throttle it there and then, wot, and because I thought I heard His Grace calling for me, I took it up to present it to him, expecting to hear his grateful arhhhhhhh, pussy! when I handed it over. Mugg was sitting dead at his terminal, eyes closed. Without their twinkling light it was shocking to see how old his face was. A man surely more ancient than the man I knew.

Thinking that eventually, when some Bunnyship finds us at last, the Bunnies will want to bury him in his splendid cathedral in Bunnyopolis, and quite right too, I dug a shallow grave – surrounded by wailing cats while I did so, I may add – dressed him in his robes, then pulled the workings out of the replicator, it being of convenient coffin size, bunged him inside and shoved the whole package under the crumble in front of the melaleuca tree where his moggs are wont to shoot the evening breeze. I also placed a pair of my spare arms in there, so that they may protect him as I did in life. When the job was done I walked out across the plain towards CbN's one and only mountain, that big white cloud hanging over its shoulders as always. I felt nothing. Thought nothing. Then ι came back and started to read Mugg's booky-do, which I have now done. Amen.

AFTERWORD

by J. W. Mathis

This part of the Afterword was written upon the day that was December 31st, 2199 A.D.

Mugg was only ¼ of the way into his *Lesser Book of Bunnies* when he died. Plenty more blither-on about Bunnies had he lasted a while longer! Damned pity! The episode I miss most concerns the attempted German takeover of Bunnyland in the early '80s. Kaiser Schmernercreutz had been busy for years making his so-called 'Little Germanys' in the mid-spirals. Then he turned his attentions to Bunnyland, sending an expedition which allied itself with a raggletaggle of minor Bunny warlords and met with a surprising success. For a year there was actually a German-in-a-bunnysuit as Shogun – Helmut Bunny von Bunnys he called himself! SWINE!

The Archbishop and myself led a resistance to this regime, knowing as we did that their only policy was to prepare the way for the Kaiser's own appearance, when the switcheroo would be pulled that would turn dear old Bunnyland into an infinite 1930s Germany. This simple process, involving the deposit of charged isoenzymes creating an unstoppable atom-to-atom chain reaction, could easily enough be reversed. So we set up a factory for the manufacture of 'charged Bunny-land material', the idea being that if the Germans managed their trick, just as they sat down in their beer-&-sausage halls,

349

we would sprinkle our magic dust and turn everything Bunnyhoo again. Of course, then they could have changed it back, all the wretched Bunnies becoming Germans for a while, but then we would have changed it back again, ad infernitum! There is, of course, the added problem of infinity to add to this scenario, but I gave up trying to work that out long ago, ehwot!

Our factory, sad to say, was raided by the Gestapo. They took Mugg and I to B'bubbadub Palace – the most chilling thing I ever saw was the swastika flag hanging from the balcony where Shogun Scats had surveyed his endless dominion – and locked us up until the Kaiser arrived. When he did, rather than whip out his portable torture chamber, he proved rather chatty, full of nostalgia about our rallying days, telling Mugg about his unshakeable religious faith. Poohell! But I refused to acknowledge his vile Hunnish existence, which put him in a stamping Hitlerite fury. Cackling like the lunatic he is, he gave out a yard of German, then shot us with a queer-looking antique phaser. This, it turned out, was a prototype weapon developed by Byron Joop in the 2080s, designed to rid the world of Hittites by zapping them byebye back to their own time. Unfortunately, all it did was zap them as far back as 1972 to Gateshead, a grimy industrial town in the North of England, which they then were unable to leave, ever! So – having been shot with this weapon ourselves, naturally, that is where Mugg and I ended up.

Our time in Gateshead was in many ways the happiest we ever spent together. Freed from the responsibilities of his office, the Archbishop was less cantankerous. We lived in an end terrace behind a betting shop – the Archbishop celebrated his 100th birthday there. Dimme, but we found it dashed exotic! Working class culture of the 20th Century! Splendid!

This wasn't quite my own epoch, but damned close, and I

had a ball. I worked in a garage for a while, then took employment operating a lathe at Clarke Chapman's factory down by the Tyne. The Archbishop kept house, read, helped out with a Sunday school. Of course, the town was rotten with Hittites, zapped there by Joop. All were dressed just like the flat cap locals, fag-in-the-gob an essential accessory, but they couldn't do without their curly Hittite beards. One had a chariot in his doorway, which excited much comment. They claimed to be a Welsh sect and were generally believed. But Mugg shouted 'Oi, bull wrestling tonight, Harry!' whenever he passed one in the street, sending them a-scuttling guiltily off. Owh, but they weren't bad fellows!

Towards the end of our year there 2 dozen Bunnies turned up, zapped by that same confounded phaser during an uprising against the German Shogun. One of these was Priscilla Muffy, an Elvisite High Priestess, but also a scientist of some standing. With her expert help I tinkered together a monstrous time machine in the lavatory of our outside yard. It took some while to get working, much to the fury of his Muggship, who found living in an end terrace with 24 6-foot rabbits beyond his social abilities, especially as they'd come equipped with 5 sets of sexualparts, which meant 10 (or more!) were COR! DOING IT! at any one time. Priscilla and I . . . oooo, less said about that the better: a wink'll do, ehwot!

Problem was how to testdrive our time machine contraption! Then one afternoon a man from the betting shop stepped in to use our lavatory and as soon as he pulled the chain was zonked across time and space to the carrot kiosk in Rumbaba Plaza. He was sent back with a note from Angie, the new Shogun, saying that she had beaten the Germans and had them bundled on trains heading to infinity . . . and pleasey-do, said sweetiepaws Angie, could we have our Bunnybish back? We formed a queue outside the lavatory and one by one pulled the chain. I was the last to leave. Bunnyland was waiting with open arms.✶

The Archbishop also planned, I see from his pencilled notes, a further section of his book to be entitled *The Lesser Book of Bishboshing*. This was mainly intended, I think, as a primer for future missionaries in as yet undiscovered countries, based on his considerable experience in single-handedly building up the Universe's largest Christian community. In his early days he mainly impressed with his uncanny abilities to cast devils out of the Bunnies. They were and are sorely afflicted with this disease and the Archbishop was an ace at fixing them. Myself, not being a Bunny, never saw any of these devils – though as Mopsy I frequently had to pretend to. Double helpings of wowwee teriff when Mugg touched a Bunny between the ears and said in a quiet voice: 'PLEASY-DO BEGONE, YE FOUL SPIRIT!' And it was gone! Pouff! Leaving the rabbit hopping about and his friends applauding. A very great and singular man was my friend and employer, ehwot!

This is the subject that fills the conversation of the cats – Mugg, his character, his relationship to me, etc. Those cats not activated during his lifetime pump the other cats for info. They want to know all about him.

I confess, when I activated their talking boxes I was intrigued as to what they would talk about – to each other rather than just to me. I was listening to them this morning and was disturbed by the extent of the respect they show for the

---

✶ In the Bunny victory over the sausage-eaters even Kaiser Schmernercreutz was kicked onto a train. Typical of Werner he cheated his way to freedom – if that word can be used where a Nazi is concerned – by shooting himself with Joop's Send-a-Hittite-to-Gateshead gun. Thus, he followed us through our lavatory time machine back to Bunnyland and hid in a bunnysuit until he could contact his agents – this not for another 11 years. Traumatized by this experience – a bunnysuit can warp a proud man – for which he blames yours truly, Werner has sworn revenge. Cum soon, Werner – I am waiting!

late Archbishop. One, I noticed, though not speaking, crossed itself every time Mugg's name was mentioned. It suddenly struck me that they thought Mugg, ludicrous as this may seem, was God Almighty. I dug out those photos of the old gent who was here before us – him skiing on the mountain, him sitting in the sun, him with a Solperine pal – put them back on the mantelpiece and picked up a cat by the scruff of the neck.

'DO YOU KNOW WHO THIS IS?'

Meows.

I shook it like a frustrated policeman. 'I SAID – DO YOU KNOW WHO THIS IS?'

Meows.

I tried it with every cat to hand, all with the same result.

Beastly of me, I know. The pussies are worried enough as it is. They have been watching the scope for days – the one from our wonky shuttle, now hooked up in the workshop. There is a German fleet out there, perhaps THE German fleet, and it could be that they are coming our way. I have been taking my big phaser to bits, cleaning it, zooping it up, walking along the corridors pointing it at nothings like a nit in an old flick.

All my life, ever since I looked upon the world as J. W. Mathis in Flanders Field 281 years ago, I have feared death, suffered from the frights something terrible at the thought that this consciousness of mine, with no logical biological foundation, might just stop . . . BUMP! But now I look forward to death, and it will surely come soon. When I found the Archbishop sitting before this terminal, dead as a post, I began to bleed, to fill up with blood – during my one-man funeral service I spouted the stuff from every crack, showering the poor thing's makeshift coffin! I thought the bleeding was merely an emotional reaction to Mugg's death. But it is getting worse. Blood is clogging me up. My eyes, nose and ears were streaming with it last night. Inside my head is one great thick clot. It doesn't matter how much of the disgusting stuff I pick out, there's always more! When I took out that old typewriter I keep in my buttocks I hosed it down for an hour, but still little clots kept sloshing from its workings. I smell like a condemned butcher's shop! And not a spoon in sight! Oh, for a bout of spoons lasting 1000 years – anything but this! Dammit, the Germans must come! Werner where are you, man! I can't die here, meaninglessly, like this! – I must die in battle! Please God, let them come and I shall fulfil my destiny at last!

This part of the Afterword was written by telepathic connection to a portable antique typewriter upon the day that was
January 13th, 2200 A.D.

The bleeding was bad enough, but then for 2 weeks I was in the most terrible pain. My whole body throbbed with agonies and I prayed and prayed to the man in the photographs for it to stop. But it would not stop. When the cats in the workshop started howling during what was usually a catnapping time, I knew they'd seen something on the scope. The Germans! They were coming at last! But I could hardly move!

I don't know why I did it. I had no thought about why I was so doing. But I did it anyway. I picked up my electric screwdriver, the one I always tinkered on the cats with, and started unscrewing my left arm. Then I understood the nature of my pain. Inside my hollow metal arm was a flesh-&-blood-

&-bone one. The rest of me was the same. I had turned into a real man. The pain was my metal bolts and dislodged cogs cutting into my newly-formed flesh.

I gave no consideration to the miracle of this. I just was glad that the pain would now stop. It took only an hour to drop the bits of J. W. Mathis, False Man, onto the floor. Who was this new chap standing before the mirror examining his wounds? Was it still me? His face was like no mask I had ever worn.

The Germans had landed, 50 battleships' worth, on and around the mound a mile away across the plain. I could see them from the kitchenette window as I dabbed my sores with TCP. Little point in doctoring myself, I thought – I'll be dead in a minute, ehwot! Ha! Ha!

My bib-&-tucker was hardly the proper thing for a soldier to die in, but I put it on anyway, filled the pockets full of zizzers, plucked up my big phaser and set out across the plain to meet the enemy. A few shite creatures, who I'd obviously missed during my last clean-up, came running away from the approaching German troops. They passed me, blowing raspberries, ho-hoing at my imminent demise. I didn't waste juice on them.

That cloud that was always on the mountain wasn't there today. Surest bet on the planet! But its going allowed me a view of the summit. Never saw that before. Funny how nature is more piquant just before combat, I thought, and remembered some fairly ikky WW1 poetry, which I muttered as I shot at my first Germans – the bushwacking beggars were crouching down among the knapweed! KRAUT SWINE! LET ME SEE YOUR UGLY MUSHES, EHWOT! HA! HA! ZAPPATYDOODA!

I expected a rush of return fire. But there was none. The Boche went quiet and I kept on walking deeper into their lines through the eye-high weed. I cut across to the old huts which the shites had made their home. A familiar sound! Egad! Haven't heard that in yonks, wot! The engine of a Merkel-Schnatz rally car. I strained for a view. Dimme! I'd recognize that determinedly-hunched-over-the-wheel shape anywhere, anytime! It was Werner in a replica of his old auto, skimming through the weed towards me – and, just like a boggn Nazi, playing Wagner at full blast. Wotho!

I trotted towards him, but soon halted for breath, being unaccustomed to the techniques of using lungs. I was squiffy, my eyes blurry. I pressed them and saw stars. Then with eyeballs sore but again operative I saw a cloud up above me – bless me if it wasn't the one missing from the mountain! – And on a ridge between me and the abandoned city a young lad was waving. Not a Hun? No. A pretty English youth with strawberry curls standing beside the melaleuca tree. Our old replicator leaned upon the tree. The Merkel-Schnatz brrrrum-brumm-med✱ closer. Couldn't see it now, just its dust and a wall of knapweed. I had the phaser pointed at where I thought it would emerge from the weed. Germans were advancing behind me, taking up positions among the huts. There were thousands of the rotters out there. Iron men too, not fleshy so'n'sos like me!

'MUGG!' I shouted to the boy.

'BUNNYHOO!' he yelled back. 'LOOK WOT'S HAPPENED TO ME!'

'I SEE, YOUR GRACE – BUT PRAY OBSERVE, IF YOU WILL, YOUNG SIR, THAT A NO LESS REMARKABLE METAMORPHOSIS HAS BEEN VISITED UPON ME, EH-WOT!'

From the cloud above us came the sound of beating wings. Loose downy feathers floated down. The cloud thinned. Wings beating in my face, laughter, clucking, bright light, hymn-singing and then the Merkel-Schnatz skidding out of the dry crackling weed. Oh, God help me!

✱ The engine wasn't right. The carbs, I think.

Appendices

*

Universal Chronology
✳ 1901–2199 ✳
Compiled by J. W. Mathis, False Man

1901
Death of Empress Victoria of British Empire (OOP)✳ Peewermums begin sending themselves as gifts to the Poshly Doo People

1910
Bunnyland's sham Democracy founded: Genghis Floppity elected Bunnyboss.

1914–18
First Great War (OOP)

1916–18
J. W. Mathis is built (OOP)

1916–22
David Lloyd George Prime Minister of Britain (OOP)

1922–33
Baron Werner Schmernercreutz wins Le Mans 24-hour race 11 times (OOP)

1933
Adolf Hitler becomes Chancellor of Germany (OOP)

1934
Gracie Fields appears in 'Sing as We Go', the greatest film ever made (OOP)

1939–45
The Second Great War (OOP)

1942–45
J. W. Mathis a prisoner in Colditz Castle, Germany (OOP)

✳ Our Original Planet.

1945
Death of Lloyd George (OOP)

1950
J. W. Mathis marries Clarissa Devney (OOP)

1950–70
Peewermums conquer and cultivate 1,000 planets in Mid-Spirals.

1952
J. W. Mathis appears in his first film role, as Bonk the Robot in Pnarvelt's *'Robot Planet'* (OOP)

1960
J. W. Mathis almost plays Sergeant Pierre Plumé in Kubrick's *'Paths of Glory'* (OOP)

1966
J. W. Mathis leaves Planet OOP on *Nobby Stiles 3*

1982
British P. M. Thatcher privatizes the British Space Stations, creating the Empire Corporation (OOP)

1999
Zoblar the Greatest eats 95% of the Crumladeevarsalaginderfardeeroons

2000
Birth of Chaffinch Chaffinch, grandfather of Muggeridge, Chaffinch Hall Suffolk (OOP)

2005–17
Plagues on OOP. 2 billion die. (OOP)

2010
First Shite Creatures reported.

2015
Cod Wars with the Bollockmen.

2045
Donaldbane Frazer founds the Scotmars Colony.

2054
Lower Buckleberry, first English Village Spacestation, built. 844 villages follow during later half of the century.

2060s
The Connie & Pam era. Happiest time in OOP's history. (OOP).

2067
Second Coming appears on OOP and is Crucified.

2070–85
J. W. Mathis in the service of the Peewermums.

2077
Octopusfrogs become first recognized alien visitors to OOP.

2078–83
Indonesian Conflict otherwise known as Third Great War. (OOP)

2083
Birth of Muggeridge Cod Robin Chaffinch, future Archbishop of Bunnyland. The Lovely Anita becomes P. M. in England (OOP)
First contact with Osbernots.

2085
No official announcement made, but the Lovely Anita becomes Queen of England (OOP)

2088
Byron Joop Jr's ill-fated time experiment brings entire Hittite Empire from OOP's past. Hittite Wars begin.

2090
The Lovely Anita declares herself a goddess and assumes total power over non-Hittite territory.

2086–2010
Hittites conquer every inch of OOP except for a few English stately homes, Benidorm and Pitcairn Island.

2099
The Lovely Anita invites the Hittite *Pankus* or ruling council to Chaffinch Hall and vaporizes them.

2100
Death of Daddyfingers and Tracy Chaffinch.

2104
Pope Lassie converts to the Hittite religion, appearing on his balcony in Rome linking hands with the great god Tesheb.

2105
Death of the Lovely Anita.
Dougal McMars sells first Martian package holidays to Bunnypeople, inspiring the 'tartan craze' in Bunnyland. Shogun Benedictus Floppity tests his power by illegalizing tartan.

2106
Mugg Chaffinch arrives in *Billingsgate-on-Sea*

2109
Mugg Chaffinch tried for war crimes. Innocent verdict is Universal scandal.

2113
HMS Thorpe-Le-Soken destroyed by enemy action.
J.W. Mathis dug up on *Billingsgate-on-Sea*. Meets Mugg Chaffinch for the first time.

2115
General Sir Humbert Windbraker presumed lost after Little Green Men destroy *HMS Frinton*.

2117
Mugg Chaffinch ordained.

2129
King William of E.E.S. deposed. A clone of the Lovely Anita becomes Queen Empress. Other clones are dispersed to English Space Villages, where they lead parish councils.

2131
Mugg Chaffinch chaplain on Patel & Thombs Megasuperdupermarket. Anita of *Billingsgate-on-Sea* gives birth to her & Mugg's lovechild, the future Admiral Starfish Chaffinch

2133–2198
Mugg Chaffinch is Archbishop of Bunnyland

2135
Bunny renegades under Snaggler Bains destroy *HMS Cromer*.

2149
J.W. Mathis arrives in Bunnyland. Mopsy elected Bunnyboss.
Birth of HRH Hippity Rumbaba III

2149–64
Cathedral of Bunnyopolis, largest cathedral in Universe, built and embellished.

2150
Hittites disappear. (OOP)

2151
Mopsy signs Bunnyhoo Treaty making peace with E.E.S. and outlawing renegades – though the Shogun later adds the words 'without Bunny ears'. Near-successful revolt of Bobo Tufts. Shogun Scats hold on power slipping.

2153
Battle of the Asteroids. Mopsy destroys German fleet. Death of Dagon Hattusilis Chaffinch.
Mopsy re-elected Bunnyboss. 6-month-long Sexual Parts Festival in Bunnyland.

2154
Death of Anita, last clone of the Lovely Anita. Her hair is planted beside the Pink Pools of Bilickers 296/D.

2157
Yorgo 'Superrabbit' Robinson conquers 80% of the Bilickers system of planets, incorporating it into Bunnylania. Scotsmen declared extinct.

2158
Death of Shogun Scats and Warlord Tufts.
Archbishop Chaffinch baptizes 100,000 rabbits in Lake Twinkie.

2160
Sparky Botchaby accidentally-on-purpose blows up the Schnorbitz Galaxy.
Last male child born to be born in an English Space Village, Chips Foggerty-Snaith on *HMS Widdercombe*.
Mopsy abdicates as Bunnyboss.

2163
80,000 20-metres-high Thin Elvis clones, all made from the same strand of hair, establish Graceland Colony in outer spirals of Kipper Galaxy.

2165
First of the Little Germanys seeded by Kaiser Schmerner-creutz.

2166
Admiral Crissie Glossop gives birth to Solperine octo-tuplets, all girls.

2170
Chips Foggerty-Snaith executed for 'making snide remarks'.
The Old Men riots on Bilickers 234/9D.

2172–79
War in Bunnyland. No Bunny warlord powerful enough to assume Shogunate.
Thumper Presley emerges as Shogun, but promptly dies.

2173
The Admiralty Purge.
Admiral Satsuma Chaffinch killed by bomb in shuttle-craft on Bilickers 333/A19.

2180–91
5th Carrot War between Bunny factions at opposite ends of infinity. No reported casualties.

2181–2
The Anschluß. German attempt to annex Bunnyland.

2183
Admiral Crissie Glossop, retiring to Graceland Colony, discovers all the thin Elvises have gone fat.

2194
HRH Hippity Rumbaba III becomes Shogun of Bunnyland.

2199
Elvisite Bunnies under Rocky Parsley colonize the depopulated OOP.

2200
Death of Archbishop Mugger-idge Chaffinch, Cats-by-Nowhere.

Shoguns of Bunnyland
in the 22nd Century*

Benedictus Floppity	2098–2109
No Overall Control	2109–2121
Hippity Rumbaba II	2121–2137
Dr Buckie Scats	2137–2158
Hopalong Croons	2158–2160
Dutch Wobbubbit	2160–2163
Snaggler Doekillers Jr	2163–2165
Thumper Presley	2165–2172
No Overall Control	2172–2179
Thumper Presley	2179
F. Klausly Whilicker XIV	2179–2181
Helmut Bunny von Bunnys	2181–2182
Angie and Norbert	2182–2189
Angie	2189–2194
Hippity Rumbaba III	2194–

* This in no way implies that the Bunnyland Shoguns had control over the Bunny Space Empire (Bunnylandia), always a mish-mash of pirates, petty chiefs and March Hares, acknowledging no leporine authority or several at once. Under the present Shogun, Hippity Rumbaba III – long may he reign – the shogunate holds greater power over the empire than at any time since Benedictus Floppity.

Clan Chaffinch

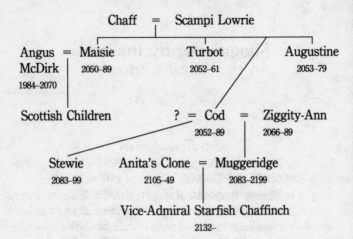

Chaff = Scampi Lowrie

Angus = Maisie   Turbot   Augustine
McDirk   2050–89   2052–61   2053–79
1984–2070

Scottish Children   ? = Cod = Ziggity-Ann
               2052–89   2066–89

Stewie   Anita's Clone = Muggeridge
2083–99   2105–49   2083–2199

Vice-Admiral Starfish Chaffinch
2132–

The Neo-Chaffinches

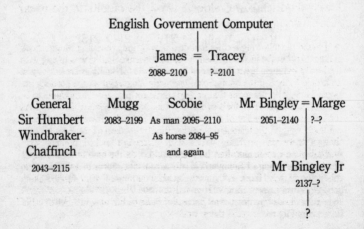

English Government Computer

James = Tracey
2088–2100   ?–2101

General   Mugg   Scobie   Mr Bingley = Marge
Sir Humbert   2083–2199   As man 2095–2110   2051–2140   ?–?
Windbraker-   As horse 2084–95
Chaffinch   and again
2043–2115

                               Mr Bingley Jr
                               2137–?

                                 ?

Mugg's Bunny Recipes *

Curried Bunny

INGREDIENTS:
5 rabbits. 15 dessert spoonfuls of currypowder, 40 large onions,
360 snidderfreens, 15 cloves of garlic, 5 lemons or one medium-
sized spoglet, 6lbs of butter, 10 pints of milk, one small shovelful
of ground cloves, one small shovelful of salt, one plidarion.

MODE:
Pleasy-do disembowel, skin & wash the rabbits in the usual

---

* I found the following recipes muddled in with the printout of Mugg's book
and could not resist including them here. It is possible that he was toying with
the idea of writing a breezy cookbook for cannibalistic Bunny gourmets, or just
an article for one of the many Solperine foody mags. But as the portions are
rather large, it occurs to me that perhaps these recipes were memoranda to be
sent to someone cooking for a synod or some such ecclesiastical jamboree. As
for the moral incongruity of an Archbishop of Bunnyland eating members of
his flock, so doth the shepherd – neither the Archbishop or the Bunnies ever
thought there was anything wrong with it, though cooked Bunnies were
unavailable for comment after the event! Indeed, as the tone of these recipes
illustrate, the eating of Bunnyrabbit was a constant source of amusement to
rabbit eaters, none more so than the Archbishop himself, who giggled like a
schoolgirl every time rabbit was served at table. Finally, I should say that I
have partooken of portions of all but one of these dishes at some time or other
and can highly recommend them, wot!

way. Cut up thy rabbits neatly. Place snidderfreens in zizzer & shoot one each into the rabbit parts. Mincey-do your garlics, chop-chop the onions – finely does it – & fry these in 3lbs of butter until the colour of a sunset on Higlashamere. Scrub curry-powder into rabbit parts, then fry in 3lbs of butter until tis the golden of a sunrise on Higlashamere. Bung into Bunnystewingpot with boiling milk & salt. Let it steweth for the length of 1½ of Bishop Meavey's sermons – slowly does it – till the liquid is reduced by half. One hour before serving, pleasy-do bung in the lemons (or spoglet). Throw the plidarion away, twas never needed. This is scrummily sufficiently-doos for 30 personages, or 2 Solperines.

Tip:
Why not brand the ears of the rabbits with the names of your guests and use them as place settings?

Boiled Bunny with Gurge

INGREDIENTS:
30 rabbits, 1 medium-sized gurge, water.

MODE:
The bestmost rabbits for boiling are 3–5 years old. Pleasy-do check that claws are smooth and sharp, if not thee hast an old rabbit. If in doubt, ask rabbit its age. Induce rabbits to take shower. Shoot rabbits with stun gun, as they are best boiled alive, but tis more Christian if they be unconscious. Putteth rabbit into sufficient hot water to covereth it to the ears – a ceremonial kettle-drum is adequate, or why not beg-steal-or-borrow a sacrifical water cabinet from your local museum? Boil

away gentlesomely for 4 hours. Leave larger Bunnies in an extra hour. Having dished the rabbits, pour liver sauce upon rabbits. Then, using the protective clothing and ear-muffs, squeeze the gurge until it drips no more. Sufficient for 150 persons.

Tip:
Never eat boiled bunny during the month of March. Permanent loss of sanity can result.

Bunny & Busby Ragout
(A campfire feast!)

INGREDIENTS:
5 rabbits, 5 busbies, 1 bag of flour, 15 sliced onions, 2oz B'bbbbbb, 12 guinea pigs, pepper & salt, 5 bay leaves, butter.

MODE:
Pleasy-do slice onions & bungeth into stewpot with flour and butter. Place pot beside fire, stirreth well while singing hymns. Add gravy till mixture is consistency of cream. Bungeth in thy rabbit parts & guinea piggies. Simmer until almost tender. Then pour the boggn lot into thy shaved busby, place busby in stewpot for 3 hours.

Tip:
Remember to thank the Lord after meals as well as before.

Bunnydevil Pie

INGREDIENTS:
1 large or 3 small devils, 2 large onions, 1 guinea pig, 2 litres of blessed veg stock, salt & pepper, fistful of plain flour, sage, dash of oil, 1 bad Solperine egg, holy water.

MODE:
Stand by with fine net soaked in holy water when your Archbishop or parish priest is casting out devils. Catch devil. Put devil in pot with veg stock. Drown devil. Remove horns. Throw stunned guinea pig into pot. Leave to simmer. Roll out pastry into an oval on a floured surface. Cut a narrow strip to fit around pie dish rim, plus 2 more pleasy-do to make a cross atop the pie – vital this, or vomiting will result. Bung devil into pie, cover with crust, bake for 30 mins, hot as you can.

Tip:
Verily, disbelievers will find in their pie only the guinea pig.

Rabbit Surprise

INGREDIENTS:
1 rabbit

MODE:
Invite a plump healthy rabbit whom you have always disliked to dinner. Hit between ears with hockey stick upon arrival. Skin, wrap in foil and bungeth into oven.

Tip:

Never swallow whiskers – always check thy plate for them, as 1 whisker can grow up to 80 miles long in your intestine. Plusly, never eat a rabbit to whom you owe money, or a rabbit who is your marriage partner or a bishop.

STEVE WALKER

21st CENTURY BLUES

READ ABOUT IT BEFORE IT HAPPENS!

The Book of the Century,
Being the Life and Times of
Chaff Chaffinch, the Famous
Stylite, Sometime Archbishop
of Canterbury, Leader of the
Revolution of '24, Saviour
of the World, Etcetera, Spoken
by Himself, Mostly in the Year
2099, Up a Pole in Ethiopia,
Written Down by his Long-
Suffering Disciple and Lost
Soul, Tadese Mblook.

21st Century Blues is the brilliantly inventive and funny book
that was the basis for the amazing radio comedy series that
dared to lift the skirts of the next century for a sneak preview
of the outlandish shape of things to come . . .

HODDER AND STOUGHTON PAPERBACKS